IMMERSIVE

THE ELITE TRIALS

IMMERSIVE

BECKY MOYNIHAN

BROKEN
BOOKS

Published by Broken Books
www.beckymoynihan.com

ISBN-13: 978-1-7327330-5-3
ISBN-10: 1-7327330-5-8

Cover design by Becky Moynihan
Cover model by Neostock
www.neo-stock.com

To the hopeless and oppressed,
to the weary souls and heavy-hearted:
You are worthy.

THE DREAM

The dream always started with running and a countdown.

Heart pounding, legs churning, I raced to escape.

Only twenty strides to go.

But no matter how fast I ran, he always stopped me. I could feel the heat of his gaze on the nape of my neck.

Run faster!

Five more steps until the treeline. Mum was maybe a handful of yards beyond that. If I called out, she would hear me. But I didn't yell her name. Instead, I counted aloud as my feet whisked me away from him.

"Four, three, two—"

"Why are you counting?"

At the boy's voice, always startling in its familiarity, I skidded to a halt. Drew in a tight breath. Slowly turned. And there he was, all gangly limbs, wildly unkempt hair, and golden eyes. Shorter than me, he stared, curious but sad.

I shrugged my bony shoulders and answered him despite the incessant need to run. "Counting distracts my mind. Sometimes my thoughts drown me, and I have to escape them. So I run away before they swallow me whole."

His eyebrows scrunched together. My fingers twitched. I wanted to smooth the puckered skin but didn't move. I knew I should, though—not toward him but away. Every time I lingered and talked to him, my chest started to ache.

Run, my mind demanded.

But it was too late. I couldn't run. My feet were rooted in place. His eyes. Gold. Piercing. Haunting. I couldn't look away from them.

Run! He's misery and pain. Heartache and betrayal. A lie. He'll destroy you.

Did I really believe that, though?

Then the tears came. They always did, because my body knew what I was going to do next. I backed away. "One." Just one more step and a tree would separate us. Hide me. Free me from this inexplicable agony puncturing my heart. I slid backward . . .

Panic flared in his golden eyes. "Don't go. Please." He reached for me. "Lune, I need you."

I need you.

Why did guilt writhe in my stomach every time he said those words?

Why did I feel like screaming, crying, punching the tree that I was inching behind? I was leaving again. Why was I leaving? No. Stop. He needed me. But my body wasn't my own. It was moving farther away, forcing me to lose sight of the boy.

"Lune," he pleaded. Begged. "Lune!"

"I'm sorry," I whimpered, letting the tears fall unchecked. "I'm so sorry."

"Lune, *please!*"

"I—" My voice gave out as I choked on a sob.

"LuLu."

The trees swallowed me whole. Suffocated me. Stole my vision.

My heart pounded fiercely.

"LuLu, wake up. It's just a dream."

I bolted upright, the boy's name bursting from my lips. "Bren!"

"Shhh," my mum whispered, smoothing my hair back as I gulped in cool night air. I blinked away the moisture from my eyes and took in my surroundings. Moonlight illuminated the black bars on the windows. A pale, threadbare blanket covered my legs. Cast in shadow, a face I knew well—and yet didn't—lingered beside me. She smiled softly. "You'll alert the men."

It wasn't the warning that made my breath hitch but the fact that my mum, my *mother* was here, comforting me as only she could. When I lay back down, she guided my head to her lap, stroking my hair some more. I'd yearned for this very thing ever since the day I'd been stolen from her, but now that I knew, now that I understood what she went through this past decade, it felt odd. Like being touched by a stranger.

I caused this.

When I'd followed Bren into the woods all those years ago, the Recruiter Clan had found her, too. Had kidnapped her. Brought her to Asheville. My mother had been less than a day's journey from me for the past eleven years and I never knew. Never knew that Iris had been raised here. Never knew that I had not one sister, but *two*. And a brother.

All because of me.

Something in my mind had unraveled the day Bren was shot by Skervvy. Having my memories restored, leaving my friends back at Blue Ridge Sector, enduring Ryker's ultimate betrayal, being reunited with Mum and learning what she'd suffered through—too much. My unbreakable brain fractured. I couldn't use my Visionary ability, couldn't form a mental tether with Bren to see if he was still alive. The only time I ever saw him was in my subconscious—in my dreams. Even then, I only saw younger versions of him begging me to stay.

And I never once did.

I always ran. I knew now that I was running from the guilt and accompanying pain. But no matter how fast I ran, I could never escape my mind. It cast judgment on me in the form of nightmares, reminding me again and again of my failures.

Thirteen days. Almost two weeks of not knowing what happened to him. Each minute of unknowing was a lifetime. A knife to the heart. A pulsing ache.

But it was my own fault.

If I hadn't fled The Ridge with Ryker, he wouldn't have used me to distract Bren, then sell him out to the Recruiter Clan. I should've stayed under the mountain like Bren wanted me to. I could've watched over him from afar, using my abilities—safe, where I wasn't a distraction. And now . . .

Now I was broken. And numb to what awaited me. I would endure the same fate as my mother and every other woman here.

To be implanted with mutated DNA.

My second day here, Mum had explained what females were required to do if they wanted to be fed. Any resistance was met with a swift trip to "The Cells." I had asked what happened there, but no one would tell me, not even Mum. The mere mention of The Cells struck fear into the hearts of these women.

But what they did talk about was their duties. If their assigned chores were completed by sundown, they earned a warm shower and hot dinner. And with most of them pregnant, they would do practically anything for those two commodities.

Thankfully, the clansmen didn't touch the women—not in

that way. It was the only mercy in this screwed-up breeding operation. An injection was all it took to impregnate the captive women over the age of eighteen, to keep them from running away. For what mother would leave her child behind, test tube baby or no? At least, that's what my mum believed.

Iris. Sweet Iris.

She was one of them—a DNA experiment.

The numbness lifted, enough for a solid weight to smother my attempts at breathing.

Don't think about it. Don't think about anything. Block out thought.

Feel, don't think.

No!

Feeling made me think of Iris locked away in a cell, alone and terrified.

Feeling made me imagine a bullet ripping through Bren's body. Made me see him fall. Was he dead or alive? Unknown.

"I can't," I gasped, clutching at the bear tooth necklace Bren had given me—a familiar comfort. If I used my Visionary ability and found nothing, if I searched for them and they no longer existed . . .

"Can't what, LuLu?"

I looked up into hazel green eyes identical to mine. Identical to Iris's. I hadn't told her that Iris was being held and possibly tortured by the man who called himself my father. I hadn't explained my countless scars. I hadn't confessed that I fell in love with the very same boy who kidnapped me eleven years ago. I couldn't. Not now. Maybe not for a long time.

It was too much. Too much *everything*.

And so I whispered, "Nothing."

Because I could do nothing for myself or anyone else.

Block out feeling. Just exist. You are nothing.

Where was the girl who fashioned sticks into swords? Where was the girl who plunged into lakes to slay water dragons?

She drowned.

WATER IS MY FRIEND

"Lune."

I felt the warning nudge but didn't bother looking up. I flipped another page and burrowed my nose even deeper into the book, my dark red hair a curtain around me. Nothing, *nothing* would distract me from this story I'd thoroughly lost myself in—a world filled with pirates and sword fights and a swoon-worthy love interest.

For the first time since childhood, I was reading a book. Actually, this was my second book in a week—the other one took me a total of forty hours to get through since my reading skills were still weak. But once I started, I couldn't stop.

Binge-reading, my mum called it. I smuggled the book with me everywhere, even into the communal bathroom. Sleep became an afterthought—I only succumbed to exhaustion when the moon vanished over the old correctional center's rooftop, making words on a page impossible to see.

Books offered me something I'd only ever dreamt about: freedom. Not physical freedom, but freedom of the mind, which was something I desperately needed. Books allowed me to escape reality and immerse myself into a world unbound by chains. In fact, the main character of my current read captained her own ship on the high seas where the only walls were the quarters she slept in at night. Endless possibilities filled her horizon and I marveled at the unwavering way she steered her destiny.

Adria, my bunkmate—my very *pregnant* bunkmate—nudged me again, a quick elbow jab to the ribs. "Skervvy's coming," she hissed, forcing me back to the real world. I avoided looking at her distended stomach, or acknowledging that she was only a year older than me. "Remember what he did last time?"

My upper lip curled as I recalled the altercation. He had slammed me up against a wall in the mess hall, saying I should watch my surroundings and not the waste of paper in front of my face. A guard had stopped him from harassing me further, but I'd seen the look in his eyes.

He wasn't finished with me yet.

He blamed me for the death of his partner, Thane—the creep who'd felt me up more than once during their attempts to capture me. Maybe I should feel a touch remorseful for the bloody, grisly way he died, but I didn't. Not when Bear, the loyal wolf dog who'd trailed me up and down the mountain, had been a casualty. Not when Skervvy had taken out his vengeance on Bren.

Crap. I was thinking about him again. And thoughts bred feelings. Before I could shut down the emotions, tears clogged my windpipe, cutting off my air supply.

"Is the book *that* good, or is my nearness causing the abrupt mood shift I'm sensing from you?" a male's voice crooned in my ear. I stiffened as Skervvy's nose rubbed against my exposed neck. Every cell in my body shrieked at the invasion, at the show of dominance. He didn't want to violate me like Thane had, but he waited with bated breath for me to react.

If I did, he'd release his need to inflict pain. My upper arm was still recovering from the throwing knife he'd sunk into it two weeks ago.

I didn't reply, which I knew aggravated him. These days, it was the only form of rebellion I could muster. Somewhere inside of me, the desire to unleash myself on him for all he'd done, all he'd stolen, simmered hotly. But that would require energy—and emotion. And I had none to spare. Staying on my own two feet while I performed the daily tasks required of me took all the stamina I had.

Just yesterday, as we'd stood side-by-side folding laundry, I'd confessed to Mum, "I should feel happy being reunited with you. I've thought of little else for over a decade. But I—I just feel . . . empty."

She had smiled sadly in understanding. "You are grieving. Grief is like a sandpit with no bottom. It'll swallow you whole if you don't fight the pull. Escaping reality through books will provide some relief, but don't forget to live, LuLu, no matter how bleak things are."

In response, I'd picked up my book and burrowed into it again so she couldn't see the spark of anger on my face. Shouldn't mothers make everything better? Couldn't she distract me? Or reassure me that she had a plan to escape this prison where women were forced to pop out mutated *babies?*

Apparently, she was retired from baby-making and had been appointed to den mother, meaning she looked after the needs of the children and pregnant women. The role was only given to women of exemplary behavior, Adria had told me, which meant that my mother had willingly submitted to the men ruling over her.

I wanted to hate her for it, but I couldn't. Iris was a lot like her: kind and gentle, docile and naturally subservient. There was strength in kindness, but I'd rather be vicious if it meant freedom from those who dared oppress me.

Which was why I refused to play Skervvy's game. The more

I could aggravate him, the more he'd reveal his weaknesses to me. I may be numb with grief, but I wouldn't let this place bury me. Soon, I would figure out how to escape, and how to get help freeing the others imprisoned here. There was no other option.

"Soon," I whispered.

"What was that, girly? You mouthing off to me?" Before I could reply, Skervvy ripped the book from my grasp. I shot up from the rusted bench Adria and I had settled onto for recreational hour, squinting as the sun above Skervvy's head struck my eyes. My hands curled into fists when I caught sight of his wicked smirk. A taunt. A challenge.

Don't do it, don't do it. Don't react.

Just exist.

His dark gaze flicked to the book, then returned to mine. I could practically see the dusty wheels inside his empty brain turning, somehow formulating an idea. "Beats me why the boss allows you women to have these books. If it were up to me, I'd destroy them all. Starting"—without taking his eyes off me, he cracked open the book—"with"—his hands gripped the two halves—"this one."

Crap. *Crap!* I lunged for him, but it was too late. The sickening sound of paper ripping tore through the afternoon air as he severed the spine in two. My numb state of mind vanished as shock jolted through me. Rage quickly followed, loosening my tongue. "You son of a—!" I swung my fist at his jaw. The fleshy impact sent pain streaking along my knuckles and up my arm.

Stars, I wanted to do it again. And *again.*

A feral grin pulled at my mouth. It faltered a second later when Skervvy returned the look, silently gloating that he'd won. I immediately straightened and neutralized my expression, but the damage was done. I had played right into his hands like the complete reactionary fool that I was. And now, I would face the consequences.

Skervvy spread his arms wide and slowly turned in a circle. "You all saw it." His voice rang across the small courtyard, no doubt to gain the guard's attention. From the corner of my eye, I saw my mum slowly rise to her feet. "She acted in violence without cause and must be disciplined."

Without waiting for the guard's approval, he snagged my upper arm and hauled me against him. As my chest bumped into his, I stiffened, preparing to pry myself loose, but his fingers dug into my arm and squeezed. I clenched my teeth, refusing to cry out.

Push past the pain. Push past the—

He tossed my destroyed book to the ground and intentionally stepped on it, tearing pages free. They scattered over the dirt yard. I had to look away, had to blink several times so tears wouldn't escape. The courtyard was eerily silent as Skervvy dragged me toward the only exit, which led into the bowels of the correctional center.

I didn't dare look at my mum as we passed by her. Our captors probably didn't know that she was my mother, and it needed to stay that way. Connections were dangerous in a world bent on exploiting people.

"Before the Silent War, this place used to hold criminals," my mum had explained to me my first day here. "And now, the criminals are holding this country's next generation. I fear for our future, LuLu."

Fear.

And fear has a tendency to turn into violence, wouldn't you agree?

I understood the point Dr. Moore had been making now that

my memories were back. Fear, if left unchecked, was the path to insanity. Renold had told me over and over that fear was weakness, yet he'd raised me to be afraid, to react to every little threat. But what purpose did my fear serve? If he really was planning on using me as a weapon, wouldn't my out-of-control emotions be a hindrance?

While Skervvy pulled me around a corner and proceeded down a flight of stairs, I let myself think of Iris. She was so shy and timid. I couldn't envision her as a weapon. But myself? Yes. I was reckless and stubborn, which oftentimes made me stupidly brave. And I did things—unforgivable things—when I was backed into a corner. What scared me most was what I would do under the right pressure.

Because deep down, I knew . . .

I knew I was capable of becoming a monster.

You adapted to a harsh environment in order to survive. It's why you're here today. Don't be afraid of who you were, who you still are, Lune.

But would Bren have said that if he'd known the full extent of my mission, that I was meant to *kill* him if he failed to do his? A part of me had considered that outcome in order to protect Iris. I knew now I never could have gone through with it, but there was still that dark, desperate corner of my mind willing to do horrible deeds.

I would snap Skervvy's neck if it meant freeing my mum from this hell.

What did that make me?

A murderer, I could practically hear Catanna mock in my ear. *But you always knew the price of freedom, didn't you? Death to innocence, death to ideals. Death to love.*

12

Because I had sacrificed love for freedom more than once. Not allowing myself close relationships in Tatum City, pushing Bren away again and again, fleeing Blue Ridge Sector at the first available opportunity—all good things that I had destroyed. And for what? All I'd ever received in return was more shackles.

Maybe I was going about this freedom thing all wrong. Maybe I had to accept that one girl couldn't accomplish the impossible—on her own, anyway. I needed help, but I'd betrayed the only people capable of providing it. And Bren . . . Bren wouldn't come for me. Because he was . . . he was . . .

I zeroed in on Skervvy's floppy brown hair as anger twitched through my muscles. He *shot* Bren. The urge to shove him down the remaining stairs couldn't be suppressed. I reached out and—

He whipped around, the abrupt action foiling my aim. I pitched forward and would have tumbled down the steps if he hadn't jerked me to a halt by my arm. His maniacal laughter echoed in the stairwell as I righted myself. "I knew there was still a little spitfire inside you. But losing your cool over a *book?*" He made a disgusted noise. "Doesn't matter. You snapped. Now you'll get to see what happens to insubordinate females."

"Insubordinate is a big word," I mused aloud, ignoring my brain when it told me to shut up. "I'm surprised your tiny mouth could handle—"

Crack.

The sharp sound registered; the pain didn't.

And then it did with a vengeance, streaking across my cheek where Skervvy had backhanded me.

"Fight me all you want," he said with a hard edge I'd never heard before, "but I won't abide a sassy-mouthed woman."

I didn't respond, though words pooled on my tongue. I didn't touch my cheek, though it throbbed like a second heartbeat. He yanked on my arm and we continued down another flight of stairs, then a dank hallway half-lit by flickering bare bulbs and lined with steel doors. This must be The Cells. When we reached the end and he unlocked one of the doors, I remained silent. When he shoved me inside and darkness enveloped me, I didn't fight.

Because he'd revealed his weakness to me.

And when the time was right, I would exploit it.

The steel door slammed shut.

"Enjoy your new home, girly," Skervvy singsonged from the other side. "This one's specially reserved for feisty, non-pregnant females such as yourself. I'm afraid there are no books to keep you company, but you *will* have visitors. Many of them."

It was his words, not the cackling laughter as he departed, that sent chills down my spine.

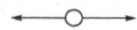

Scratch.

Squeak.

Scratch, scratch.

Days without food, bedding, and light weren't what unraveled my sanity.

It was my many promised visitors.

The rats.

And not just any rats. Giant mutated rats called vorax that feasted on dead flesh. The problem was, they didn't seem to care that I wasn't dead yet.

They nibbled on my pants and hair, sometimes on my fingers when I fell asleep. I would wake up, screaming from nightmares of rodents the size of saber cats gnawing off my hands. So I stopped sleeping.

I knew what they, the Recruiter Clan, were doing. Breaking my spirit. My will to fight back. But they didn't know about my time with Renold, how he would whip and beat me with sticks, plunge needles into my flesh, tear down my self-esteem with a single word. I had years of abuse, years of conditioning under my belt.

And yet, even the sub-basement of Tatum House had been clean. Renold wouldn't have allowed rats and mold to fester inside his prized dwelling place. Here, the air reeked of rat poop and stagnant dirt. The moist earth I sat on had seeped through my pants and was caked under my fingernails from when I'd taken care of my . . . needs. So, I essentially wallowed in crap, animal and human alike.

These conditions were degrading. Inhumane.

But it was the constant scuttling and scratching and squeaks of hunger that slowly tipped me over the edge.

A few rats won't be the end of you, Lune Avery, I scolded myself.

Unfortunately, there were more than a few. I couldn't see them but it felt like there were at least a dozen—close enough to detect, far enough to avoid my boots. For once, I welcomed the company of my thoughts and the torture they brought. Better than dwelling on how big my furry guests were.

I thought of Mum. Was this how they broke her into submission? Isolated, starved, driven to madness.

I thought of Bren, but the pain was still too sharp, like a shard of ice wedged between my ribs. I blocked out his memory with vindictive thoughts of Ryker instead. First, he'd been a mystery, then a pain in my butt, then a friend. Now he was enemy number one. If

I ever got out of here, I'd hunt him down with my Visionary ability and make him pay. He was probably tucked inside Tatum City, taking over my Elite Guardian duties. I wondered what story he'd told Renold to explain the failed missions.

Stars, what if this outcome had been his mission from the start? Anything was possible.

Bang, bang, bang.

"You alive in there?"

The rats scampered off as I flinched at the too-loud noise. Even if I'd wanted to respond to Skervvy's flippant question, I couldn't. My tongue was swollen and plastered to the roof of my mouth from lack of water. Never in my life had I felt thirst and hunger like this, so intense that my stomach was trying to flip itself inside out. A fresh wave of cramps grabbed me. I curled into a tighter ball, slowly breathing through the pain.

"Ahh, are you hungry? That's the price you pay for insubordination," Skervvy mocked. "Here, I can at least give you some water."

I swiftly raised my head in anticipation of cool liquid coating my parched throat. My eyes willed the door to open, to allow me a glimpse of light. Maybe I'd be gifted with a whiff of damp air unsullied by feces, too.

But I waited. And waited. I knew Skervvy was still there— he was muttering curses and smacking something against what sounded like his palm. I attempted to swallow. And failed. My hands shook with the need to hold the perspiring cup of life-giving water. My chapped lips trembled as I imagined pressing the cup's rim to them.

A crackling noise reached my ears, then . . .

"Hey, Axe, water in cell fourteen." Pause. "Yeah, the works.

She hasn't been properly initiated yet."

I held my breath, too focused on the word water to care about who he was talking to or what else he was saying.

Water.

Water.

Clear, perfect, quenching—

The room erupted.

I instinctively squeezed my eyes shut as slivers of ice pelted me. Hissing, I lurched into motion and blindly crawled toward the steel door. The hail, or whatever it was, stung my exposed skin. I scrambled faster until both palms were flattened against the door. I hauled myself upright on unsteady legs, pushing and pounding. My weak cries were lost in the explosion of sound destroying my cell.

"Skerv . . . open . . . door!"

"What?" he yelled, mere inches from my face yet so far away.

". . . said . . . wanted . . . water!"

Water?

I stopped pounding as the words sunk in. As I became fully aware of what was happening. Freezing cold water was raining down on me with such force, it felt like needles stabbing my flesh. I renewed my assault on the door, screaming at him to let me out as the deluge continued without end, bruising my skin, seeping inside of me until I knew nothing but water.

But water is my friend, not my enemy.

It was all I had left.

When the downpour finally ceased minutes, hours, or maybe days later, I was still on my feet. Still pressed to the door. My knuckles were bloodied and my throat scraped raw. My body was limp and shivering uncontrollably. But I was still standing. Still *fighting.*

A sense of purpose burned hotly within me, something that had been missing since arriving here.

Because Skervvy made a mistake.

He chose the wrong tool to break me.

RATS & BACKSTABBERS

Time bled into countless streaks of pain.

The vorax came back after the water switched off, more active than ever. In fact, they seemed excited that I was half-drowned. It meant I was that much closer to death, my pruned body slowly being prepped for a grand feast. One managed to bite through the pant material right above my boot before I could kick it away. With a shriek of rage, I sent the rodent soaring so far that it smacked into the wall. His buddies then proceeded to tear into him as he lay stunned in the squelching muck that was now my cell floor.

An indefinite amount of time later, Skervvy returned. "You still alive?" he yelled.

I stayed silent. Mute. Like I did all those years in Tatum City to survive. I would use his weakness against him soon enough, but I didn't have the strength for a confrontation at the moment. I knew what he wanted though. Knew because I had been raised by a man just as sadistic as he was. Their torture methods may not be the same, and their temperaments were different, but they both sought one thing.

Submission.

They wanted me to beg.

I wouldn't. Ever. I would rather die in this putrid hole.

"I can hear you breathing," Skervvy cut through my thoughts.

"Did the vorax chew off your tongue?" Cackling laughter. "Here, let me get rid of them for you since I'm such a nice guy." *Beep.* "Axe, let 'er rip!"

I braced for the stinging rain. None came. Instead, white hot light tore across my vision. I slammed my eyes shut and raised trembling hands to shield them. A multitude of squeaks rose to a feverish pitch. I couldn't help but open my eyes. I needed to see what those disgusting rodents were up to now. As soon as I did, I wished to the sun and moon and a billion stars that I hadn't.

They were everywhere. And huge. The size of small cats. Blinded by the lights, they rammed themselves into the walls, frantically clawing their way to a thin grate. As they squeezed through the metal bars, patches of matted fur and pink skin glistened under the fluorescents. Saliva rushed into my mouth. I gagged, unable to vomit with an empty stomach.

Another feeling rose right behind my tongue. A ball of panic. It grew and hardened until the only thing left to do was scream.

And pound on the door.

And scream some more. I broke my fingernails in an attempt to pry my way out.

Now I was crying, prepared to spill traitorous words from my lips. Pleading words. Weak words. *No. You are not weak, you are not weak.* I bit my tongue until I tasted blood.

Even after the last rat left my cell, tears rolled down my face. I resorted to silence once more, resting my forehead against the cool metal door. I expected to be plunged into darkness now that Skervvy was finished with his fun. The burning light remained. It stayed on for hours. Maybe days. A pulsing headache formed. Sucking my energy. Stealing my sleep.

Time bled into more pain and suffering.

Never in my life had I craved darkness as I did now.

I jerked awake as pain lanced up my arm. Noting that I'd slid into the sludge once again, I glanced at my throbbing hand. Blood dribbled from a puncture wound on the fleshy part of my palm. And there, inches away, was a vorax about to take another bite.

At the sight of its long, yellow teeth, something inside my brain flipped. Adrenaline surged through me and I lunged for the creature. As I wrapped a hand around its bulbous belly, the animal shrieked and promptly bit me again. The thought of rabies flitted through my mind, but I was too far gone to care. Gripping its neck, I squeezed.

I knew that I was beyond weak. Knew that I was acting crazy. But I'd had enough.

"Die, you disgusting vermin," I growled, exhausting the final dredges of my strength on obliterating the creature. When it finally stopped moving, I studied the deep scratches on both my forearms. I couldn't feel them. Maybe I was in shock. Or maybe my overpowering hunger consumed every other feeling, including remorse at having killed an innocent being.

I paused, staring at the limp rat in my hands. Laughter bubbled out of my chest. This grotesque thing was far from innocent. It wanted to *eat* me. And now, I was going to eat *it*. I laughed harder. The creature was probably full of disease. One bite and I might not make it through the night. Or maybe it was already night. I had no way of knowing.

Tears joined my giggling fit. I had never felt this kind of desperation before—a gnawing need to survive, no matter what. There were too many things left unfinished. Too many people I wanted to help. If that meant eating raw rat meat to keep me alive for another day, then so be it.

Before I could muster up the courage, the door behind me screeched open. I tipped over, landing flat on my back. Above me, a shadowed form blocked the hallway's dim lighting. My brain expected to hear Skervvy's snide tenor, so I didn't react when a deeper male voice said, "What are you doing?"

I didn't blink. Didn't even breathe when he crouched beside me. Familiar features slid into place: heavy brows, short black hair, a moon and claw tattoo on a pale neck. Blue eyes edged in obsidian scanned my body several times. He reached down, resting a hand on mine. I remained frozen. But when he started to pry the vorax from my grip—to steal my *food* from me—I snapped.

"It's *mine!*" I snarled. The sound was so feral, my eyes widened. His did, too.

He pulled his fingers away, watching me warily. "Lune."

Startled at the soft tone, I sucked in a breath. Then ground my teeth together. "Don't. Say. My name."

The man who betrayed me—who betrayed Bren and caused all of this misery—sighed in exasperation. "You need help."

"Not from you," I bit out. When he continued to assess me with that heavy-lidded, bored look of his, I hissed, "Traitor." Not good enough. "Backstabber." Better, but the words needed more color. "You lying piece of—"

"Ryker Jones," a new voice said, interrupting my verbal assault. "Why am I not surprised to see you here, playing with my conquest?" I tried to stop it, but a shudder ripped through me at the sound of Skervvy's manic cackle.

A muscle jumped in Ryker's jaw. He studied me a moment

more before smoothly rising to his feet. "We both know you stole her from me, Skervlong, so stop pretending otherwise."

Conquest? *Stole* me?

I was going to puke, then twist off their manly jewels and shove them down their throats for treating me like a possession. After I regained my strength first. As the men continued to bicker, I tested my muscles, surprised that they actually responded to my commands. It must be the lingering adrenaline over seeing Ryker again—my friend turned enemy. Rage blanketed the hurt trying to curl itself around me.

I'm no one's friend, was the last thing he said the day he'd left me tied to a tree. Then why was he here now, trying to help me? It had to be a trick, another way to break my will. Unless he still planned on re-entering Tatum City and couldn't do so without me.

A pawn. That's all I was to him. Well, I wasn't going to helplessly lie here and wait for him to make his next move.

While the men argued, I slowly rolled over and crawled into the corridor's shadows—still holding the vorax. It was the only weapon I had. Plus, if they were both Sensors, the darkness wouldn't stop them from finding me. I was maybe a handful of yards down the hallway when I heard the scrape of boots, then fingers tangled in my hair and yanked my head back. "Where do you think you're going, girly?"

I did the very first thing I could think of. I twisted, ignoring the pull on my hair as I shoved the dead vorax into Skervvy's face. "Watch out!" I screamed, shaking the furry body before throwing it at him.

It worked. With a yelp and a curse, he scrambled back, releasing his hold on me. I bounded to my feet and ran. Then promptly smacked into a wall as my legs buckled. No! My body was failing me at the worst possible moment. My jagged nails scraped and snagged on the cement blocks as I fought to regain my footing, but I was trembling too hard. The lack of food and sleep—such simple yet vital things—would cost me my chance at escape.

An arm snaked around my neck and jerked me upright. I fell back against Skervvy who quickly wrapped me up in a chokehold I had no way of breaking. "You're speaking my love language, girly," he crooned in my ear as I struggled for breath. "Pranks are my specialty. The dirtier the better. But that was especially dirty. And, flipping phlegm wad, you smell *awful*."

For a second, I thought he'd release me, but he simply cackled. Of course he did. Secretly, he probably *liked* the smell. "Are you sure," I wheezed, fruitlessly prying at his arm to acquire more air, "that it's not you?"

Bad timing, bad timing. I shouldn't have preyed on his weakness while in such a vulnerable position. Sure enough, his hold tightened. I choked and was just about to claw at any piece of Skervvy flesh I could reach when I heard, "Release her."

My sight wavered, making the image of Ryker impossible to see. Then came a metallic *click*.

"*Now*, Skervlong."

"You won't shoot," Skervvy replied in a stupidly amused tone. Was he really that dumb? "Boss's orders."

"The boss ordered me to remove Lune from solitary confinement and have her cleaned up. He wants to see her. Now."

"I'll do it. I'm the one who brought her in. I've got visiting privileges."

"Not anymore. She's being transferred into my care, and if you don't let her go in three seconds, I'll have no choice but to report you."

Skervvy snarled. His forearm flexed against my windpipe and I saw stars.

"Three."

I couldn't breathe at all now. My eyes widened, but I couldn't see.

"Two."

A loud rush filled my ears.

"One."

Everything fell away. The arms. The support. The ground. Pain spiked through my hip bone and shoulder as I reconnected with earth. I dragged in air to avoid passing out. My ears were still ringing, my eyes watery as someone began lifting me up. I threw an elbow back, which did absolutely nothing. My body was weaker than it had ever been before.

But I could still speak. So I proceeded to do what I did best. "Put me down, you spineless, dumber-than-wood slimeball." I paused to assess the insult. I could do better. "I'd rather be kissed by a vorax than breathe the same air as you."

I left the ground anyway as either Skervvy or Ryker swung me into his arms. At this point, I didn't know which was worse. "When you least expect it," I continued, "I'm going to find something pointy and skewer your—"

"Shut up, Lune."

Ryker, then.

"Don't tell me to shut up," I growled, rather weakly. To compensate, I added, "Jerkwad."

"Real mature."

"I don't have to be," I shot back, blinking until his stupid chin swam into view. "Apparently the only thing I have to do now is pop out a litter of *babies*."

Every inch of his body that was pressed against mine hardened. "That's not going to happen."

Relief and hope tripped over themselves in my stomach. I hated how quickly my body wanted to believe his words. I knew better though. "What are you going to do? Carry me out of here and all the way back to Tatum City?" Acid dripped from my syrupy sweet tone.

He glanced down at me with a frown. "Not exactly. I need you for something first."

I gaped for several seconds, unsure whether to laugh at him for thinking I'd actually help him or scream in his face for acting so calm after what he'd done to Bren. I settled on hissing, "Whatever you have planned, you can shove it. I'm done following you, listening to you, and helping you. Anything you command me to do, I'll do the opposite."

"Not if you want to see him again."

It was as if he'd dropped me.

My body fell, fell, fell and wouldn't stop. My brain spun but couldn't grasp the words. Their meaning. The implications. The emotions that I should be feeling. None of it was registering. I couldn't think or breathe. My chest began to burn, but not from lack of air. No, it was anger. And hatred. Because this was the cruelest thing he'd ever done to me.

"You're lying." I had meant to coat the statement in venom, not floundering hope. A stupid, foolish hope that he was telling the truth. That Bren was still alive.

"I'm not lying."

Stars, the fire in my chest was too much.

I struggled, albeit weakly, against his grip. "Put me down."

And, surprisingly, he did. As soon as my feet touched solid

ground, my knees wobbled. I crumpled into a heap. I didn't care. The floor was a whole lot cleaner than what I'd just left behind. I stared at the chipped, yellowed tiles, unable to place where I was—still not caring.

"You're lying," I whispered again, but with even less conviction. I wanted his words to be true too much.

A metallic clank reached my ears a second before water burst over me. My heart lurched into my throat. I instinctively flinched, expecting another stinging deluge. Awareness returned as the steady downpour warmed comfortably. The communal showers. I glared up at Ryker anyway, but didn't find a smug expression or even a blank one. He was . . . he looked . . .

Sympathetic.

Screw your fake sympathy, you backstabber.

His face settled into neutrality a moment later. "He's alive."

My teeth chattered, but not from the cold. My adrenaline had come back. The urge to use it, to plunge into my ability and find Bren for myself—to make absolutely certain that he was alive—trembled through me. I hugged my knees to my chest in an attempt to keep myself from floating away. I didn't trust Ryker to watch over my body while I searched, not as I had with Bren.

Inhaling slowly, I straightened my spine and stared holes into Ryker. "Prove it."

His lips twitched as he crossed his arms. "I will. After you help me with something."

"How do I know this isn't a trick?"

Without warning, he tossed a small object at me. Wary, I almost batted it away, but my hand reflexively reached up and caught it. Heavier than I expected, I examined the metal object more closely. Copper. Round. Half the length of my thumb.

27

A bullet.

"That was in Bren's back. I took it from beside his living, breathing body while the clan's doctor wasn't looking."

I dropped it.

Clank, clank.

The bullet rolled toward the shower drain.

I slammed my palm on top of it. Why, I had no idea. This thing had been in Bren's *body*, damaging precious parts of him. It was evil. Destructive. I hated it.

But it was a piece of him.

I carefully closed a fist around the bullet and cradled it to my chest.

"This doesn't prove anything," I managed to croak.

"It's the best I can do for the time being. But I promise that you'll see him if you agree to a task."

My eyes narrowed suspiciously as I looked up at him again. "What task?"

Ryker glanced away, which was surprising enough. But when he violently shoved his hands into his pants pockets, his next words became that much more ominous. "You won't like it, but it's the only way you're getting out of here."

THE TASK

"Ow!"

"It's just a shot. Suck it up."

"Yeah, but you're doing it wrong. When was the last time you shot someone without intending to kill them?"

"I'm not laughing. You're not funny."

"I wasn't trying to be." I rolled my eyes, exaggerating the movement so the needle was no longer visible. After the vorax bites and scratches, I should be grateful that Ryker had thought to vaccinate me, but my hatred of needles dried up any thankful comments. Besides, thoughts of revenge were still forefront in my mind. If he could betray Bren—who supposedly used to be his *friend*—he could easily betray me again. My distrust of him had reached a whole new level. Pulling me out of a cell and cleaning me up didn't equal absolution.

As my legs dangled over the bathroom counter's edge, suppressing the urge to kick him in the kneecap was difficult. I managed, only because I didn't want him to jab me in the eye next with that needle. "So what's in it for you?" I asked.

"What?" He slid the needle out of my arm and pressed some gauze over the small puncture.

"If I complete this *task*, what do you get out of it?"

He hesitated, avoiding my gaze by fussing with a bandage. "I'll possibly earn the Recruiter boss's trust—or as close to trust as he gives. He needs to know where my allegiance lies or neither of us will be leaving this city."

"That's something you should have thought about *before* killing two of his men. Or tying me up to a tree in the middle of nowhere. Was your plan to let me rot there? Maybe provide a snack for the local wildlife?"

"No, I was coming right back. No one was supposed to find you. But . . . my mission hasn't exactly gone according to plan," he grumbled, crouching to check the bite wound on my leg. "We should be in Tatum City by now."

"I've been stuck in here for two weeks. What took you so long?"

"That's how long it took to get an audience with the boss. His attention has been elsewhere and getting him to listen hasn't been easy. He wants me to prove my loyalty and that takes time."

"I thought you were loyal to the Supreme Elite," I couldn't help quipping. "You also said you weren't part of the clan anymore. Does Renold or the *boss* know about this task you want me to complete?"

His eyes slowly rose to mine. Even from his hunched position, he was intimidating. I should have kept my mouth shut. "If you want to see Bren and get out of this city, then you'll say nothing, absolutely nothing. You're a nobody. A simple girl I found who has no clan or loyalties. If you open your mouth just once, *just once*, it could ruin everything."

Stars above, I wanted to snark all over his threatening words right now. It was physically painful to keep my lips sealed together. I managed to rein in the sarcasm, but was unable to stop myself from blurting the one question that had been plaguing me for the last two weeks. "Why did you give Bren to the Recruiter Clan?"

He studied me for a long time. I refused to look away, even when tears threatened to well up from the intense staredown. Finally, *finally*, he said quietly, "We shouldn't be discussing secrets in this building. But after you meet the boss and complete your first task, I will tell you, I promise. And my promises are binding."

First task? My suspicion radar was beeping loudly now.

After a moment of tense silence—and failing to read his inscrutable expression—I sighed. "Fine. I don't have the energy to bicker with you anyway. So what's next?"

"It's time for you to eat something so you don't pass out and ruin this whole operation." He snapped the first aid kit shut and strode for the exit, pausing inside the doorway to glance over his shoulder. "Coming?"

Typical Ryker. Didn't offer me a hand down. Didn't wait as he turned and disappeared around the corner. Sometimes his unpredictableness was predictable, and that could be used against him. I just had to figure out how to exploit it in case everything he said was a lie. In case he had no intention of letting me leave this place, and I was forced to break out everyone I cared for by myself.

The gentle pitter-patter of rain hit me first. Then the musky smell of damp wood still burning. I tilted my head back, relishing the feel of raindrops rolling down my face as I greedily inhaled the fresh air. Although I was blindly walking into this meeting with the Recruiter Clan's boss, I exhaled a relieved sigh at being allowed outside.

My gratefulness switched to squirming discomfort when I

opened my eyes and noticed that Ryker and I weren't alone. A certifiable horde of tattooed, mostly bearded men observed me with mixed expressions—none of them kind. Some were neutral while others leered menacingly. And some smirked, perusing my body with their eyes, their intentions more than clear.

Not wanting to appear weak, I straightened to my full height, planting my feet shoulder-width apart. Immediately, my thighs shook with the effort. I curled my hands into fists, raising my chin. I was no longer starving, but days without food and rest had taken their toll. A good strong wind would no doubt topple me over.

I am not weak. Show no fear. I sifted through every chant I'd ever told myself.

But I was a lone female surrounded by testosterone-driven males. Underneath the charred odor of wood burning in waist-high barrels, I could practically smell their hormones raging. No wonder the women were locked up—not just to keep them from running away, but for their own safety.

Were any of these men Berserkers? If they had the Sensor gene, that would make them little more than predators, controlled by their mutant abilities. They could be regular, unmutated humans too, but I somehow doubted that. The gleam in their eyes was too feral. Animal.

Strong fingers wrapped around my bicep. Under less hostile circumstances, I would have yanked my arm away. But, for the time being, I welcomed the touch. It reminded me that I wasn't *completely* alone. Hopefully.

"They are under orders not to touch you," Ryker's voice rumbled in my ear. He spoke louder for the next part. "And if they do, they will lose a hand."

Once again, if I weren't surrounded by a pack of barely

restrained, hungry-looking men, I would have reacted—this time with a wicked smile. I expected the twenty or so men to lead us someplace out of the rain, but no one moved. They were waiting for something—or someone.

An uneasy silence settled over the group as the minutes ticked by. Strands of dark red hair clung to my cheeks. I didn't dare brush them aside and draw even more attention to myself. Thunder rumbled in the distance, buzzing through the soles of my boots.

And then, as if responding to a silent command, the men suddenly parted. Ryker tightened his hold on my arm. A bear of a man strode into the clearing, his wide shoulders almost knocking into the men on either side of him. When he spotted me, he paused. Even with the sky a bleak gray and the flickering fires casting eerie shadows across his face, I could make out the color of his eyes.

They were shockingly blue. Surrounded by a ring of black.

And they were smiling at me with pure delight.

I would have passed out on the spot, uncaring if my head smacked against the fissured cement at my feet, if it weren't for the death grip on my arm.

Because it was *Ryker*.

His eyes were staring back at me from an older version of himself. A version that had a full beard and dark blond hair pulled back into a messy bun. With the shiny gold loop in his left ear, tattoos running up both bare forearms, and gun belt hung loosely at his waist, he looked like a pirate from the book I'd been reading. Despite all that, the eyes, heavy brows, and strong nose were exactly the same as Ryker's.

This must be his father.

And since the man commanded every last drop of attention from the men around him . . .

Holy crap, was Ryker the boss's *son*?

"Apologies for not coming to see you sooner, lass, but I've been a bit busy as of late with a newly returned clansman," the man said in a deep voice almost identical to Ryker's but with a decidedly more jovial tone. "How did none of my men stumble across a pretty thing like you all these years?"

"I told you," Ryker replied before I could—not that I was going to. "I found her south of here, just past Tatum City, hiding in a secluded grotto. She's been living off the land and is trained in weapons. An excellent choice."

The burly man eyed me head to toe as if sizing up a breeding mare. Which was why I didn't refute Ryker's words. Didn't even breathe. If this was Ryker's father, he was in charge of the "Operation Mutant Baby" program. Stars, I wouldn't let that good-natured smile fool me.

But there was something else, too. Something familiar that had nothing to do with Ryker and everything to do with the way he looked at me. Goosebumps pricked my skin beneath the clean white shirt I wore.

He crossed his beefy arms the same way I'd seen Ryker do countless times and finally focused on his son, freeing me from his heavy gaze. "So how is it that she was dragged in by Tom Skervlong?" he asked. "Why not bring her here when you showed up on my doorstep with my wayward son?"

Wait. His wording didn't make sense. It implied that he had *another* son. And the only person I could think of was . . . Bren. Unease churned in my stomach. Bren's parents were dead. Drowned. *Murdered* by the Recruiter Clan. Nothing made sense anymore. My knees wobbled and I quickly locked them before I went crashing to the ground.

"She is fiery and headstrong," Ryker said, but with a slight edge this time. "I couldn't carry Bren and manage her at the same time. But she will learn. As for Skervlong, he's been stalking what is mine for weeks now. He stole her from me the first chance he got."

Ryker's father lifted a meaty hand to stroke his beard. "So you found a girl with spirit. Just like your mother, eh, boy?" He chuckled, then threw back his head and roared with laughter, clapping the shoulder of the man next to him. The other men joined in until the only two not participating were me and Ryker.

The laughter died as quickly as it began. The boss crossed his arms again and smirked at his son. "Always so serious. Are you sure you're mine, boy?" Ryker's grip on my arm tightened to the point of pain. I started to pull free when words directed my way stopped me cold. "Is it true then, lass? Are you willingly giving yourself to my son?"

Willingly giving—

Wait. What?

Everything stilled then—the clansmen, the rain, my heart—as I registered what he said. Time itself paused as the man closely watching my every move waited for an answer. But my lips were frozen shut, my mind stuck on a loop.

Ryker had warned me not to speak. Said I had to go along with everything that happened if I wanted to see Bren again. But *this?* I didn't know what "willingly giving yourself" meant exactly, but my imagination was doing a good job of guessing.

The moment of indecision lasted a second too long. The boss's two-toned eyes narrowed. Then, ever so slightly, Ryker shifted. That small movement might as well have been a shove. He was nervous. *Ryker* was nervous.

If I said no, what would happen? Even scarier than that, what would happen if I said yes? But decision time was over. Every instinct shouted at me to run, but I couldn't. And so . . . and so I jerked my chin in a sharp nod of affirmation.

Crap.

The man chuckled. Then said two words that shot ice through my veins. "Prove it."

I wasn't given time to fully digest his command. In the next instant, Ryker whirled me toward him. My weak knees buckled, but he slid an arm around my waist, pulling me tightly to his chest. I stiffened, preparing to shove him away, to growl at him for manhandling me, but his hand lifted and gripped the nape of my neck. My eyes flew to his in surprise.

Before I could make sense of the emotions flitting across his face, he leaned into my personal space. His breath was a wisp of air on my ear as he whispered so quietly I almost missed it, "Make it real. You know what's at stake."

My heart gave a hard thump when, instead of retreating, he pressed his mouth to my jaw. Panic rose, wrapping around my throat as his intentions penetrated my brain. Crap. Oh crap. No, I couldn't do this. I loved Bren. *Bren.* I couldn't—

But it was too late.

I felt warmth a second before his lips slanted across mine. Every muscle in my body locked up. I jerked back, breaking the kiss. Hot anger throbbed in my skull. My eyes shot hellfire as I prepared to yell and curse at him for kissing me. But when he dug his fingers into my damp hair, tearing free a few strands, I saw the look of pure desperation he was giving me.

"Please," he breathed. I felt his fingers tremble, felt the arm supporting me quake as he asked for my permission. Why? *Why* was he doing this to me? He must know about my feelings for Bren, so why make me give myself to him? I didn't receive an answer. He simply said *"please"* one more time, using my body as a shield so the men couldn't read his lips.

Whatever his reasons, I knew he was concocting a plan, one that would hopefully keep me out of the correctional center and reunite me with Bren. I had to see him again. Had to see with my own eyes that Bren was still living and breathing. If kissing Ryker was the cost . . .

But by agreeing to kiss him, I could be throwing away my relationship with Bren. This could destroy our love. The decision was a hot brand searing into my flesh. I could lose him forever, but . . . but I had to hope that he would understand. Had to hope that we could heal from this and become stronger. Because a kiss from Ryker meant nothing to me. I would do this for Bren and face the consequences, knowing my heart belonged to him.

So I gave Ryker a look laced with warning. But a look giving him permission all the same.

He didn't hesitate. His mouth recaptured mine in the next breath. He moved with purpose. Pushing against my lips. Forcing them open. Demanding I yield to him. I did. Then stifled a gasp when his tongue thrust through, sweeping across mine. Testing. Tasting. It was foreign. Smoky yet sweet. Not unpleasant when I knew it should be. He continued to slide his tongue along mine, exploring every inch he could reach, as if claiming it—*me*—as his.

Claim.

It's a predator thing, Bren once told me. *Also a Sensor thing if not kept in check.*

A frantic fluttering of wings exploded in my stomach. A feeling I most *definitely* didn't want. A feeling of complete and utter betrayal. I didn't want to be claimed—not by Ryker, no matter what my traitorous body felt.

My hands found his face. Moved to our joined mouths. I pressed my thumbs against his bottom lip, asking him to stop. I couldn't . . . I couldn't do this anymore. My heart was being mauled and shredded. This *was* affecting me, despite my best efforts to act like it didn't. After a moment, he withdrew, but only enough to break the connection. His breaths were ragged, warm across my mouth and cheeks. The hand on my back slid up my spine, the action gentle yet almost . . . possessive.

An ache built in my chest. A twisted ball of confusion and misery.

Because I couldn't tell.

I couldn't tell if this was an act . . . or real.

THE BOSS

"Bring out Skervlong!"

The bellow of Ryker's father snapped me out of the strange trance the kiss had plunged me into. I became all too aware of the milling crowd, the penetrating looks and low rumble of words exchanged between the men as one of them took off to find Skervvy. An awkwardness I'd never felt before draped over us like a damp blanket. Or maybe the feeling stemmed from standing next to Ryker after what had just happened. There were so many words that needed to be said, but couldn't. So many emotions that needed sorting, but wouldn't.

I refused to dwell on them, wanting to pretend it didn't happen. But Ryker made that impossible—he wasn't looking at me, but I could sense his attention on me all the same. He had a *lot* of explaining to do after this.

The tension grew unbearable as the minutes ticked by, as the rain intensified and thunder boomed. But no one moved. Eventually, there came a scraping of boots against rock and the men parted to let Skervvy through. He strutted into the middle of the circle, then placed a fist over his heart and sketched a quick bow to Ryker's father.

"Boss," he said. "How may I be of assistance?"

Boss. So I'd been right. Ryker truly was the son of the

Recruiter Clan's boss. But he'd warned me away from the man, said he was worse than Renold. Yet he'd brought me to this meeting like a lamb to the slaughter. A cold flush shivered through me. The urge to bolt was a wild thing in my chest.

Before I could so much as twitch, a hand wrapped around mine. Startled, I jerked away, but the hand held fast. I looked up at Ryker, my eyes accusatory and brimming with anger. He shook his head, then deliberately slid his fingers through mine, clasping our hands together.

"Tom Skervlong," the boss said, breaking our staredown. "Is it true that you took my son's intended mate and tried to claim her as your own?"

Saliva built in my mouth, acidic and nauseating. Something twisted and wrong was happening here, words and rules that didn't make sense to me. Intended *mate?* My mind was coming up with all sorts of weird conclusions, at the forefront a crazy notion that these men saw themselves as animals.

Ryker had admitted that his moon and claw tattoo meant "nocturnal predator." Were the clansmen a pack of *wolves* or something?

While Skervvy defended himself—which he was doing a poor job of—Ryker's father tugged at the gold loop in his ear, a bored expression on his face. He glanced at me and, catching my stare, winked. It was such a *Bren* thing to do that my heart skipped a beat.

This couldn't be Bren's father. For one, they looked nothing alike, not a single trait. There was a good chance this man had raised him, though. They shared the same easy-going exterior while concealing untold secrets within.

His attention snapped to a still rambling Skervvy. "Enough," he said.

Skervvy immediately shut up. The boss took his time ambling toward the tall, lanky man who had done nothing but bring me pain. He circled him once, then twice. To his credit, Skervvy didn't cower. His hands balled into fists, though. Thunder shook the ground, as if seeking to alleviate the tension.

The boss circled one more time before facing the man who couldn't quite hide his nervousness. He cocked his head, the edges of a smile shifting his beard. "So what you're saying, Tom, is that you decided to challenge an alpha for his female without following the proper protocols. You know what that means, of course."

Skervvy's eyes widened comically. "N-no, boss. It wasn't like that. I was just following your orders. She was roaming the area, so I—"

"Are you questioning me, Skervlong?" the boss interrupted. "Are you *challenging* your head alpha's word?"

Skervvy shook his head vehemently, swallowing hard. He opened his mouth, whether to deny or apologize, I would never know. With lightning quick reflexes belying his size, Ryker's father rammed a fist into Skervvy's gut. The thin man bent over, groaning loudly. I gasped as the boss lunged forward and locked Skervvy in a chokehold.

"Doesn't matter either way, Tom. First you shoot my returned son in the back, then you spend two solid weeks sitting on your rear and gloating about a catch that was never yours to steal. May this serve as a reminder to you *all*," Ryker's father boomed. "No one breaks the code without invoking challenge from me."

Skervvy bucked and writhed in the boss's ironclad hold like a rabbit caught in a snare. Strangled sounds left him. He was pleading. Begging. Like he'd wanted *me* to do. But his words fell on unsympathetic ears, and he was no match for the heavily muscled older man. My mouth dried as I watched the man who had chased and abused me, who had shot Bear and Bren, turn red in the face. His eyes bugged out, his expression open terror as oxygen was squeezed from his lungs.

I waited for the inevitable moment when he would go limp and collapse to the sodden ground, but I wasn't expecting a *crack!* as the boss broke his neck. My blood ran cold. I was no stranger to death, but watching the man I had wanted to kill die by another man's hands was gut-wrenching.

At the undeniable truth behind the vicious thought, a violent shiver shook me.

Catanna was right. I was a murderer, my heart inked black by the color of revenge. I had wanted to end Skervvy with my own two hands. Now he was dead and I was numb—but not from shock. No, I was devastated that I'd lost the chance to enact my own version of justice.

I must have made a sound—maybe a whimper of disappointment—because Ryker turned me toward him. His look was questioning, asking if he'd need to catch me before I fell. I knew my eyes were wide and easily mistaken for fright, but my jaw was hard. He noticed. His brows slowly ticked upward. Then he nodded as if he understood. Of course he did. I had seen him kill more than once.

"Come with me," he said quietly. I didn't resist as his hand tugged on mine, as he led me around the group hovering over their dead clansman. But my eyes tracked the crumpled form on the ground. They remained glued to Skervvy's wide, sightless gaze until the crowd swallowed him whole.

Remembering words he'd once said, I couldn't help muttering, "Never underestimate desperation and the wily ways of women."

42

He should have taken his own advice.

No one stopped us from leaving, and as soon as we were alone, I jerked my hand free of Ryker's. For a split second, I thought about running.

His shoulders stiffened as if he'd read my mind, but he kept moving. "Don't try it. You might not see them, but we're still being watched. Closely."

My fingers flew to my neck, feeling for the bear tooth necklace Bren had given me. Its familiar presence brought me a small measure of comfort. Not like the comfort its rightful owner gave, but enough to slow my erratic heartbeats.

Even if I wasn't afraid of being tracked down by a pack of wolf-men, I couldn't run, not when my mum was here. And I wouldn't leave Bren behind. Soon, I would see him. And then I could release the flood of emotions that threatened to gush down my face at any second.

As if to taunt my resolve, the sky chose that moment to split open. The gentle rainfall became a downpour. Streaks of lightning lit up the street, revealing roots and leafy vines overtaking the urban landscape.

We walked in silence for several minutes, our focus on avoiding countless puddles, debris, and rusted trash cans dotting the streets. At one point, I skirted around the broken hull of a piano. My clothes were now plastered to my body. I realized then how revealing my white shirt was. No wonder the men had ogled me with such hunger in their eyes.

Ryker had found new clothes for me to wear after my shower. What if he chose the too-tight outfit on purpose, to show me off to his *pack*? Now that his tongue wasn't down my throat, reason had returned, along with my fierce distrust of him. I replayed the words "intended mate" over and over in my head. All of the men seemed familiar with the phrase. Did that mean there were others? Other women kept in a place outside the correctional center for . . . for what purpose?

The men's pleasure?

My heart thumped madly once more at the prospect of being prostituted. Such a thing was unheard of in the controlled confines of Tatum City, but I knew it existed. Knew that *claiming* could mean—

Oh stars.

Now I couldn't breathe. That sodden blanket was back, this time shoving itself down my throat. Ryker could be taking me to a new prison even worse than the last. And this *task* I was meant to do. I thought the kiss had been the task, but he'd hinted at more than one . . .

"What's wrong?"

I almost fell into Ryker, the lack of oxygen and my overall weakened state getting the better of me. His hands rose to steady me, but I managed to sidestep his touch. A buzz formed in my fingers and toes, a feeling I knew all too well. Adrenaline. The need to run. To *react*. I locked my knees, refusing to give in to the urge. "Where are you taking me?" I asked, my voice low with suspicion.

He cocked his head like a dog, as if trying to puzzle out what manner of crazy person stood before him. When he continued to study me in silence, my patience unraveled.

"Are you taking me to Bren now?" More silent scrutiny. The buzz tingled up my legs. "If not, then take me back to the correctional center so I can be with the other women." As his look morphed into one of surprise, alarm spiked through me. "Fine. I'll go back by myself."

I whirled, my only plan on returning to relative safety, when he grabbed my wrist and tugged me back. Without hesitation, I swung a fist at his face. He ducked. "Let go of me!" I yelled, panic pitching the words too high. My fingers formed claws as I prepared to rake my nails across his cheek. He caught that wrist, too.

I was so weak. *Weak!* I thrashed against his grip like a wild beast, shouting my fury, screaming my fear and helplessness. In a flash, I was lifted, borne over his shoulder. My legs were pinned to his chest as he carried me with purposeful strides down the darkening street.

"Ryker, let me go. *Ryker!*" I realized now that the dam had burst without my permission. Despite the wet hair smacking my face and blood rushing to my head, I knew my tears were falling in droves to the broken cement below.

What felt like only seconds later, I was sliding to my feet. It was darker here. A blank space between two tall buildings. Even *more* secluded. Before he could restrain my wrists again, I slapped his cheek with all of my strength. Alarm jolted through me and I sucked in a gasp. At any moment, I expected to be slapped in return. But when he made no move against me, I shoved him. His back hit the brick wall behind him. "You did this," I cried, striking his chest. Again and again. "You did this!"

He didn't stop me. Which only enraged me further.

The anguish. The confusion. The frustration. It needed *release*.

"Fight back, Ryker. Punch me. Kick me. Don't—" I shoved him again. "Just—" My boot connected with his shin. "Stand there!"

I growled like a rabid animal and charged, fully intent on beating him to a pulp for all he'd done. But when our bodies collided, he wrapped me up in his arms. I fought his grip. Cursed him. But he didn't relinquish his hold.

As if a lever had been pulled, the shouting became sobs. Great heaving ones that robbed me of strength. With no other choice, I sagged against him, utterly spent and unable to stop my tears from soaking his shirt. And then it clicked. The realization that he wasn't simply restraining me. He was . . .

Holding me.

His large hand was cradling the back of my head, firmly pressing my cheek to his chest. Then the words registered. Thin and hushed. "I'm sorry. I'm sorry." Over and over he said them. He continued to say them as he rocked me, holding me like a wounded child. He said them like he cared, like he actually freaking *cared*.

I wanted to black out then and never wake up. Because this— *this*—was all too much. But the darkness never came. Only numbness after the tears stopped falling. So I quieted. Ceased fighting. I felt Ryker pull back and search my face, but he wouldn't find anything. My mind, as well as my heart, had retreated into a dark corner where pain couldn't touch them. It was the only form of control I had left.

Where he took me next was a smear of thin, dank hallways and creaking stairs. Cracked plaster came and went. Flickering bare bulbs. Chipped banisters and faded rugs. And then I was sitting on an old leather couch with a wide tear in the cushion. A cup was pressed into my hands. Fingers curled over mine.

Fine. He could touch me. He could show me he *cared*. But I would do nothing, *nothing*, until he gave me some answers.

"Talk," I rasped, not bothering to clear my throat. He tapped the cup. I refused to drink. "Tell me what just happened and what's going to happen, or I'm done."

More of that insufferable silence.

Then, "Okay, I'll tell you."

46

I met his stare. And showed him with a glance just how much I didn't believe him.

He rose from his crouched position and paced a few times. He was nervous. Ryker hardly ever revealed outward signs of emotion. When he stopped, his gaze drifted to what looked like a kitchen, giving me a clear view of his flexing jaw. "I'm the son of Rollie Jones, who is head alpha and King of the Recruiter Clan. As the prince and only heir, I was raised to lead the clan someday. That is, if I'm willing to challenge my father and win, which is my birthright."

There was a beat of silence, then, "Prince?" I deadpanned. "Like the ones from fairy tales?" This was crazy. And he expected me to believe him?

He gave a self-deprecating snort. "Hardly."

"A *cursed* prince is more like it," I muttered. "Prince of the Jerkwads."

"You're not wrong," he admitted, which surprised me. His expression hardened. "A group of men deemed 'inferior' were cast out of Tatum City decades ago, commanded to follow the Supreme Elite's orders in exchange for food, medicine, and comforts that we struggle to produce out here. Over the years, the Recruiter Clan has grown into a pack comprised mainly of men with animal-like traits. But we are little more than grunts to the Supreme Elite, good for guarding his city and recruiting others to his cause."

"You mean kidnapping," I interrupted. "Stealing children from their homes. And now, I've come to find that you're stealing the *mothers*, too. Did you know about my—" I stopped myself from revealing that my mum was here. Who knew what he would do with that kind of information.

He looked away again, this time at the ratty brown rug under his boots. "I know about your mom," he said quietly.

I shot off the couch. The cup I'd been holding clattered across the scuffed hardwood floor. My vision blurred from the sudden movement, but that didn't stop me from taking a threatening step toward him. "You knew?" I hissed, fisting my hands. "You *knew* she was stuck here this whole time and didn't tell me?

"Yes," he said, once again not defending himself. Which suited me just fine.

"I'm going to kill you." I took another step toward him, unsure what my plan of action was. All I knew was that my fists burned with the need to punch something and Ryker's face looked like the perfect target.

But he raised steely eyes to mine, rooting me to the spot. "Yeah, well, you'll have to get in line, Princess. Just about everyone wants a shot at me right now."

My head jerked back as if he'd struck me. "Whoa. Okay. Now that I know you're a *prince* and that your clan thinks I'm your intended mate or whatever, under no circumstances can you call me *princess*. Got that?" The room tilted to the right and I stepped with it, almost leaning too far. Crap, the pesky black spots wouldn't go away.

"Sit down before you pass out on my floor," Ryker demanded, his voice sounding farther away than it should.

"*You* sit," I mumbled, even as I took a shaky step toward the couch. "Sit, like the dog that you are. Don't expect any treats though."

"Glad to know Skervvy didn't break your terrible sense of humor. And just so you know, it's an insult to call our kind dogs. Think twice before uttering that word around here." He about-faced and strode down a hallway, returning before I could snark

48

some more. A wad of fabric was shoved into my hands. "Put this on before you get sick."

I frowned and glanced at my trembling arms, too heated in the moment to realize how cold I was. "You're not going to undress me," I warned, scooting closer to the couch and away from him.

He snorted. "I will if you keep dripping water all over my rug."

"It's butt ugly anyway."

His lips twitched into a faint grin, which reminded me of our kiss. Nope. I was *so* not going there. I fisted the clothing and stormed for the hallway he'd come from. Well, stormed *after* my boot caught on the butt ugly rug. I heard a soft snicker as I tried to cover up the graceless move. My cheeks burst into flame despite how cold they were.

There was only one door to choose from, so I wasn't surprised to find a bedroom. With a bed. The sight drove lead into my veins and an overwhelming ache to sleep. But I couldn't. I still had too many questions, and I *needed* to see Bren.

Another door inside led to a bathroom—which I had no desire to enter. I imagined I must look awful. Shutting the door to the hallway, I habitually felt for a lock but found none. My nose flared with irritation. If Ryker came barging in while I was dressing, stars help me . . .

He disappeared from my thoughts as I struggled with my water-logged boots. When I'd finally stripped down to my underwear, I was breathing heavily, like I'd run a couple miles uphill. The task of pulling a dry shirt over my head almost made me whimper. I eyed the pants on the bed that looked a few sizes too large, then inspected my shirt's hem, which fell to mid thigh.

I was decent enough for what my body and mind screamed at me to do. I could no longer resist the pull. I sprawled face-first on the bed, uncaring that the blanket smelled musty. I only cared that it didn't reek of rat. Relief deadened my muscles. Just a few minutes of indulging in this luxury I had missed beyond reason. My eyes slammed shut, cementing my decision. Immediately, my brain switched off.

IT WAS AN ACT

The feeling of something in my hair dredged me from the endless dark pit I'd succumbed to. My first thought was of falling asleep in the filthy cell and waking to a vorax crawling in my hair. I shrieked, blindly shoving the disgusting rodent away from me.

When fingers wrapped around my wrist, I wildly swung a fist, seeking out Skervvy's face. My knuckles connected with flesh, but not in the area I was aiming for. Sharp pain zipped up my hand at the hard impact, jogging some sense into me. My eyes jerked open. To pitch black nothing. Panic sucked the air from my lungs.

Instinct had me aiming for a location I had a better chance of reaching. I half expected to meet the thickness of his thigh, so when I hit my intended mark, a masculine grunt of pain drowned out my surprised gasp. I quickly drove the heel of my palm upward, connecting with Skervvy's chin. Twisting out of his hold, I scrambled away.

Then promptly tipped over an edge and fell.

Oof! My shoulder struck solid ground, not the mucky dirt of the cell. Had he moved me to a new location while I slept? I rose onto my hands and knees, feeling my way across what felt like a wooden floor. Ahead, a faint light bloomed. I scrambled toward it, my heart jackknifing in my chest.

Just a little farther and I would be free of Skervvy's maniacal clutches.

A handful of feet to go.

I gathered my strength and stood, racing for the light, charging toward freedom. I burst into the hallway and paused. Where were the other cell doors? Unless . . . unless he'd moved me to a place where women were claimed. A streak of fear bolted through me.

Crap. *Crap!*

Straight ahead, a white door with peeling paint beckoned. I dashed toward it, not daring to survey my surroundings. I expected a guard to pounce on me from a shadowed corner at any second, so I willed my legs to pump faster. I all but slammed into the door, my heartbeat a wild thing as I wrapped shaking fingers around the handle.

I turned it. Yanked. The door was stuck. Locked! I stopped breathing when I noticed five separate locks decorating the door. I fumbled with them. *Snick.* One down. *Click. Scrape.* Only two more to go.

A throat cleared. Tingles of dread froze me in place.

"Where are you going?"

At the sound of his voice, a voice that was very much *not* Skervvy's, awareness and memories finally caught up with me. Including the realization that I wore nothing but a *shirt.*

Crap on a cookie.

"What was that?"

Stars, even my mouth was betraying me. I slowly straightened and, with as much dignity as I could muster, turned toward the room. And a very annoyed Ryker.

Oops. I'd punched him in the jewels. Then again, he deserved it. I struggled not to smile. Okay, I was smirking a little. His expression darkened and he prowled toward me like I was trapped prey. I scowled at him, widening my stance as I prepared to strike again.

But he threw me off balance when his look slowly bled into wicked amusement. Instead of swinging a fist, I tried to push him back. He easily caught my wrists, pinning them to the door above my head. My mouth popped open. When he didn't stop there, when he pinned *all* of me to the door and pressed his leg between mine, I sucked in a harsh gasp.

His head came down and I had just enough sense to jerk mine to the side. His lips landed on the shell of my ear. I tried and failed not to shiver as his breath warmed the side of my face. But it was his leg, his *leg*—wedged between mine where only a flimsy pair of underwear stood in his way—that sent my pulse into overdrive.

"Ryker," I breathed. Stars *above!* I had meant to snarl his name, not purr it like a kitten. What was happening to me? And *why* was he doing this? Revenge? Settling an old score with Bren? Because it was working. I was questioning the depth of my loyalty and love for Bren.

And I hated every doubtful moment.

Ryker shifted, rubbing his body against mine in ways that were far too intimate. I chomped down on my lip to keep from groaning aloud. "Good," he whispered, the word teasing my hair.

My eyes snapped open. I immediately stiffened, that one word a splash of ice water to the face. He was *enjoying* my inner—or maybe not so inner—turmoil.

Before I could fight against his hold, he slid his fingers through mine and tightly gripped them. "We have company." I barely caught the warning, but when it registered, my eyes widened further.

Oh. *Oh.*

I shivered again for an altogether different reason. Some-one—probably his father—was watching this very *public* display of affection.

And I was only wearing a shirt!

After a lingering moment, Ryker pulled back but continued to hold my hand as we faced the room's other occupant. Sure enough, the boss lounged on the couch, a booted leg propped over his knee. Both arms were splayed across the back cushions, and he wore a lazy grin, boldly taking in my apparel—or lack thereof.

"She's perfect for you," he addressed his son. "That feisty spir-it will serve you both well. I'm surprised though. After the last un-suitable female you picked, I thought you were doomed to repeat the mistakes of my brother."

Ryker's grip on my hand tightened, his fingers trembling. With anger? Nervousness? Or was it fear? But when I dared peek at his expression, it was blank.

"I've learned my lesson," he replied, his tone bland. "And I have you to thank."

The boss guffawed. "You'll have to do a lot better than that, boy. You ditched your clan for Tatum City. Two years I've been without an heir, wondering if you'd ever return. I need proof of your renewed loyalty, not flattery." His eyes swiveled to me. "But where are my manners? We haven't been properly introduced."

When he rose from the couch, the already small space shrunk even more. His boots thundered across the wooden planks. When he stuck out a hand, I offered him mine, wondering if his grip would crush my bones. But he did something completely unexpected and bent to kiss my knuckles.

As he straightened, his voice became smooth as silk. "I am head alpha and King of the Recruiter Clan—better known as 'the boss'—but you may call me Rollie, my lady. After all, we're almost family."

A charmer, then, when he wanted to be.

Just like Bren, my inner critic hissed.

No, not like Bren, I argued back. Bren didn't snap men's necks simply to prove his dominance. At least, I hoped he didn't.

I steadied my voice before saying, "I'm Lun—a. Luna." I inwardly grimaced, unsure why I'd given him a fake name at the last moment. Besides, it was too similar to my real name.

Rollie cocked his head. "Luna. Meaning 'moon.'" He glanced at Ryker's neck, then touched a spot on his own where the same moon and claw tattoo was inked—the symbol of their clan. He barked a quick laugh. "It's a sign. Though I sense you do not carry the predator gene. What are you exactly?"

"Um, I'm . . . human?" I shrugged, feigning ignorance. If he knew what I could do, he would no doubt use me like he had with Bren. A worrisome thought took hold. What if Ryker told his father about my abilities to prove his renewed loyalty? He didn't know everything, but he knew enough. His fingers briefly squeezed mine as if in approval of my answer. Which didn't help me know whose side he was on.

"So where did you meet my prodigal son?"

The subject change threw me off guard. A cold sweat immediately dampened my palms. Was his father testing our stories to see if they matched? "I met Ryker at—"

Rollie waved a hand dismissively. "Not that one. My boy, Bren."

If this was meant to trip me up, it was working. My mouth formed words, but nothing came out.

His eyes did that glowing thing I'd seen Bren and Ryker's do, like an animal's reflecting the moonlight. Were all Sensors capable of this trick? I wondered if he did it on purpose to intimidate me. His mouth slowly curled into a smile. Yup. Definitely on purpose.

"Sadly, I missed the spectacle, but many of my men said they witnessed you throw yourself at Bren the night he was brought home," he said casually. "Under different circumstances, this would please me greatly, but he betrayed us. Honoring the code is the one thing I ask of my clan. Not only did he break that time and again, but he refused our clan's mark. He must be punished for his crimes. You would do well to forget about him. Whatever feelings you once had for Bren must now be directed toward my sole heir, who I've overlooked for far too long."

He looked at Ryker, but there was no pride or warmth in his expression. It was dark. Bitter. Despite his words, there was a deep tension between him and his son. I recalled something Jaxon had once said about Bren.

He was being hunted by the Recruiter Clan boss who valued him more than all of his goons combined.

Did Rollie care more about Bren than his own flesh and blood? Enough to want Bren as his heir instead? Maybe Bren's punishments would be less severe then—or worse, if his betrayal had hit the boss on a deeper level. Either way, I had to see him as soon as possible. I didn't know how to save him from this terrible mess, or know if Ryker had a plan to do so, but there was something I could do right now. Something reckless. And irreversible. But something that would speak volumes.

"I will accept your clan's mark," I said firmly. I expected surprise, and got it. Rollie's eyebrows flew up while Ryker's head whipped my way. Before either could say a word, I added, "But with your permission, I'd like my moon tattoo without the claws.

As you pointed out, I'm not a predator."

The Recruiter Clan's boss studied me shrewdly, searching for signs of treachery.

What he didn't know was that my *real* name actually meant "crescent moon." My mum had told me the story of my birth many times and I'd never forgotten. Under a sliver of moon and a thousand twinkling stars, she had labored, unable to make it back to the community's safety before the pain became too great.

But she hadn't been alone.

I could envision what he must have looked like that night. Face etched into fierce lines of protectiveness, he bravely stood guard over his wife and unborn child, worried that predators would come investigate the screams. When I came into the world, he wasn't able to see or hold me for several minutes, too busy fighting off a mutated beast. His first saber cat kill. Definitely not his last.

The memory of his loss struck me then, like a swift kick to the heart. I firmly pushed aside the gruesome images before I was forced to relive that terrible day.

Inking a moon onto my skin wouldn't be accepting the mark of a clan who'd torn me from my mother. The symbol would remind me of my humble beginnings, of the beauty that was found in the darkest hour. Of the love I had known, the fruition of bravery and sacrifice.

By accepting the moon, I would be embracing my parent's legacy. I couldn't think of a more fitting reason to permanently stain my skin than that.

Finally, after a full minute under his gaze, Rollie nodded. I couldn't tell if he saw through my ploy—his expression remained blank—but he turned to Ryker and said, "See to it," then unlocked the door and exited without a sound.

After his departure, I thought the room would feel bigger again. Nope. Ryker was still staring at the side of my head, and with everything that had happened between us today, I couldn't bear to face him. Gah, we were still holding hands! I tugged mine free and quickly rubbed my sweaty palm on my . . . shirt. Crap, I'd completely forgotten about the lack of pants.

"What are you doing?" Ryker said softly, yet I almost jumped out of my skin.

My focus stayed on the shirt as I muttered, "Uh, your hand was warm. I think a pound of sweat just went through my—"

"No. What are you *doing*, Lune?" he cut in, facing me squarely now. At the incredulity in his voice, I almost looked up, but didn't dare. "You don't have to get a tattoo."

"Yes, I do. You said we need your father's trust. But I'm not doing it for him. Or you." I paused, knowing I shouldn't look up, but wanting to see his face for what I said next. I lifted my eyes. "I'm doing it for myself. And for Bren, so I can see him again."

Ryker's expression was always impossible to read. This moment was no exception. His jaw gave him away, though, the muscles bunching as he ground his teeth together. He was mad, I knew that much, but I wasn't sure who the anger was directed toward.

"I care about him," I continued when he remained silent. "I'm sure you already knew that though." His eyes darkened, making my stomach lurch. He couldn't really be mad about . . . Ah crap. "Today was an *act*, Ryker. Nothing more. I did what you wanted me to do so I could see Bren again."

"Oh?" he snarled. The hairs on my arms raised. "So your thundering heartbeats were an act?"

"Yes." I stopped breathing, trying to stop my heart from skipping as well.

"And the way your body responded to my touch. An act?" He leaned into my personal space, almost stepping on my toes.

I quickly retreated, realizing too late that he'd backed me against the door again. My eyes narrowed to slits but he didn't stop. His hand rose toward my face. I stiffened. He paused. But only for a second. His fingers gripped my chin, and I growled a warning. Ignoring it, he tilted my head up, lowering his until a scant inch separated our lips. When his breath feathered over my skin, I couldn't hold back a shiver.

"Is *this*," he whispered gruffly, "an act?"

Stars above, I didn't know *what* this was, only that it made me feel vulnerable and confused. And if I was brutally honest with myself, I did find Ryker attractive. He stirred my blood and made me want things I shouldn't.

Like right now, as his other hand slid around my waist and pulled me flush against him. He shifted, rubbing his bottom lip over mine in a slow caress. Waiting for me to make a move. To prove that this wasn't an act. My heart was undeniably pounding, my body urging me to be reckless. To embrace the danger I craved. To allow myself to lose control and revel in the fall.

But there was Bren.

Bren.

My comfort. My rock. My haven.

There were still so many things I didn't know about him, but he'd only ever kept me safe. He had fought, bled, and sacrificed for me. Had told me I was strong, had believed in me, had protected me at all costs.

Who would I be if I betrayed him when he needed *me* now? A coward, that's what. Selfish and weak. That wasn't who I wanted to be.

I could feel that Ryker wanted me. The lines of his body were taut with pent-up need. His lip quivered against mine with barely restrained desire. But were we *right* for each other? All we did was argue and fight. We were like two deadly knives, sharpening each other's edges, when we both needed someone who could soften them. Maybe he wanted this act to be real for the same reason I had.

To *feel* something other than hurt and pain. To escape the loneliness. To distract an overactive mind from an uncertain future.

But I wouldn't let him use me that way, and I wouldn't use him.

I couldn't. Not when—

"I love Bren," I blurted.

MOON TATTOO

It took all of one second for him to register the statement.

Then, before I could do little more than gasp, he whirled us around. We were halfway across the room and nearing the hallway when I realized where he was taking me. Fear drained the blood from my face.

"Ryker, no." I pried at his fingers on my arm. They were cemented in place. We were only a few steps from our destination now. I peered into the inky darkness, a wall of panic bearing down on my chest. "Ryker. *No.*"

I was about to start fighting in earnest when he grabbed both my arms and pressed me against the wall. I jerked a knee up, but he anticipated the move and I struck his outer thigh instead.

"Lune, stop. *Stop*," he hissed. "I would never hurt you like that."

"Why else would you be dragging me into a dark room, huh?" I yelled. "You're mad that I'm not giving in to your *charms* or whatever, so now you'll force yourself on me."

As soon as the words left my mouth, I wished I could take them back. I'd never seen Ryker so angry. My returning glare shriveled up, and I struggled not to cower. His fiery gaze quickly shifted to the wall beside me. "I am *not* my father," he said, his voice deathly quiet. "I will never be like him."

I stilled and waited for him to continue. When he didn't, I

broke the tense silence. "Then why—?"

He held up a hand. "I'll tell you once we're on the other side of that door. Not a moment sooner. If you want answers, you'll have to trust me with your honor."

The urge to sass bubbled up. The need to remind him that he'd given me no reason to trust him. Besides, if he didn't trust anyone, then trusting him was probably stupid. He *had* released me from that cell though and promised to let me see Bren. I had to hope that there was more to this than becoming his intended *mate*. "Fine. But if you make a move on me while we're in there, you can say goodbye to your jewels."

The anger on his face faded to confusion, but he stepped back anyway, allowing me to enter the room on my own. I rolled my eyes. How chivalrous. When the door sealed shut behind us with a soft *click*, the room plunged into darkness. I readied for his attack. None came.

A switch flicked on. Near the bed, an ancient-looking lamp made of multi-colored glass illuminated Ryker's expression. It was back to being unreadable. "I'm not going to touch you," he said. Then added, "Unless you allow it."

"Fine," I replied curtly, crossing my arms. Ryker's attention drifted to my legs. Crap! I lunged for the pants still draped over the bed and tugged them on. They must be his, judging by the material pooling at my feet. I tied the waist string as tight as I could, placing hands on my hips in case the pants slid off. "Now start talking."

He gestured around the room. "It's soundproof in here, a precaution I made several years ago. Our kind has keen hearing, and I'm not the only one living in this apartment building. Spouting your undying love for the clan's number one traitor could ruin everything we're trying to do."

Okay, that made sense. "Why did you kiss me?" I was done with vague responses. Either he told me the truth or I was going to take matters into my own hands.

"Proclaiming you as my intended mate was the only way I could think of to prove my renewed allegiance to the clan. But they needed to *see* the genuineness of my claim, and what better way than public affection? The boss has every reason to doubt my loyalty. When things went south a few years back, I left for Tatum City shortly afterward without explanation. He thought I'd chosen a new alpha, forsaking his legacy—like Bren did. I'm lucky he didn't throw me in a cell too."

I squinted at him, trying to figure out his angle. "Is that why you handed Bren over to him? To gain back his trust?"

"That's one of the reasons. Yes."

"How come it didn't work then?"

"Because he thinks we're secretly conspiring together."

"Are you?"

Ryker snorted. "Hardly. Bren hates me."

"Why?"

A muscle jumped in his jaw and the floor received his undivided attention.

"Ryker, just tell me. If you want me to cooperate, this is the price. Answers."

"I can't tell you everything."

"Why not?"

He looked at me, his stare hard. "Because I don't trust you."

I gave him a hard look of my own. "That makes two of us. But if we're going to get out of this craphole, we have to."

He huffed his annoyance but didn't disagree. In fact, I was struck mute when he opened his mouth and said, "Bren blames me

63

for what happened to his sister three years ago. I transferred her to a new location in the city for safekeeping, but a few clansmen with a vendetta against Bren found her while I was away. They—"

He heaved a sigh and scrubbed a hand down his face. "Let's just say it's a good thing Bren caught her scent when he did. He found her at the house several minutes before I did. By the time I got there, Bren had already set his plan of escape into motion. Blood was everywhere. Broken furniture. I thought the clansmen were trying to kill them both. Not thinking, I told him to take his sister and run."

Ryker's face pinched, as if the memory pained him. Perhaps angered him, too. "While I killed the three men for crimes they hadn't actually committed, Bren ran. But I didn't expect him to leave the city for good, and I never saw Isabella again after that. It's why the boss still doesn't trust me. She was my responsibility and I lost her. Therefore, he lost Bren, his greatest asset. At first, he thought I'd killed them and hidden their bodies. Now he thinks I helped orchestrate their escape. On top of that, most of the clan is still ticked off at me for killing those three men and wouldn't mind putting a bullet in my head."

Deafening silence settled between us. I couldn't speak, not when my brain was so busy putting the pieces together. He must have brought Bells to that white house we'd holed up in on the outskirts of Asheville. Bren must have told Jaxon and the others at Blue Ridge Sector that Ryker was the boss's son, which explained why he'd been locked up and questioned. Did Bells know he was at The Ridge for two months? And if Rollie had been using her to blackmail Bren into doing his dirty work, then why had Ryker been allowed to move her?

The pieces clicked into place.

Oh. *Oh.*

"Holy crap," I whispered. My eyes flew wide. "Did you choose Bren's sister as your intended mate?" Holy. Crap. "Wha—How old was she? Like . . . *twelve?*"

Gross.

Ryker had the audacity to roll his eyes at me. As if I were being dramatic! "She was almost fourteen. And think of it more as a betrothal. A promise. We hadn't completed the bonding ritual though, so technically, I had no claim on her. Plus, the men were jealous of Bren's standing with the boss. When they found Isabella unprotected for the first time in eight years . . . Well, use your imagination."

Stars, I didn't *want* to use my imagination. No wonder Bren, who so desperately tried to protect his sister, was so mad at Ryker. At the same time, I knew the feeling was mutual. Did Ryker actually care about Bells?

I plopped onto the bed. What a messed up situation. I was about to ask him if Bells had been forced into this "betrothal" when I remembered something she'd told me. *I can't help but be drawn to the tortured soul types though. They feel everything so intensely under all that dark brooding.*

No way. Had she been referring to *Ryker?* And then I was laughing. Loudly. Deep belly chuckles. I fell back onto the mattress, clutching at my stomach. It was so screwed up that I found the whole thing hilarious. When I was able to pry open my watery eyes again, an irate Ryker was hovering over me.

Oops.

"I'm sorry," I wheezed. "I'm not laughing at you, I'm laughing with—" I sat up and cleared my throat, struggling for control. "Never mind. Um, so can you take me to Bren now?" I winced. Maybe I shouldn't have asked that question so soon after laughing in his face.

"No."

Great. Now he was going to punish me for—

"We have to do the tattoo first. That way the boss won't question your intentions if you're found in restricted areas. Hopefully not, anyway. And the men will think twice about bothering you. It was . . . it was smart thinking, offering to accept our clan's mark."

I fiddled with the bed's musty blanket as guilt pricked at me for some reason. Maybe because I wasn't used to being the deceiver. "I'm not accepting your clan's mark. Not really," I admitted. "I'm accepting my own." Telling him the truth about it was the least I could do after everything he'd told me. And I still planned on prying many more answers out of him before we left this city.

When he didn't respond, the urge to peek at his face almost strangled me. Instead, I jumped up, feigning excitement. "So, what lucky person gets to jab a needle into my flesh? Can't wait." Crap. Needles. *Needles!* Maybe I couldn't do this after all.

"Me."

"You?" I squeaked. I tried to swallow and failed. A delusional part of me had assumed the clan's doctor would do it. Had thought anyone, *anyone* but Ryker would. Because the thought of him so close to me after all we'd done . . .

Smart thinking, indeed.

I finally managed to swallow. "Fine, let's get this over with. So—" I waved a hand around like an awkward idiot. "Where will this torture session take place?"

"Here."

"Here?" I blinked at him dumbly.

He gestured at the bed. "Have a seat. Soundproof room, remember? This way no one will hear if you scream." With that, he disappeared into the bathroom, leaving me to gape like a stupid fish. Was this payback for laughing at him? Because it was good. He came back with a small kit and unrolled the contents on the bed. A shallow dish, rubbing alcohol, cotton balls and cloths, a jar of black ink, a box of matches, and . . . needles.

I looked away, inhaling slowly to steady my heartbeat, but it was too late. My pulse was soaring through the roof.

"You sure you want to do this?"

I nodded, crossing my arms, then quickly uncrossed them. "Just don't make it too big."

"Where do you want it?"

Oh. I probably should have thought about that. Heat warmed my face. The tattoo needed to be in a location Ryker could reach without removing any of my clothes. A crazy idea popped into my head. I shoved it away, but it only came back, persistent and decisive. My delusional mind was officially broken.

Here goes nothing.

"Can you . . . can you tattoo over a scar?" I picked at my nails to distract myself from the needles winking in my peripheral.

"Yes. I've done it several times."

Right. He had at least ten tattoos scattered over his body—and maybe more that I hadn't seen. Any number of them could be hiding the countless scars on his torso and back. I dragged in a breath and spoke my request before I could lose the nerve. "Then I want it right here, directly over the C shape." I pulled back my hair from the left side of my face, revealing the scar Catanna had given me.

I almost bolted from the room when he blurted, "Your face? You want a tattoo on your face? *I* wouldn't even go that far."

"Oh, that's good to know, thanks," I deadpanned. "Anyway,

a mark I purposefully choose is preferable to one I had no control over."

Whoa. Where had that come from?

Apparently, Ryker was just as shocked. And, ah crap, why was he staring at me like that? Like he completely understood and couldn't believe I felt the same. Okay, this was getting awkward really fast.

I sat on the bed, careful not to send the needles rolling my way. "Okay, so inside the crescent moon shape, could you add star constellations? Should I draw it for you or something?" Not that I could draw.

"No, I've got this." He came around and sat to my left. Reaching toward my face, he paused, silently asking for permission to touch me. Surprised that he kept his word, I nodded without rolling my eyes. He tucked the hair behind my ear, inspecting the scar on my temple. Tension thrummed through me. If he noticed my stiff posture, he didn't let on. He also didn't shy away from touching me now that I'd given him permission.

We were alone. On a *bed*. And my emotions were still heightened and confused.

Stars above, this was the worst idea I'd ever had.

I flinched as he disinfected my skin, the sharp bite of rubbing alcohol stinging my nose. Silence settled between us—the very uncomfortable kind. Thankfully, it didn't take him long to sketch the tattoo's shape over my scar, only a couple inches in height and width. Rollie and his men should have no problem spotting the mark, though. If I tied my hair back, the tattoo would stand out nicely against my pale skin.

What came next was a blur. A flash of needle. A spark of flame. A swirl of ink. Blue, black-rimmed eyes steadily focused on the needle tip dangerously close to my—

"Wait! Wait, wait." I leaned a safe distance from the needle, waving it away. Ryker had the audacity to look annoyed. "How badly will this hurt?"

"Bad," he said without inflection.

I rolled my eyes. "Oh, that's so comforting."

"I've reached my empathy level for the day. There's not much room for it in my DNA."

"That's interesting. Bren's a Sensor too and he's plenty empathetic."

He scowled. "Don't start comparing me to Bren. You'll be sorely disappointed."

"I'm not. I just don't think you should use your mutated genes as an excuse to be a jerk."

His eyes narrowed in warning, and I bit the inside of my cheek. I really shouldn't be antagonizing him right now. "You know nothing about me," he said, quiet anger in his tone.

"You're right, I don't. Just like you don't know much about me, only what you've observed."

"Apparently." He paused, slowly cocking his head in that dog-like way of his. "Why did you allow me to kiss you?"

My jaw slackened. Really? *Really?* Was he going to press that sore spot until he got what he wanted? What *did* he want anyway? "First, promise to tell me why you brought Bren here instead of directly heading back to Tatum City, and how you plan to leave this place."

"I promise."

I raised an eyebrow, waiting.

"I promise to tell you right after you tell me about the kiss," he amended.

Ugh!

"Fine. At first I allowed it because I'll do anything to see Bren again. But then I allowed it because . . ." Heat rolled up my neck as the truth settled into my bones. Crap. This was going to suck. Better to just rip it off like a bandaid. "I allowed the kiss because I'm reckless and drawn to dangerous things. You're like a shot of adrenaline, and for a moment, I gave in to the temptation. I wanted to feel something besides pain. But . . . but you're *bad* for me, Ryker Jones. And I'm bad for you."

And now I needed to crawl beneath the bed and burrow under the floorboards.

This was the perfect time for him to use my confession of weakness against me. If he was looking for revenge against Bren, all he had to do was press the issue. Maybe I'd stay strong . . . but maybe I wouldn't. My mask was paper thin, my walls even thinner. I had always thought fear was my biggest weakness, but maybe I had an even greater one.

I shot off the bed, but Ryker's hand was already around mine, keeping me from running. "I—I can't," I stammered. "This is not—"

He tugged me down to the mattress again. I sat, my back ramrod straight, my stomach tied into knots. He reached for my chin. Instead of turning my head toward him though, he faced it forward. "Hold still," he simply said.

Then poked the needle through my skin.

I squeezed my eyes shut and bit my lip as hot pain spiked through my temple. When the needle retreated, I sucked in a ragged breath, thoughts of kissing Ryker long gone. I swore loudly. He snickered. Now I wanted to punch him. "Holy crap, that majorly sucked."

He shrugged, then poked me again. "Enduring pain is better than feeling dead inside. At least this way, you know you're still alive."

I frowned, surprised to hear him share something so deep. But when he dug the needle in again, I refrained from commenting. The crescent moon shape could easily become a shriveled banana if I moved around too much.

"From the start, my mission was to hand Bren over to the Recruiter Clan if I suspected his loyalty was compromised," he said, surprising me once more. "I almost didn't when I saw what was in his backpack, but something didn't add up. That map drawing I'd been given led me straight to his location, which can only mean one of two things: He works for that place under the mountain, or he's a double agent and they found out. Which still doesn't explain why someone wanted me to take you and leave, but either way, I wasn't going to let him return to Tatum City. There's too much at stake."

When he paused to wipe the blood and excess ink from my temple, I quickly interjected. "What's at stake? What was in his backpack?"

"I'm not at liberty to say."

I pursed my lips, grappling with some not-so-nice words. "Let me guess, Renold's orders?"

"Yes."

"Why does he keep me in the dark about *everything*?"

"At first, I thought it was because he didn't trust you, but now I think it goes deeper than that. I think it involves what you can do, and the power you'd have over him with that kind of information." His fingers directed my chin to face him. When our eyes met, he said, "Since I'm being so accommodating and answering your questions, how about you tell me what else you can do besides track Bren?"

"Tell me your plan for leaving this place first," I shot back, raising my brows in challenge. The action tugged at my fresh wound and I grimaced.

He shook his head and sighed, but without the regular annoyance. "Let me finish the tattoo and get you in to see Bren first. If we make it back without getting locked up ourselves, then I'll entrust you with my most guarded secret in exchange for yours."

If he wasn't still holding my chin, my mouth would have fallen open. I wanted to believe he was simply manipulating me so I'd divulge my Visionary abilities, but . . . but this felt real. Like the mask was off and he was letting me see a side of himself that no one else saw. I swallowed, the sound loud in the silence. I nodded without comment.

He went to work on the tattoo again, deftly poking a curved line down the scar on my face. The pain was terrible, a constant, scraping burn. But Ryker was right. Pain was better than feeling dead inside. My driving need to fight for a better future had returned in full force. He might have plans to leave this place, but I was formulating a plan of my own.

And I would give him no choice but to help me complete it.

PURE GOLD

Bren was somewhere beneath my feet.

Instead of a locked cell, he was being held in the city's sewers. There was only one entrance and exit to his prison: a manhole in the middle of a dead end street.

When I asked Ryker what would happen if someone caught me down there, he simply said, "Don't get caught."

Great. At least during the day, most of the clansmen were asleep. When the sun lowered, they came out in droves, and when the moon vanished, so did they. Nocturnal predators, indeed. It was now early morning, the sky and buildings cast in shades of gray as the rain from yesterday continued to pelt the streets.

I pulled the hood of my borrowed jacket further over my head, trying to remain invisible and mask my scent. But I was in my own shirt and pants again. If someone looked closely enough, there was no disguising my feminine figure.

In the distance, Ryker spoke to the man guarding Bren's underground prison. He was making a deal of some kind with the clansman. Hopefully. I was waiting for his signal in case things went south, poised to flee back to his apartment.

Thoughts of Bren's living conditions made my stomach roil. Did the vorax visit him down there too? "Oh, Bren," I breathed, my heart aching for him and all he must have endured the past few weeks. And it ached for what I had to tell him. What would I say, exactly? *"I'm Ryker's intended mate now, but only for pretend. Anyway, I let him kiss me, and I sort of felt something. But I didn't want to."*

Yeah, this wasn't going to be pretty.

Separating from the guard, Ryker headed toward my hiding location while the clansman adjusted his jacket and went the opposite direction. Leaving the manhole unattended.

Ryker slid into the cramped space beside me. "It's done," he whispered.

"How did you get him to leave?" I spoke just as quietly. "I thought they were all mad at you."

"Only when I have nothing to offer. I just happened to have something he wanted."

"What did you give him?" I peered up at his profile.

"Medicine from the correctional center."

My brows rose. Smart.

He looked down at me. "We have twenty minutes before a new guard shows up for his shift. You sure you want to do this?"

"Absolutely," I said, even as my heart nervously skipped a few beats. "Are you? We're risking a lot."

"A promise is a promise," was all he said. Then, before I could block him, he carefully pried my hood back. I stilled as he pushed aside my damp hair to inspect the completed tattoo. After a tense moment, he lowered his hand and glanced at the street. "It suits you. Don't get it infected while you're down there."

I nodded, unable to respond. His actions were confusing me again, and stars above, I *really* needed to see Bren now. Ryker ticked his head in a *follow me* gesture, making sure the coast was clear before casually slipping into the street. I tried to mimic his confident strides, transitioning my gait to a man's. He peered back at me with a frown. I shrugged and gave him a *you should have let me practice first* look.

He shook his head without comment and scanned the dark buildings for signs of life, no doubt listening with his keen senses. My eyes stayed glued to his back, my focus on making as little noise as possible. When Ryker paused, I stiffened, prepared to run. Then I noticed the tall, chain link fence blocking our path that I'd assumed would be unlocked. A giant padlock sealed its gate shut.

Crap. Why didn't the guard—?

Before I could finish the thought, Ryker was already moving, scrambling up and over the fence. He landed softly on the other side, straightening to stare at me expectantly. I stared back, my mouth agape.

"You've got to be kidding me," I muttered, rolling my eyes. Just like climbing a tree, right?

Ugh.

I stepped back and took a running leap. Metal, slippery with rain, bit into my skin. I knew that I was making too much noise, knew that my movements were clumsy from lack of exercise, but I made it to the top. Bren would have caught me on the way down, but Ryker stepped back as I gracelessly landed.

Okay, I was officially comparing them. I couldn't help myself.

Ryker was already crouched near the manhole when I turned. He waved me over, motioning for me to grab the lid. We barely managed to lift the unwieldy metal circle. The abrasive edges dug into my callused palms as I dragged my side a couple feet before letting go, puffing out a strained breath.

Nervous excitement swirled in my gut. I almost jumped into the black hole right then in my overwhelming need to see Bren. Ryker grabbed my arm as if sensing the idiot move. He shook his head, pulling me down as he bent to pick up a small rock, then dropped it into the hole. I held my breath, waiting for the rock to crack against cement. But it dropped. And dropped. Finally, I heard a faint *plink*.

All went silent except the pattering rain.

I met Ryker's solemn look, mouthing, *"Holy crap."* He nodded, gesturing at the metal ladder rungs attached to the hole's side. I didn't waste a moment, already slinging a booted leg over the side. I was about to lower myself down when a hand squeezed mine.

I glanced up to find Ryker's face inches away. His eyes slid to my lips. I sucked in a breath, frozen at the thought of him kissing me. I silently asked him not to, hoping he would honor his word.

He leaned forward, but instead of kissing me, lightly brushed his cheek against mine to whisper, "You have ten minutes. I'll tap on the ladder three times. Don't be late." When he pulled back, he added so quietly I almost missed it, "Be careful."

As I descended, I cleared my mind of Ryker. The rungs were slippery, and after almost falling to my death, I slowed, gripping the metal until my fingers throbbed. I wasn't sure what to expect when I reached the bottom. A pit of mud, maybe. Or Bren wrapping me in his arms with a shout of joy.

But when my boots landed on the ground, it was solid except for rain water running down the middle of the worn concrete. The only light was from above, so it took my eyes precious seconds to adjust. There were shapes moving in the shadows. Rats—or vorax. And the smell was overwhelming, a mixture of damp earth and rotten eggs.

My nose wrinkled, but I released the ladder and entered the sewer tunnel, following the water's path. Weaponless, I sought out the only comfort I had—my bear tooth necklace. I grasped the tooth as I navigated the underground lair.

Several yards in, a thin strain of light from above illuminated a large form hunched against the wall.

My entire body stiffened.

What if it wasn't Bren? What is this had all been a sick game to lure me down here so a giant mutant beast could eat me for breakfast?

The form shifted. I jumped, blindly reaching for the ladder. My fingers met air. I was too far away and the beast was probably faster than me. I tried not to panic, but fear barreled through me. My breaths came in spurts. When the form shifted a second time, I couldn't hold in a tiny shriek.

"Lune?"

At the sound, everything in me clenched tightly. That voice. That deep rolling timbre. More gravelly than usual with a strong note of disbelief, but I would know that voice anywhere.

My heart turned over and I stumbled forward, tripping over loose bits of rock. Without hesitation, I splashed through the sewer water. Nothing mattered. Nothing mattered but getting to him. When I saw him, when I *really* saw him, I started to cry.

He was bare-chested and shoeless. The stubble on his jaw and cheeks had grown into a dark beard. And he was slumped against the wall as if he had no strength to stand.

But he was still beautiful. So very beautiful.

"Come here."

My breath hitched at the quiet request, but I couldn't seem to move.

"Please, Lune," he begged. Pleaded. Just like in my dreams. "I need to know that you're real."

His words squeezed the air from my lungs. I had the overpowering urge to run then. But this time, I wouldn't be running away. I lurched forward, demolishing the space between us—space that I had cursed and hated for tearing us apart. I didn't stop until his warm body was beneath my fingertips. Until my hands were running over his face, down his chest, exploring every inch they could find. Making sure he was whole. Alive.

I was on my knees before him, drawing him to me. I pressed his cheek to my chest and held him there, comforting him the same way he'd comforted me so many times. My fingers found his back, tentatively seeking out the damage, afraid to hurt him. When they felt the raised skin where he'd been shot, I choked out a whimper. "I'm so sorry. I'm so sorry, Bren."

With a loud, rattling clank of metal, he finally moved. His arms came around me, squeezing me to him until my ribs groaned in protest.

But I didn't care. I loved the pain in my bones. Loved the ache spreading across my chest. Loved every second of discomfort if it meant we were together again.

"It wasn't your fault, little bird. I never should have tried to get away. But we were surrounded and I couldn't free you on my own. I just . . . I can't believe you're here. I didn't think I'd ever see you again."

It took me a moment to realize he was crying. His breathing was harsh. Anguished. Relieved. His legs came up, boxing mine in as if to keep me from disappearing. I clung to him with no intention of letting go.

This.

This was right.

There was no confusion. No doubt.

It was a knowing. An assurance without thought.

My heart simply knew.

This was home.

Too soon, he eased back, raising his hands to cup my face. "Say something, Lune. Please tell me you're okay. Did they . . . did they do anything to you? Are you hurt?"

My lips parted as I prepared to reassure him, but the words wouldn't come. I couldn't lie. The secrets had to stop, and I couldn't expect the truth from him if I let fear keep me from being honest in return. But this was going to suck. Really, really suck.

"I . . ." My stomach cramped. Looking into his concerned eyes physically hurt.

Stars above, just say it!

"Ryker kissed me and I let him," I blurted in a rush. Then gasped. Hearing it out loud was so much worse.

Bren stopped breathing. His golden irises shone bright with emotion.

"And . . . and I agreed to be his intended mate. It was the only way he could sneak me down here."

Tears burned my eyes as I helplessly watched him absorb the news. Confusion, shock, horror, then hurt leached the color from his face.

The look of utter betrayal was the hardest to watch.

A thousand apologies sprang to my tongue, but we didn't have time for them right now. "That's not the worst of it, Bren. They're breeding women here. The kids are then being transferred to Tatum City—maybe other locations, too. Did you know? Did you know that my *mother* was here all this time?"

His eyes widened. He still didn't speak.

My fingers squeezed his, trembling as dread sleuthed through my veins. "Bren, please," I whispered. "Please say you didn't know."

He blinked, panic and shame paling his skin further. "I-I knew. I knew about the women and children. But, Lune, I—"

A gasp ripped through me. Now it was my turn to feel the gut-wrenching punch of betrayal. I dug my nails into his palms, trying to pry his hands off my face. "Let me go. Let me go, Bren!"

He only slid his fingers into my hair, anchoring me in place. "Just wait, Lune. *Listen.*" I glared, ready to spew venomous words, but his expression grew determined. "I knew about them for *years*, unable to help them. I hated not being able to save them. Hated that I left them, that I wasn't strong enough. I hate myself every day for my failure.

"That's why I went to Tatum City, the source of the problem," he said, his voice hushed and urgent. "But I swear I didn't know about your mom. I never visited the correctional center because I didn't . . . I didn't want to know who was in there. You have to believe me. When I met Iris, though, I began to suspect. What were the odds that she'd end up in Tatum City too? But I couldn't tell you about the breeding program. It's connected to my mission, and I'm not auth—" He froze. I watched with growing alarm as his expression pinched. His neck muscles spasmed like he couldn't breathe. Like he . . .

Ah crap.

"You have a restraining chip in again." It wasn't a question.

He nodded, conveying with his eyes how sorry he was.

I searched his face for signs of falsehood, but found none. There was just pain. Raw, honest pain. Guilt pressed down on me. Here he was, suffering in a rat-infested sewer, and I had done nothing but cause him more agony. I sighed. "We still have a *lot* to discuss, but I believe you."

He practically deflated, heaving a sigh of his own. "I'm sorry you got dragged into this mess. I can never apologize enough. I'll spend the rest of my life making it up to you, however short that may be."

I frowned. "Don't talk like that. We're both getting out of here. Besides, I'm the one who left Blue Ridge Sector. That was *my* choice."

A deep groove formed between his brows. "Yeah."

We fell into an uncomfortable silence, and I wondered where his mind was taking him. Maybe to thoughts of Ryker, the man who'd helped break me out of his home. Who'd forced him to reconnect with his past. Who'd kissed the girl he loved. I didn't know what to say, so I said nothing. I simply pressed my thumb to that deep groove and smoothed it out.

He studied me for a long moment, regret and sorrow evident in his eyes. I worried that he'd push me away again like he did after I'd lost my memories. My heart fluttered in panic. He must have sensed it, must have made a decision because he suddenly tilted my head and kissed my cheek. The contact was feather light, his lips soft and tentative. But it was enough to undo me.

At my quick inhale, he pulled away, as if afraid he'd made the wrong move. I touched his face, feeling the newness of his beard, urging him on without words.

When he tipped my head again and brushed a kiss to my other cheek, a wave of fierce longing washed over me. My hands fell to his shoulders and a pathetic sound left my throat, but I didn't care. He was kissing me. *Kissing* me. Even after what I'd admitted.

His warm mouth roved up my jaw. I bared my neck, silently urging him to kiss a path there too. He did, swirling his tongue against my skin as he went, completely wrecking me. I groaned weakly, utterly lost to his touch. His lips nipped at my ear and I shivered with pleasure. But when his rough beard scratched my left temple, I couldn't hold in a pained hiss.

Bren jerked back, surprised. My eyes popped open and so did his. I knew the moment he spotted my new tattoo. "Lune. What is this?"

I reached up to cover the mark with my hood, but he caught my wrist. I shrugged offhandedly, but he wasn't fooled. If anything, my tripping heartbeat gave me away. "It's . . . we had to earn Rollie's trust. Bren, it's not what you think."

"Not what I think?" he growled, eyes blazing. "You have the Recruiter Clan's mark on your *face!*"

Crap, he was more than mad. He was furious.

"It's not their mark," I said calmly, trying in vain to soothe his rage. "I had Ryker alter it—"

"*Ryker* did this? I'm going to kill him. I'm going to—"

"Bren!" I cried, alarmed at his vicious tone. Hearing him so unhinged sent fear pumping through me. Not for myself—for *him.* "You can't kill Ryker. We *need* him. Without his help, we'll never get out of here. Please." I threaded my fingers into his matted hair. "I can't stand seeing you like this. Channel that energy into escaping this place."

At that, his shoulders slumped and he looked away. "I can't."

"Can't what?"

He released me and gave his wrists a shake. The jangling noise startled me, and I stared stupidly at the metal cuffs and links securing him to the wall. "I can't escape," he replied.

It was his tone that jarred me from my stupor. The unmistakable note of defeat. I studied his expression, horrified at what was written there. "No!" I snapped, and roughly grabbed his face, forcing him to meet my eyes. "You are *not* allowed to give up, Brendan Bearon. I don't care how bleak things look or how impossible it seems. We all lose our way at times. We make mistakes, we fail, and we fall. Then we get up again. But giving up? Don't. You. Dare."

Clank, clank, clank.

Ryker chose that moment to tap on the ladder.

Our time was up.

No!

A tremor shook me so hard, my teeth chattered. "I-I can't leave you. Not like this. I don't know what to do."

Bren gave me the saddest smile. It tore out a piece of my heart. "Yes, you do," he said, and ever so carefully tucked a lock of hair behind my left ear. His finger traced the crescent moon tattoo. "You've gotten this far. Don't stop now. You're capable and strong—so very strong. I've always believed in you. But . . . but I wanted so badly to . . . to . . ."

"To protect me? Save me?"

He nodded, a pained look on his face. "But I can't seem to save anyone. Look at me." He rattled the chains attached to his wrists. "You don't need me anymore."

"Yes, I do," I said firmly, hating that the one person who'd lifted me up over and over again was crumbling before my eyes. He was losing faith in himself. "And you can still save me. But now it's my turn to save you."

Clank, clank, clank.

Louder this time. More urgent.

My heart rate sped up. I wasn't ready. I would never be ready to leave him. But I stood anyway, taking more time than I should. "I have to go, but I'll be back. Here, take this." I started to remove Ryker's jacket, but Bren stopped me with a shake of his head.

"I can't take that. They'll trace it back to you." At my helpless look, he attempted a reassuring smile. It fell flat. "I'll be okay, little bird. Sensor blood runs hotter than most. Now go before you get caught."

As I turned, he grabbed my hand. I blinked, surprised at the firm hold.

"Wait. There's one thing I need you to do for me, Lune," he said urgently, demanding my full attention. He had it. "Contact Jaxon. You know how. Tell him my mission has been compromised—the traitor works for Renold. Tell him that it's now or never. And, Lune? Do what you have to do. Fight to be free; save yourself. Just promise that you won't sacrifice yourself for me."

I shook my head incredulously. "I can't promise you that."

"I'm not worth it," he said forcefully, his hand trembling. "I'm not as strong as you think I am. I only pretend that I am to make myself feel better, and to hide the ugliness inside. I hate what I've done and don't deserve to be saved."

My eyes ran over him, every inch that the thin light touched. He was beaten down, worn out and tired. Drowning in his demons. Buried in guilt. His heart was shrouded in shadow, tormented and heavy.

But underneath all of that darkness was a heart of pure gold.

I could see it even if he couldn't. That warm light was what drew me to him in the first place. And it wasn't fake. Despite being a spy and having the ability to charm the evilest of villains into trusting him, that gold center of his was real.

I began to pull away, watching him strain against the chains as he continued to hold on. His fingers slipped from mine, leaving me achingly cold and bereft. I turned away. My boots were poised to climb the ladder when I finally said, "You're worth it to me."

I knew he heard.

Two steps from the top, a large hand reached down to help me out. I accepted without thought. But as he hauled me over the edge and I regained my footing, I looked up to discover . . .

It wasn't Ryker.

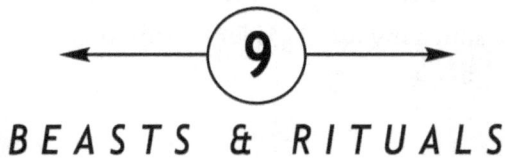

BEASTS & RITUALS

"Hello, lass."

I flinched back and the Recruiter Clan's boss released my hand. There was no way I could run from this bad situation. Blocking the chain link fence were five other clansmen, two of which had a grip on Ryker. His father picked up the manhole cover as if it weighed nothing and slammed it in place.

He straightened, wiping the dirt from his hands. "I'm not surprised to find you here. Bren always had a magnetic charm that was hard to resist. Pity that you are so thoroughly under his spell. But what I didn't expect was to find my son here."

At the cool glare he slid Ryker's way, warning bells clanged through my skull. That look. I'd seen it many times before—but on Renold's face. I knew what it meant. "I just needed to say goodbye," I said, attempting to draw his attention. My chin lifted when Rollie trained that look promising pain on me. "I wanted closure and Ryker gave me that. As a . . . as a bonding gift."

Crap. I didn't even know if that was a thing. But he'd mentioned a bonding ritual, so it was the best I could come up with.

The boss raised an eyebrow. "How generous of him. I didn't know my son was the sharing type. But if that's the case . . ." He lunged forward, shoving my shoulders. Instead of hitting the ground, though, a pair of hands broke my fall. Before they could release me, Rollie said, "Have at her, boys. Your prince likes to share."

There was a moment of hesitation, but when he added, "I'm rescinding the code, men. Don't waste this opportunity," the hands tightened, pawing at my jacket.

I froze, paralyzed by the sound of a loud *whoop* as a couple more of the men surrounded me. One ripped my hood back, pulling out strands of hair in the process. My eyes found Ryker's. His teeth were bared, muscles taut, but he wasn't fighting to break free. When his gaze flicked to the boss, my stomach twisted. I understood then that I was on my own.

Fine. I'd show them determination and the wily ways of women.

I snapped my head back. Even as I heard a shout and the crunch of cartilage, I was moving for my next target. I kicked in a kneecap. Punched a throat. I managed to get in a few more hits when the groping hands became violent. Fingers gripped my hair and wrenched my head back. I rammed my leg into the man's groin in front of me before my limbs were grabbed from all sides and I went down, down, down.

They shredded the jacket from my body. Tore at me, leaving behind blood and bruises. I bowed my back off the ground, screaming, fighting with everything I had. "You're animals!" I yelled. "Monsters. *Beasts!*"

"Enough!" a deep voice bellowed. The men immediately stopped their assault. The weight on my chest lifted as they fell back, and I scrambled out of reach. I shook all over as I stood. My heart pounded so hard, I thought it would rupture.

Before I could react, fingers grabbed my chin. Turned my head. "You accepted our mark," the boss said, pulling my hair back from my face. "This changes things."

He whirled me around, still holding my hair. "From now on, no one touches her but my son," he barked. "Those who break the code will pay with their lives. She's a part of our clan now. Spread the word." I flinched as his heavy boot stomped on the manhole cover. "You hear that down there? *No one* touches her."

With a flick of his wrist, he commanded the men to release Ryker. "My son and his intended mate may freely roam the city, all except this underground cell. As a reminder that my orders will not be disobeyed, even by our future princess . . ."

I heard the quiet rasp of steel. But what he did next happened so fast, it was over before I could fully register the sharp tug. He shoved me again, and this time, Ryker caught me. I didn't move, didn't breathe as I waited to feel pain.

"I want the bonding ritual done by sundown, boy," Rollie said over my shoulder. Ryker nodded. "When it's complete, bring her to Pack's Tavern. She and I need to have a little chat."

The men filed through the gate behind their king, one remaining to guard Bren's prison. When the only sound was the pattering of rain, I allowed my hand to drift upward, seeking out the damage. Ryker beat me to it. His fingers slid over my shoulders, gathering something before pulling away. I looked down at what he held.

Long strands of dark red hair.

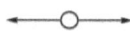

I stared at the pale stranger in the mirror.

The girl had a cut on her cheek. Purple smudges under her eyes. A black sliver of moon speckled with stars cupped her left brow. Her jagged hair, dark auburn beneath the dim lights, barely dusted her shoulders. Her full lips were pinched, bled of color. But her eyes . . .

That clear spark of determination was familiar.

"Who's tough?" I whispered to her. "That's right. You are."

And for the first time ever, she nodded back, knowing the words were true.

"Let me cut it for you."

"No."

"Stop being stubborn. I've been cutting my hair for years. I'll make sure it's even."

"Oh, so that chunk missing in the back was done on purpose?"

He quickly ran a hand over his head, seeking out bald spots. "I don't have a—" Ryker caught the gleam in my eye and dropped his arm with an irritated sigh. All too easy. "I'm surprised you're in such high spirits."

"It's just hair." I shrugged. "Better than losing my head."

And I'd seen Bren. He was alive and well. Or as well as could be expected under the circumstances. That look of defeat, though . . . Stars, I had to get him out of there and soon.

"What is this bonding ritual we need to do?" I asked, closing yet another empty cupboard in Ryker's kitchen. My stomach growled loudly, still recovering from almost being starved to death.

Ryker tossed me something. Dried meat. Not my favorite, but I'd eat just about anything right now. "You ask about the ritual instead of demanding what my best kept secret is that I promised to tell you?"

"It'll keep for a while longer. Is this squirrel meat?" I

grimaced, but ripped off a piece anyway. "Sounds like this bonding thing is a pressing matter. How long will it take?"

"Not long."

I stopped chewing and eyed him suspiciously. "I still love Bren, Ryker. This better not be something weird that involves taking off our clothes and—"

"Despite what you think," he interrupted, giving me a hard stare, "we're not animals. Maybe rough around the edges, but we have rules to live by, a code of honor. Women here are seen as lesser, yes, but a chosen mate is revered. She is untouchable once under the head alpha's protection. You earned that honor, so you will be respected."

I made sure to give him the biggest eye roll on the planet. "So chopping off my hair was a sign of respect?" I stuck another wad of squirrel into my mouth, muttering, "Sign me up for a lifetime of bad hairdos."

"No, that was a warning. You got off lightly. Everyone has to obey the head alpha's orders, even his queen."

I blinked. "You have a mother?"

He looked at me like I'd lost a few brain cells. "Of course I do."

"No, I mean, is she alive? Does she live here?" Or was he a test tube baby like Iris? The thought turned my stomach. I set down the remaining squirrel meat.

He jerked his chin toward the bedroom where we couldn't be overheard. When the door was closed, he began to pace. I leaned against the wall and crossed my ankles, settling in for a story. Hopefully. Something told me he didn't talk about his mother often.

"How good are you at keeping your mouth shut?" he said, still pacing. I hurled a scowl at his back.

"For eleven years, I didn't tell anyone that I was kidnapped and beaten by my adoptive father," I said baldly, since he already knew.

He stopped in the middle of the room and watched me with those intense blue eyes. I struggled not to squirm. "So you'd hold up under torture?"

I gaped. "T-torture?"

"If the boss finds out what I'm planning, I'm dead. And if I'm dead, there's no point in keeping you alive—unless he uses you for the breeding program. So tomorrow, when he has a little *chat* with you, nothing I say can be repeated."

"I won't say anything. You're my ticket out of here and into Tatum City, remember? I wouldn't jeopardize that."

"I thought you didn't want to return," he said shrewdly.

"I don't," I admitted. "But it's as you said. I left someone behind."

I couldn't leave Iris all alone to suffer the same fate I did. But I needed help, and having Ryker as an ally was a good place to start.

He approached and I straightened, unsure of his intentions. When he grasped my wrist, I stiffened, but didn't pull away. "Swear a blood oath to me that you won't tell a soul, and I'll tell you everything."

When his thumb slid over my inner wrist, I whispered, "What are you doing?"

"Checking your pulse for a lie."

"Oh." I swallowed, all too aware of how close he was standing. "Okay, fine. But what's a blood oath?"

Instead of replying, he let go and reached behind him, pulling out a knife. Without hesitation, he dragged the blade across his right palm. Blood immediately welled up, and I stared at him incredulously. "Your turn." He flipped the knife, offering me the handle.

"What? No. This is . . . it's unsanitary. What if you have a disease?"

His expression flattened. "I don't have a disease. Do you want me to do it for you?"

"*No,*" I practically shouted. "Definitely not." Grimacing, I took the knife still wet with his blood. This was stupid. But I needed answers. I sighed, muttering, "This better not turn me into Wolf Girl," before neatly slicing my palm. I watched as an old scar split open, blood bubbling to the surface.

Ryker quickly grabbed my hand and pressed our palms together, sealing in the blood. My first instinct was to pull away, but he linked our fingers, squeezing until my knuckles whitened. He withdrew a slim cord from his pocket and wrapped the length around our joined hands. The cut on my palm began to burn as he cinched the cord tight.

When he was done, he resheathed the knife and placed his thumb over my inner wrist again. "Do you swear to uphold this blood oath on pain of death?"

"Ryker," I whispered, and his eyes settled on mine. "You're creeping me out."

He blew out a breath, annoyance in his tone as he said, "Do you swear or not?"

"Fine. I swear."

"Say it," he growled softly.

"I swear to uphold this blood oath on pain of death. There, happy?"

"I'm never happy."

"You need a hobby then. Something relaxing. Fishing, perhaps."

His brows lowered. "This is serious."

I schooled my expression into seriousness.

He remained silent long enough for me to feel uncomfortable. Probably a tactic he learned from his father. "You were never supposed to enter this city, and I was meant to quickly leave after handing Bren over," he began, dropping my wrist but still keeping our bound hands locked together.

"I underestimated Skervvy's need for revenge and his desire to prove himself, though—he always wanted to be an alpha. When he took you and Bren's backpack containing the box, I had to formulate a new plan. The Supreme Elite's orders were explicit: make sure Bren completes his mission or complete it for him. Without you and that box, he'd never let me back inside Tatum City."

"What's in the box?"

"Serum vials of some kind. Similar to what the people under the mountain interrogated me with. They tried to pry answers from me about my mission and alliances, but I proved resistant to their methods."

Cold dread shivered up my spine. "Was the serum in the box yellow?"

His eyes narrowed. "Yes. Why?"

I hesitated, knowing that I was treading on dangerous ground. If he really was loyal to Renold, then this could end badly for me. But what if I could sway his allegiance? I fiddled with my necklace, watching his face for signs of deception. "Ryker, what is Renold *really* up to?"

"He doesn't tell me everything, but—" He paused, studying our linked hands as though tempted to undo this whole blood oath agreement. Finally, he looked up. "I'll tell you what I know if you explain to me what your ability is. And not the short answer. Every last detail."

"Okay."

He blinked. "Really?"

"It's the only way we're both going to get what we want. So, yes, I'll tell you." I plowed ahead without preamble, knowing that I could be playing right into Renold's hands. But I didn't know what else to do. It was time to take a chance. "I'm a Visionary. I can see things happen before they happen, predicting an opponent's move before they make it. I can also seek people and objects—and not just by tracking. I can tunnel into my mind and form a tether with what I seek, actually *seeing* the object or person.

"Oh, and I can telepathically communicate inside people's heads." I shrugged. "I'm still working on that part though."

To say he was shell-shocked was an understatement. It *did* sound pretty crazy. His mouth opened and closed several times. "Prove it," he whispered, as if dreading the very thing he was asking.

It was my turn to study our clasped fingers. "I, uh, I can't."

"Why not?"

"Because . . . because when I thought Bren was dead, I just . . . I don't know."

"You broke."

My nostrils flared as I glared up at him. "No, I didn't."

"You did."

"I didn't!"

"Then. Prove. It." Each word was a challenge, mocking the foundation of my strength.

I threw him an angry look but slammed my eyes shut, breathing deeply. Searching for my source of calm and control. *Focus on his stupid face. Focus on his annoying voice. Focus, focus, focus . . .*

His scent came to me then. Earthen. Smoky. Like a campfire. Awakening memories I'd much rather forget. But they unlocked something else, too. A feeling of being sucked inside myself. A feeling still very much foreign and a bit frightening. In the pitch black, an invisible tether formed, drawing me to him. I resisted the pull at first, not wanting to get stuck in his head. Fear of what I'd find was a deterrent yet a curiosity. But the tug was insistent, and I plunged ahead.

Into a tangle of intense emotions.

His emotions. A swirling wall of anger, pain, loneliness, and . . . desire.

I felt like an intruder.

I knew Bren or Iris wouldn't mind me in their heads.

But Ryker?

I whispered his name into the void, then louder when there was no answer. Nothing happened. Frustration built. I was *stronger* than this. Dominic, my teacher at The Ridge, had said my mind was a steel trap, stronger than any he'd ever felt before.

I'm not broken!

I know you aren't.

At the sound of Ryker's voice in my head, I coughed in surprise. When I'd connected with Bren and Iris in the past, I had heard them speak out loud—not *in* my mind. With Ryker, the words had echoed, filling my ears as if they were my own thoughts.

Something rubbed against my face, snapping me back to myself. Instead of meeting Ryker's eyes, his black shirt swam into view. It was right there. Plastered to my cheek. What the—? Crap. I was *leaning* on him, his arm around me for support.

"That happens sometimes," I mumbled, wiggling out of his hold. When I didn't get very far, I gestured at our joined hands.

"Can we—?"

I needed space to clear my head. If the desire he'd been feeling was for me, I would have to be more careful. Bren may have all but given me permission to do what was necessary, but I wouldn't play with someone's heart. Including mine. I knew how painful betrayal felt.

Ryker unwound the cord, appearing deep in thought. When our palms separated, my cut began to throb. I headed for the bathroom to clean it, but he stopped me with a hand on my arm. "Let me."

I almost demanded to know why, but he was already moving and I was suddenly exhausted. The bed called to me and I responded, plopping onto the edge. Before my eyes could drift shut, he returned with a first aid kit and knelt in front of me. Speechless, I simply watched as he flipped my hand over and cleaned the wound with practiced movements.

Who was this man? It certainly wasn't the Ryker that I knew.

I prepared to ask where the rude side of himself had wandered off to when he started to speak in low tones. "Two years ago, I made a deal with the Supreme Elite. I was to become your Keeper and contend in two Trials to earn what I asked for. But when I failed the Rasa Rowe Trial, he reset the terms. Once Bren's mission is complete and you're safely returned, he'll give me what I want: an enhancement serum that'll allow me to challenge and defeat Rollie. He's been questioning the boss's loyalty for years and wants a new leader anyway."

He glanced up at me, pausing for several uncomfortable moments as if debating my trustworthiness. I didn't dare look away. "When I'm head alpha," he said quietly, "I can enact my most guarded secret. Free my mother."

I gaped, completely dumbstruck. That was the *last* thing I expected him to say.

"But maybe the enhancement serum is already within my reach," he continued. "Once I get that box back, I could use one of the serum vials to inject myself. Without it, Rollie is too strong to defeat. I could speed up the process and challenge him now before returning to Tatum City. His rule has to end."

"Whoa, wait a minute. That's your plan? Earn the boss's trust so you can get close enough to steal the box of serum back?"

"We can't move forward without that serum," he replied. "It's the key to reentering Tatum City and what I need to fulfill my own mission."

I bit my lip, replaying his words. "So let me get this straight: everything you've done up to this point has been to free your *mother?*"

He inclined his head. "As I said, we're not so different. You wanted to escape an abusive, controlling father and reunite with your mother, correct? So do I."

My mouth fell open. Stars, we really *were* the same. Except he was willing to sacrifice Bren in the process.

Was *I?*

Even entertaining the thought sent panic spiraling through my gut. No, I wouldn't sacrifice him. Or Iris and Asher. I wouldn't sacrifice *any* of the people I cared about. There was a time when I would have, when my heart was hardened and I'd do anything to achieve my lifelong goal of freedom. But the price was too high. The guilt of destroying someone's life to better my own was a weight that would forever burden me.

I still had recurring nightmares of killing Catanna—maybe always would. Destroying more lives would destroy *me*. I couldn't allow myself to make cold, calculated decisions like Ryker did. I wanted to be more like Bren, willing to save others even if that meant my own hopes and dreams would never be met. But maybe I could do both.

With Ryker still loyal to Renold, though, the chances of rescuing the people I loved were slim. I needed to prove that the Supreme Elite was a monster. But what if he didn't care?

As he finished tying gauze around my hand, I said, "I'll help you. But whatever you do, do *not* inject yourself with the serum from that box. It's not what you think it is. I believe it's a memory-blocking serum, and I think Renold's planning on using it to control the memories of kids brought into Tatum City."

He frowned. "Why do you think that?"

"Because he used it on me."

Silence settled between us. I half wondered if he already knew. An instinctual urge tingled through me, a desire to dive into his head again and dig out the truth. I nervously chewed on the inside of my cheek. Stars, that would be a handy, albeit terrible ability to have.

Ryker stood with the kit. "Get some sleep. We'll work on a plan after you're rested. I'll take you to the boss at sunset."

He was halfway across the room when I asked, "What about the bonding ritual thing? Shouldn't we, you know, do that?"

At the door, he turned, showing me his still bloody palm. "We already did."

PACK'S TAVERN

I tiptoed into the bathroom and silently closed the door. Every move I made was calculated, focused on the utmost stealth. Even if the room *was* soundproof, my tentative alliance with Ryker was too fragile. I couldn't chance waking him. Hopefully he was adjusting to the afternoon sleeping hours better than I was.

As I slid the shower curtain closed and settled into the tub, doubt—and traces of fear—trickled through me.

The last time I attempted long distance communication, I'd spiked a high fever and Bren couldn't wake me. What if . . . what if I got lost inside my head? On top of that, Jaxon probably didn't want to hear from me. I was the reason his girlfriend got shot—I didn't even know if Yukiko was still alive, despite Ryker's reassurances. I had also jeopardized his home's safety by leaving without permission. Not that they were going to *let* me leave. Still, The Ridge had given me shelter and I'd made several friends. In return, I'd betrayed them all.

Did they hate me?

The concept of caring was still new. In Tatum City, I grew used to people knocking each other down so they could rise. Backstabbing was expected. But at Blue Ridge Sector, people worked together. Even as an outsider and possible threat to their home, I'd been offered help and friendship. Losing that filled me with regret.

I'd destroyed another good thing in my quest for freedom.

I blew out a sigh and cranked the shower handle, cringing more from the noise than the cold water spitting on me. If Ryker came bursting in, at least I still wore my underwear. He had a knack for catching me off guard. I rested my head on the tub's edge and closed my eyes, focusing on what I needed to do. If Bren wanted me to contact Jaxon, then maybe he had a plan for getting out of here, too. And maybe The Ridge would still help me, despite what I'd done.

A smidgen of hope replaced the fear. Casting aside doubt, I submerged into my mind.

With all of my memories intact, I thought stretching my consciousness for miles and miles would be easier than last time. I could clearly recall Jaxon's goofy expressions and flamboyant voice. But there was still a pesky wall of hesitation separating us, worry that he would refuse to listen and cast me out of his head.

Do it for Bren.

He didn't have anyone to watch his back and had foolishly taken on this complex operation all on his own. But he didn't need to be alone. He had me, whether he wanted my involvement or not. *I* would watch his back, and I wouldn't fail.

Who's tough? I internally whispered. *You are.*

You are.

You are.

I sent the words spiraling into the abyss. They filled my head and strengthened my resolve. They expanded, thinning the wall. Suddenly, they punched through the barrier, hurtling past the living room and a sleeping Ryker. Past brick and wood, narrow hallways and stairs. I cleared the building and soared into the gray sky, passing through raindrops I couldn't feel. I let my subconscious guide me, knowing it instinctively knew where to go.

But it brought me somewhere I wasn't expecting.

In the forest on the outskirts of Asheville, my mind delved into Jaxon's. I was immediately assaulted. Not with the usual emotions, but with thoughts. Impressions. A million possibilities streaked by like lightning. I struggled to remain connected, the sensation similar to holding my breath underwater for too long. I held on, determined to make my voice heard.

Jaxon. Jaxon! Can you hear me?

The impressions quieted. Emotions poked through. Surprise. Curiosity. Excitement. "Lu Bear, is that you?"

Relieved, I internally laughed. The sound of his voice—jovial as always without a trace of anger—soothed an ache inside of me.

"Whoa, this is trippy," he said aloud. "Where are you? Why does it sound like you're in my head?"

Because I am.

"Okay, I'm officially jealous of your telepathic powers. Also, don't be nosing around in there. I'm a very private person."

Laughter echoed around me again, and this time, not just mine.

For a beat, silence floated between us as I worked up the courage to ask about Yukiko. If she was dead, I'd never forgive myself.

"Lune, you still there?"

Um, yeah. I just . . . How is—?

"She's okay," he replied, perceptive as usual. "A little salty. But Sensors heal quickly."

I almost lost the connection then, so overwhelmed with emotion.

Jaxon, I'm so sorry. I didn't know—

"You can apologize later, escape artist. I'm starting to get weird looks over here."

Just talk to yourself in your head. I'll hear it. That way you won't creep anyone out.

"Oh, I'll always talk to myself and creep people out," he replied. Then his voice became echoey as we spoke mind to mind. *So what's going on?*

I got right to the point, unsure how long I could stretch my abilities. *I'm stuck in Asheville. So are Bren and Ryker.* I told him the short version of everything that had happened, repeating what Bren had wanted me to share. *And, Jaxon? I think Bren has given up on himself. I don't know what to do. I just . . . I need your help.*

Worry pinged through me. It took me a moment to realize the emotion wasn't mine.

We already have people on the ground, Lune. After you escaped, Dr. Moore and the others were frantic. I sent out a drone and finally spotted you a few days ago. We've been preparing ever since. Just hold tight. We're coming to extract you and bring you home.

No, wait. Wait, Jaxon. I can't go back yet. Ryker and I are planning to—

Before I could fill him in, a force shoved me so violently that I blacked out.

When I came to, nothing made sense. The taste of rust trickled down my throat. Short gasps reached my ears. A burning headache throbbed in my skull. I was hot. Then cold. Flashes of light flickered behind my closed lids. I pried my eyes open, blinking as water dripped from my lashes. Something tickled beneath my nose and I swiped at the spot. Red coated my fingers.

I heard a metallic *hiss* and sharp intake of breath. A curse. Several curses. Arms wrapped around my back and under my legs. I was lifted, borne into a dimension that was becoming more and more solid. Real.

This is real.

I had to repeat the words over and over until the room stopped spinning and my mind settled.

Ryker placed me on the bed, then was gone and back again a second later. He wiped at the blood, scanning my face and body, trying to understand what happened. I focused on his expression, failing to read the strong emotion written there. And then it clicked.

He was afraid.

For me?

"I th-thought the room was s-soundproof," I said past chattering teeth.

"Not in the bathroom." He threw a blanket over me. "I could hear you through the wall, struggling to breathe. I thought . . . I thought you were—" His lips thinned. He stepped back and turned, jerking both hands through his hair. "What happened?"

"N-nothing. I must have g-given myself a bloody nose when I f-fell. I'm fine." Which didn't explain why I was taking a shower in my underwear. Crap. I frantically searched for a way around this pending conversation. Ryker couldn't know what I was up to. If he knew a rescue team from The Ridge was heading to Asheville, he might inform his father. Or worse, lock me up again so I couldn't screw up his plan.

I focused on his back, his very *naked* back. The pants hanging dangerously low on his hips didn't help matters. Feeling a blush rise to my cheeks, I forced my gaze upward to the exit wound where I'd shot him. Not even three weeks later, the damage was almost completely healed. A few inches to the left and his thorn-covered rose tattoo would have been ruined. I blurted the first thing that came to mind. "Why a rose?"

He peered over his shoulder, giving me a look that said my sanity was coming into question. "What?"

I waved my fingers. "Your rose tattoo. Is there a meaning behind it?"

He shrugged and cleared his face of emotion. "It's a reminder that beauty can be found in the most unlikely of places. And there, she can thrive, even among those who would tear her apart."

I could tell there was more to it than that, but I didn't pry further. Still, I doubted the story was about a rose. More like a person. Maybe his mother.

Or maybe, just maybe . . .

Bells.

"Repeat the plan."

I groaned loudly. "I already did. *Twice.*"

"Do it again." He reached for my hood, scowling when I batted his hand away.

"It's still raining outside. I want it up. Besides, no one will touch me now, whether they can see my mark or not."

I could have sworn he internally rolled his eyes. Ever since finding me in the bathtub, he wouldn't stop . . . hovering. Like a mother hen. The image that popped into my head made me snicker.

His frown deepened. "The plan."

"Fine. So bossy and annoying," I muttered, knowing full well he could hear me. "Step one: don't divulge traitorous information during my meeting with the boss. Step two: calmly leave the meeting while locating the box of serum with my tracking ability. Step three: secure the box in the billowing folds of my jacket"—the second one Ryker had to give me—"without looking suspicious. Step four: don't get caught."

"And then we'll leave through the underground tunnels and make for Tatum City," Ryker added. "Once inside, we'll deliver the box, and the Supreme Elite will give me the correct serum necessary to challenge the boss for head alpha."

Except, that was *his* plan. Not mine.

I watched as he checked the bullet chamber of his gun, expertly sliding the weapon into the holster at his waist. This wasn't the first time I'd wondered why he didn't just walk up to the boss and pull the trigger. But there was actual substance to this whole "code of honor" thing of theirs. Rules I barely understood. "And so you'll continue to blindly follow Renold's orders then. Do his dirty work, be in charge of kidnapping women and children."

They weren't questions. I was challenging him, trying to gauge his moral compass. I still didn't know if he had one or if he simply did what served him best.

His movements slowed. "If that's what it takes to guarantee my mother stays free, then I'll do what is necessary."

My eyes narrowed. "Do you think your mother would approve of those terms?" When he didn't respond, I pressed further. "If you had the chance, would you set the others free?"

He stopped and looked at me. "They ensure our survival. Out here, we don't have the means to produce our own food, clothing, or medicine. Tatum City is our only trading source. If we jeopardize that, we'll die."

"Then why not just take your mother and leave the Recruiter Clan?

He scoffed. "And go where? You've seen how dangerous it is out here alone, especially when someone has it in for you. Clans form for a reason. Stay loyal to your clan and you might survive. Did you know that the small community we found you at no longer exists? They've moved on, probably to join a larger community outside the Recruiter Clan's reach."

Tightness built in my chest. My childhood home was gone? I could barely remember the days of hunger, leaky roofs, and constant threats of danger. But there had been happy times too. Whole families living together, striving to eke out an existence their children could thrive in.

I debated telling him everything. About Renold's plans to build an army, about the safety found at The Ridge. But would he side with the people who'd kept him locked in a cell for two months? I cleared my suddenly dry throat, choosing my words carefully. "What if I told you there was another way?"

"I'd say tell me later when we're out of this mess. Our focus needs to be on this mission, not fighting the system." He shrugged into a black leather jacket and opened the bedroom door, slipping into the hall.

"So stay out of your way, is that it?" I mocked, marching after him.

"That's it," he replied without looking back.

Fury washed over me. Before he could leave the apartment, I slammed the door shut he'd just opened. "Maybe *you're* the one oblivious to the world. You only see how it's always been. Maybe it's you who's an ignorant insider. And maybe, just maybe, you should stay out of *my* way."

I shoved past him and exited the apartment, not sticking around to witness the ire no doubt plastered on his face. Let him stew and wonder if I was going to sabotage his plans. Served him right for all the lives he'd ruined in his single-minded goal to defeat his father.

A heavy tread came up alongside mine. "They can't see us arguing," Ryker muttered. "Our intentions are still under suspicion." I ignored him, descending the three flights of stairs in cold silence. Just as I reached the building's main entrance, he grabbed my arm, forcing me to stop.

"Don't touch me," I warned, jerking free

With a growl, he recaptured my arm and backed me against the wall. "We don't have time for this," he snarled as I contemplated kneeing him in the groin. "I thought you wanted out of here. I thought you wanted to see your sister again."

My heart seized. "You knew? Stars above, you knew this whole time she was my sister? What *don't* you know?" Wait. "Did Renold find out about her because of you?"

Okay, I was going to kill him now.

He gave me an indignant look. "There's certain lines even *I* won't cross. Of course I didn't tell him. But there were other people in Tatum City closely monitoring your movements."

One person in particular.

Lars.

Bile burned my throat. What was happening to her at this very moment? Was she still locked away, alone and afraid, at the mercy of the madman who'd raised me? I ached for her and hoped she could endure whatever he had in store for a little while longer.

I swallowed my growing panic and lowered my voice. "I *do* want out, and of course I want to see Iris again, but there are people here who need help too. I can't just turn a blind eye and do nothing."

"You can and you will," Ryker hissed, invading more of my personal space. "Because if the boss catches wind that you're plotting to release the captive women and children, I won't be able to stop him from ripping you limb from limb. And he will. I've seen him do it."

I envisioned the burly man choking Skervvy and shuddered, blinking away the image before I reheard the snap of his neck. "Maybe saving them would be worth the risk. Because I don't think I can live with the alternative."

He stared at me for the longest time. I barely breathed, praying I was getting through to him. He shook his head. "You're insane."

I shoved him away and stomped out of the building into the soggy evening. "Better insane than selfish," I shot back, knowing he wasn't far behind. Instead of wasting more energy on him, I mentally burrowed into my ability, feeling the tug that would lead me to Rollie.

If Ryker had one glaring flaw, it was overconfidence that I would follow his every move simply because he held all the cards. Well, it was time to exploit his weakness. I was done following him. From now on, I would make my own decisions.

Pack's Tavern was in the debilitated heart of Asheville. The farther in we went, the stronger the smell. Rotten garbage and who-knew-what-else littered the narrow, vine-strewn streets. While the buildings grew in number, so did the city's population. Perched on crumbling walls or loitering in groups, the men fell silent as we passed. Some followed us, but kept their distance.

Cars made visibility low, their rusted hulls practically touching as they sat waiting for owners who would never come. One of them was being used for target practice. A group of young teenagers whooped and hollered, dangerously brandishing their guns. They paused in their revelry as I approached. My chin lifted despite the nervous fluttering in my stomach. Did these boys fend for themselves? Were they deprived of parental guidance and left to become wild animals? The thought of Bren and Ryker growing up like this didn't sit well in my gut.

As I drew even with them, one stepped into my path. I stopped, reaching for daggers that weren't there. The boy was maybe thirteen, dirty with even dirtier clothes. I recognized his puffed-up confidence for what it was—a need to prove something to his peers. I would have put him in his place if it weren't for the gun pointed at my boots.

He flashed crooked teeth. "How about you let me make a woman out of you, pretty thing?" Several whistles and catcalls followed. Ugh, group hazing at its finest. I debated removing my hood so they could see the tattoo, but they abruptly quieted. I scanned their faces, which were no longer looking at me.

From behind, a hand wrapped around mine. I recognized Ryker's firm grip right before he said, "Touch her and you'll never make a woman out of anyone." If the boy wet his pants, I wouldn't be surprised. Part of me wanted to laugh at all the male stupidness, but another part wanted to pull away and handle this on my own. Instinct told me that word of my disrespect toward the *prince* would spread quickly, though.

Ryker was right about us needing to present a united front. These boys might be intimidated by him, but if *I* didn't obey him, why should they? He was only one man, after all. One who'd disappeared for two years without explanation. Even I could see how that must look to them. Like he didn't care about his clan. Like he didn't take his role as prince seriously.

How Ryker planned to win them over someday as head alpha was beyond me. It also wasn't my problem. I couldn't get distracted with worrying over his life when there were already so many people I cared for in trouble. Out of everyone, Ryker was in the *least* amount of danger—or so I told myself. I saw the way his father looked at him though, like a king demanding loyalty from his subject, even if that meant beating the crap out of him.

The same way Renold looked at me.

We left the gawking boys behind without further incident, but I wasn't given time to relax my tense shoulders. Up ahead was a two-story brick building, so dirty and worn that the front was a nondescript, muddy brown. The sign over the grimy yet surprisingly intact glass door read: P-A-K T-A-V-R-N—still legible despite the missing letters. But it was the dogs on either side of the entrance that had my attention. Both were huge with black muzzles and ears, the rest of their fur a tawny brown.

Just like Bear.

A vision of his death hit me before I could stop it. Ryker took the lead, tightening his hold on my hand when I slowed. Both animals stood as we approached, but instead of greeting us with wagging tails, they let loose a flurry of barks. The vicious sound snapped me back to reality.

"No hesitation," Ryker muttered, throwing me a quick glance as the dogs strained against their chains. "Not in the lion's den. The only way out of here is to be as ruthless as they are. Don't give them a reason to tear you down and feast on your weakness."

"Wow," I murmured, mustering bravado I didn't feel. "You're really great at this whole reassurance thing."

He didn't bother with a reply, which was a good thing since my ears stopped working the moment he pulled open the door and I saw what lay within. A couple dozen rough-looking men occupied a spattering of mismatched tables. Every single one of them was staring at me. Even the deer heads on the walls seemed to be looking at me.

The smell of the place—smoke, sweat, and testosterone—punched me in the gut, and I almost hurled. Spanning the back wall was a long counter with stools. None were empty. I stopped counting after thirty men when the room's hazy corners swallowed the rest.

The silence was thick. Weighted. When a chair loudly scraped against the hardwood floor, I almost jumped. Ryker squeezed my fingers in warning. Boots stomped our way. I already knew who it was before my eyes found the broad, bearded man with an easy-going smile and piercing gaze.

"Ryker. Luna. I'm surprised you made it on time," the boss's voice boomed. "Under the circumstances, I wouldn't blame you for being late. Am I right, boys?" A chorus of shouts and lewd comments erased any confusion I had. If he was trying to unsettle me, then he chose the perfect thing to say. Flames fanned my cheeks, and by his chuckle, he noticed. "Come. Sit with me."

Ryker stiffened. "I thought this was supposed to be a private conversation."

His father slanted him a look. "You know that's not how we do things around here. No secrets. What's the number one rule?" He swept his arms wide as he addressed the room again.

Men from all sides answered as one: "Honor the code, respect the clan!" Cheers of camaraderie and clinking of glasses followed. I didn't fail to notice several glares thrown Ryker's way.

Rollie faced us again. "If you are to lead this clan one day, son, those hidden agendas of yours must stop. The men respect a transparent leader, not a snake in the grass." He ushered us to a corner table with red-cushioned seating in the shape of an L. I slid across the cracked leather, unease slithering through me when Rollie took one end and Ryker the other, leaving me trapped between them.

To distract myself, I mulled over the term "snake in the grass." It described Ryker perfectly, but hadn't the boss raised him to be one? He was to listen and not be seen—and probably report back with what he heard. Maybe he wanted to tarnish his son's reputation so he couldn't succeed him someday. Or maybe the King of the Recruiter Clan simply didn't trust his men.

Either way, the last thing I wanted was to become the princess of these morally questionable men, some who no doubt had a personal hand in kidnapping me and my mum. I could fake the union if I had to, but I'd never let it become real.

"Is it done?" the boss said, breaking through my ruminations.

Instead of replying, Ryker unwound the bandage from his hand, then reached over and undid mine without asking. Ire at being manhandled simmered beneath my skin, but I managed to keep from kicking his shin. A man plunked three full glasses on the table as Ryker turned our hands palm up, displaying the blood oath cuts—or *bonding* ritual.

Rollie scrutinized the marks. Without warning, he grabbed my hand and brought it to his face. I inwardly recoiled as he inhaled deeply. I was all too aware of the entire room watching us with bated breath, probably hoping the bond was a fake so they could tear into me. Stars, is that what would happen if the boss thought I was pretending? I fought off a shiver of dread.

A second later, he returned my hand to the table and picked up his drink, smoothly standing as he raised his glass in the air. "My son, Prince of the Recruiter Clan, is officially a bonded male!" he shouted to the room. "May their betrothal remain unbroken, sealed within the blood they have shared. May no one separate them on pain of death. They have my blessing. Good health to them both!"

"Good health!" the men chorused, raising their own glasses.

Still processing all that was said, I didn't react when Ryker pressed a drink into my hand and wrapped my fingers around it. I peeked at him, tentatively following his lead when he brought his own glass up. "Good health," he said to me, before tipping his drink back.

"Good health," I muttered, quickly scanning the room to confirm my fear. All eyes were on me. Eager. Waiting. I brought the questionably clean glass to my lips and took a sip. Expecting water, I almost spewed the contents across the table. Fighting against every sane cell in my body, I grimaced but managed to swallow.

The liquid burned like acid down my throat. A fit of coughing overwhelmed me, and when I blinked the tears from my eyes, it was to see every single man in the room roaring with laughter. Well, then. Even more disturbing was the heavy warmth that settled into my gut.

Before I could ask what the drink was, Rollie returned to his seat and said, "If there's one thing my men are good at, it's making moonshine! It helps get us through the cold winters and days when game is scarce."

Game. I wondered if he meant animals or *people*. Probably both.

"I'm assuming you don't have spirits in that walled city of yours, right, lass?"

"The elites drink wine on occasion, but I've never—"

Ah. Crap.

The smooth-talker managed to get my incredibly stupid tongue wagging.

On the table next to mine, Ryker's hand curled into a fist. I was done for.

"Secrets destroy trust, Luna. If you are to be a member of this clan, we need to be honest with each other," Rollie said conversationally, then leaned toward me and whispered, "Or should I call you *Lune?*"

I stared at my drink, refusing to comment. But my tripping heartbeat was proof enough of his words.

"I think it's time for tonight's special entertainment," the boss bellowed, startling me. Ryker laid a firm hand on my arm. I refused to look at him too. "Axe, if you'll do the honors."

Axe. Why did that name sound familiar?

As I heard the distant sound of clanking—like metal being dragged over wood—I remembered. The faceless man who'd tortured me for hours on end in that dank cell. And then I saw him: a stout bald man with tattoos covering his skull, along with several piercings in his face and ears. He carried a chain. No, he was *pulling* a chain, forcing something out of the tavern's hidden depths and into the murky light.

One look at the man who materialized from the shadows and I was on my feet, pushing against the table that separated me from him. I heard my glass tip and lose its contents. I felt Ryker's fingers dig into my skin. Yet I was blind to everything but the golden-eyed boy who shuffled closer and closer. Close enough for me to see the tattered state of his pants, the dirt and bruises on his skin. The weary lines on his face and the resigned slump of his usually proud shoulders.

My mouth betrayed me. I could no more stop the word that came from it than pause the beating of my heart. "Bren," I whispered.

His eyes shot up and locked onto mine.

BIG BROTHER

Bren didn't fight to reach me. After that split second of open emotion, he quickly looked to the floor. He was still trying to protect me, but it was too late for that. Rollie knew of our past connection, and somehow knew who I really was. I doubted Ryker had told him, but maybe he'd tortured the information out of Bren. How else could he have found out?

"Sit down, lass. You're only making this worse for him."

I barely registered the boss's words as Axe wrapped Bren's chains around a sturdy beam—a position that left him vulnerable to a roomful of hostile men. Ryker yanked on my arm, forcing me to sit.

"Here's what I know," Rollie continued calmly. *Too* calmly. "A couple months ago, one of my young lads reported seeing you and my son leaving Tatum City together. Said you killed two of my men but spared his scrawny hide. That was a mistake. Never hesitate to finish the job if you want to cover your tracks."

He took a swig of moonshine, watching as a few clansmen gathered around Bren. They didn't touch him, but their close proximity was enough to make me nervous. Something told me they weren't allowed to physically harm him unless their boss gave the word, though.

"Here's what I don't get." He absently toyed with the rim of his glass. "Why all the secrets and sneaking around? We don't hide what we do here. We make do with what the world has thrown at us, fighting against the predator gene that threatens to consume the last of our humanity.

"Don't look so surprised," he added with a chuckle. I swallowed as he cast that easy-going grin my way. "We know we're beasts, barely men at all. Some of us embrace the simplicity of our animalistic nature, and others despise it. Bren has always hated how we round up women and children, breeding and selling them like cattle.

"But here's what you don't know." He paused, waiting for me to give in. To look him in the eye. I did. "You're working for the devil, and the devil doesn't care what his servants endure—only that they do his bidding. He who holds the power holds the world in his hands, eh?"

Shock jolted through me. Was he referring to Renold? Did that mean he considered *himself* a prisoner too? But he was on the outside—a *king*—free of walls, cages, and chains. Unless . . .

"What is he to you?" I couldn't help but ask.

Ryker tensed. I could practically feel his desire to knock me out so I wouldn't ruin his master plan. But I knew now that he was afraid, well and truly afraid of his father. Which meant he wouldn't interfere. I was afraid of the big bear-of-a-man too, except I suddenly understood him a little. There was a primal, backward method to his madness, but his actions sort of made sense—unlike the man who had raised me for eleven years.

"Ah." Rollie threw me a wink of approval. "You're asking the right question. And there's a simple answer to that one: family. It's hard to turn your back on family, wouldn't you say?"

At first, I was too stunned to react. Then my throat seized, an involuntary act as my body registered his words before my brain did. "You're—" I swallowed hard as saliva rushed into my mouth. "You're related to . . . Renold?"

Rollie tipped his glass toward me in a salute. "He's my big brother. 'R' names run in the family, a tradition we've upheld for generations." He pointed at himself. "*Roland. Ryker.* Jones is an alias, a way for big brother to separate himself from what he deems *lesser.*"

His amiable expression slipped, and he curled his upper lip as if tasting something sour. "Renold thrives on control. When he made plans for the Elite Trials over three decades ago, I helped him, creating challenges that would separate the strong from the weak. Strength, speed, precision? I came up with that motto." He snorted. "But my presence threatened his carefully-constructed system. I had a loyal following of recruits who were eager to contend in the Trials and climb the ranks, become *alphas* as they were meant to be. But there can only ever be *one* head alpha."

He slid his eyes to Ryker. "I was barely a man when Renold banished me and my recruits. He said that we were *made* for the outside. That first winter, I lost a dozen strong men to frostbite, starvation, and wild animals picking them off during the night. I'd find their frozen, half-eaten corpses on the streets. So I struck a deal with the devil himself, honoring every single demand, and became king to a pack of beasts in order to survive. But for *what?*" He banged a fist on the table. I flinched, sucking in a gasp.

The room quieted as all eyes turned toward their leader. But what I didn't expect to see was sympathy on their faces instead of fear. I wondered how many of these men were his original recruits.

"I bet big brother made us into a bedtime story: Beware of the wild men who prowl outside the electrified wall. They seek a way inside to devour naughty children." He barked a humorless laugh.

"But you see, lass, we're not the enemy. We've been wronged, lied to, and cheated out of a better life—because of our DNA. That's right. Genetic makeup we have no control over. Unfair, don't you think? It's all my brother and father used to talk about. So how is it that the two boys I raised, who *both* carry the predator gene, are allowed inside the golden city? But then I realized"—he tapped his bearded chin as if trying to solve a puzzle—"there's a wildcard now."

I stilled, refusing to blink or even breathe.

"If I'm right, I may finally have the upper hand after all these years. My big brother—so in control, so meticulous and unwavering in his goals—may have given me the tool necessary to fix this broken cycle. I just need to know one thing, lass." His expression sharpened, voice falling flat. "Did he send you here to dethrone me?"

The blood slowly drained from my face. His question hit way too close to the mark. I knew without a doubt that if I said yes, he'd snap my neck in a split second. My eyes burned with the effort to hold his gaze. Before the silence could drag, I quickly said, "No, sir."

For one unbearable moment, I thought he could see through my flimsy mask. The need to protect my vulnerable throat overwhelmed me. I grasped my bear tooth necklace. His eyes tracked the movement, then lifted to mine again.

"So where *do* your loyalties lie?" He jerked his chin at Ryker. "With him? I'll admit, watching you two cozy up together was cute, but my eyes tell me one thing and my senses another."

A sly grin tugged at his mouth, and he pointed a finger at Bren. "With him, perhaps? I can't blame you. I trained them well and they're good at what they do, but they will only tell you sweet lies. They learned nothing of loyalty and what it takes to survive in this cold world. They don't appreciate the sacrifices that have to be made to keep a community together. They think only of themselves, not the clan who sheltered and protected them."

My nostrils flared as anger curdled my stomach. Screw the plan. I was done pretending. "You killed Bren's parents. You made him *watch* as you drowned them."

He shook his head sadly. "An unfortunate casualty. They got in the way of our livelihood, our *survival*. It was drowning or a bullet between the eyes. My men chose the cleaner option. The clan is only as strong as its weakest link, lass. We must stand united or we will fall, and I *won't* let that happen." A crazed gleam entered his eyes, causing the blue to glow brightly. I shrank back.

Just like that, the glow receded, replaced with a warm smile. "So you see, Lune, I need you to be on our side. My brother broke radio silence simply to ask if I'd seen you, so I know there's something special about you, something he would pay dearly to have returned."

I blinked, forcing myself not to peek at Bren and Ryker's reactions. "He . . . Renold contacted you?"

This was insane. I was considering the words of a kidnapper. A *killer*. I wanted to throw up. I wanted to scream in his face and scratch out his eyes. But I didn't. I stayed glued to my seat, riveted by what he was telling me. What he was *revealing*. That the Recruiter Clan had a vendetta against Renold and were willing to defy him. To break loyalty.

Maybe I could use that knowledge to my advantage.

"He only contacts me to make sure his operation is running smoothly, so when he radioed a few days ago and mentioned you, it was quite the surprise," he answered. "But after all these years, I still don't know what he's planning—and he *is* planning something. He and Father were always plotting while I did the grunt work. They'd disappear for days without explanation, refusing to include me."

The boss fell silent for a moment, stroking his beard, lost in thought. "He killed them, you know. Our parents. One moment, they were throwing a party, and the next, *poof!* Gone. Disappeared. That's what big brother does: gets rid of what he can no longer control."

He abruptly stood, sidling toward the room's center. Toward Bren. My heart leapt into my throat. I felt my body rise to go after him—to do what, I didn't know. But I couldn't just sit and watch him torture Bren. Ryker caught my hand and jerked me down again. I snarled at him, not caring who heard.

"Wait," he ordered, shooting me a warning look I was beginning to loathe.

"Why didn't you tell me that Renold is your *uncle?*" I hissed. "I can't believe you're related to that monster." I snorted, not hiding my abject disgust. "That explains a lot, actually."

He bared his teeth at my thinly veiled insult. "So because I share the same blood as the Supreme Elite and *him*," he said, jerking his chin toward his father, "that automatically makes me a monster, too? That's rich coming from the girl who fell for her kidnapper."

I yanked my hand free, deliberately scrubbing my palm on my pant leg. "Bren didn't want any of this. He was only trying to protect Bells."

Ryker tensed. In an eerily quiet voice, he said, "What did you call her?"

Before I could cover up the slip, the sound of clanking

metal grabbed my attention. I stopped breathing as Rollie un-wound Bren's chains and led him to our table. Bren didn't resist, but I was encouraged by the rigidness of his shoulders, the clench-ing of his fists. He still had fight in him.

They stopped directly across the table, close enough that if I leaned forward, I could take Bren's blood-encrusted hand in mine. Was the damage to his knuckles self-inflicted? I ached to squeeze his fingers and offer him a small measure of comfort, but didn't dare. I met the boss's inquisitive gaze, dreading where this was headed.

"Here's the difference between me and my brother," he said, looping Bren's chains around his wide palm. He gave them a quick jerk. "I don't so easily destroy what I love. Bren may have betrayed me by leaving with his sister, but he's like a son. And now that you're here, I'm betting he'll fall in line again."

Bren's fists began to tremble. Rollie's lips twitched. He knew. He definitely knew that Bren felt something for me, and was now using that knowledge to blackmail him into staying once more. That manipulating, son of a—

"I'd like to make a deal with you, Lune." The words sliced through my fury, leaving me shaken yet again. And the more he spoke, the more my head spun with disbelief.

"Pledge your fealty to this clan. Become its princess. Do so with *true* intentions, and I will unchain Bren right this very mo-ment. I'm done being my brother's lackey while my city crumbles. We barely have anything to show for our loyalty to him. We de-serve *better* than this. Strengthen this clan by uniting with my son. By joining forces, Renold will have no choice but to honor my de-mand for equal opportunity. What say you, lass?"

If I were breathing, my lungs would have emptied in a giant

rush. My heart fluttered like a trapped bird, because that's what this deal was. A cage to contain me. A plan to use me. I quickly glanced at Bren to find him stiff as stone. His eyes were twin yellow beams burning holes through the tabletop. If I didn't speak soon, he was going to explode. And there was no way I'd let him risk his life over this.

It was *my* turn to fix things.

I carefully cleared my throat before saying, "You really think I mean so much to Renold that he'd listen to your demands?"

Rollie barked a laugh. "I *know* so. And with you as Princess of the Recruiter Clan, dedicated to our well-being, he'll have to take me seriously for once. He can always find more men to run his secret breeding program, but something tells me that you're irreplaceable to him. I'd hate for the object of his attention to fall into harm's way simply because he couldn't see reason."

I didn't fail to catch the double-barbed threat. It was meant for me as much as it was for Renold.

But Bren caught the threat too.

"Harm her and I'll—"

Faster than I could blink, the boss snaked a chain around Bren's neck.

"No!" I lunged forward only to have an arm block my attempt at scaling the table.

Without hesitation, I whipped my head back, pegging Ryker in the face. He swore loudly but held on, immobilizing me within seconds. I continued to fight against his punishing grip as the chain around Bren's throat dug in deep.

"What will you do, boy?" Rollie goaded, dark blond locks falling into his steely eyes as he grappled with the younger man. "You think you can best me? Say it then. Say the words and we'll see who's more alpha."

When Bren remained silent, the boss laughed mockingly and released him with a shove. I ceased trying to break free, watching helplessly as Bren doubled over in a fit of coughing.

"That's a warning, lass," Rollie said, casually reaching for his drink as if he hadn't just *strangled* a man he called his son. "Betray me and he'll be the first to pay the price. So what's it going to be?"

There was no thinking this over. No choice.

If I didn't agree to his terms, he would kill me. Or Bren. Stars, it wasn't Ryker who held all the cards. His father did. But in doing what he wanted, Bren would be released from his underground prison. One step of my plan completed. It could still work. I could get us out of here. I just needed to play by the clan's rules a little while longer.

Bren lifted his head, just enough for me to see the turmoil on his face. He knew what this meant. Knew that I would do anything to save him, even align myself with the men who'd killed his parents and forced him to become something he hated. And then there was Ryker. His friend turned enemy. The person who'd endangered his sister's life and now mine. Bren knew what I would have to do.

I would have to sacrifice him—his *love*—in order to save him.

Because if kissing Ryker hadn't destroyed his love for me, becoming his enemy's mate surely would.

A sudden ache splintered my heart.

It was breaking. For him.

For us.

My body moved of its own accord, shaking Ryker's grip loose so I could round the table. In one swift motion, I knelt. Before a king.

"I swear fealty to you and your clan. I will become your princess."

Every single word was real.

FEUD

The tension was a wall.

A wall of rigid, moving, steaming muscle—that I was currently wedged between. No one spoke. Only the heavy tread of boots dispelled the silence. The rain had finally stopped, but the dark streets ran amuck with sludge and sinkholes that I kept stepping into. If only Jaxon were here to lighten the mood. He would say something like: "Okay, let's all sing a song and express our feelings. Then we can hug it out."

But no, I was on my own. I buried myself in this hole and would have to dig my way out. But what choice did I have? At least Bren wasn't in chains.

I could feel anger pulsing from him in waves. His hurt was a hurricane.

Despite the barrage of his emotions, Ryker's fury made me the most nervous. I knew where Bren's anger came from, but Ryker's? His plans were shot to dust, and I'd just made his *fake* plans real. But even if I'd wanted to follow through with his plan to sneak out of the city with the serum and leave my mother behind, that was no longer an option.

We were being tailed.

"For your protection," Rollie had said before we'd left the tavern. We all knew it was to keep us from fleeing, though. I couldn't

see the clansmen, but I knew they were there, lurking in the shadows.

Maybe when I was officially their princess, I could make a deal of my own. I thought Ryker would be the one to convince, but perhaps I could talk his father into forming an alliance with—

Out of nowhere, Ryker swore and grabbed my arm, dragging me into an alley. He didn't stop until we reached a tall, chain link fence. My back struck the links with an echoing clang. He buried a fist in my jacket and yanked me close. Shocked, I stupidly gaped as he laid into me with fierce vengeance. "Do you know what you've just *done?* We can't leave now."

Once again, I was dragged away, this time by Bren. He pushed me behind him, then went nose-to-nose with Ryker. "Touch her again," he said, low and lethal. "I dare you."

Ryker bared his teeth. "And what are you going to do about it? You know the code, *brother*. You know who she belongs to now. The bonding ritual is complete."

A growl exploded from Bren and he shoved Ryker. "She's not *yours*. You had no right to kiss her or force this life on her. She doesn't want it. She doesn't want *you*."

Ryker licked his bottom lip with a goading smirk. "Maybe she does. Maybe this is exactly what she wants. You heard her in there. Saw her bend a knee to the great alpha king. She's not pretending. This is happening."

Bren was shaking now, a hair's breadth away from snapping. At the menace in his eyes, my heart jack-knifed in my chest. "She didn't have a choice. As soon as we find a way out of this mess, she'll come back to me. To someone who can keep her *safe*."

"Back. Off. This isn't your fight, Bearon," Ryker said, his tone deathly soft. Yet he moved closer as though spoiling for just that.

A fight.

A harsh laugh left Bren. "It became my fight the minute you lured my five-year-old sister into the woods when my back was turned. When you tracked me to my home and tore apart my family. If it wasn't for you, I wouldn't be in this mess. Neither would Lune."

Ryker jerked as if he'd been slapped, but quickly recovered. "You want to do this right now? Fine, let's do it. I was *nine*. Nine years old. I didn't want a flogging or another broken bone, so I did as I was told. I wanted to see my *mother*."

"Did you tell Lune that you tracked down her mom that day? Admit it. She's been here this entire time, so I know you did it. You pumped me full of guilt the day I took Lune, but you didn't go home empty-handed either."

I gasped, stumbling against the fence when Ryker didn't refute the accusation. My heart was pounding, head throbbing as they continued to spar with words, slicing deep, cutting to the very core of their lifelong feud. I remembered Ryker's gun and searched for its shape beneath his leather jacket. If things escalated, maybe I could reach it before he stopped me. But after that latest revelation, a weapon in my hands could be deadly.

The mood suddenly shifted. Anger became something else entirely. There was hurt saturating their shouting match. They were indeed yelling now, uncaring who heard, lost to the world around them. Even me.

And I couldn't . . . I couldn't stop them. I didn't want to. They wielded truth like blades. It was a dance unlike any I'd ever seen. Raw and ugly. But, stars, it was real. They were talking about Bells now, a point of contention that had caused so much hatred and bitterness between them.

I was riveted. Rooted to the spot as Ryker jabbed a finger at Bren's chest and growled, "You took her from me. The only good thing I had in my life. You didn't even let me say goodbye."

Bren knocked the finger aside. "What was I supposed to do? Stand by while you failed to protect her from jealous, vindictive men who would do anything to see me tarnished in the eyes of their king? She was *my* responsibility. Not yours. I never gave you permission to claim her—"

Ryker shoved Bren, sending the taller man back a couple feet. "She *wanted* me. *Me*. And I wanted her. Then you took it all away." Both men silently fumed, neither giving an inch. Ryker's expression suddenly fell. "You left me here. Alone. You were . . . you were the only friend I had. And you tossed me aside like trash. Just like the boss always said I—" He cut himself off, dragging both hands through his hair.

I winced as he spun and took out his pain on the wall, his fist the inflictor. My stomach and thoughts were in knots, but I couldn't help feeling a twinge of sympathy. I knew that kind of loneliness, the hurt that could so easily turn into anger, causing further alienation.

Ryker may have started the events that led us to this point— and destroyed lives in his quest to better his own—but I understood his pain. He didn't have to suffer alone anymore. Not if I could help it.

I reached out. Not with my body, but with my mind. It was easy to form a tether with him now. I knew him. Knew his motives, his hopes and dreams. Many were self-serving, but he wasn't the monster I thought him to be. He had a heart—a big one—and it was bleeding.

The connection solidified.

You're not alone.

His back stiffened as I sent the words into his head.

I'm not abandoning your plan. But this is bigger than you and me, Ryker. People need us, and not just our mothers. I've got an idea, but I can't do it alone. I need your help.

It took several moments of heated silence, but he eventually glanced over his shoulder at me. His eyes were narrowed, searching. "How do I know you won't double-cross me?" he rasped.

Bren tensed, scanning both our faces. As it dawned on him what I'd just done, his jaw hardened. He looked away. Guilt squirmed inside me. I knew how this must seem. But instead of reassuring him like I ached to do, I ignored him. And hated myself for it. I shrugged at Ryker, smirking as I replied, "You don't. You'll just have to trust me."

He snorted, but it was devoid of rancor. For him, the sound was practically laughter. It was a start, at least.

"So it's real then?"

Confused by the question, I forced my eyes to meet Bren's. Oh stars, the look he was giving me. There was only one word to describe it. Lost. My chest practically caved in as I fought to hold eye contact. My voice was reed thin, but I managed to say, "What is?"

He gestured at me and Ryker. "You. Him."

Panic shot through me. I quickly shook my head. "No. I mean, yes. But not—" Crap. *Crap!* "We didn't do anything. Well, not what you're thinking anyway." Shoot me now! "But I fully intend to follow through with this whole princess thing. You know I have to, Bren. Which means—"

Which meant what?

Too many things that I didn't want to say out loud.

Mortification heated my face. Did he think I would *sleep* with Ryker? Holy crap, would the boss *expect* us to? My thoughts and emotions went haywire. The more I struggled to speak, the worse my guilt became.

A throat cleared and I flinched. "Meet me back at the apartment when you're done hashing this out. And don't even think about running off together. I'll track you both down myself if I have to. But you know I won't be the only one."

With that foreboding promise dangling in the air, Ryker left us.

Left us to stew in our doubts and fears and unspoken deeds.

Bren broke the silence first. "He just keeps getting in the way, doesn't he?"

"It's not like that," I whispered, my throat too tight for much else.

His sigh was short. Harsh. He looked away again. "I deserve this after everything I've done. It's only fair that I suffer this way. I can sense it, Lune—your feelings for him. You're not indifferent as you once were. And although this kills me to admit, I don't blame you. I've done nothing but cause pain with my lies and secrets. Then I was afraid, so afraid of losing you that I let fear tear us apart. You deserve *so* much better than me."

My jaw couldn't help but drop. "Bren. I don't—"

I squeaked as his arms shot out, trapping me against the fence. He didn't touch me—just curled his fingers into the chain links on either side of my head and leaned in close. Close enough that his bright golden eyes became my world.

"But I can't give you up that easily," his voice rumbled in the scant inches separating us. "This thing between us? It's not over. Once we find a way out of this, I'm fighting to win you back. And

I'm fighting for keeps, because I *won't* share you. Not even a sliver. I want every. Last. Piece." As if to punctuate the words, he fitted himself even closer. He was all around me, yet not a single part of him touched any part of me.

Shock rendered me speechless. Even after my kiss with Ryker and the agreement to become his mate, Bren still cared. Still *wanted* me. It was plainly written on his face. The sight caused an ache to build low in my gut, followed by a deep yearning to fuse my mouth to his. I lifted my hands, wanting to slide them up his bare chest and into his hair. Before they could make contact, he jerked back. Retreated a step.

I swallowed a breathy whimper and dropped my gaze, the sting of rejection hitting me hard. I deserved that. It was too soon. He probably couldn't get the image of me and Ryker kissing out of his head.

Self loathing dragged me down, threatening to yank tears from my downcast eyes. I didn't bother hiding my misery. We'd come too far for pretense. If he wanted to keep his distance, then he had the right to do so—even if it destroyed my heart.

"I can't touch you right now," he said quietly. My eyes jumped to his. "You're bonded to the prince, and if I were to lay a hand on you with seductive or violent intentions, my life would be forfeit. But more than anything, I want to touch your soft skin," he breathed. "I want to press my lips to every last perfect inch of you until Ryker is but a memory and mine is the only name you know."

Wait. *Whoa.*

If my body wasn't propped against the fence, I'd have joined the murky puddle at my feet. His words continued to strike me mute. And by the slow grin spreading across his face, I knew that had been his intention.

That *smile*. It twisted my insides yet filled me with warmth. Oh how I'd missed it.

He tilted his head in a *follow me* gesture, stuffing his hands into his pockets as if embarking on a midnight stroll. I automatically followed him, mesmerized by the straight lines of his body and the sureness of his step. It clicked then.

I'd given Brendan Bearon a challenge. A purpose. Something to fix.

And so his cocky, egotistical self confidence had returned.

Tears burned my eyes.

It was the most beautiful thing I had ever seen.

No, please don't. I didn't do anything. I didn't do anything!

I exploded upright, a scream lodged in my throat.

"Iris," I panted, frantically searching for her. "Iris, I'm coming. I'm com—" No, I realized with a sinking heart, I wasn't. We were still miles apart. Fear, *her* fear, continued to tremble through me as I shoved aside sleep-mussed hair. I stumbled across the room and yanked open the door.

Only to sprawl headlong into the hallway as I tripped over something large and solid.

Oof!

The landing should have hurt more. I glanced down and there was Bren, groggily blinking up at me. But the longer I lay sprawled on top of him, the wider his eyes became. For a second that lasted an eternity, I froze, gobbling up the sight of his freshly-shaven face and clean skin. And, stars above, he smelled good. Wait, were his hands on my hips? Yes. Yes, they were. It felt so right, yet so wrong.

But I couldn't remember why.

And then I did.

"Crap!" I rolled off of him, instantly regretting the move. By the look on his face, so did he. We had broken the no-touching rule, but all I wanted to do was reverse course so I could sniff him again. Yeah, I was probably addicted to his sunshine smell by now. "What are you—?" I began, then stopped as I recalled our current living situation. Our very *awkward* living situation consisting of two angry men, one bed, and a girl stuck in the middle. They had both insisted I take the bedroom.

Bren had an apartment one floor up, but the space had been pillaged except for a few articles of clothing that he now wore. They were a bit snug across his chest, but I wasn't complaining. After a few terse words with Ryker last night, he'd been allowed to stay here. He was sleeping on the floor though, accommodations he was probably used to at this point.

I felt terrible that he was hunkered down in the hallway right outside my door. To be closer to me?

The soundproofed room didn't have windows, but I could see from the living room window that it was around midday. I suddenly remembered my dream, so real that it must have been a vision. "Iris is in trouble."

Bren sat up while Ryker stirred from his spot on the couch.

"Renold's torturing her. I couldn't see what he was doing, but—but I could *feel* her fear. She's all alone, and—" I blew out a breath. "I have to get back in there. Right now before it's too late."

My eyes met Ryker's calculating stare. "I need unrestricted access to this city. There's a certain something that I have to find. What will it take for that to happen? I'll tell the boss whatever he wants to know. Swear whatever oaths or honor any deals he wants to bind me with. Just . . . tell me what to do, Ryker."

It could have been a trick of the light, but I could have sworn he glanced at Bren with unease. His gaze swiftly returned to mine, now neutral.

Then he said two words I never expected him to say.

"Marry me."

My mouth popped open. Deafening silence settled between us as reality smacked me upside the head. Marriage. I was being asked—more like told—to *marry* Ryker. This was real. Really real. I could finally feel it, like a swarm of angry bees in my stomach. Before I could stop them, my eyes flitted to Bren's. But his were downcast, glaring at the floor near his boots.

Surely he knew how I felt about this. If there were any other way . . .

Ryker stood from the couch and stretched leisurely as if those two words had been a simple "good morning." Bren and I remained on the floor as he strode for the kitchen, rummaging for something edible to eat.

"There's no quicker way to earn an entire night of free rein," he said over his shoulder. "Rollie created this kingdom, and with it, a set of rules. One of the most elaborate revolves around what you must do before claiming a mate. On top of that, the female is given a small window of opportunity—she can stand by her intended mate, choose another, or reject them all by running." His jaw hardened. "Not that the men ever honor her rejection."

"So," I drew out the word, trying to settle on what to say. Something safe, since we weren't enclosed in the soundproof bedroom. "Once I'm married to you, I'll be given a measure of freedom?"

"Not exactly. The night before the claiming, there's a

ceremony." Ryker cleared his throat. My stomach bottomed out when he had the nerve to look uncomfortable. What didn't I know? Ah crap, something told me this was going to be bad.

"I'm assuming it's nothing like a traditional wedding ceremony with flowers and music and fancy dresses?" I quipped, though the words came out higher-pitched than usual.

He opened his mouth, but Bren chose that moment to stand. As he stepped over me to get at the food Ryker had found, I stood as well. Then promptly crossed my arms with a huff and leaned against the wall. Dried meat again. For breakfast. Yuck.

Before Ryker could answer my question, Bren slanted him a look, saying, "The ceremonial ritual is so dangerous that not many clansmen dare go through with it. Besides that, it's barbaric. To be considered worthy of a mate, the male must fight to claim his female. For one night, anyone can pursue her. She can choose another, but he too must fight to keep her."

He pinned that look on me, slowly approaching my position. "And if he can survive the night and no one has stolen her away," he said, stopping close enough for me to feel his body heat, "he is free to claim her as his mate. *That* is the ceremony."

A shiver worked its way down my spine. "What if the female doesn't want to be claimed?"

"She can run and hide, but the choice is usually taken from her."

Fury was a whip slashing through my blood. "So women are just prizes to be won? That's sick."

"Still want to become Princess of the Recruiter Clan?" Ryker mocked around a mouthful of mystery meat.

I turned to him. "Is this what happened to your mother?"

He bared his teeth, but ignored the question. "You will be

given from dusk until dawn to roam the city. As long as you're not caught, no one will question why you're alone in the streets unescorted."

This was crazy. Any number of things could go wrong if I agreed to this animalistic ritual. But it was the perfect opportunity to enact *my* plan. One step closer to freeing my mum and returning to Tatum City. To Iris.

"Ryker?" He lifted a brow in acknowledgment, but it was Bren's eyes I sought as I said, "Tell your father that I want the ceremony done. Tonight."

CLAIM ME

I avoided a group of boys huddled around a flaming barrel. They were too busy arguing about something to catch my scent though. I purposefully slogged through several rain puddles, still uncertain how keen a Sensor's abilities were. But the more I could throw them off my trail, the better.

Thankfully, the rules mandated I be given a head start.

Good thing too, because the men who wished to challenge Ryker's claim on me had arrived at Pack's Tavern an hour before sunset—all two dozen of them. I was the prey, the lone contender against a pack of hungry mutant beasts. It was the Arcus Point Trial all over again. But this time, I was weaponless and didn't have Bren fighting beside me.

When I left the tavern, his tall frame had been lurking in the shadows where he silently observed the restless men. I hadn't dared ask him if he would challenge Ryker's claim. I was afraid that he would and jeopardize my precarious deal with Rollie. I was even more afraid that he wouldn't.

Foolish heart. So willing to risk everything for a heroic, albeit twisted gesture from the one it loved. Which was why I repeatedly considered leaving him clues so he'd discover me first. I kept thinking of him whisking me out of the city where we could start a new life.

A fresh beginning.

Just the two of us.

I clung to the selfish and unrealistic thought a moment more before letting it slip through my fingers.

My goal tonight was to find that box of memory serum. Ryker hadn't seemed worried about the ceremony's outcome, but what if everything went wrong? What if he and Bren were killed during this fight-to-claim-your-mate thing? What if I was caught stealing the serum? Either way, we *needed* that serum. It was the only way back inside Tatum City when the time came.

The next part of my plan hinged on Jaxon. Well, the entirety of Blue Ridge Sector, actually, but I was counting on Jaxon to be my spokesperson. He had a special way with words. I assumed Bren had told them about the women and children being held in the correctional center. If they meant to stop Renold from starting a war, then making a deal with the Recruiter Clan was a step in that direction.

My plan could so easily fail. Dr. Moore could refuse to listen, as could Rollie. Trust was hard to come by in this world. But if Blue Ridge Sector and the Recruiter Clan formed a mutually beneficial alliance, then destroying Renold and freeing those I cared about wouldn't just be a dream.

It could really and truly happen.

The thought sent adrenaline zipping through me. I put on a burst of speed and lost myself to the city, weaving through broken doorways and rusted cars. I touched everything, leaving false trails and marking passages that lead to dead ends. Just like I had in the Abilities Competition during my time spent at The Ridge.

I held my breath whenever male voices or footsteps reached my ears. Kept moving even though my body urged me to hide.

When my chest heaved and lungs burned, I pressed on, ignoring the pain in my sides and calves. I ran for miles, creating a confusing patchwork of trails across the city. And when I finally stopped, it was to find myself back where I'd started.

Pack's Tavern.

The dogs weren't at the entrance. Probably out searching for me.

Was it too much to hope that the building was empty?

I knew one thing for certain though. The serum was here. If someone caught me snooping, I could pretend that I was searching for a good hiding spot. I snuck around back, quieting my harsh breathing. Now if only there was an outer ladder like the one I'd used—

A rickety black stairwell emerged, glistening dully under the waning moon.

Jackpot, I inwardly crowed, knowing Jaxon would be pleased with my word choice. The stairs led straight up to a second story window—exactly the place I needed to be. *This is too easy. It has to be a trap.*

Or maybe Renold simply hadn't told his little brother how important that box of serum was. Maybe Rollie wasn't guarding it because he didn't care. Which would make its theft all the easier to pull off.

With one last look down the narrow alley I was crouched in, I dashed for the stairs. The first problem presented itself right away. Noise. The metal shrieked when my boot made contact. I bit my lip. Hard. By the time I reached the second floor landing, I tasted blood on my tongue. But there were no shouts. No whoops of glee from the savage men spotting their prize. Just silence. And one very clean window.

Surprised, I hesitated.

Trap, trap, trap, my mind chanted. *The boss wants you to find the serum so he can call your bluff and put a bullet in your head. Or Bren's.*

I batted my paranoia aside. Tonight, I was given free rein of the city. No one would question my reasons for sneaking in here. If I was going to steal the serum and use it to present my case for an alliance, it was now or never.

My fingers gripped the window and pulled. Stuck. No. *Locked.* I hissed, mentally ticking off my options. Entering from the ground floor wasn't happening. A rock would make too much noise. I eyed my borrowed jacket, wishing it was leather like the one Ryker wore. I prepared to ram my elbow through the glass, already wincing from the pain that was to come.

I drew my arm back. As my muscles tensed for the strike, the window scraped open. A hand shot out and grabbed a fistful of my jacket. No sound left me as someone yanked me inside. I hit the floor hard, my shoulder barking in protest. But I was up and spinning toward my attacker a second later.

If one of the two dozen clansmen tried to *claim* me tonight, then he was in for a smackdown. When feminine features suddenly popped up before me, I couldn't stop my fight or flight reaction in time. My fist flew toward a jaw—a decidedly female one. I heard the fleshy *smack* right before her head whipped to the side. I gasped, an apology already forming on my lips.

As I reached out to steady her, I caught a flash of straight black hair and deep blue eyes. Then a fist, followed by shooting stars. I reeled under the return attack, slamming into the brick wall behind me. My head glanced off the bricks and I groaned as more stars exploded across my vision. I wasn't given time to recover before the fist was back, burying itself in the front of my jacket.

"Shh," the woman hissed, giving me a little shake. "They'll hear you."

I didn't respond, too busy blinking away the floating lights. Soft fingers touched my cheek and I flinched, swallowing back another groan.

"Sorry," she whispered. "Knee-jerk reaction to being punched in the face."

"I'm sorry too. I thought you were—"

"I know, I know," she interrupted, moving to slide the window shut. "We don't have much time. Tell me why you're here."

"Uh . . ." This was happening way too fast. Who *was* this woman?

She looked back at me impatiently. "You're my son's intended mate, yes?" My mouth formed an O. She stuck out a hand. "I'm Evangaline. Ryker's mother. You can call me Evie."

Ryker's . . . mother.

I raised a limp hand and she shook it firmly.

"No time for chit-chat unfortunately," she went on, dropping my hand to usher me farther into the room. Which, I could see now, was an apartment. A very clean one, but overwhelmed with stuff. Paintings on the walls, clay figurines, bowls, plates, jars. Practically every surface was covered. "Tell me." Her hurried voice recaptured my attention. "How is my son?"

"Uh, he's well? As of a couple hours ago anyway."

She snorted, a sound that I'd heard Ryker make often enough. "He's fine then. The men are too eager for a good chase and won't be focused on taking him out. But I must know why you've come here. Has he . . . has he informed you of his plan?"

I debated whether to trust her or not. I didn't know what kind of relationship she had with her husband. She could very well tell him everything.

"Ryker is my world. If he picked you, then we're on the same side," she pressed, darting a quick look to a red door covered in painted flowers. "So I'll ask again. What is it that you seek?"

I noticed her tattoos then. They weren't in shades of black and gray like the men's. Like mine. They were vibrant. Beautiful. Traveling up both her arms before disappearing beneath a green flowy top. She had to be an artist—one that was trapped in a tower, which reminded me of another fairy tale story Mum had told me.

Something about that comparison made me let down my guard enough to say, "Have you seen a couple of backpacks lying around?"

Her midnight blue eyes brightened. Without a word, she scurried into another room. I could hear her grunt and curse a few times, but I didn't move—in case she came back with a gun and I'd need to throw myself out the window. A minute later, she returned, carrying three familiar packs. "My husband thinks he's so clever hiding these under the floorboards," she puffed, dropping the load at my feet, "but I know every inch of this place."

My hands started to tremble as I crouched and unzipped the packs, quickly rifling through their contents. A grin tugged at my mouth when I caught sight of my twin golden daggers. I ran my fingers over Bren's book. No sign of my bow and arrows, sleeping bag, or tent though. Worry shivered through me as I wondered what else they'd kept for themselves. I ripped open Bren's pack.

And released a huge sigh of relief.

"I've been wondering about that."

I whirled at the sound of Evie's voice, jerking the zipper closed. She laughed softly. "I detected Bren's scent on that one. I was happy to hear he still lives. After what happened with his sister and my son, I worried that the men had killed them both out of jealousy."

I blinked up at her stupidly. "You know Bren?"

Her head tilted in that dog-like way Sensors often adopted—confirming my guess that she was one. "Of course. I know everyone in this city, even if I'm not allowed to see them." Her eyes saddened for a moment, then grew animated again. "He's a good boy. So is my Ryker, once you get past the pain and bitterness. He was never the same after Bren and Isabella left. I'm truly happy that he's found another worthy of his affections, though. He's always been so lonely."

Fresh beads of sweat peppered my forehead as I felt a blush rise to my cheeks. This was now officially awkward and uncomfortable. I could only imagine Ryker's reaction if he knew about this conversation.

I carefully slung the packs over my shoulders and rose to my feet. "Um, thank you for these. It was nice to meet you. I should probably go, though. The men have an uncanny sense of smell and will probably be here soon."

My lame joke fell flat as Evie stared at me quizzically. Not knowing what else to say, I shuffled back the way I'd come. My hand was on the window when she whispered, "What does it do?"

I turned and immediately froze when I saw what she was holding. A syringe. Filled with yellow liquid. She'd taken one of the memory serum vials. When I simply gaped at her, not knowing whether to spring forward and snatch it away or run for cover in case she came at me, she sighed. Then brought the needle to her neck.

"No!" I blurted, raising my hands.

She lowered it and arched a dark eyebrow. "One way or another, I always find out what's going on around here. What's this serum for?"

Wow. Nosy and unpredictable. Like mother, like son.

"It steals your memories," I explained. "Locks them up so you can't even remember your own name." Stars, I really hoped she didn't tell Rollie.

Her expression flattened. I waited for her to demand the full story, but instead, she pocketed the syringe and nodded at the window. "You'd best be going. Hide those backpacks so they don't fall into the wrong hands."

Before she changed her mind or demanded more answers, I slid the window open. Halfway through, I paused and glanced back at her. "Don't you ever try to escape?"

Evie slowly shook her head. "No."

"Why not?" I couldn't help but ask.

She gave me a sad smile. "Because a mother will sacrifice pretty much anything to protect her child. Even her own happiness."

The next several minutes were a blur. Not because I was scrambling to put as much distance as possible between me and that building, but because I couldn't stop crying. Her parting words reminded me of Mum, of everything she'd sacrificed for her children. It had only been a few days, but I already missed her so much. And I hadn't told her that I loved her, that her memory had given me the courage to face the Trials—and come out on the other side.

I finally had to stop running. My brain was having a meltdown or something. Thinking of all the people I wanted to save, yet feeling completely inadequate to the job, had me curling into a ball. I fought the compulsion, continuing to crawl into the dark recesses of an alley, but my arms eventually gave out.

Get up, get up! It was no use. I had reached a limit I'd been unaware of. Still, I scanned the area through my tears, searching for a possible hiding spot. And not just for myself. I needed to stash the backpacks, then contact Jaxon—

A hand touched my head.

An involuntary shriek escaped me and I jerked back, promptly smacking into a wall. I looked up to see a massive form looming over me. When no features presented themselves, I decided to attack. My boot made contact with a kneecap. The form curled forward with a pained grunt. Using their superior weight against them, I lunged for the neck and threw myself toward the ground, bringing them with.

The packs broke our fall and we rolled. I came out on top and quickly pressed my forearm to their throat. "No one's claiming me unless I say so, scumbag!" I snarled, applying more force to the windpipe.

A deep rumble vibrated through my arm as the man began to choke. No, he was laughing. *Laughing?* I growled, squinting for a better look at the idiot's face. Familiar golden eyes greeted me. "Bren?" I whispered in disbelief, loosening my grip. Then again, I'd been projecting my Visionary ability and he could sense the energy. I had led him straight to me.

"You're so beautiful," he said, still chuckling, and reached up to touch my face. He paused with his hand inches away, as if remembering the rules.

Screw the rules.

I tilted my cheek into his warm palm. He stiffened, but didn't pull away—simply stared, unblinking. As if afraid I would disappear at any moment. We stayed like that for the longest time, unwilling to break the spell. Then, his thumb ever so gently swept across my cheekbone. Drying my tears. Stirring the wings in my stomach. His breath caught. The small noise awakened my desire for him with a roar.

His muscles bunched as he pushed himself into a sitting position, leaving me to straddle his waist. The air grew charged between us, fit to ignite. To reactivate the raging fire that had never gone out.

"Please," I whispered, not bothering to suppress the quiver in my voice. "Touch me. Kiss me."

Please, stars, please.

"I shouldn't." His voice was equally affected. "It's too dangerous."

"Then let me touch you," I breathed, suddenly desperate for this one last opportunity before we were forced to keep our distance. "Just for tonight while the rules allow it. Please, Bren."

When he didn't protest, I laid a hand on his chest. He shuddered and closed his eyes. Encouraged, I slid my fingers into his thick wavy hair—right where they wanted to be. A hum came from deep in his throat. He eased a hand beneath my shirt, pressing his palm to the small of my back. A thrill went through me when he gathered me close, fitting us together like two puzzle pieces made to belong.

He stilled, reopening his eyes to carefully search my face. "What about Ryker?"

"What about him?"

"You're supposed to get married to him."

"I know. And I'll do what has to be done, but *this* is what I want. You. Me."

"I won't share you," he softly growled, tightening his grip.

"You don't have to. Kiss me. Kiss me and I'll prove that you won't have to."

His head lowered. Our breath mingled. Yet he continued to hesitate, not bridging that gap I so desperately wanted him to cross. I slowly shifted in his lap and he stiffened, hissing through his teeth. Butterflies jumped in my stomach. My thighs instinctively clenched around his, and this time, it was my turn to suck in a gasp as heat barrelled through me.

In one swift move, he was on his feet, carrying me into the alley's secluded depths. His gaze was fire and passion, love and adoration. Everything that I wanted. He never once looked away as he moved. The backpack containing the box of serum dug into my spine as he backed me against a wall. I fumbled for the straps, trying to wrestle the packs free.

Bren had other plans. He reached behind me and gave a sharp yank. The wall fell away as we entered through a door. He toed it shut behind us.

His plan was better. Much better.

I dropped the packs just before he pressed me to a wall again. Feeling the length of him against me sent a weak moan rolling up my throat. His mouth—stars, his perfect mouth—finally found my skin. My head fell back as he kissed a scorching trail up my neck. My fingers clenched in his hair and he growled, low and deep, his teeth tugging at my ear as repayment. I bit my lip to keep from crying out.

"Claim me," I panted, half out of my mind for him but lucid enough to know what I was asking. "Before the others come and I have no choice. Claim me, Bren."

He balked, drawing back to look at me. The room was dark, but I could still make out the yellow glow of his irises. "Do you know what you're asking?" he replied thickly. "You would have to bind yourself to me. Submit. *Give* yourself. You want that?"

I touched his face. "I do. My heart is yours. *Only* yours. No matter what happens after tonight, I need you to know that."

"I don't want you to make a rash decision and regret giving yourself to me—"

"I would never regret it," I interrupted him, then softened my voice. "I *want* to. More than anything."

His inhale was sharp, as if he couldn't believe what I was saying. So I added, "This is *my* choice. Not something I'm doing simply because a king is forcing me to marry his son. It's you, Bren. Your quiet strength, your teasing, your crooked smile, your gentleness, your kind heart, your sayings that don't make sense. Everything you are, the good and the bad. All of it. I want it all. I want . . . I want you."

He closed his eyes for a moment, murmuring some more of those sayings I didn't understand. "If the boss discovers us," he said, slowly reopening his eyes, "he might lock us up for good. Or worse."

"Then we better not get caught," I dared challenge him. "But right now, it's just you—" I pulled his face closer to mine. "Me—" I tilted his head, kissing his ear, then his jaw, slowly working my way toward his mouth. I stopped just shy of his lips as I finished with, "And an abandoned building."

His skin practically vibrated under my fingertips. I knew he was weakening. Knew it in the way his hands tightly gripped my hips, his chest heaving against mine. The power—the control I had over him—was intoxicating. Not that I wanted to steal away his choices. But seduce him a little?

Freaking, yes.

I shrugged before trying a new tactic. My tone was dripping

with sarcasm, but I was still hoping for a reaction when I whispered, "Or you could give Ryker and me your blessing as we—"

"Never," he interrupted with a growl, that one word holding a world of anger and hurt, desperation and want. "I will never give my blessing. You're mine." He made a sound in the back of his throat. Dark. Feral. "You're *mine*, Lune Avery."

Oh.

And then he finally did it.

He claimed my lips in a powerful rush.

The kiss was intense. Possessive. Punishing. Punishing *me* for my words.

I took it, asking for more. He gave. And gave. With a fervor that was almost frightening. His scent wrapped around me, consuming my senses. I drank him in. Willingly drowning. His mouth worked mine hard.

Branding.

Claiming.

My lips parted as I asked him to claim the rest of me. Asked. Because it was my decision. And I chose *him*.

His tongue swept inside, and mine eagerly met his. I gasped as they intertwined. He explored every inch of my mouth and I his, until we were both shaking with need. His fingers found the zipper of my jacket. Mine were already tugging at the collar of his shirt. In seconds, we were stripped to the waist, our clothing tossed into the darkness.

He claimed my lips again and I arched against him, inhaling sharply when our skin met. New sensations overwhelmed me, the feel of his hard chest against the softness of mine.

More. My body craved more of him. *All* of him. Wanted to crawl *inside* of him.

His legs suddenly gave out and he dropped to his knees. As he lowered me to the floor, I expected to feel the cold bite of concrete. Instead, something soft cushioned my back. Moss. Nature had claimed this room. I grasped Bren's neck to pull him on top of me, but he halted the movement. His fingers encircled my wrists, placing them on either side of my head.

I tried to make out his face but was distracted by his eyes. They were taking in the bare skin he'd never seen before. As his gaze ran over me like a caress, my breath hitched. He swallowed up the reaction, his irises brighter than I'd ever seen them. I squirmed under his all-consuming stare, feeling exposed and vulnerable.

His eyes lifted to mine. "I'm completely undone by you."

I stilled.

His next words had me wholly enraptured.

"I claim you, Lune Avery, as my mate," he said quietly, but his voice was steady. Reverent. "From this moment forward, you are mine and I am yours. I will protect you—" He lowered his head and I watched him press a kiss to my bare stomach. A riot of butterflies took up residence there and I lost my ability to breathe. "Honor you—" His lips found my rapidly beating heart. "And love you. Until my very last breath." He kissed my mouth, this time gently, and I struggled with the overwhelming urge to cry.

I was trembling, heart in my throat and completely clueless as to how this claiming thing worked. He had labeled it a predatory act, but this—*this*—was beautiful.

And I wanted to claim him in return.

I nudged him back until he was the one lying down. His eyes tracked my every movement as I slowly straddled him. My whole body flushed under that penetrating gaze, but I still managed to say, "I claim you, Brendan Bearon, as my mate. From this moment forward, you are mine and I am yours." My voice shook with nerves, but I didn't falter once. I repeated the rest, kissing his stomach, his heart, and his mouth, lingering each time. Relishing the way he responded to my touch.

A slight weight, one I'd borne for eleven years, knocked against my chest as I shifted. I reached up and removed the bear tooth necklace he'd given me. And looped it around his neck. I rested the tooth on his chest and placed my hand over it. "You're mine now."

He wrapped an arm around my waist, rolling me under him. "You have no idea how much I love the sound of that, little bird," his voice rumbled in my ear. Then his body was on mine, pressing me into the moss. A moan left me as my brain fogged, as the world receded and all I could do was feel. His lips on my skin. Kissing. Every. Last. Inch. His strong yet gentle hands exploring the contours of my body for the very first time.

He built a fire in me. Then soothed the ache.

He stole my breath completely.

He loved me. Until I only knew him.

As my heart swelled to bursting and the feelings overflowed, I cried out. The love I felt for him in this moment was bigger than words. This was my soul's desire, for as long as I could hold onto it. Maybe we'd have an hour. But maybe we'd have a lifetime together after facing the challenges ahead of us. I greedily soaked up every precious second of time with him. Because he and I both knew how much time enjoyed tearing us apart. But this moment . . .

It was ours.

YOU ARE BRAVE

"Jump."

I wrinkled my nose.

Bren gave me a devilish grin. "I swear I'll catch you."

"Or maybe I'll just up and fly," I purred, enjoying the easy banter we'd fallen into. "Why can't I have the ability to fly instead of haunt people's brains?"

Laughter burst from him. Light and carefree. Happy. "Come on. You totally made this jump during the Arcus Point Trial."

"Yeah, but I had a saber cat trying to *eat* me then." I rolled my eyes but backed up a step. Then ran toward the rooftop's ledge. As I soared through empty space, knowing certain death awaited six stories below, exhilaration gave me wings. All too soon, the neighboring rooftop came up fast. I stuck the landing. Sort of.

True to his word, Bren caught me before I face-planted into concrete. I laughed as he swung me around, pretending for a moment more that dawn wasn't approaching and this wouldn't have to end.

"They'll have a hard time tracking us up here," he said, setting me down only to twirl me. I bit my lip in a vain effort to stop from smiling when he reeled me back in and started to dance.

"What are you doing?"

He quirked a brow. "Dancing."

"And avoiding the inevitable?"

He dipped me low, whispering in my ear, "Don't remind me."

"Bren."

"Hmm?" We were off again, leaving me breathless and far too happy on a night that could still go terribly wrong.

"Bren, we need to discuss this."

We slowed. Then stopped.

He sighed, gently tucking hair behind my ear before saying, "Okay."

"When Ryker arrives, we have to act like this never happened."

"I know." He gave me a tight smile, but it quickly fell.

I fingered the leather cord around his neck, then slipped the bear tooth beneath his shirt. "I know it'll be hard, but I really do have a plan. Promise not to leave me behind, even if things go south."

Bren had found an epic hiding spot for our backpacks, but I couldn't help worrying that he'd take the box of serum and re-turn to Tatum City without me. He was compromised, but I didn't doubt that he'd try to complete his mission anyway. And that scared the crap out of me.

"I will never leave you behind again, little bird. Things are dif-ferent now."

"Why? Because we had—" My mouth snapped shut. I was *so* not ready to say that word. But now I was thinking about what we'd done. How patient and attentive Bren had been. How incredible he'd made me feel—like the center of his universe.

His fingers distracted me as he plucked something from my hair. When he held up a cluster of *moss* with an insufferable grin plastered on his face, my cheeks caught on fire.

"You're so adorable when you blush," he teased. I scowled,

but had to bite back a giggle when he suddenly turned me in his arms and sat. We stretched out on the rooftop, my legs between his, my back resting against his chest. He kissed my temple as I placed my head on his shoulder.

We stared up at the starry sky in peaceful silence. I didn't press him further. Not right now. Later. There would be time for all of that later. I hoped.

"To answer your question," Bren said, surprising me, "things are different because of the promises we made. I don't take them lightly. Claiming a mate is as binding as marriage—maybe more so, since I now consider you my other half. My soulmate. I will defend, respect, and cherish you until my very last breath."

Tears smudged the stars from the sky. One second, I was elated by his words, and the next, a sick wave of nausea swept through me.

"Hey." Bren tilted my chin toward him, revealing his worried frown. He wiped away my embarrassing tears. "I'm sensing fear. What happened? Do you regret—?"

"Don't you dare say it, Brendan Bearon," I said sternly, but my voice shook. "I could never regret what we shared. I'm just scared. Scared because I've never loved someone this way before and I can't lose that. I can't lose *you*."

His eyes held sympathy. I knew he understood. His fingers traced my jaw before tipping my face up to his. "You won't lose me." He pressed his lips to mine in a slow caress, soothing my fear.

"You can't promise that," I whispered against his mouth. When the kiss grew more heated, scattering my thoughts, I pulled back. I made sure he was looking at me as I said, "You're still planning on returning to Tatum City, aren't you."

It wasn't a question.

His gaze dropped, but I brought a hand up, brushing my knuckles across his cheek. When his eyes lifted, there was so much turmoil inside them that I wanted to cry.

"Please don't, Bren. If Renold knows you're a spy, he'll torture you. Maybe even kill you. You can't go back. It's too risky."

He sighed and wrapped his arms around my middle, pulling me close. "Someone has to make a stand, Lune. I've been preparing for this moment my entire life. It's my chance to atone for my sins. Knowing I put children in there, knowing I destroyed their families . . . I have to make it right, little bird, or the guilt will eat me alive."

I trailed my finger up a vein in his forearm, deep in thought. "What if . . . what if the guilt won't go away until you forgive yourself?"

He didn't say anything for several moments. "Guess I'll have to carry the guilt for a little while longer then."

Oh, Bren. His pain was palpable. If only he'd let me carry some of that burden for him.

I jerked as an agitated male voice tore apart our little cocoon. "So I swoop in all stealth mode, expecting to rescue you two from a manhunt, only to find you schmoozing under the stars? I'm disappointed, guys. Real disappointed. And a bit nauseated at all the ooey-gooey crap."

Bren was already on his feet, blocking my view of the intruder before I could so much as twitch a finger. Just as quickly, he lunged forward and tackled the man. No, they were hugging. *Hugging?* What in the—

"You came," I heard Bren say with relief. As I stood, they separated but still clasped each other's shoulders. I squinted for a better look at the newcomer, barely making out dark skin and short black hair on top of a solid black outfit. It was the dazzling white teeth as he grinned that had shock zipping through me.

"Jaxon," I blurted incredulously. "How—?" I trailed off as he took three giant steps and swallowed me in his arms. I was too surprised to protest when he lifted me off my feet.

"I'm glad you're here, Jax, but you chose the worst possible moment to attempt a rescue," Bren said from nearby. "Two dozen men are on the hunt for Lune tonight. It's only a matter of time before they catch on that I'm with her and track my scent instead—especially Ryker. I'm surprised he's not here already."

Jaxon stepped back and peered down at me sternly. "How come you left The Ridge with that doofus? He's bad news. And you," he said, pausing to scan Bren's body. "I thought you were in serious trouble. What am I missing here? 'Cause my remote-controlled drone doesn't have voice detection."

I gaped at him, feeling heat rise to my cheeks. "You've been *watching* us?"

His hazel brown eyes narrowed. "It's my job, remember? Sleek, panther-like drone? Now stop giving me that koi fish look and spill the beans."

I started to explain what happened the day Ryker showed up at Medical when Bren suddenly grabbed my arm and dragged me behind him.

"Someone's here," he said, squaring off with the northern edge of the roof. "I sure hope you're armed, Jax." I peeked over Bren's shoulder only to have him nudge me out of sight again. I stared at his broad back, feeling both the urge to kick him and hug him for being so protective.

"Uh, about that," Jaxon muttered almost nervously. "My covert operation ended up with a stalker sidekick. You have to understand, she's been impossible ever since Lune disappeared. She was ordered to stay at camp until we could extract you two, but . . . but she snuck in after me, man. I didn't know until it was too late."

Bren slowly turned to his friend, every muscle on his frame taut. "*Who?* Jaxon, I swear. If you—"

"Jaxon, I think I heard something. It could be one of the clansmen, and I can't—" A gasp. "Bren!"

Alarm flared through me at the sound of that decidedly female voice.

Bren jerked, whipping toward the voice. And swore.

He rushed to help his sister over the roof's ledge, glaring daggers at Jaxon the whole time. Crap, there was a ladder. Our hideout was more accessible than we thought. Bells threw her arms around her brother, talking so fast I could barely catch the words. She also wore solid black, her dark brown hair weaved into a thick braid.

I thought about using the moment to speak with Jaxon about my plan, but the timing was all wrong. Neither side would listen under these circumstances. This was incredibly dangerous for all three of them. They were in this predicament because of me and needed to leave the city *now*.

Even Bren. *Especially* Bren.

But he would have to leave me behind.

Despair punched me in the gut. The violence of the emotion stole my breath.

Focused on breathing through the pain, I didn't see her approach until arms were enveloping me in a hug. Probably feeling my distress with her Empath ability, Bells crooned little nothing's into my ear, gently rubbing my back. Still unused to female touch, it took me a moment to return the embrace. But when I did, I had the strangest urge to cry my eyes out.

"I had to come," Bells said softly. "I'm scared witless to be back here, but shortly after you left, it hit me. You didn't escape The Ridge to betray us. You went to save my brother because you love him." She hiccupped, pulling back to blink at me with sad, amber brown eyes. "I'm right, aren't I? And then I realized how pathetic I've been, hiding behind parties and dresses and books. I've been too scared to fix things like you and Bren are, and I felt ashamed. I'm so sorry that I'm not more brave, but I'm trying now."

"Oh, Bells." I drew her into another hug. Tremors rocked her slim frame as she broke down in tears. It was a dangerous thing to be overly sensitive in a violent world, but that very thing was also her strength. Kindness—empathy toward others—kept humans from tearing each other apart. But those gentle souls—like Asher, Iris, Mum, and even Bren—needed protecting, oftentimes from themselves. They carried too much so others wouldn't have to.

"You *are* brave," I reassured her. "You survived and never stopped believing in the goodness of others. That takes a lot of courage. Everyone has their own battles to face, but they don't all look the same."

"Lune's right," I heard a new voice say.

Bren cursed again, but didn't move to block me this time. I realized why a second later as Ryker slipped over the roof's ledge, leveling a gun at Jaxon's chest. A growl formed in the back of my throat. Bells stiffened against me but didn't pull away.

Blue eyes rimmed in black swung my direction, but Ryker wasn't looking at me. His intense gaze was wholly focused on Bells as he said, "You've always been brave."

Bells gasped and jerked around. When Ryker saw her face, he froze midstep. They wordlessly stared at each other. No one dared move while his gun was still trained on Jaxon. He seemed to have forgotten about it, about everyone and everything. Except Bells.

He finally blinked, swallowing hard. "Isabella." Her name was soft on his tongue. My brows crept upward. His eyes flitted over her again. "You've grown."

She collected herself, raising her chin defiantly. "I just turned seventeen."

His mouth lifted in a ghost of a smile. "I know."

She gawked at him a moment, obviously tongue-tied, then blurted, "Can you put away the gun, please? You know how I hate those things. And I go by Bells now."

Ryker glanced at me. "So I've heard," he simply said, then shocked my socks off by lowering his weapon. "You all need to leave. Now. Everyone except Lune. The men aren't far behind me and won't hesitate to shoot first, ask questions later. If they detect your presence, they'll chase and capture you."

"Too late. I can sense someone close by," Bren muttered, striding toward me. "We'll take the long way down, over the roof-tops. Chances are we'll still have to fight our way out, though. *All* of us. We have what we need, so let's get out of here."

"*I* don't have what I need," Ryker interjected. "And Lune's going nowhere without me."

Bells gasped, then quickly clamped a hand over her mouth. I grimaced, realizing how terrible Ryker's words must sound to her. And I didn't have time to explain.

Not when Bren rounded on Ryker and snarled, "Why do you want Lune so badly? And for heaven's sake, why did you give me up to the *boss*? You hate him. You know what? Screw this. You've always had questionable motives and I won't let my mate be a part of them."

Ryker reared back, shooting us both death glares. "Your *what?*"

Crap on a *cat*. Couldn't these two chill out already?

A shoulder nudged mine. "Mate, eh?" Jaxon whispered. "Kinky. I like it. So does that mean you—"

I elbowed his arm. Hard. Bren was in so much trouble for this. I was going to yell at him, then bite and lick him. Wait.

Get it together, you love-sick fool!

"Guys, stop!" I hissed, placing myself between them. "I agree with Ryker. You all need to leave before it's too late. But I have to stay and so does he. I've got a plan, and as long as we—well, when we do the—when I become *princess*, everything will be fine." Well, that was painful. I turned pleading eyes on Bren. "You have to leave, too. If the boss finds out what we did, who knows what the punishment will be. You know how it feels to have a loved one used against you."

Despite my reasoning, he looked ready to throw me over his shoulder and apologize later. I was gearing up to deliver some choice words when Bells let out a startled squeak. I turned toward the noise. And almost swallowed my tongue.

She was out in the open. Unprotected. With a gun pointed at her head.

And the one holding the gun was none other than the boss.

"No one's going anywhere," he drawled, his tone convincingly amiable. If it weren't for the chips of ice in his eyes, I'd think he was in a good mood. Lightning quick, Ryker raised his gun. And pointed it at his father. Rollie almost looked bored. "Shoot me and she goes down, too."

Jaxon shifted beside me, slowly unholstering his weapon. I grabbed his arm and squeezed. He froze. What I couldn't do was stop Bren if he decided to attack. He hadn't moved a muscle, but fury poured off the taut lines of his body. I scrambled for a way out of this that didn't involve bloodshed. But came up empty.

"How did you get up here?" I blurted, desperately needing to divert his attention. "You didn't use the ladder, and I didn't see you jump."

He threw me a smirk. "I own this city. No one knows its secrets like I do—not even my traitorous son. The deal still stands, by the way. I don't care if you gave yourself to another man like a tramp. You *will* marry my son. That's right, lass, I heard everything. It didn't take you long to betray me, and I *told* you who would pay the price. Bren will be taken care of, but first . . ."

He paused, soaking in the fear and trepidation oozing from our pores. "But first, I have to take care of my son's weakness. I warned him that females were treacherous to a man's heart—they steal it, make it beat for them, then skewer it to the wall—but he didn't listen. My mate, *my mate*," he growled, losing his composure, "betrayed me tonight. I never wanted to be like my brother, but I won't let love blind me from doing what's best for the clan. If you're all against me, then I'll destroy you—starting with her."

Rollie steadied the gun, his focus solely on Bells. Yet his words were for me. "You can't save the girl, lass, but return what you stole from me and I'll consider sparing Bren's life." The blood drained from my face. "Where are the backpacks, Lune?" he roared, spittle flying from his mouth.

My pulse went sky high, pounding in my skull as he cocked the gun's hammer. Adrenaline whooshed through me. I felt sick. Helpless. Powerless. And yet, I was angry. So very angry. I had the greatest urge to reach out with my mind and demand he lower the gun.

The feeling intensified. It thrashed in my chest, a wild instinct I couldn't control. Couldn't shake. My sight narrowed to him. Only him. The rush surged through me like a raging river, threatening to sweep me away.

And I couldn't.

Hold.

On.

I was screaming. The sound a galewind. A twister in a storm.

It hurt.

I needed to release it. Let it go. Before it swallowed me whole.

My mouth opened. The inferno charged.

Then, as though immersed under water, the faraway voice of Ryker shouted, "*Stop!* I challenge you for head alpha."

THE CHALLENGE

My limbs twitched with aftershocks as I watched father and son strip to the waist.

The guns had been tossed aside. Barely a word was spoken after Ryker had challenged Rollie. The King of the Recruiter Clan had looked shocked, then furious. But he honored the code he himself had instilled, allowing Bren to reach for his sister and pull her to safety.

Bren kept darting worried glances at me, probably from sensing the strange manifestation I'd just experienced. Beside me, Jaxon had reversed my hold on his arm and now firmly held mine, keeping me from shaking right out of my skin. He was frowning, but remained tight-lipped as we watched the men prepare to fight. I ached to step forward and demand we reach an agreement that didn't involve violence, but I knew it wouldn't make a difference.

This wasn't the time for negotiations and alliances.

This was Ryker's moment to prove himself. To free himself of an abusive father and reunite with an imprisoned mother. Judging by the scars on his back, he'd been waiting his entire life for this moment.

But the challenge was premature. He wasn't ready—or so he believed. After seeing his reaction to Bells being held at gunpoint, though, maybe her presence alone would give him the strength needed to defeat Rollie. He cared for her. A *lot*. Bren wasn't the only one fighting to protect her anymore.

A commotion to the left caught my attention. Three clansmen clambered onto the roof, and Jaxon whipped out his gun. Before a shootout could commence, Rollie whirled, bellowing, "No weapons! There will be a ceasefire as you all witness this challenge for head alpha. We fight to the death in hand-to-hand combat. The loser is not allowed mercy. Anyone who interferes forfeits their lives."

The men nodded, pounding fists over their hearts. "Honor the code, respect the clan," they said in unison, casting suspicious glares at Bren and Jaxon. Despite the hostility permeating the air, there was also a palpable sense of anticipation. They were excited about this fight.

Jaxon holstered his gun, muttering under his breath, "Honor the crazy, respect the cult, is more like it."

Although I agreed, Rollie was without a doubt dedicated to the clan's survival, and he was nowhere near ready to give up his throne. Which was why fear gripped my throat. Ryker may be younger and fitter, but his father was a boulder of dense muscle.

Sure enough, I heard the boss jeer, "You're not fit to rule, boy. You're a disappointment and I'm ashamed to call you son. Bow out now and I'll spare your life, for your mother's sake."

Ryker simply shook his head. "We fight. It's time to end this."

The king's lips peeled back in a silent snarl. "So be it."

Then he rushed his son.

Ryker faced the attack the same way he would any other vicious predator—with a bored air. At the last second, he jerked back. Rollie's powerhouse punch sailed past his shoulder. He expended little energy as the boss pursued him across the roof with savage thrusts and kicks meant to maim.

We followed at a safe distance. A part of me didn't want to watch, but I couldn't look away. I knew Bells felt the same. Her hands were pressed tightly to her mouth, eyes round and unblinking. Bren had a firm grip on her arm as if afraid she'd try to break up the match. Smart. She probably would in the name of this newfound bravery she'd discovered. One blow from Rollie could kill her.

Scratch that. One blow from *either* of them could. Ryker finally made a move, punching his father's jaw with an audible *smack*. Blood sprayed from the older man's mouth.

Jaxon did a little cheer, whisper-yelling, "Go, Team Ryker!"

I glared at him.

He shrugged innocently. "What? He may be a douche, but you wouldn't believe the stories I've heard of daddy-o. My money's on the broody one."

"Money?" I waved a hand dismissively. "Never mind."

I was too focused on the stunned look both men were giving each other. My guess was that Ryker had never hit his father before. His eyes flicked to the blood spattered on the rooftop. Rollie used the distraction. A *crack* rent the air—the sound of bone giving way.

Ryker doubled over, clutching at his ribs. Bells whimpered. I clenched my teeth, willing him to get up again.

Push past the pain.

I had never seen a father injure his child before—only ever experienced it. Watching was worse than I'd imagined. Before Ryker could recover, Rollie's fist plowed into his cheek, almost bringing him to his knees. He staggered, bent at the waist, but remained on his feet. And from that position . . .

I saw the move coming, but Rollie didn't.

Ryker's arm swung in a perfect arc.

And delivered a powerful uppercut. Straight to the chin.

The king toppled.

Ryker was on him in a heartbeat. Pounding his face. Repeatedly. Like a demon possessed. He roared. As if in pain. As if he hated what he was doing but couldn't stop. Blood spurted onto his neck. Cheeks. Coating his hand. I was frozen by the violent display—agony mixed with hatred.

I didn't see the next move coming.

No one did.

How could we have? From day one, Rollie had spouted the importance of open honesty, of honoring the code and clan. So the last thing I expected. The very last thing . . .

Was for him to break it.

Out of nowhere, a knife flashed. He plunged the blade into Ryker's back. Bells screamed and wrenched free of Bren's hold. He lunged for her, but fear had given her wings. She sprinted forward, her brother in hot pursuit.

The panic in his voice as he yelled her name broke me from my trance. I charged after her. So did Jaxon. But we were all too late. Too late to stop her from flinging herself at Ryker. Too late to stop Rollie from blocking her path and delivering a powerful backhand.

The blow was so brutal, her body spun through the air. She crumpled into a fragile heap.

"No!" Bren roared. He slid the last few feet to her prone body. His hands fluttered over her but didn't make contact, as if afraid to touch her. As if afraid that she was . . . dead.

I dropped next to Bren and immediately felt for her pulse. My own was pounding so savagely that it took me longer than necessary to find what I sought. "She's alive. But her neck might have been injured. I wouldn't move her."

Bren made a sound in the back of his throat—part relief, part "I'm going to beat that man's brain in." I grabbed his arm. He shook me off with little effort, his Sensor strength raging. He stood, preparing to attack. A warning shout burned on the tip of my tongue, but Jaxon tackled him from behind.

"*Prohibere. Opus tibi est viveret,*" he fiercely whispered to Bren. I couldn't understand, but it was enough to calm Bren down, allowing me to breathe again.

Then I remembered Ryker.

Ryker!

If he was dead, we were so screwed.

My eyes found him just as Rollie plowed a boot into his gut. I winced at the pained groan, at the coughing that no doubt sent fire streaking through his wrecked body.

But he was alive. *Alive.*

His back was smeared red where he must have taken out the knife. I searched the rooftop and found the discarded weapon a few yards away. But what if Rollie had more? He could easily slit Ryker's throat in his vulnerable state.

Ryker must have thought the same thing, because he staggered to his feet. The man had many flaws, but a low pain threshold wasn't one of them. He spat blood and pressed a hand to the purpling bruise over his rib cage. "You're going to pay for hurting her."

Rollie's laid-back demeanor was gone. His expression was feral, wild like an animal. A wolf. A Berserker? "You won't take this clan away from me. I've worked too hard, *too hard* to let my good-for-nothing son have it. There's only one head alpha. One *king.* And it's going to be me."

Ryker's eyes took on a weary light. "No matter what I did, I was never good enough for you," he said dully. "It took me forever to figure out, but I know why now. She loves me and not you, and you can't stand it."

His father stiffened, slowly curling his hands into fists. "I dare you to say that again."

Oh crap. There was no way Ryker wouldn't—

"She. Doesn't. *Love*. You."

Yeah. That.

Like a rope stretched too taut, Rollie snapped. He barreled into Ryker, sweeping him clean off his feet. When his injured back slammed onto the rooftop, phantom pain shot up my spine.

"It's all your fault," the boss roared in his son's face. "I should have killed you years ago so she'd see *me*. Her mate. Her husband!"

He struck Ryker's face again and again, a succession of hits that left the younger man dazed. And all I could do was watch. Helplessly watch as he took the beating. Tears of frustration dripped off my chin.

Desperate for a way to stop this, I fixed pleading eyes on Bren. His gaze was locked on Ryker, but I could see the glistening trail down his cheek. He was crying, too.

Crying for the boy he'd grown up with.

The sight almost crushed my lungs.

But what cracked my heart wide open was seeing a broken Ryker staring at an unconscious Bells. He never once looked away from her.

And it was his sacrifice that made me do what I did next.

I gave Bells' limp hand a gentle squeeze, then slowly rose to a crouch. I sucked in a breath. Let it out. In. Out. Then bolted for the discarded knife. A startled yell followed my pounding footsteps, but I didn't look back. Within range, I dropped into a skid, all of my focus on scooping up that knife. Success. My fingers wrapped around the cold handle. I only had one shot at this. *One*. I couldn't fail.

I jumped up and pulled my arm back, zeroing in on my target.

This was it. One thrust of the arm and my life was forfeit. But Bells and Ryker, Bren and Jaxon. They would still be alive.

I stared at the spot between Rollie's eyes and tensed my muscles for the throw.

Then choked back a gasp.

Evangeline. Evie. Ryker's mother. Was right behind her husband, poised to plunge a needle into his neck.

Before I could see her do it, something slammed into me. A shock of pain lit up my chest, and the air left my lungs in a giant whoosh. Death by bullet, then. One of the clansmen must have taken the shot. But shouldn't it hurt more than this? The sensation was like being squeezed by a spectacularly strong pair of arms.

Wait. I *was* being squeezed. Bren had me in a death grip. If he didn't let up soon, my bones were going to rearrange themselves.

"Bren," I squeaked. "Bren, I'm not going to throw it. Please . . . let me . . . breathe."

"I'm furious with you right now," he quietly growled, but let me go.

"Punish me later," I said distractedly, nudging him aside to scan the scene I'd missed.

Circling the scene was Jaxon and the three clansmen, all pointing guns. An unconscious Bells and Ryker made up the middle. Evie and Rollie were dead center. Staring at each other.

"How? Why?" I heard the boss whisper. He blinked lethargically. "What did you . . . do to me?"

With an effort, she raised her chin. "I knew you'd take my

betrayal out on our son, so I escaped and followed your scent. You went too far this time, Roland. You know what he means to me. He's my world. I couldn't let you destroy my world, so I . . . I had to destroy you."

He stumbled back, shellshocked. "Wha—? How could you—? Evie. My love. Why have you always loved him and not me? I tried to make you happy." He reached for her, but she shook her head and stepped aside.

"A pretty cage is still a cage, and you never once asked me what I wanted," she said, tears of hurt and anger trickling down her face. "I don't know how long the serum takes to work, but you're going to lose all of your memories. And I'm glad. So glad. I will finally be free of you."

Rollie made a strangled noise, then suddenly swayed, shaking his head. "What's happening to me?" He backed up, eyes bulging as he noticed his blood-encrusted hands. "Where did this come from? Why can't I remember?"

He was panicking now, swiping at the blood, moaning when it wouldn't come off. And all the while, he continued to back away. Toward the roof's ledge. I opened my mouth, but Bren laid a hand on my arm. Staying my words. The rooftop was silent, not a single soul offering to help the floundering man as he stumbled against the raised lip. He didn't cry out as he flailed. As he tipped over the edge. And plummeted to the cracked cement six stories below.

I felt detached from my body—a spectator—as my feet shuffled across the roof. A numb acceptance stole over me, an understanding. His life was forfeit the moment he'd broken the code. There was no guilt over what happened. Only justice.

But I needed to know for certain.

I reached the ledge and peered below. As I did, the first golden rays of morning sun swept across my face, nearly blinding me. But I had seen. My fears were put to rest.

"The king is dead," I said.

TREATIES & TRAITORS

Word spread like wildfire that Rollie had fallen—literally.

The three clansmen who'd witnessed the challenge also passed on news of their king's unforgivable betrayal. There was an uproar. The men refused to give him an honorable burial. And they were shaken enough to listen to the most unlikely of persons: their queen.

And, stars, she could talk. Too bad the king had never treated her as his equal. She was cunning, yet considerate. Firm, yet forgiving. She, with her Sensor blood and knowledge of their ways, understood the men far better than I ever could.

Not that I wanted to speak to them or become their princess. Now that Rollie was dead, there was no need to follow through with my plan—at least the princess part. Besides, Ryker was in no condition to claim anyone even if he wanted to. I glanced up at the tavern's wood-beamed ceiling where I knew he rested. His mother had insisted on keeping him close, and Bells—after regaining consciousness—hadn't left his side. Not once.

Both Bren and Jaxon had grumbled, were *still* grumbling, but I secretly approved of Bells and Ryker as a couple. Had I not been claimed by the hottest man alive, though, I might have been jealous. There was something exquisitely intense yet achingly vulnerable about those two when they were together. I wondered how people felt about me and Bren. We knew Jaxon's opinion, at least: a bit nauseated.

I snorted loudly.

"Earth to Lu Bear," he singsonged, waving a hand in front of my face. "Care to join the conversation?"

"Only if it doesn't involve Ryker and Bells' love life."

The sip of moonshine he took practically showered my lap as he sputtered out a laugh. "Did you just use the L word? She's just a baby! If anything, it's a case of Stockholm syndrome."

I rolled my eyes even as Bren nodded in agreement. I kicked his shin under the table and he shot me a confused look. "I don't know what kind of syndrome you're talking about, but she's not a baby. You just don't want her with the big bad wolf. Anyway, I told you his side of things. His methods were questionable, but his intentions were honorable. Mostly."

Neither of them looked convinced, but at least the hatred toward him had dissipated. I guessed taking on the boss so Bells wouldn't get shot had earned Ryker a few points. Jaxon swigged more of his disgusting drink, eyeing the packed room for a moment before whispering, "Do you think they'll cooperate?"

I surveyed the boisterous crowd who seemed happy with receiving a few days off from their duties. Upon her husband's death, Evie had decreed that no one should leave the city until further notice. As far as I knew, they'd listened. Probably out of curiosity more than anything. But I worried for her. Ryker too. If one of the clansmen decided to challenge them for head alpha, neither were in a position to fight. Evie was scrappy, but even the punch she'd laid on me lacked technique.

"They have to," I answered Jaxon. "Things are going to change for the better. If they don't like it, they can leave."

He chuckled, patting my shoulder. "If only it were that easy. This is why you won't be making the speeches."

"Hey." I whacked his arm, feigning offense.

Bren snickered softly. When I glared at him, he simply leaned toward me and nuzzled my neck, inhaling deeply. My annoyance evaporated as warmth infused my cheeks at his public affection. "I like your direct approach," he purred, his breath stirring my hair. "You can practice it on me if you want."

Holy stars. This man and his wicked tongue.

And then that tongue flicked out, catching my earlobe. Heat pooled between my legs and I squirmed in my seat. Several heads chose that moment to swivel our way. Crap balls, could they sense my body's reaction to his touch? Okay, I was so out of here. Negotiations could wait.

I was about to crawl over the table and make a break for the exit when I heard a growl. Not a human one or even animal, but a mechanical sound that cut through the tavern's chatter.

All eyes went to the glass front door.

"My baby's here!" Jaxon crowed, jumping up and practically skipping toward the entrance. I saw Evie rise too, so I followed suit, Bren at my heels as we tailed a jubilant Jaxon. I didn't need a Sensor ability to feel the tension in the room. Animal instincts were kicking in—fight or flight. Hopefully neither would happen this evening, but if they did, I was slightly reassured by the weight of my daggers crisscrossing my back.

Bren had surprised me with the leather holster shortly after Rollie's death. I'd almost wept. Dresses and jewelry couldn't compare to being gifted a fine quality sheath for your favorite weapons. My lips had shown him my appreciation. He'd seemed happy.

The first thing I noticed after exiting the tavern was the

monstrous black vehicle. Round lights on the front pierced the evening gloom. And was that a gun mounted on top? Jaxon was stroking the vehicle's side, crooning sweet nothings. I caught the words "baby" and "did you miss me?"

The engine cut off and the doors opened. When I recognized who hopped out of the driver's side, my heart rate quickened. Spiky black bangs were flipped aside as she rolled her dark, almond-shaped eyes. "I won't even bother to compete with that," she said in response to her boyfriend's antics.

Her gaze sliced to me, and she froze. I held back a wince, wait-ing for that pale face to twist in anger. Waited for her to stomp over and yell at me for jeopardizing the home she so fiercely protected. She did approach, but her neutral expression made it impossible to predict what she'd do. Would she shoot me the same way she'd been shot?

I braced for impact, refusing to cower or run. I deserved whatever punishment she wanted to—

Yukiko slammed into me, wrapping her arms around my back to keep me from falling. She was shorter by a handful of inches but had no trouble keeping us upright as she squeezed me. The stern, no-nonsense girl who could have died because of my stupidity was *hugging* me. "Thank you," she mumbled against my shoulder. "For keeping our secrets and saving Bren."

I was too shocked to do or say anything. Over her head, I saw Jaxon watching us. He clutched at his heart and pretended to wipe away tears, mouthing, *"So sweet."*

She released me and cleared her throat. "I like the new hair-cut." Her eyes widened slightly when she caught sight of the tattoo on my temple. "Nice ink. You'll have to let me know who did it in case I want something done."

Oh crap. I highly doubted she'd want the guy who *shot* her to stick a needle into her flesh.

Thankfully, I was spared from answering with the arrival of more Ridge people. Heavily armed guards—hopefully none of the ones who'd shot at me and Ryker—made room for Dominic and Dr. Stacey to approach. I gave my old instructor a tentative smile which he easily returned, pulling me into a quick hug.

I had to blink away tears. All of this acceptance from the people I'd betrayed was overwhelming. I wondered if this was how Bren had felt when I'd forgiven him for the part he played in my kidnapping.

"We need to have a long, lengthy chat," Dominic said and leaned back, his gray eyes sparkling with excitement. "Bren radioed that there were new developments with your abilities?"

"Uh . . ."

He waved away my dumbfounded response. "We'll have time to explore that later, but right now . . ." He stepped around me and held out a hand toward Evie. "Evangeline Jones, I presume? I'm Dominic Holland, emissary to Blue Ridge Sector, a division of Homeland Security. I'm here on behalf of my colleague, Dr. Carl Moore, who oversees The Ridge."

She shook his hand with a firm grip but offered a warm smile. "I've heard rumors of your mountain city. Is it true that everyone has access to clean water and three square meals a day?"

He returned her smile, launching into a description of their home similar to the one I'd been given upon arrival. I felt some of the tension in my shoulders ease as Evie ushered us inside the tavern where negotiations for peace and trade between the Recruiter Clan and Blue Ridge Sector would commence.

Dr. Moore had chosen well in sending Dominic to speak for

him. When Jaxon had helped me radio The Ridge's leader two days ago, convincing him to form an alliance with the clan hadn't been easy. But when I'd secretly used my telepathic ability to tell him about the box of memory serum in Bren's backpack, he was willing to listen to my plan.

Not only would the alliance free the imprisoned women and children of this city, but it would draw out The Ridge's traitor. Because whoever was working with Renold was also a part of Blue Ridge Sector's inner circle. Who else could have orchestrated my escape and shown Ryker exactly where to find Bren? If they knew plots were being hatched against the Supreme Elite, this was the perfect opportunity for them to spy.

It took everything in me not to glance over my shoulder as I reentered the building, because the person who'd stabbed Bren and drugged me could very well be walking into Pack's Tavern on my heels.

"So what triggered her new ability?"

"I can't say whether it's new or not, just that it was unlike anything I've ever felt before," Bren replied to Dominic's question.

Dominic had taken me, Bren, and Dr. Stacey to their camp just outside the city for a more private conversation. The site had been cleared out earlier and was now little more than muddy tire tracks, boot prints, and a couple camouflaged tents.

The negotiations meeting last night had been somewhat successful. A peace and trade treaty had been signed, but with several stipulations. I had wanted to share the news with my mum, but the clansmen had demanded they be given a second chance where the women and children were concerned. Several of them wanted to start families but hadn't dared with the dangerous ceremony ritual hovering over their heads. The risk had been too high.

Now, they sought redemption, thinking all would be forgiven with a few manners and promise of unlocked doors. I had wanted to scoff at first, but paused, remembering how I'd forgiven Bren— and Ryker—for all I'd endured.

Forgiveness was a powerful thing.

Time would tell if the men deserved the women and children who decided to stay. But the queen ordered our silence on the matter. She alone would share the news and give them choices, ensuring their safety, whatever they chose. She, to my utmost shock, was staying. Without a family to return to, the city was her home, for better or worse. Apparently, she'd only ever wanted to be free of a jealous, possessive husband who beat her child.

"It was in reaction to Bells being held at gunpoint while the boss shouted at her to return something she stole," Bren continued. "Then I suddenly couldn't move, overwhelmed by the blast of her emotions. It felt like Lune was pulling all of the surrounding energy to her, immersing herself in it." I lifted my brows at the way he'd described my manifestation.

Dominic scratched his head, further ruffling his sandy brown curls. "Her ability is immersive then," he murmured. "She reshaped reality to create her own."

"And how did you feel afterward?" Dr. Stacey asked, her green eyes assessing me in that doctorly way of hers. "Different than your other manifestations?"

"Yes. With past projections, it felt like I was giving energy. The more I gave, the more nauseous or feverish I'd feel. But this time, I was shaky, like coming down from an intense adrenaline high. And it was . . . it was like *taking* energy."

"Interesting that your abilities are so different from mine despite us both being Visionaries," Dominic mused. "I would say that every human with the mutant gene has something in common though. Emotion. Or adrenaline, to be exact. It's the key to triggering or enhancing our abilities." He frowned in thought. "What did you steal from Rollie Jones that would cause you to project so intensely?"

Silence fell as I gauged the interest levels of my three companions. Only Bren and now Dr. Moore knew that I'd stolen back the memory serum. Not even Ryker knew. But I still didn't know how many people knew about the box of serum in the first place. Dr. Moore had seemed genuinely surprised to learn about the contents of Bren's backpack. He hadn't known, and after feeling the emotions firsthand while inside his mind, I believed him.

I hadn't spoken to Bren about it yet, but he must have been aware of what he carried. Still, I wasn't ready to jump to conclusions. I needed to carefully play this out, consider each person from The Ridge a possible suspect.

Someone had stolen the new batch of serum from Dr. Bradfield's lab. Someone with high security clearance. Multiple people could be involved in this operation. I could be surrounded by traitors in league with Renold right this very moment. The thought of Dominic, Dr. Stacey, Bren, Bells, Jaxon, and Yukiko working with that monster made me want to vomit. They all seemed happy with their home at The Ridge, but appearances could be deceiving.

I didn't believe Bren was the traitor. My heart—and instincts—told me it was impossible. Unfortunately, evidence was currently stacked against him. If I'd been completely wrong about him this entire time, I already knew my heart would shatter into a million pieces.

And I wouldn't bother trying to put it together again.

I wiped sweaty palms on my pants, doing my best to ignore Bren's searching gaze as my heart hammered. What would he do when I revealed what I knew? But before I could utter a word, thunder rumbled in the distance. When it grew louder and closer, I rose from the tree stump I'd been sitting on and scanned the treeline. That sound. It was awfully familiar. Like . . .

"Yeehaw!" Jaxon cried as he burst into the clearing. On a charger. I squinted for a better look at the animal. Something was wrong with the thing. For one, it was incredibly tiny. And the pale fur was smooth. This must be a common horse. I'd always been curious about them, but now that I'd seen one, it was underwhelming compared to its mutated counterpart.

Yukiko arrived at a less reckless pace, barking at her boyfriend to control his mount. His inexperience showed as he yanked on the reins, causing the horse to balk, then paw the air. He yelped, tightening the reins even further. They were either going to tip, or Jaxon was going to fall and get trampled. I lurched forward and grabbed the reins, forcing Jaxon to loosen his death grip. The animal's front hooves thumped to the ground.

Jaxon let out a relieved sigh, murmuring, "My hero," but my attention was on the white mare. I had seen a flash of her large teeth. They were squarer than a charger's, but I assumed they could still tear through flesh. Namely mine. If only I had a—

Someone tapped my shoulder. I stiffened but didn't look away from the animal's dark brown eyes. A hand materialized before me, holding an . . . apple?

"No thanks," I said softly, careful not to spook the horse. "I'll eat it later."

A familiar chuckle stirred the hair near my ear. "It's not for you," Bren said, reaching for a rein to free up one of my hands. He placed the apple on my palm, then cupped my hand—like I'd done with him the first time he'd met a charger. I pressed my lips together as nostalgia washed over me.

He directed my hand toward the horse's mouth, and although instinct had me tensing up, I trusted him. With my *life*. He would never intentionally put me in harm's way, which was why he couldn't be The Ridge's traitor. He couldn't! The thought stung like a hundred needles driving into my flesh.

"Relax," he whispered teasingly. "They can smell fear."

I narrowed my eyes. "If I lose a finger, my daggers will ensure you lose a body part too."

He paused, as if considering. "Which one? Because you might miss certain parts of my—"

"Ugh, stop, you egotistical maniac."

"Why, because you know it's true?"

Yes. "No."

"Throwing up in my mouth now," Jaxon grumbled from his perch on the horse's back.

Crap! We really needed to stop having these conversations around him.

Bren only snickered and nudged my hand into motion again. When the apple was directly beneath the horse's nose, I braced for impact. But the strangest thing happened. The mare lipped the offering gently. No flash of teeth. No predatory gleam in her eye. I felt the tickle of whiskers, then the apple disappeared as she munched contentedly.

A surprised laugh left me. Bren continued to cradle my hand, turning it to rest on the animal's neck. The coat was even softer than it looked. I stroked the fur, marveling at the difference be-tween horse and charger. An ache suddenly formed in my chest. I missed Freedom. And despite her sharp hair and dangerous teeth, I wouldn't have her any other way.

On impulse, I wrapped my arms around the mare's neck and pretended, just for a moment, that prickly fur was jabbing my skin. When I eventually let go, my cheeks were wet. Bren gave my arm a squeeze before leading the horse away. I wondered if he missed his grumpy, pain-in-the-butt charger, Stalin.

A throat cleared.

"I hate to interrupt this touching moment," Jaxon said, hav-ing dismounted while I was sniffing back tears, "but we have things to discuss. We would have been here sooner if you hadn't taken my baby." He mock-glared at Dominic. "Ryker's mom let us borrow the royal horses. Cool, huh? Oh, speaking of the brooding prince, he's finally up and causing problems already. Typical. Told his mommy all about the horrible way we treated him during the two months he was in our holding cells. Big baby."

I snorted at his colorful description. Although, that did sound like Ryker. "Is he against the alliance?"

Jaxon shrugged and, rather stiffly, situated himself on a tree stump. "Not exactly. We explained why he couldn't have been al-lowed access to The Ridge. I mean, it's not like we were going to give him the tools necessary to crack open the mountain and steal away all the people with abilities. He seemed willing to listen with Bells there." He rolled his eyes. "Does he always stare like that? 'Cause he looked about ready to eat her, and it gave me the heebie jeebies."

Bren paused on his way over, looking more than a little peeved.

"Relax," Yukiko said, taking a seat next to Jaxon and waving for us to join them. There were six of us now, all part of the inner circle. Five of which could be traitors. My stomach gave a sickening lurch. "Nothing's going to happen between those two with the amount of guards stationed right outside the door."

I squirmed, remembering Ryker's kiss and touch. Maybe we should be a *tiny* bit worried for Bells. "There's a window in the back—"

"Covered," Yukiko assured. "They aren't going anywhere. Besides, we might need him."

"For the Tatum City mission?" I guessed.

"Yes. We need to know what he knows. Find out if Renold really does distrust Bren enough to imprison or kill him on sight. If Bren goes in knowing the full story, maybe he has a chance of—"

"He doesn't need to go in," I interrupted. "Only Ryker and I do."

If silence was weighted, I'd be pinned to the ground right now, struggling for air.

I forced my eyes to connect with each and every one of them, saving Bren for last. Their reactions were vital. Dominic and Dr. Stacey seemed surprised. Yukiko and Jaxon looked more than a little alarmed, the latter gaping with his mouth open. And then there was Bren. Oh Bren. Storm clouds swirled in those golden eyes.

"Explain," he said through gritted teeth.

And so I did. I told them about my mission for Renold, how he'd questioned Bren's loyalty even then. I told them about Ryker's, how he was my Keeper and meant to safely return me—with or without Bren. I told them everything the boss had revealed, that Renold was indeed planning something big but hadn't even told him.

"So you see," I said, unable to hold Bren's stare any longer, "Renold doesn't trust anyone, least of all Bren, and it's too dangerous for him to return. But he definitely wants me and Ryker back. We could easily explain away our long absence by saying we were kidnapped, but escaped. Then Ryker completed his mission by tracking down Bren and delivering him to the Recruiter Clan. And if no one radios Renold about his brother's death, he can be assured of Ryker's continued loyalty."

"Wait." Dominic leaned forward. "His brother? As in, Ryker is the Supreme Elite's—?"

"Nephew."

He blew out a stunned breath. "We didn't know that. So who's to say Ryker *isn't* still loyal to his uncle?"

"Doesn't matter."

His forehead wrinkled in confusion.

"He won't risk being cut off from his mother again. Or Bells," I added, still avoiding Bren's gaze. "With the proper leverage, he'll help us complete this mission."

Silence settled over the camp again, each person mulling over the information I'd dumped into their laps. The question was, did they trust *me* to complete the mission?

Bren stood and started to pace, yanking agitated fingers through his hair. "I can't let you go in alone."

"I won't be alone."

"Let me rephrase. I can't let you go in without *me*. I still don't trust Ryker."

I jumped up as the moment of truth finally arrived. I hated, *hated* what I had to do next, but I couldn't waste this opportunity. My knees shook as I rebutted with, "Oh, but I can trust *you*?"

He jerked toward me, his expression a mess of shock,

confusion, and hurt. I bit my lip, determined not to cry. "What's that supposed to mean?" he asked softly.

"It means that you're hiding something. From all of us." I turned and produced a backpack from behind my tree stump. It was mine, but I'd added one additional item to it when Bren had been occupied earlier today. I undid the zipper and revealed the box of serum, watching his face closely. Guilty or not, he was a good actor, a good *spy*. I couldn't let my guard down. "You never explained where you got this. You never told me if you stole it from Dr. Bradfield's lab so you could give it to Renold."

He blinked several times, shaking his head. "I didn't steal it. There was one detail about my mission that *no* one knew about: the contents of the package Renold asked me to pick up. His mission for me was simple: wait at a predetermined site for a package to be delivered, then return. I stayed there for two days. When nothing happened, I decided to rig a tripwire so I'd be notified when someone arrived. The alarm went off the evening before I left.

"But that's why I told you my mission's been compromised," he continued, almost pleading with me to believe him. "No one at The Ridge knew the exact dropoff location, so when someone inside gave Ryker the coordinates, I knew they must be working for Renold."

When he finished, there were tears in his eyes. They were in mine too, because I wasn't finished.

"Since no one else knew, you have no alibi." My laugh was flat. Empty. "I begged you to be real, Brendan Bearon. But you still have secrets, and I . . . I don't know what's truth or lie."

Bren's expression fell. I wondered if he sensed my pain. The pain I felt for doing this to him.

I looked down at the box. "Maybe we'll never know who stole

this serum, but I know one thing for certain: I don't want it in Renold's hands." I opened the lid and pulled out a vial, sweeping a glance at the faces around me. "So I'm going to destroy them."

The serum slipped through my fingers and struck the ground. When it didn't break, I stomped on the glass with the heel of my boot. A pop and tinkling sound filled the air. Everyone was on their feet now. Dr. Stacey gasped. Dominic looked shell-shocked, staring at the broken vial with such intensity that I worried he was having a stroke.

He suddenly swayed, inhaling a ragged breath. "I-I had a prediction. A solid impression as to how Lune will defeat Renold. But she has to confront him personally. She has to endure more hardship before he'll reveal his secret—"

His words ended in a strangled gasp. He jerked away from Dr. Stacey who'd come to stand beside him. And then I saw it. A quick flash of silver. It was there and gone again so fast, I could have been mistaken. But when Dominic continued to gasp and cough, clutching at his throat as if unable to draw air, I knew.

I knew who The Ridge's traitor was.

I CAN FEEL IT

Dr. Stacey met my stare.

Watched me pass the box of serum to Bren and slowly unsheath my daggers.

She bolted.

I charged after her.

As she dashed into the treeline with sure swiftness, I realized how drastically I'd underestimated her. The inconspicuous doctor, quietly earning her patient's trust, was the ultimate spy. More than a spy, actually. She had multiple skill sets.

She was wicked fast. Fast enough to stab someone at a party without anyone noticing. Fast enough to jump me from behind, inject me with paralyzing serum, and be ready to play the doting doctor half an hour later.

And she was smart. Smart enough to use her high security clearance to open Ryker's cell door and lead him to my location in Medical.

Crap. *Crap!*

It all fit. She was the only person who knew where to find me that morning. And she was in close communication with Dr. Bradfield. Close enough to steal serum from his lab without anyone noticing—or maybe even leave The Ridge for a couple hours without raising suspicion.

She had said Bren didn't want my memories restored until after he'd left, because it would be *easier*. Had that been a lie?

Now wasn't the time to figure everything out, though. She was twice my age, but she might as well have springs in her shoes. I resheathed my daggers to free up my hands. We needed her alive for questioning, and my best bet was to tackle her from behind.

Suddenly, she disappeared. I didn't even have time for confusion as my boot caught nothing but air. And then I was falling, crashing, tumbling down a steep hill. I tried to loosen my limbs, but my hands instinctively shot out to break my fall. Pain stabbed up my right arm as my wrist bent under the impact.

I didn't scream. I was too busy trying not to get impaled on a stick or tree branch. When I finally reached the bottom, I hit the ground with a jarring thud. Air whooshed from me. I couldn't breathe, but I struggled to pick myself up anyway, inwardly chanting my old mantra.

Push past the pain. You are not weak!

Every bone in my body protested the movement, but the thought of Dr. Stacey reaching Tatum City and telling Renold all that she knew numbed the pain. I scanned the forest floor, thick with greenery that could easily hide a thin, scrappy woman. Hide. Which was exactly what she would do. I forced myself to still.

To *listen*.

The slightest of sounds came from the left. I crouched low, advancing on the noise with caution. It could be anything. A squirrel. A wererabbit. A saber cat. But it was her, facedown and motionless. Dead? No. Her back slowly rose and fell. Unconscious, then. I debated what to do. Carrying her to camp wasn't an option. My wrist was probably sprained, and there was no way I could drag her up this hill.

Maybe I should bind her hands and wait until she woke up, *then* drag her to camp. Her shoelaces could be used to secure her wrists. I bent down and untied one. I was halfway through the loops when her boot kicked up, smacking my cheekbone. As I landed hard on my butt, something flashed. Silver and thin, like a needle. I grabbed ahold of it.

With my injured hand.

Hot agony streaked up my arm, and I couldn't hold back a scream this time. My good hand joined the struggle for the needle as Dr. Stacey put everything she had behind the attack. The needle inched toward my face. She was strong, but lacked my conditioning. I was on my back with an injured wrist, though.

My only choice was to endure a moment of intense pain. A single moment and it could all be over. At the thought, adrenaline snapped through me. I welcomed it eagerly, knowing the rush would mask some of the pain. But if I couldn't endure it . . .

Game over.

There was no time for doubt. I rolled, throwing her aim off balance. She renewed her efforts just as my good hand fell away. The pain didn't register at first, shock softening the blow. But when nothing but a sprained wrist separated me from possible death, I felt it.

The pain paralyzed me.

Push past the . . .

Just one more second . . .

My fingers wrapped around my salvation. A metallic whine rang in my ears as I whipped my dagger free and brought the handle down on Dr. Stacey's head. *Crack!* She immediately sagged, crumpling to the ground unconscious.

I stared at her for several seconds to make sure she wasn't

faking, then released a delirious laugh. "Take that, you needle-wielding, backstabbing traitor."

Bren found us two minutes later, his wild-eyed gaze scanning every inch of me. I was flat on the ground, my ankles crossed and fingers laced over my stomach. A firmly trussed-up Dr. Stacey was still knocked out cold nearby.

"Ousted your traitor," I called up to him casually, watching his face filter through a gambit of emotions. "I spared her for questioning. Thought you'd like that. How's Dominic?"

"Don't know," he muttered distractedly, folding his long legs as he sat down next to me. He reached out and, when I didn't flinch, gently trailed his fingers over my bruised cheek. A ghost of pain bloomed.

"You're hurting," Bren said, his voice reed thin as if my pain were his. "Where else are you injured?"

"I'm fine," I began, but he cut me off.

"Don't do this, Lune. Don't prove to me how tough you are, how nothing can break you. It's okay to tell me you're hurting. Physically. Emotionally. I can feel it. Right"—he pounded a fist over his heart—"here."

I brought my hand up to cup the side of his face. After a moment, he turned into the touch and pressed trembling lips to my palm. I ached to erase the worry lines on his brow. To erase the *hurt* between us.

"I can feel your hurt too," I whispered. "I'm sorry for what I said earlier. I had to find out who was working for Renold."

He sighed against my skin. "I'm sorry too. I can't expect you to trust me if I keep you in the dark. I'll ask Dr. Moore for permission to tell you everything. I don't want there to be any more secrets between us. Deal?"

"Deal." A weight I'd carried for far too long lifted. "Now please let me hold you."

Without hesitation, he lowered himself beside me. My arms shot out and wrapped around his neck, hugging him fiercely despite my injuries. "Only if I can hold you back, little bird," he murmured, drawing me even closer.

That night, we mourned the loss of a friend and mentor. By sunrise, my eyes were nearly as swollen as my wrist. Bren took Dominic's shocking death the hardest. I cried for him as well. Another adult in his life snatched from him too soon. We quietly agreed to bury Dominic beneath a towering pine, knowing we couldn't transport his body to The Ridge anytime soon.

We had to press on with the mission—he would have wanted us to. But it wasn't easy, not when his killer was yards away, still breathing.

And I knew it was unrealistic, but when Dominic had taught me to believe in the impossible, I had foolishly hoped that maybe, just maybe, we would all make it through this alive.

I KNOW WHAT YOU NEED

"What was in the syringe? Answer me. *Answer me!*"

The shout thundered through the clearing. I flinched, despite myself. The heat, the *rage* rolling off Bren, put me on edge. I didn't fear him. I only feared how his actions would haunt him later. But I didn't interfere with the interrogation. Dr. Stacey had valuable information and I hoped Bren twisted every last drop of it from her.

Yukiko cleared her throat before he could shout some more. "Take a breather, Bren. Your emotions are too high."

He turned and growled at her. She growled right back. I couldn't stop myself from smirking. Stars, that girl had balls. I'd give her a fistbump if Bren wasn't watching.

She shoved their communication device at him. "Radio Dr. Moore. He needs to be briefed on the situation, and we need to know whether our orders are still the same." She glanced at me. "After Dominic's impression, I'm thinking not."

Oh, right. Dominic had clearly said I needed to be *in* Tatum City to stop Renold.

The reminder only made Bren more angry. I thought he'd explode—maybe tear apart the camp since he couldn't tear into our prisoner—but he simply marched for the treeline and disappeared from view. I lingered for a moment, then decided to go after him.

Jaxon grasped my elbow before I could. "Just let him have a

few minutes to blow off steam and punch things without an audience," he said quietly so Dr. Stacey couldn't overhear. "Dom meant a lot to him. And then there's that vision about you. The last thing he wants is for you to be in Tatum City again."

"I know," I whispered, my throat tightening with grief. "I don't want to go, but I *have* to. And not just because of Dominic's vision. My sister's in there."

He nodded his understanding, but there was an undeniable sadness to him as he wandered a short distance away. I had the urge to comfort him too, but Yukiko chose that moment to start up the interrogation again.

"Why did you kill Dominic?" Her tone was even, the complete opposite of what Bren's had been. And instead of towering over Dr. Stacey's chained, disheveled form, she crouched to meet her at eye level. "How could you kill someone so kindhearted? Someone who only wanted to help others?"

Dr. Stacey's usually pulled-back, tidy hairdo was now a brown, matted halo around her bruised head. Despite her disheveled appearance, I'd never seen her look more confident. She swallowed with difficulty, her throat no doubt bone dry. We hadn't given her any food or water, a fact that didn't make me feel guilty. "I didn't want to, but he gave me no other choice," she rasped. "The high dose of opioid I injected him with was quick and efficient. He didn't suffer for long."

Her explanation was so *clinical*. No sign of remorse. Did she even care about her patients, or was that all an act too? The thought made me sick.

"What about Lune?" Yukiko went on, still managing to conceal her emotions. "Is that why you tried to kill her at The Ridge? Was she a threat to your plans?"

Dr. Stacey's expression hardened. "I didn't try to kill her—only scare her into leaving Blue Ridge Sector. After Dominic confirmed Lune as the girl from his prediction, it was too dangerous to let her learn how to use her abilities. But she stayed. Now she's even more of a threat to the Supreme Elite's master plan. I should have disobeyed his orders and eliminated her when I had the chance."

Ignoring the last bit, I stepped forward, capturing her attention. "When's the last time you contacted him? Does he know about his brother's death?"

Her stare was cold and unblinking. Unnerving. I switched tactics, playing on her ego. "What *is* Renold's plan anyway? Form a brainless army? And then what? Make a few Trials contenders conquer more territory for him so he can expand his city? Sounds a bit delusional to me."

She laughed coldly. "I wish I could tell you, if only to see the look on your face. Unfortunately, I can't say a thing."

"Can't or won't?"

"Can't," she purred with a smirk.

Yukiko swore, then stood. "She must have programmed and injected herself with a restraining chip." She paced while Dr. Stacey looked on in amusement. As if she'd won.

"I'll cut it out of her," I said. All eyes jerked my way. I shrugged, feigning indifference even as my stomach rolled. "What? I'm good with a knife. Just tell me where to cut."

I made to unsheath one of my daggers, watching as Dr. Stacey's eyes rounded. Then, as if in afterthought, slipped a hidden knife free of my pants pocket. Jaxon started protesting, but his girlfriend held up a hand.

"It's a good idea," she said, observing me closely. "Can you manage with your left hand?" A strangled sound left Jaxon.

I fiddled with the wrap around my right wrist. "The incision might not be as clean, but I'll make do."

The diamond stud in Yukiko's nose winked as her lips quirked. Without a word, she stepped aside, allowing me access to the prisoner. As I approached, I flipped the knife a few times, noting the way Dr. Stacey's throat bobbed.

I hunkered down in front of her, cocking my head. And studied her *clinically*. I pointed the blade's tip just beneath her chin. "Is the chip lodged near the vocal cords? I should be able to reach it without nicking an artery. Probably."

"Yeah," Yukiko said. "Just don't slice too deep or you'll damage the cords. We need her to talk afterward."

Dr. Stacey was noticeably shaking now. I felt a tremor in my own limbs, but I wouldn't let that stop me. We desperately needed the information she possessed. I steadied my hand before resting the blade against her pale skin. She flinched away, the action causing a thin line of red to bubble up.

"I suggest holding still," I murmured while positioning the knife over her vocal cords. "You're a doctor. You know how delicate the throat area is." Without further warning, I cut into her flesh. Despite my words, she jerked against her restraints. I grimaced, holding in a hiss as blood spurted, some landing on my face. "Yukiko, hold her down!"

A hand clamped over Dr. Stacey's shoulder. The other captured the back of her neck and squeezed. "This is for Dominic, you slimy worm," Yukiko growled. "Finish it, Lune."

The blade dug in again and Dr. Stacey screamed. A cold sweat doused my skin as she tried to thrash and buck, further injuring herself. Doubt set in. Panic. What if I killed her by accident? Too much blood already ran down her neck and into the black V of her shirt. I bit my lip until the taste of iron coated my tongue.

Maybe I couldn't do this after all.

When a voice panted, "I can't do this," I paused, thinking I'd spoken aloud. But then came the words, "I'm sorry, darling, I just can't. I'm not . . . I'm not strong enough after all. I'm not worthy. I—" Dr. Stacey let out a wail, gnashing her teeth together. She seized up. Convulsions shook her. I slid the knife free.

"No!" Yukiko shouted, grabbing the woman's face. Shock ripped through me when I saw white foam at Dr. Stacey's mouth. Was she having a seizure? But I hadn't nicked anything vital. She should be fine. This shouldn't be happening. Yukiko shouted some more and Jaxon was suddenly there, his face sallow as he looked on helplessly.

"Suicide pill," he whispered. "There's nothing that can be done."

It was all over in seconds. Dr. Stacey's green eyes stared sightlessly at the blue sky above.

Nausea barrelled through me. As saliva rushed into my mouth, I stumbled to my feet and lurched toward the woods. At the first bush, I heaved up my breakfast, simultaneously coughing and sobbing. After last night, I didn't think there were any tears left in me. But here they were, pouring down my face as I plunged into the trees, needing to escape those eyes and what I'd just done.

Too much death. I didn't care if she deserved it. I just wanted the deaths to stop.

For several minutes, I wove an aimless path through the woods. Or so I thought. I'd unconsciously followed my gut to Bren, stopping a few yards away only to stare at the long line of his spine. He'd taken his shirt off and sat at the grassy bank of a stream-fed pond.

Such a beautiful display of life on a day so full of death.

Water cascaded over a rock ledge on the far side, masking the sound of my approach—to an ordinary human's ears. Bren's shoulders tensed when he heard me, but he didn't turn. My eyes traced the slightly raised scar in the middle of his back. Where Skervvy had shot him.

Another dead person.

I made a sound. Half whimper, half sob. Bren immediately whirled, jumping to his feet. When he saw me, the device in his hand hit the ground with a faint thud. He swallowed the space between us in three large strides. His hands lifted but froze, as if uncertain where to touch first.

"So much blood." Panic tightened his voice. "What happened?"

Steel bands of guilt wrapped around my throat. I shook my head.

Frustration lined his eyes as he yanked trembling hands through his hair. I caught sight of his knuckles. Bruised. Bloody. "I can't do this, little bird. I just can't. Not with you. I'm not strong enough."

I sucked in a gasp, feeling lightheaded at his choice of words. So similar to Dr. Stacey's. Another dead person. "Please," I whispered. "Please, don't say that."

He cast me a helpless look, letting his arms fall. "I can't control it, Lune. My instincts scream at me to protect you. It's so strong that I can barely think straight. I've been distracted and making mistakes, causing more harm than good. All I want to do is wrap my body around yours and shield you from the world."

His shoulders drooped. "When you're hurt, I go mad with fear. I'm not strong enough to fight my reactions, and I know they push you away. They only make you want to prove how strong you are on your own."

He dropped his gaze in defeat. "Never in my life have I been so scared of losing someone. Dominic's loss is a stab wound that'll heal. If I lose my sister, I'll keep on living but the wound won't ever fully heal. But you? Losing you would rip out my heart. I couldn't survive that. And now you're a part of the mission. You're returning to the very place I can't protect you, and I . . . I don't know what to do, Lune. Please tell me what to do."

Don't go on the mission, I so desperately wanted to say, but that would make things ten times worse. We were both set on going, and nothing we said to each other would change that.

His pleading words filled me with the worst kind of guilt, though. Saving others was his purpose, his path to redemption, and I was walking right into the lion's den. But it was more than that. The more he loved someone, the more he feared for their safety. I hated that I was forcing him to carry this burden, but I also worried that fear of loss controlled him.

If he didn't face that fear, it could drive him insane.

"Bren?"

I almost told him. Almost shared my own fears—the fear of losing control and becoming a monster, the fear of others paying the price for my freedom. But he would worry. He would beg me not to return. And I had to. I had to go back for those very reasons. I wouldn't cower in the face of fear any longer.

So I sought comfort in a way that would ease our worries without words. In a way that could be considered cowardly, but I needed this. I needed *him*. And he needed me. "Please hold me, Bren. Touch me, kiss me. Just hold—"

He took the offering, cupping my face before placing a gentle kiss on my mouth. His touch was achingly sweet, but I wanted us both to forget, just for a moment, that fear and death and missions that could go terribly wrong existed.

I pulled away. His look was both surprise and dejection, but he quickly caught onto my intentions as I fumbled to unbuckle my dagger holster. He reached to help me, but hesitated.

I captured his hand, slowly guiding it to the leather strap across my chest. His eyes flared bright as he deftly undid the buckles, his gaze heating with each passing second. The holster gave way and I let it thump to the ground. I silently communicated what else I wanted out of.

"Jaxon or Yukiko might come looking," he said hoarsely, even as his fingers drifted south toward my shirt's hem. I wordlessly lifted my arms in challenge, and I could have sworn he purred. He took his time, which annoyed me at first. I wanted everything off. Off! But he made the wait worthwhile, trailing his fingers up my stomach as he went, setting off a flurry of wings inside of me.

By the time my bra and shirt hit the ground, I was a trembling mess. I quickly tugged at my pants, but he wasn't finished with the torture. He stilled my frenzied movements by curling his fingers into the waistband. I let out an embarrassing moan as his fingers dipped further in before releasing the button. When he slid my pants down, he lowered himself as well, dropping to his knees before me.

"I know what you need," he said softly, undoing my shoelaces, then slipping my boots and pants off. "You need loving. And maybe tomorrow, you'll need saving and protecting, but right now"—he leaned forward—"you just"—he pressed a kiss to my navel—"need"—his tongue circled the area, leaving a trail of delicious warmth—"loving."

Yes, I internally groaned, digging my fingers into his hair. *I want to burn.* A rumble from low in his throat vibrated through me as he kissed my stomach harder, his stubble scratching the sensitive skin.

My head lolled, eyes drifting shut as I reveled in the feel of his lips. They kissed a straight path upward, until they got distracted. Noises came out of me—weird, awkward ones—but I couldn't seem to care. His hands joined in, rubbing up my thighs and hips, smoothing over my rib cage. The more he touched, the more I wanted. And I wanted to touch *him* too.

I urged him to stand, but when my hands found his skin, there was no restraint. I grasped his face and kissed his mouth hard, pulling away only to come back for more. My teeth grazed his bottom lip and he groaned. Wanting to hear the sound again, I sucked his lip into my mouth and bit down. He came alive with a roar, pressing my body so tightly to his, I lost the ability to think.

Sharing this closeness with him was unlike anything I'd ever known—a dizzying mix of weakness, euphoria, and power. I had all the control, yet had none. And I was beginning to crave the feeling. Bren hurriedly removed his pants, the last item of clothing between us falling away.

When he swooped me into his arms, I yelped. His steps were sure, swift, as he carried me to the pond's edge.

"Bren, what are you—?"

I squeaked as he plunged into the pond without pause. The cold water struck my backside and I squirmed to be let down. But when I scrambled for shore, he caught my waist and dragged me to deeper depths. Despite the shivers racking my body, I couldn't help but laugh a little.

Playful Bren was exactly what I needed.

My laughter ended in a gasp as he lifted my left thigh and slowly guided our bodies together. At the sensation of becoming one, my lips parted, eyes sliding shut. I let him take control, let him love me the way he wanted to. I was malleable, a creation of his making. My raging heart beat for him. His world was mine, and nothing else existed.

When he threw my reality into orbit, I clung to him, knowing he was solid and real. My rock. And when I fell, he was there to catch me, to pull me close again.

Our breathing was ragged, our bodies still twined together when he said, "I can't promise to never let fear control me. Just like I can't promise to always be reasonable in my need to protect you. But I will *always* think of your wants, needs, and desires. I will always fight to better myself for you. And at the end of each day, we'll face our fears head on. Together. We'll face them together."

Just like he was facing his fear of water right now. For me. I wrapped my arms around his neck and pressed my cheek to his shoulder. He kissed my hair, gathering me close before murmuring, "Thank you. For not giving up on me. For thinking that I'm worth it."

I breathed in his unique scent of pine, leather, and sunshine. The scents of nature, warmth, and hard labor. The scents that made me feel at home. They *were* home. My home.

"I will never give up on you, Brendan Bearon," I promised.

No matter what.

GOODBYES

I rubbed my throat again.

Restraining chips were no joke. Now that I knew everything about the Tatum City mission, it was necessary for me to be chipped. All I had to do was voice details of Blue Ridge Sector's plans and my windpipe sealed shut, like the inner code could read my thought patterns. Creepy. Jaxon said the device was modeled after Darth Vader's abilities, whatever that meant.

And no wonder Dr. Stacey had panicked when I'd tried to remove hers. It was smaller than a grain of rice, and she probably would have bled out before I could find the thing. Dr. Moore was especially proud of this particular invention, saying it was some of his best work.

But his usual excitement had been absent this morning as he'd radioed his final orders. News of Dominic's and Dr. Stacey's deaths had hit him hard. His words had been firm and filled with warning as the seriousness of this mission took root.

There were still so many unknowns, but we were going in. All *three* of us. Bren, Ryker, and I.

And now with the chip in, the danger ahead felt all too real.

Jaxon glanced back at me from the driver's seat of his "baby." He didn't miss the way I massaged my vocal chords. An impish grin spread over his face. "I dare you to stick your head out the window."

The vehicle struck a pothole. Next to him, Yukiko whacked his arm. "Get serious and watch the road."

He winked at me before turning around. "That's your job, baby cakes!"

Beside me, Bren nudged my shoulder. He too wore a mischievous smile, as if racing to our doom was somehow exhilarating. I held back an eye roll. "Go ahead," he said over the engine's roar. "I'll spot you."

"Huh?"

"I'll hold your legs down. Keep you from being sucked out."

My eyes widened a bit, a thrill going through me. We were all crazy. "We're not going *that* fast."

"We are now," Jaxon crowed, punching the accelerator. The force pressed me into my seat. "It's now or never, Lu Bear! Final stretch before the checkpoint."

All eyes were on me now. Expectant. Waiting. Like it was an initiation or something. My competitive nature set in, the desire to prove myself worthy. I wouldn't disappoint them.

I peeked behind me at Ryker who, after being stabbed only a week ago, insisted he was well enough for the mission. And for having been beaten to a pulp, he didn't look too bad either. His brows slowly ticked upward as if to say, "Well?"

I rolled my eyes this time, glancing at the vehicle's final occupant. The bruise on her cheek had lightened to an ugly yellow-green, the same color as mine, but that didn't stop her from beaming at me. "Do it, Lune," Bells encouraged, bouncing in her seat. Or maybe that was another pothole. "Then tell me how it feels since I'm too chicken to do it."

She bit her lip and cast a sidelong look at Ryker, as if worried he'd think her pathetic. But I could have sworn there was a faint smile on his mouth. I still wasn't used to it—his smiles or seeing them together. There was a change in him. He was still rude and grumpy most of the time, but around Bells, there was a stillness. A contented aura I'd never felt before.

Like her presence soothed the beast inside of him.

I faced forward and announced my readiness. My old habit—the leg-jiggling one—chose that moment to return. Bren barked a laugh. I froze, desperately trying to catch and bottle that sound. I doubted I'd hear it again anytime soon, not with what awaited us.

He tapped my knee, leaning close to whisper in my ear, "Go fly, little bird. I'll catch you if you fall."

My heart fluttered with excitement. At the whine of a window sliding open, I tucked my feet beneath me. A blast of air stirred my hair, blurring my vision. I stood on the seat anyway, shooting up, up, up until my head went through the roof.

I planted both hands on the vehicle's warm black hide, ignoring the deadly machine gun inches from my fingers. When it hit me how fast we were going, I sucked in a gasp. The whistling air snatched the sound away, just like it tore at my clothes and hair. I could barely breathe past the intense rush.

So it was true after all.

Cars really were faster than chargers.

Shock rendered me mute. Then I was laughing, whooping to the sky.

Below came answering whoops.

"Warrior Princess!" Jaxon shouted.

I threw my arms wide and let my head fall back as I roared, "I'm a beast-taming, kick-butt warrior princess!"

Saying goodbye sucked.

Now that I thought about it, I'd never had to say goodbye to anyone before. I had been torn from the people I loved time and again, but I'd never had the chance to hug them farewell, share a few tears, or utter parting words. No wonder Bren chose to quietly slip off for his missions. I almost wished for that option right now.

But I wouldn't, no matter how painful it was. Because *not* saying goodbye hurt just as much. I still hadn't seen my mum. With so many changes and the precariousness of the new alliance, Evie couldn't chance word spreading of the Tatum City coup. For this to work, Renold needed to believe all was well with the Recruiter Clan—and his brother. There had already been mutterings amongst the clansmen, some questioning their new leadership—especially those recently returned from outside jobs. With Ryker gone, it was sure to get worse.

The task ahead for the queen wouldn't be easy. Not only with the clansmen, but freeing the women and children of their cages. Most didn't have homes to return to—or wouldn't remember where to find them.

If I made it back—*when* I made it back—I hoped to find my mum settled at a community far from here. Or maybe Blue Ridge Sector would take her and my siblings in. Then there was Iris. Sweet Iris. More pain clenched my heart. When all of this was over, I *would* reunite my family. I could almost picture us all together. Me, Mum, Iris, and a little boy and girl I had yet to meet. We were hugging and laughing.

Happy and at peace.

Tears streaked across the image.

A hand rested on my shoulder. I blinked the tears away before facing Bells. Her eyes were watery too, having come from saying farewell to her brother. I didn't see him nearby. He must be collecting himself, something I sorely needed to do as well. But I accepted her embrace, relieved when the urge to cry didn't overwhelm me.

"We're sisters now," she said with a trembling voice. "I always wanted a sister. Bren's great and all, but he can be overprotective. And we have *nothing* in common. You'd think since he reads poetry, he'd be into my romance novels." Her laugh ended in a sniff. "I'm trying to be brave about this, Lune, I really am."

I held her tightly. "You *are* brave. Emotions don't make you weak. They make you human. Your brother taught me that."

A throat cleared. I already knew who it was as I gave Bells one last squeeze and stepped back. "Oh, wait," I said, reaching into my backpack. My fingers closed around a slim rectangular object. I hesitated for a moment, loathe to let it go, but I'd be foolish to smuggle such an item into the city with so much at stake. "Keep this safe for me until I return?"

The unspoken promise settled between us. She nodded, eyes welling again as she accepted Bren's book of poetry and hugged it to her. Ryker looked more or less unaffected by all the tears, but I'd seen the way he'd embraced his mother after she asked him not to go. I hadn't heard his reply, but she hadn't stopped him from leaving.

And now, three years later, he was finally getting to say goodbye to Bells.

As they walked a short distance away for privacy, I lingered like a creep, curious what they'd do.

"My bet is on Captain Grumpy Pants," Jaxon said, slinging an arm over my shoulder.

Yukiko snorted, moseying up to my other side. "You didn't hear her going on about him for three years. My bet is on Bells."

"Settle the tie for us, Lu Bear. Who's gonna make the first move?"

I wrinkled my nose. "Uh . . ." I openly studied the pair, feeling less like a creep now that I had creeper company. Ryker's dark head was bent and Bells was staring up at him with rapt attention. Were they even talking? Their lips didn't appear to be moving, but their eyes sure said a lot.

And then, out of nowhere, Bells shot up onto her tiptoes and planted a swift kiss to Ryker's mouth. When she pulled back, he didn't react.

"Ahh, poor Bells," Yukiko murmured.

Even from here, I could see the flustered look on Bells' face. She whirled, seeking escape. Two steps later, he grabbed her arm and swung her around.

"It's like watching a soap opera," Jaxon breathed.

As Bells' lips parted in surprise, Ryker cupped her face and returned the kiss. She practically melted against him, grasping his shirtfront to keep from falling. He looped an arm around her and crushed her to him. Their movements became more urgent. Ryker dug his fingers into Bells' hair as he deepened the kiss. When his tongue touched hers, she all but tore his shirt from gripping so hard.

Holy hotness. A blush scorched my cheeks.

"I'm disgusted but can't look away," Jaxon whispered. "His tongue has skills. I think he *is* eating her."

Yukiko snort-laughed. "Take notes."

"What, you're not satisfied with our makeout sessions, sweet pea?"

"I'm just saying. It never hurts to try something new."

He chuckled darkly. "Noted."

Oh gross. I so needed out of here.

I ducked beneath Jaxon's arm. Shaking my head when he barely noticed, I went in search of Bren. If that was their attempt at lightening the mood, it worked. But the fear that I might never see them again still lingered. This time tomorrow, Ryker, Bren, and I could be dead. Iris, Asher, and thousands of others could be trapped inside Tatum City.

Forever.

The three of us were their only chance at freedom. Once inside, the mission involved letting our allies in to take over the city. My telepathic ability would come in handy for that, and thankfully, the restraining chip didn't hinder me from communicating mind-to-mind. No matter how long the mission took, I was to remain in contact with the outside.

If Renold saw through our ploy, though, it was game over. He was paranoid and only trusted what he could control. Which was why our fake stories were so important and why I couldn't stop worrying over Bren's. There were too many holes in his. If he said the wrong thing, the words would trigger his restraining chip and raise suspicion. Ryker's story was the closest to the truth, but even he was injected with a chip—after much protesting, of course.

We couldn't pull this off without outside help, but Dr. Moore wouldn't risk the safety of Blue Ridge Sector. Concern over Renold's supposed army and his retaliation had The Ridge leader on high alert. The less we were able to say, the better. But if Dr. Stacey had contacted Renold in the days preceding her death to warn him of the new alliance, we were so screwed.

"Hey." Bren's voice pulled me from my troubled thoughts.

"You all right?"

The old habit of masking my feelings surfaced. But I'd just told Bells not to be ashamed of hers. It was time I started taking my own advice. "No," I said honestly, looking up at him. "I'm scared."

His sympathetic expression plucked at my tender emotions. Before I could blubber like a baby, he wrapped me up in his arms so completely, I'd never felt more safe. "I'm scared too. More than you know," he whispered against my hair. "But I know it won't do any good asking you to stay here. If I'm willing to risk my life to save others, then I can't ask you to do any less. So I'm finally going to suck it up and deal."

His words wrung a grin from me, despite everything.

"Trust me when I say I won't be taking any unnecessary risks when we're in there," I said, my voice muffled against his shirt. "I have too much to live for."

He stroked my hair, kissing me softly before saying, "Me too, little bird. Me too."

The sun was directly overhead by the time we departed with nothing but the backpacks and weapons we'd received from Tatum City—and what was left of the serum.

Winter was long gone, spring in full bloom. Pink and white flowers covered many of the trees, emitting a sweet fragrance. I wanted to stop and enjoy their smell, to tilt my head back and soak in the sun's rays.

I was about to do just that when Ryker grumbled, "Keep up."

Déjà vu hit me. I remembered him uttering those very same words when we'd left Tatum City three months ago. My eyes narrowed on his back and I stuck out my tongue, for old time's sake. Bren snickered beside me.

"You have no idea what I had to put up with while we were

tracking you," I muttered.

He cocked his head and frowned in thought. "You know, I don't think I wanna know."

Yeah. Probably not. Especially the naked cabin incident. I might not be able to stop him from rearranging Ryker's face for that one.

Bren twirled something in front of my nose and I jerked back. He chuckled, taking my hand to place a delicate white flower with pink edges on my palm. "An apple blossom," he murmured. "Their scent reminds me of you. When I first met you in Tatum City, it's what you smelled like."

I brought the bloom to my nose and inhaled deeply, a smile playing on my lips. He tucked a strand of hair behind my left ear and I directed the smile his way. But the adoring look on his face quickly turned to dismay. He swore softly. Ryker heard, immediately backtracking.

"What's wrong?" he said, scanning the woods on either side of the road.

"Lune's tattoo," Bren replied. "We have to cover it up somehow."

Ryker shook his head. "Let the Supreme Elite see it. We'll add to the story and say Lune was forced to swear fealty to the Recruiter Clan before the boss would let us leave. Renold would expect such a power play from his brother. I'll assure him that Lune's loyalty remains with Tatum City. As long as he doesn't catch wind of Rollie's death, he should believe that I'm still loyal as well."

"And are you?"

Ryker's eyes narrowed. "Am I what?"

"Still loyal to Renold? He has that enhancement serum you so desperately wanted, after all." Bren fisted his hands in challenge.

Ah crap. *Now?* When we were only a mile from Tatum City's gates?

"I don't need it anymore," Ryker threw back, widening his stance. "Or did you forget that the head alpha is dead?"

"Yeah, but how long do you expect the men to follow a *female?* No offense to your mom, but how will she keep order when the men get unruly? They only know one form of punishment and I doubt she's up to the task."

Ryker suddenly lunged at Bren. I shouted a warning, but Bren was already prepared. They exchanged a few blows, each hit harder than the last.

This wasn't happening. This wasn't happening!

"Stop it, you two. Stop!" I screamed, pulling at their arms. Bren immediately stopped and checked me for injuries, probably remembering the last time I'd tried to break up their fight.

Ryker swooped in, aiming for Bren's neck. My eyes widened in horror at the flash of silver.

"No!" I grabbed for the needle but was too late. Ryker jerked back, leaving a stunned Bren behind with the syringe's contents already in his system. "Bren, are you—? Bren!"

He dropped like a stone. I flung myself beside him, frantically searching for a pulse. My heart drummed wildly, but I found what I was looking for and quickly rose to my feet.

"Why would you *do* this, you son of a—" I shoved Ryker with all of my pent up fear and frustration.

He knocked my hands aside as I attempted another shove. "He's fine, Lune. Just a mild sedative."

"Why? *Why?*" I lashed out and kicked his leg. He growled a warning to which I jeered, "Was he getting in your way? Was he right about the enhancement serum? Bells will never forgive you for this!"

"Stop," he barked, catching my wrist when I made to slap him. "You know more than anyone that this had to be done. The Supreme Elite won't believe Bren's story. He's a dead man the second he steps foot inside Tatum City. I did you a favor and took care of the problem. The fight was just a distraction so I could sedate him. You're welcome."

"You're . . . you're *welcome?*" I roared, twisting my arm free. "You used me to betray him. *Again.* I want to tear your stupid head off and feed it to your clan!"

He sighed as if weary of the conversation. The *nerve.* I was going to let the vorax eat his fingers and toes! "I'm sorry I had to use you. You might not like my methods, but they're effective. This way, Bren is still alive and can help my mother with the Recruiter Clan while I'm gone. In time, you'll understand that I made the right move. Now contact your Ridge friends to come get him before he wakes up. We need to reach the gates before he can stop us."

I could only stare in dumb shock as he removed Bren's pack, then dragged his unconscious body off the road and into the woods.

My mind must have shorted out for a bit, because the next thing I knew, Ryker was gripping my arm and leading me away. I snapped back to reality, jerking free. "I'm not leaving him."

Ryker grabbed both my arms, giving me a solid shake. "*Think,* Lune. Don't let this all be for nothing. Without the box of serum, he can't enter the city. He's *safe.* I know you want that. We don't need him for the inside job. Everything he was planning on doing is something you can do."

He dropped his hands, but his gaze remained steady. "If you want to see this mission through, then you'll come with me right now. Bren was always going to be a casualty. This way, he won't have to."

Without waiting for a reply, he turned, leaving me with yet another impossible decision. He held all the cards now, Bren's backpack containing the serum firmly in his possession. As tempting as it was to knock him unconscious and handle the mission alone, I couldn't. With Bren out of commission, I needed his help more than ever.

I glanced to where Bren lay hidden. This was his life's mission. Leaving him behind was the ultimate betrayal. Would he ever forgive me?

At least he'll be safe.

And I would rather have him angry with me for all of eternity than see him destroyed at Renold's hands.

Pain. Pain filled every pore of my body as I followed after Ryker.

What I wouldn't give to see Bren's beautiful face one last time.

But I didn't have the strength to say goodbye.

WELCOME HOME

The first thing the gate guards did was search us.

Thoroughly.

I grimaced as hands brushed down my thighs. They took Ryker's pack and mine, but when they tried to take the one containing the serum, Ryker gripped the thing with an ironclad fist.

"No one is to touch this," he said with authority. "Supreme Elite Renold Tatum's orders."

The guards glared at him, but one spoke into his ear communicator to confirm the order. They ushered us forward without a word. It was a three mile hike to Tatum House where I assumed we were going. Two guards flanked us, hands on volt guns at their waists.

The silent tension grew.

A couple miles in, my palms began to sweat. I wiped them on my pants, glad that I wore a thin thermal shirt on this warm day. Still, a damp trail trickled down my back as well. I tugged the bear tooth free of my shirt and tightly fisted it. Bren had given the necklace back to me earlier today in case questions arose about our relationship. But now it didn't matter.

Out of nowhere, my knees threatened to buckle as grief grabbed my heart and viciously yanked. I clutched at my chest, expecting to find a Bren-sized hole. "I left him."

At my whispered words, Ryker shot me a look.

He's mine and I left him. I left my soulmate.

"Keep it together," Ryker muttered, sliding a glance to the guards.

I didn't want to. I wanted to fall apart. I'd left my rock, my comfort, my *safety* behind. I might never see him again, and I hadn't said goodbye.

When the house came into view, a new kind of misery writhed in my stomach.

Everything looked the same.

The trees, the gravel road, the expansive front lawn. Benny and Lennie, the two giant lion sculptures, still guarded the iron and glass front doors. I didn't dare touch them, not when the guards were observing my every breath. Dobson, the house's middle-aged butler, already had the doors open, stoic as ever. Normally we'd trade a few barbed comments, but not this time. Not when everything looked the same yet felt so different.

Or maybe it was me. *I* was different. Because when I'd entered Tatum City eleven years ago, everything felt big. But it wasn't my world anymore. This was simply another set of walls to overcome. To break down.

Once inside the house, I took in the polished wood, marble, archways and chandelier with one swift glance. I wondered if Renold would keep us waiting. Draw out the suspense and misery—a favorite tactic of his. When Dobson stepped around me, I followed him into the bowels of the house I so deeply loathed. The Winter Garden's exotic plants even failed to brighten the stifling space.

I had forgotten that I'd have to speak to the elitists darkening these halls. Nothing had changed for them, but I was a different person now with a wealth of knowledge. Keeping my true self hidden would be harder than ever.

When Dobson stopped just outside the banquet hall, I fought off a cringe. Lunch hour had passed, but that didn't mean I wasn't walking into a room full of elites. Just once, I wished to stride into the enormous space with its ridiculously long table, roaring triple fireplace, and soaring barrel-vaulted ceiling with a semblance of *real* confidence.

Today wasn't that day.

Be brave. Be strong.

I am not weak, I inwardly chanted. It was the best I could do. I straightened my spine. Tipped up my chin.

And stepped into the room.

A set of eyes immediately pierced mine. Only one, belonging to the sole occupant of the room. Seeing their icy familiarity was like ripping open an old scar. I bore the pain, drawing closer and closer to the man at the center of all my fears. To the monster who'd shredded my back and tortured my mind.

To the devil himself.

Sapphire rings flashed as Renold gestured for us to be seated. I didn't hesitate, making for the seat of honor to his left. I could have sworn his white-blond eyebrows lifted in surprise as I smoothly pulled out the high-backed chair and settled myself on its blue velvet cushion. Ryker sat across from me on Renold's right.

When he placed his long, elegant hands on the table, old habits drew my gaze to them, like a moth to flame. A very deadly flame.

A sliver of fear crawled up my throat. I quickly tore my eyes away only to meet Renold's pale blue ones.

He smiled that secret smile of his, as if he knew every last dark corner of my mind. "Welcome home," he said, his lightly accented voice smooth and cultured as always. He looked at my wrapped wrist, but his attention lingered the longest on the crescent moon tattoo I'd made sure to expose. "It would seem you've had quite the adventure."

An open-ended statement. One that would receive an open-ended response.

"I have," I replied neutrally. "We both have."

His smile dipped a little. "But it was successful?" He turned his attention to Ryker, and I finally allowed myself to breathe.

"Yes, sir," Ryker said, lifting the backpack off the floor. "With your permission?"

Renold nodded, watching closely as Ryker undid the zipper. If only there was a syringe prepared inside. If only Ryker plunged the needle into his uncle and pumped him full of memory-blocker serum. But all he did was carefully set the box on the table. As Renold pulled back the lid and peered inside, nausea swirled in my gut. What did it mean that he wasn't keeping the serum a secret from us?

He swiftly closed the lid and waved Dobson over, who took the box with a bow and left the room.

And just like that, the serum was out of our grasp.

Razor-edged silence blanketed the room.

Then, "There's a few vials missing and so is Mr. Bearon." Renold steepled his fingers, leaning back in his chair. "Seems you two have a lot of explaining to do."

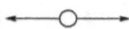

Two hours.

Two hours of masking my inner turmoil, of talking about Bren as if he meant nothing to me, of painting him as a traitor.

I was seconds away from completely losing it.

At least I was finally free of my adoptive father's penetrating gaze. Time would tell if Renold believed our stories, but for now, Ryker and I had the rest of the day to ourselves.

Exhaustion pulled at my limbs as I marched down the hall, but fury drove me forward. Feet away from my destination, a door whipped open. And there she was, Renold's daughter. Rose took one look at my murderous expression and immediately snapped her mouth shut. Still, she flipped back her platinum blonde curls and sneered at my travel-worn clothing, telling me with her big brown eyes how pathetic I looked.

I couldn't care less what Rose Tatum thought of my appearance.

Our old feud was meaningless compared to everything I'd experienced the last few months. I knew now that her barbed words were nothing more than a little girl's jealousy. That and she was wretchedly bored. I didn't have the time or patience for such things. So when she threw back her shoulders and stepped into the hallway, ready to do her worst, I stormed past before she had the chance.

I heard her splutter in protest, but I was already through my bedroom door, cursing when Ryker strode in behind me without invitation. I wanted to slam the door and show them both my wrath, but Rose would no doubt tattle on me. I settled for firmly shutting it in her shocked face.

I turned on Ryker, hissing, "I don't want to talk to you."

"Lower your voice," he softly growled, jabbing a finger at the door.

"I don't *care*."

His brows lowered. "We need to work together on this, Lune."

Together. Like Bren had wanted.

Tears sprung to my eyes. I jerked around, desperate for some privacy. The dam was bursting and I did *not* want Ryker to see. My old room came into focus, with its cheery yellow walls and bright peach furnishings. I sat on the canopied bed.

"Leave." The command was pitifully small as my throat closed. I bent, fumbling with my boot laces. A tear slipped free, splatting onto the hardwood floor.

"Lune."

No. No! He knew.

"Leave," I snarled past quivering lips. Another tear joined the first.

A weight settled on the mattress beside me.

When he said, "I'm sorry," my chest cracked wide open.

A choking noise left me. I tried to stop it, tried to clamp my lips tight, but it was no use. As the stuttering sobs built in volume, I felt Ryker's arms around me. He shifted our positions until my mouth was pressed to his chest—to muffle the calls of distress. He held me there, slowly rocking me as I released my anguish.

My overwhelming guilt.

For leaving Bren.

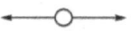

The tether snapping into place was immediate, jerking me off the bed and through the house's wall. I mentally soared west, over the barracks, past the lagoon and French Broad River, and to the densely-wooded part of Tatum City so few ventured into. A cage sprung into view. Arcus Point. I flew over it, heading straight toward a short cement structure.

Fear pinged through me, almost breaking my concentration.

I fought the urge to pull back, to disconnect from her before I was sucked inside that building.

But no, I *had* to. Had to know if she was okay. Especially now. Now that I knew she was inside a bunker filled with . . . with . . .

The tether yanked me past the steel door and I mentally screamed. Screamed all the way down, down, down through layers of concrete and shadowy corners filled with monsters. Waking nightmares. I saw cages. *Things* inside them. Mutated beasts. Magnawolves. *Saber cats.* Pacing, roaring, clawing to get out.

But there was something else too. *Other* things. Stars, no. No! There were humans. Locked in cages.

Bam!

I jerked to a halt and everything went dark. I panicked, struggling to see before a beast got me.

No, no, no. Focus. Focus!

Alarm flitted through my mind. "L-Lune? Is that you?"

I stilled at the sound of her sweet voice. *Yes, Iris, it's me. I'm back. I'm finally back.*

REUNIONS

I thought Tatum City hadn't changed.

I was wrong.

There was a newfound tension, a wariness. Not the kind I'd known for eleven years, where the citizens fought to climb the ladder of success on the backs of their neighbors. No, this feeling of distrust was more palpable. Searching. Burning. Goals weren't one-and-the-same anymore.

Asher had been right.

The people were scared but finally asking questions. Good thing too since I knew where the missing people were now. No wonder we hadn't been able to find them all these years. So few had access to the bunker where the mutated beasts were kept, and no one in their right mind would try to break inside.

Whispers followed me down the halls, from the lips of elites and staff members alike. About my scars, Renold's brutality, my three month absence, and what I must have endured. The former still made jabs, questioning my worthiness at earning an Elite Guardian title. But not all of them. Some were curious, even awed as I strode on by. As for the staff—the *lesser* of Tatum House—their expressions were all the same.

Hopeful.

Like they knew I'd returned to change their lives for the

better.

Like I had the strength, the *power* to make a difference.

If they only knew how weak I felt.

My orders as the city's Elite Guardian were simple. I was to oversee the other guards, making sure they did their jobs. But I was also supposed to survey the city and report back with any suspicious behavior. Renold especially wanted me to keep an eye on the villagers—which was to my advantage. They were exactly who I needed to see.

Ryker was to remain by my side at all times, still my Keeper. My shadow. And no doubt intended to keep me in check. He had loyally reported my activities to his uncle before our mission, and would continue to do so now. I could only hope that he was on our side and wouldn't screw this whole thing up.

The moment I took a step outside the creepy house, I was filled with bone-deep relief. After not even a day of obsessively worrying over Bren and Iris, I was dying for a distraction. I promised myself that I'd personally contact Bren by nightfall. Jaxon said he was all right and wanted to speak to me, but I just . . . I needed a little more time. My emotions were still raw, and I couldn't afford another meltdown.

The urge to throw my head back and soak up the sun's early morning rays overcame me. But Ryker's elbow nudged me forward. Ugh. Some things never changed.

"Did Renold mention anything about upholding his deal with you yet?" I asked him quietly as Trials trainees and stable hands openly gawked at us. I adjusted the dagger holster across my chest, the one thing from the outside I couldn't bear to part with.

"Actually, yes," he replied, his voice low and even as he chased away the curious looks with his usual glare. "Half an hour ago, I ran across him in the hall. He said the serum was almost ready. That's all he said."

Great. Mysterious as ever.

"And Iris?" he asked.

"He said she's safe." And I didn't dare press him for details. The first thing he'd ever punished me for as a child was asking a question. I already knew she was alive—I had checked on her again this morning—but I still didn't know what he was *doing* to her. She had tried to tell me, saying something about needles. Both times I'd contacted her though, she'd fallen asleep, her mind feeling sluggish. Drugged?

At least I knew where she was. Now I just had to find a way inside.

No problem.

Nervous anticipation kicked in when we rounded Tatum House and I caught sight of an achingly familiar two-story structure. My throat closed. Two of my favorite things were inside that building. At least, they *should* be. Asher was alive, the last I knew. But he'd been snooping around a lot lately, spreading rumors and asking questions. He knew the price. Knew that people disappeared for less. But he'd done it anyway, for me.

Stars, if anything happened to him because of me, I wouldn't survive it.

Fingers of fear suddenly clutched at my chest and I broke into a jog, needing to see him more than anything in the world. My only human friend for a decade—my *best* friend—had to be all right.

I was aware of Ryker hissing at me to slow down, but there was no way. I barreled inside the stables, my boots clapping against cement. When the familiar scents of charger sweat and raw meat struck my nose, I skidded to a stop. Ryker cursed, barely avoiding a bodily collision. Dust motes floated in the air, flashing in the morning light. I blinked past them, searching, searching . . .

"Thinking about me?" a voice said from behind. A voice I had grown up with and heard change from a boy's squeaky alto to a man's smooth tenor. I stiffened, not because he was at my back—the vulnerable part of me I never left exposed—but because it took all of my willpower not to whirl around and throw myself into his arms, then sob my heart out.

Ryker mumbled something and brushed past, heading for his charger's stall. I remained where I was. One false move and I would lose it, right here where the occupants of the stable could see. So much for avoiding a meltdown.

Asher cleared his throat. I peeked over my shoulder to catch him tip his chin at the second floor loft. Stable hands sometimes slept up there, but it should be empty this time of day. I made for a ladder, assuming he would take another.

At the top, the space was packed with piled-up crates, and I couldn't see him. But then he was there, his tall, lanky form sliding into view. He approached me slowly, as if I was a skittish animal—the same thing he'd done countless times before, always mindful of my moods.

The Ridge believed he was an Empath.

Could he hear my thoughts? Did he know about his abilities but kept them a secret like I had?

I still hadn't moved. I could only stare as the dust motes cleared, giving me the perfect view of his boyishly handsome face. He looked the same, with ash-blond hair that stood up every which-way and sky blue eyes that crinkled at the corners.

He smiled.

And there were those deep dimples that I'd missed so much.

My nose scrunched up as the burn started. There was no stopping them. Tears were *definitely* coming. And fast. As the first one filled my eye, his arms opened. An invitation. One that I didn't hesitate to accept.

I stumbled forward and all but fell into his embrace, pressing my mouth to his shoulder as a hiccup left me. His frayed, hay-scented collar was quickly soaked with my tears. His arms were solid, work-worn hands steady as they rubbed my lower back. I let him comfort me in the stillness, listening to the muted animal and human sounds from below.

Eventually, he whispered, "Where's Bren?"

I squeezed my eyes shut as pain lanced my heart.

"Oh, Lune." He held me tighter. "Is he . . . is he . . . ?"

I inhaled a shaky breath and pulled back. "He's not here. I have a lot to tell you, but it's not safe to discuss in the open like this."

He nodded, his dimples winking as he chewed thoughtfully on his lip. "Same routine? Special knock and password?"

Drying my cheeks, I agreed. "I have a night shift the day after tomorrow. Meet you then. But after that, we have to find someplace safer. I won't risk your family."

His head bobbed again. "What should the password be?"

I looked him square in the eye, knowing without a shred of doubt that he could be trusted. Wanting him to know it, I said, "Freedom."

He blinked, thrown off by my word choice. Usually I selected something completely ludicrous. His lips curled into an impish grin. "I like it."

My answering smile was just as wide.

We didn't linger. There was no telling who might be spying

on my movements. I grimaced, remembering that *Lars* was skulking about somewhere. On the ground floor once again, I paused to take in the familiar noises I'd missed. Creaking leather, jangling metal, horse-like grunts.

Crap. I hadn't asked about Freedom!

My boots pounded a rhythm down the main aisle. Curious equine heads emerged from their stalls, but my vision had narrowed to a fine point. There was only one charger head I wanted to see. Before reaching the end, I stopped and strained to hear a sound—*any* sound—from that last stall I knew so well.

But all was silent. So devastatingly silent.

My feet were lead weights bolted to the floor. I couldn't bear the sight of an empty stall. Or worse—a trainee saddling her up for a run around the track. It was too much to hope. Too much to expect my charger to still be there, waiting for me. But that was the crazy thing about hope. It was stupidly persistent.

I made a kissing noise. In reply came the faintest of rustling. My heart jumped into a gallop. I made the noise again, this time louder. When a squeal rent the air, my chest all but exploded. I moved, even before her chestnut head popped out to greet me. Because I would know that sound of joy anywhere.

She remembers me, she still loves me. She remembers me, she still loves me.

Fresh tears blurred my vision as I approached, belatedly realizing that I'd forgotten a slab of meat. I probably shouldn't chance it for our first reunion, but when she strained against the stall door to reach me, I shoved caution aside. I touched her nose, the only soft spot on her entire body, chuckling as she breathed in my scent and exhaled gustily. My arms ached to wrap themselves around her prickly neck, but there were too many witnesses.

I hadn't forgotten where I was—the city that preyed on weakness.

Renold wouldn't hesitate to hurt or even kill her if it meant keeping me in line. And I intended to uphold my promise to her. She would taste freedom, feeling it race through her mane and thunder under her hooves.

So I reined in my happiness, carefully stroking her face, but without the affection I desperately wanted to give. I whispered her name. Not her birth name, but the one I'd secretly given her. "Hey, Freedom."

She nickered contentedly, eyeing me with those keen yellow irises so similar to a lion's.

I managed to saddle her without bursting into tears, the familiar motions bringing back countless memories. Bruises, cuts, spills, close calls. But also tender ones, even peaceful ones as she'd shown me nothing but devotion. I hadn't appreciated everything she'd given me before, too focused on training and earning my freedom. But now, every sound she made—every muscle twitch and tail flick—was a gift.

This. *This.* Could all be gone in a blink of an eye. I hadn't cherished the small moments, the moments that brought tiny glimmers of peace, joy, and happiness. Maybe I hadn't been free, but I'd been alive. And I should have lived *every* second to the fullest.

I wouldn't make that mistake again.

Starting now, I would live each moment as if it were my last.

"Come on, girl," I crooned in Freedom's ear, unlocking the stall door. "It's time for us to fly."

There was eternal silence and ringing emptiness.

Then there was hurt. A yawning black pit.

So huge that I felt lost inside my head.

No. *His* head.

Bren, I—I'm so—

Please don't. Please don't say it.

Silence. The kind that collapsed my lungs and left me floundering for air.

I thought I could do this, Lune, but I can't.

More silence.

It stretched and stretched until I was firmly pushed from his mind.

THE MEETING

Fog blanketed the evening of my first night shift.

Perfect.

Freedom stomped a hoof, blowing a ploom of air from her nostrils. After only two days of riding, I already had fresh cuts on my palms. I welcomed the sting, a reminder that I was alive and with my beloved charger. But time was running out quickly for Iris. A day ago, something terrible happened, blocking me from communicating with her.

For two days, I'd checked her condition at least a dozen times with no problem. She was either asleep or alone and afraid. But on the last occasion, she'd been in a world of pain. I'd snapped back to my body and spent the next hour sobbing for her. After that, I hadn't been able to reach her mind.

And then there was Bren. His pain was different, but no less potent.

After that botched attempt at contacting him, I hadn't tried again. He needed space to lick his wounds—and maybe punch a few trees. But fear also kept me away. Fear that I'd ruined our relationship for good. I couldn't stand to hear him say that it was over, that *we* were over. I was a coward who couldn't face the consequences of my actions.

Hopefully tonight would provide answers, or at least a

distraction.

I handed Freedom's reins to Ryker, still astride his dark bay charger, Napoleon. If a guard questioned my whereabouts, the answer was simple: I was taking a bathroom break. A very long one. Dinner hadn't agreed with my stomach.

"Loop around the village a couple times, then meet me back here," I reminded him, checking for guards nearby.

"Half an hour," he said firmly. "Don't be late."

I nodded distractedly, waving him off as I darted for cover. How many of the guards were Sensors? I'd need to be more careful considering they could see in the dark and probably *smell* me. Which made me think of Lars again. Where *was* he? I hadn't seen him once. Maybe he'd tripped and fallen on his saber. That would solve one of my problems, at least.

Slipping through the village undetected was easier than I remembered, probably due to the fog. But maybe partly due to my new title. I felt a tad untouchable, overconfident that I wouldn't get into trouble, which left a sour taste in my mouth. My elite status was already going to my head. Did all the elites feel this way? Powerful? Invincible?

Ugh.

I hated it. Hated *myself* for feeling those things.

But it was addicting, and I could understand now why so many elites scrambled for more. Having control—no matter how superficial that control was—did something to you. I couldn't deny the rush it gave me, so similar to adrenaline. And if I was an adrenaline junkie . . .

Stars help me.

The weathered green door of Asher's house materialized out of the fog. I switched my disturbing thoughts off, poised to knock when the door suddenly slid open. As Asher's head popped out, I jerked back, swallowing a startled squeak. Instead of ushering me inside, though, he stepped outside—the first time I'd ever seen him break curfew.

I immediately waved for him to go back where it was safe, revealing the pack of food I'd brought. But he simply shook his head and tucked the offering inside before sealing the door shut. When he pressed a quick kiss to my cheek and grabbed my hand, I was too surprised to resist as he led me behind the house.

He moved with ease through the narrow, cobble-stone alleys, pausing at multiple intervals to listen. Obviously he'd taken this route before. My best friend, the simple, rule-following stable hand, really *was* The Ridge's inside man. And that fact terrified me. He squeezed my fingers as if picking up on the emotion. Crap, he probably was.

Had he always been this capable and I'd simply never seen it?

We didn't go far, stopping at a house tucked among flowering trees, which hid most of the front from view. Asher scanned the area before he approached the door and gave the wood a quiet rap. One. One, two, three. Our special knock.

My jaw dropped.

The door cracked open an inch. "Code word."

"Freedom," Asher murmured.

What. The. Crap.

Okay, I was officially freaked out. But as the door swung inward to let us through, I followed my friend inside. Because it was time. Time for me to take a chance on others. Time to trust and work together with them. I couldn't do this alone, and if Asher trusted these people, then so would I.

The house was almost pitch black when I entered. Since

electricity in the village was turned off at night, this was normal, but not even a candle lit the way. As we were ushered into the unknown depths, I itched to hold one of my daggers. The word *trap* played through my head. But Asher, kind and dependable Asher, was at my back. I drew comfort from that as our faceless host disappeared into the thick darkness.

Asher nudged my shoulder, redirecting my steps just as my boot knicked something—a piece of furniture. His hand lingered, guiding the way. He seemed to sense that things had changed. That I wouldn't reject his touch as I once had. Trust and vulnerability would always be hard for me, but letting others in felt good. It chipped away the cold wall of anger and resentment I'd built around my heart.

From ahead came a faint *creak*. It could have been a loose floorboard, but when a cool draft hit my face, I reached for a weapon. Asher stayed my hand.

"Look," he whispered.

I frowned, unable to see a thing. Fear tickled my throat as the inky room pressed in on me. This was a bad idea. Asher was acting strange and . . . and then I saw it. A flicker of color. Orange. A candle? But that couldn't be right. Because it was coming out of the—

A glowing hand rose from the floor. I flinched and bumped into my friend, who simply patted my arm reassuringly. Sure, this was fine. People popping out of the ground was totally normal. Except I knew about zombies now. If this person at all resembled one, I was chopping the thing's head off.

I warily watched the mysterious hand pass a candle to our host, then vanish below again. It took me a moment to realize I was being waved toward the strange hole in the floor. Wait. They wanted me to go *down* there? I mentally resisted even as my feet carried me forward.

Bad idea, bad idea, bad idea.

Then, *Trust them. Trust Asher! He wouldn't hurt you.*

I peered into the abyss and spotted a ladder. Okay, so it wasn't a grave. I could do this. The entire climb down, I didn't breathe, expecting hands to grab my clothing and drag me deeper, deeper, deeper. But when my boots landed on something solid, I was surprised to discover concrete.

After a quick peek to make sure Asher was descending, I ventured inside. A short tunnel opened up into a large, underground room packed with . . .

I stifled a gasp.

Men. Women.

They must be villagers.

Lots of them. Maybe twenty or so.

And by the looks on their faces, they all knew who I was. Some appeared as wary as I felt, but most had that hopeful look. Like I was their savior or something. And here I thought it would be the other way around. That or they would bury me down here.

When Asher was once again at my back, our host—a middle-aged man with thinning brown hair—stepped forward. "It's good to see you in one piece, Miss Tatum. We—"

"It's Lune Avery, actually," I interrupted, feeling heat creep up my neck as brows furrowed in confusion. "I'm not the Tatum's daughter. It's true they adopted me, but I was stolen from my home. My mother is still out there."

Murmurs of surprise filled the room. Besides Bren, I hadn't told anyone in this city of my past, not even Asher.

Our host's faded brown eyes were warm as he said, "I'm sorry to hear that. We saw your scarred back at the village dance, and the food you shared with one of our own. It was Asher who convinced us to trust you, and since he's nothing but honest, we agreed to this meeting. It is safe to talk openly here. This room, built before our time, is all but soundproof and free of hidden voice communicators. We have a few other meeting locations too that we use on rotation. When you and that outsider, Brendan Bearon, disappeared almost four months ago, a revolution was born. We've been planning and organizing ever since."

"Planning what?" I whispered, holding my breath. Yes, I was feeling it too. A spark of hope.

"To give a voice to the people," Asher answered, coming up beside me. "We want to send a message that our days of silence are over. When a person goes missing, we'll speak up. When someone's abused, we'll help them. We want fair payment for the work we do—proper food, lodging, and medical treatment. And if the Elite Trials truly are rigged like Bren said they are, then we can't rely on them to better our stations."

He turned to me with that contagious smile of his. "We all deserve an equal chance, and to have a say in our future. So whatever the Supreme Elite is doing, we want it to stop. It's time we stood up for ourselves as you did that night of the Winter Gala, and work together as you and Bren did in the Trials."

"Here, here!" several voices murmured, excitement rippling through the crowd.

Excitement stirred in me too. Bren had been right. The oppressed people of Tatum City were ready to rise up. They could help us free Iris and the others trapped inside the bunker. Their numbers could even the great odds against us. My only allies weren't miles away out of reach anymore. They were *here*, standing right in front of me.

But even though I was proud of what my best friend had accomplished, I still feared for Asher's safety. All those years of talking him out of entering the Trials, and now this? His mother and siblings needed him. But didn't mine need me too? And I was still risking it all. Maybe that was the point. We were doing this *for* them, which meant we were willing to make the sacrifices necessary to secure their futures.

Even if that sacrifice was our own lives.

Sorrow filled me. *Oh, Bren, I understand now. I understand completely. I'm so sorry that I took that away from you.*

As hard as it was to see those I loved willingly put themselves in danger, the alternative was even worse. They were fighting for what they believed in, and I would honor that.

I returned Asher's smile with a slightly wobbly one of my own before facing the others. "I'm glad to hear that you want to fight back, because I have a lot to tell you." I shared *everything* with them, speaking mind-to-mind with Asher when my restraining chip interfered.

By the time I was done, they knew about the missing people in the bunker, Renold's possible plans for war, and his secret breeding program. I explained my Visionary ability and how many of them could have abilities of their own. And I told them about Blue Ridge Sector, our new allies.

The need to take action shivered through the room, but we had to carefully bide our time. The prisoners inside the bunker were at Renold's mercy. We had to free them before they could be used as leverage against us. When they were safe, we would set our budding plan into motion.

After confirming a time for the next meeting, it was late. *Too* late. I gave Asher a quick hug and hurried to the spot I'd left Ryker.

Fog still hovered above the ground, distorting his features, but the blue flash of his eyes cut through the gloom.

"You're late," he hissed, his body a wall of coiled tension.

Without a word, I mounted Freedom and picked my way through the black streets. Beside me, Ryker seethed, but he knew better than to argue publicly. I could have formed a mental connection and told him everything. Instead, I let the silence drag between us, making him wonder. Making him worry. Because at the end of the day, I still didn't know if my wildly unpredictable friend would choose to save this city or *his*.

Eventually, when Antler Hill Village was a speck in the distance, I sent Ryker a message. *We have an army. On the inside.* It was short, but unmistakably clear.

I allowed my hope to soar.

A week went by.

Two more underground meetings.

A plan took shape.

And then . . .

TURNING POINT

"Do you know what this is about?" I muttered to Ryker, giving Freedom one last pat before we joined the throng in Village Square. He shook his head, using his glare more than his body to part the masses.

Villagers and elites alike mingled, their unease palpable. A mandatory meeting this time of year had never happened before. The only time the lesser and the esteemed were required to be in the same place was for the annual Elite Trials, but the event wasn't for another half a year. Something big was about to happen, and it probably wasn't good.

The viewing screen used for the Arcus Point Trial switched on, displaying the arrowhead insignia. There was a commotion directly beneath the elevated screen, guards dressed in blue surrounding what looked like a villager. Several gasps and murmurs filled the air.

I squinted for a better look, pressing forward. The man was slouched, head downcast with hands behind his back. Beaten? The answer became clearly visible as his form flickered to life on the wide viewing screen above.

There were more gasps and cries, but mostly stunned silence.

Blood was caked in the man's thinning brown hair, his face so swollen that I almost didn't recognize him. But I did. He was the kind host from our first underground meeting.

"Citizens of Tatum City," a voice boomed. I jerked around, searching for the source. He was on a raised dais, the midnight blue cape he wore for the Trials draped across his shoulders. Gold and sapphire rings flashed in the morning light, his wife Blanca and daughter Rose behind him as he spread his arms wide.

The Supreme Elite held the pose, waiting for everyone to acknowledge his presence, to show their loyalty. One by one, the people around me slapped their left shoulders before thrusting their arms straight. Bile rose in my throat, but through sheer force of will, I repeated the sign of deference. Although Renold's eyes weren't on me, I knew I was being watched, and now wasn't the time to make a stand.

"Citizens," he repeated, lowering his arms. "We gather here today not to celebrate, but to mourn. One of our own, the man you see on the screen, has betrayed us all. He seeks to destroy everything we stand for. Our way of life, our pride and joy, the city that was designed to keep its citizens safe from the dangers of the outside world. But he's not the only one. There are insurgents among us, perhaps the person standing right next to you."

A panicked murmur swept over the crowd. Faces turned to each other in suspicion. *Fear.* I could have sworn Renold smiled, but his troubled frown returned before I could be certain.

"In the past," he said, hushing the masses, "malcontent was dealt with swiftly and quietly. But my generosity has been taken for granted, and the betrayal has gone too deep this time. From now on, we must *show* that disloyalty is not tolerated. Anyone who seeks to undo what my forefathers have painstakingly built will be publicly disciplined."

With a wave of his hand, he drew our attention to the screen once again. Guards were securing the beaten man's restraints to a wooden support beam. When they stepped away, the man slumped, but the beam forced him to remain upright.

A fizzle of bright blue caught my eye.

The guards. They were carrying volt sticks. The weapon was rarely used, its electrical charge higher than a volt gun's. I had only ever seen handlers use them to control the mutated beasts.

Oh stars.

"Ryker," I breathed, helplessness washing over me. His shoulder brushed against mine in silent acknowledgment. "Why wasn't I informed of this?"

As an Elite Guardian, I should have been the *first* to know. Unless Renold knew what I'd been up to this past week.

"He must be warning you too," Ryker responded, confirming my fear.

This was happening because of *me*? Stars. The guilt. It coiled around my chest, tightening until I could barely breathe.

Before I could come to terms with it all, the four guards lunged. Blue electricity zapped along the rods as they found their target. The man immediately convulsed, his muscles stiff with shock. Screams rent the air. Mothers covered their children's eyes. A few pushed to get away, but there were more guards. Surrounding us. Boxing us in. Making us watch.

I was frozen solid. Completely helpless. Unable to look away.

When the man slumped against the wooden beam, hanging limply from his restraints, a hush fell over the crowd. A silent question saturated the air that no one dared ask. But the longer we stared at the unmoving form projected on the viewing screen, the clearer the answer became.

Frightened whispers of "He's dead" reached my ears. A cold

numbness trickled through me. I knew there would be casualties—
I wasn't disillusioned anymore. But I hadn't been prepared to see a
man electrocuted to death simply for believing in a better tomorrow.

A moan rose up from the crowd.

It wasn't over.

As one body was carried away, another was brought forward.

And this one. This one I knew at a moment's glance.

But I must be dreaming. Stuck in a waking nightmare. Because this. *This.*

Was impossible.

I pinched myself. Hard. Hard enough that tears pricked my
eyes. But the vision of *him* didn't disappear. This couldn't be. He
was far away from here. Safe.

"Wake up, you idiot. Wake up!"

Fingers squeezed my arm. "Quiet," Ryker hissed in my ear.
"He's watching you."

Who was watching? I didn't care. I didn't care about *anything*
except the man being chained to the very same spot someone had
died just seconds ago.

An amplified voice, a voice that I *hated*, started speaking. He
listed the man's crimes against the city. There were many. A guard
tore the shirt off the man I loved. I flinched, almost feeling the material tear from my own skin. I checked the viewing screen. His face
was turned away from the crowd, the exposed lines of his back the
only thing I could see.

That was my soulmate, restrained and helpless.

My other half. He needed me.

A ringing. A screaming. A storm of emotions barrelled
through me.

Ryker gave my arm a shake. "He can handle it. This is a test. Stop reacting." But I heard the doubt in his voice. The panic. That his friend, his *brother*, was about to die.

And his emotions added more fuel to mine. They were my weakness. My ruin. I felt and thought too much. But I didn't care. I didn't care if the whole world knew how to destroy me.

Because he already was. Brendan Bearon—the one who'd taught me to love fiercely and believe in something greater than myself—was destroying me by destroying himself.

I couldn't let that happen. Every inch of me railed against that outcome. So when I saw the *whip*—the same one I'd felt across my back for over a decade—and saw the guard position himself behind Bren to destroy a perfectly beautiful part of him, I exploded.

"No!" I surged toward him, shoving aside anyone and anything that separated us. Arms shot around me, pinning my flailing limbs. "Let me go, Ryker!"

I thrashed against his grip like a wild beast, cursing him for holding me back.

I knew he'd betray me again!

"Lune Tatum." The sound of my old name, my *fake* name, made me pause for a moment, just long enough to hear Renold say, "*You* will do it. Deliver thirty satisfactory lashes and Mr. Bearon will live to see another day."

A lightning bolt to the chest couldn't have shocked me more. I seized up, replaying the words over and over, but I couldn't grasp them.

Renold repeated his demand. "My daughter, our esteemed Elite Guardian, will have the honor of delivering justice. After all, it is her duty to defend this city, inside and out. Hand her the whip."

I knew what he said, but I still didn't understand.

I grew aware of my surroundings. The gaping faces. Everyone was watching me. Of course they were. They wanted to see what I would do. To see if I would remain loyal—or disobey a direct order. This moment was pivotal, a turning point in the game for control over this city. Would I rise up? Or would I crumble under the demands of a dictator?

When I didn't move, Ryker nudged me forward. He practically carried me, my feet dead weights, the people soundlessly parting to let us pass.

Bren's back grew sharper as we neared. The only thing marring his smooth skin was the faint scar where he'd been shot. I was still a shell of confusion, unwilling to believe the order I'd been given. But when he looked over his shoulder at me, when I saw his beloved face, reality sucker-punched me.

This was real. *He* was real. Somehow, Bren was in Tatum City and I was being told to mutilate his back.

Someone—the guard—pried my fingers apart, placing a cold object on my palm. I looked down. Stars, I shouldn't have. There was the whip. In my hand. *The* whip. There were nicks on the handle where Renold's fingernails had gouged the leather while he'd beat me.

My hands started to shake. I tore my gaze away, fixing wide eyes on Bren.

And then he did something terrible. With a whispered, "It's okay," he gave me permission to whip him. To *destroy* him.

Tears distorted his features. Tears of hurt. Of *anger*. I was suddenly mad at him for being so calm and accepting of this. I wanted him to beg me not to do it!

I flung the vile whip as if it were a snake, spitting, "I can't. I won't."

If Renold meant to unearth my true loyalties, then he'd won. But I wouldn't give in to this ultimatum, this deal that would destroy my heart. Bren would live another day. I just had to find another way.

"Guard, pick up the whip," Renold said without inflection, as if he knew all along I wouldn't go through with it. "For my daughter's weakness and inability to do her duty, Mr. Bearon will receive double the lashes. Proceed with the whipping."

My heart forgot to beat. "No, *don't—!*"

The whip's high-pitched whine cut through my words, slicing the air and into Bren's flesh. I sucked in a gasp, too stunned to move. But when a thin red line slowly formed across his back, my knees gave out. Ryker bore my weight, refusing to let go. I stared at that cruel line. Stared and stared.

With a crack, the whip came down again. This time, Bren tensed, gripping the chains attached to his wrists. Blood trickled down his back and soaked his pants. But he didn't cry out, even when the whip's metal tip struck his rib cage, tearing free a chunk of flesh.

I bit my lip until a metallic tang coated my tongue. The pain wasn't enough to dull the throbbing ache in my chest.

Sixty lashes.

Five down, fifty-five to go.

I couldn't do it. I couldn't stand by while his back was pulverised to raw meat. Screw the consequences because it was time to fight back.

I lunged at the guard. Startled by the abrupt move, Ryker's hold on me slipped. I stumbled but quickly righted myself. As the guard's head turned my way, I plowed my fist into his face.

Blood instantly spurted. He yelled and dropped the whip to

clutch at his broken nose. Before I could deliver another blow, I was picked up off my feet. Ryker's hold was punishing this time, so tight that I couldn't breathe. I tried to headbutt him, kick his kneecaps—anything I could reach. But there wasn't enough room.

Despite everything we'd been through together, I wanted to kill him right now.

"Let me go," I snarled as he dragged me back. The crowd wasn't so silent anymore. Some were yelling, but I was too enraged to make out their words. Ryker's arms loosened enough for me to breathe again. "Why are you doing this?"

"I'm keeping a promise," he growled back. "He told me to protect you if he couldn't."

I would have barked a crazed laugh if I wasn't so angry. "But I'm trying to protect *him!*"

"Proceed with the whipping," I heard Renold say above the rising chaos. "Ten extra lashes for my daughter's insubordination."

That did it.

He was doing this to destroy my weakness. He thought *Bren* was my weakness.

But I suddenly knew without a shred of doubt that the complete opposite was true. Brendan Bearon was going to make me stronger than I'd ever been before.

It was like turning a handle. Simple. So simple. And then the raw fury poured free. It swept aside my fear and helplessness, drowning the weaker emotions until my vision bled red. I embraced the wild wave crashing through me, letting it fill and consume me. I remembered feeling this once before. On a rooftop when all I wanted to do was stop a madman from shooting an innocent girl.

And here it was again, energy rushing to my aid, answering my unspoken cry for help. But I wasn't helpless. No, there was something in me, something powerful and dangerous that wanted to be unleashed. It was a part of me, begging to be used.

To be wielded like a weapon.

I could stop this and save Bren. I simply had to believe that I could.

Energy shot through me like pure adrenaline, pulling me under, yet granting me power to rise. With Ryker's arms anchoring me to earth, I finally let go. I let myself lose control completely, giving it all to the ability raging through me. I was floating, wrapped in a watery bubble of protection.

I was invincibility. Power.

Not a girl. Or an elite. Or even a Visionary.

I was something else entirely in this moment. A being unlike any other.

I didn't recognize my voice when I spoke next. It was like hearing myself from inside a pocket of water. My body, along with everyone else's, was on the outside. But my subconscious was here, controlling what I said and did. I could see everything, though. I saw the irate guard pick up the whip again, his desire for vengeance clear. He was planning to take it out on Bren.

But I wouldn't let him.

"Stop," I said. The single word was neither a shout nor a whisper. But commanding. I gave him no choice but to listen. My order was absolute.

The whip paused midair. The guard froze. Didn't so much as blink. But I knew that once I let him go, he'd resume tearing up Bren's back. Hurting the man I loved. My soulmate. So I formed a tether with his mind. Dove into his consciousness.

And tore him apart from the inside.

He screamed, the only thing he was able to do. Blood trickled from his nose and ears.

It was the color. The color red—sliding down his chin and neck—that made me blink. Made me realize.

I was *killing* someone.

Stop, stop, stop!

I pounded against the bubble separating me from my body.

But even as I threw myself against the mental shield, I could see that it was too late.

The man's eyes fogged—that dull, glassy look I couldn't seem to escape—before he tipped over, landing on the ground with a great thud.

The noise jerked me back to myself. The reuniting of mind and body was like smacking into rock. Short, strangled gasps left me while my heart raced a million miles a minute. I was crashing. An adrenaline junkie coming down hard from a high. My knees gave out, but arms kept me from falling.

And then . . .

Everything returned.

The sound of screaming. Renold yelling, "Arrest her!"

The smell of fear. I could sense it everywhere, in and around me.

Did they know?

Were they fleeing because they knew that I'd killed someone. With my mind?

My body was jostled, lifted up. Hands grasped at my clothes. Guards. Pulling my arms, restraining my wrists. But Ryker held on. More frenzied shouts. More faces. Not guards this time. Villagers. They swarmed around us, blocking the light and my last glimpse of Bren. They grappled to reach me, shoving the guards aside. Blue electricity lit up the chaos and a villager fell. Two more took his place.

They tore me from Ryker. Sidestepped the lunging guards. I didn't resist as they dragged me away. Didn't care what the nameless faces planned to do with me. I deserved their punishment after what I had just done.

I was slipping, slipping away from the havoc I had wreaked.

The last thought I had before darkness pulled me under was that I'd truly become the one thing I'd fought so hard not to become. What I feared more than anything else.

A monster.

MONSTER

Fog swirled around a dark form. One I could never see but knew all the same.

"Hello, Catanna."

"Hello, Princess." A pause. "It's been awhile. What's on your mind?"

"I . . . I killed someone. On purpose this time."

Silence.

A dark chuckle. "Was the price you had to pay too high?"

Another pause. Then a whispered, "I don't know."

I was so close to the surface. So close to waking. But the voices followed me there. Elites and villagers, friends and enemies. They banded together against me, knowing that I was the greatest threat of all.

"*Murderer*," one jeered.

"*Monster*," another hissed.

"*Berserker*."

Wait. No. Not that. A murderer and monster, yes, but insane? I didn't *allow* my ability to control me. Did I?

"*Berserker!*"

"No. No, please. I swear I'm not!"

Something brushed aside strands of my hair, coaxing me from my nightmare.

"It's okay, little bird. You're safe."

My eyes snapped open. I immediately winced as a headache throbbed at my temples.

When my searching gaze found Bren's face inches from mine, I gasped and rolled over, scrambling to create distance.

"Stay back," I said hoarsely, throwing out a hand when he slowly sat up. "It's not safe. I'm not—"

A flickering candle on a scuffed table, the room's sole piece of furniture, caught my attention. Nausea swept through me. "The bunker. They took us to the—" I started to shake with fear. "The beasts. Where are they? Where—?"

Fingers touched my cheek.

"Bren!" Shocked to discover him so close, I pulled away again, backing into the wall. He continued to pursue me on his hands and knees in nothing but a pair of dark pants. I froze, struggling to put together the missing pieces. It was the pain tightening his eyes that jogged my memory. "Oh stars, Bren. You were whipped."

He shook his head. "It's okay. I'm okay."

"No. None of this is okay." I swallowed my rising panic, darting a look around the room. Seeking escape.

"Lune, we're not in the bunker. Several villagers took a stand and distracted the guards so we could get away. Asher and a few others smuggled us into an old wine cellar during all the chaos. Please, look at me."

He was close enough to touch now. I scooted sideways along the wall. "You shouldn't have come. I wanted you to be safe."

"That's my line."

"Well, it's my line now too!"

His hands captured my face. I grabbed his wrists, but even in his weakened condition, he wasn't letting go. "Look at me, little bird." I couldn't deny the quiet command. When I met his eyes, tears immediately threatened to spill over. The familiar sweep of his thumbs across my cheeks jerked the tears free.

"I understand why you left me behind," he said softly, catching each tear that fell. "And I tried to accept it, but I couldn't. Every second you were in here without me was a waking nightmare. I could barely breathe, let alone think. And even if turning myself in was the stupidest thing I've ever done, I had to come for you, no matter the cost."

"Yeah, and you almost got whipped to death, you big idiot." He flashed a sheepish grin. I should have been mad at him for his reckless behavior, but only felt relieved that he was alive and speaking to me. I raised tentative fingers to his face. When he turned his cheek into my palm, I blew out a shaky breath. "So you . . . you don't hate me for what I did?"

"Nothing you do could ever make me hate you."

My heart skipped a beat, then another as I remembered why I'd been running from him. I yanked my hand back and batted his away. Stunned, he let me slip by him. But before I could jump up, his arms shot around my waist. "Please," I pleaded, fighting his hold only for him to draw me closer. "Please, Bren. I'm dangerous. Evil. I—I killed someone. You need to go!"

He banded an arm across my shoulders, pressing my back to his chest. "No, little bird. I know what you did and I'm not going anywhere. I'm not afraid of you."

I trembled from head to toe, wishing I could tear free of my wicked mind and reactive body. But Bren held me together, forced me to stay. A steady rock at my back. "You should be. I lost control. I'm a monster." Once I admitted it out loud, I couldn't stop. I repeated the words over and over, the note of hysteria in my voice climbing.

"You're not a monster," he said, his breath hot against my neck. "You're not a monster, Lune! Just listen. Listen and let me tell you something."

He sighed, falling silent for a moment. I stilled, curious at his shift in mood.

"I was twelve years old when I shot someone for the first time," Bren said. The open admission quieted my racing mind. "I'd just learned how to use a gun and Rollie trusted me enough to let me bring it on a mission. But I messed up. There was this kid I was supposed to lure away, same as always, but . . . but his dad caught me. I panicked. Pulled a gun on him. But he pulled one out too. And all I could think was that if he shot me, who would protect Bells? So I . . ."

He cleared his throat, then sighed again. "I shot him. It was a fatal gut wound. He . . . he bled out, but not before witnessing me drag his son into the woods, unable to do a thing."

A shocked silence settled over us. He continued to hold me, but his muscles were as rigid as mine now. I got the feeling that he didn't allow himself to remember that dark moment very often. I could understand why. It was horrific. Some part of me wanted to recoil from him, at the innocent blood that stained his hands. Who knew what else he'd done in the name of survival.

But maybe that's what he wanted. For me to view him as a monster so I wouldn't view myself as one. Always the hero, ever willing to sacrifice himself.

A noble effort. Although the admission didn't make me feel

better about myself, I was relieved that he knew exactly how I felt.

And so I accepted his embrace and comfort, allowing my body to relax against him. "Maybe there's a monster inside all of us," I whispered. "And we must decide whether or not to free it."

Eventually, he said, "Maybe we do."

"It should be me."

I narrowed my eyes at my best friend. "You can't do it, Ash. You're too well known. You'll end up as the city's next missing person. Or worse."

"Yeah, but isn't that a risk we're willing to take? Besides, I've got one of those faces."

I frowned. "Huh?"

He gestured at himself. "You know, the doesn't-stand-out-in-a-crowd type."

"That's totally not—"

"He kind of does," Bren said with a shrug.

I sent a glare his way. "You're not helping."

He cleared his throat, unsuccessfully hiding a smirk. "Look, we only need him to disguise himself as a handler until he's inside the bunker. Then he can open the main doors and let the rest of us in. If he gets caught, we'll simply rescue him with the other prisoners when we try again."

My mouth opened, then quickly snapped shut. I wanted to argue against this plan until they were too worn out to fight back, but infiltrating the bunker was the only option we had. If I had to pick someone to sneak inside, it would be Asher. Renold wasn't currently looking for him and I trusted that he could get the job done.

But the protective side of me hated this plan with a vengeance.

I ducked my head to hide the conflicted emotions, jabbing a finger at our makeshift, paperless map. "Let's go over the bunker's floor plan again." I adjusted a rock and a few sticks on the worn table, suddenly doubting the snippets of layout I'd memorized during my mental connections with Iris. I needed to check on her again. My tether hadn't been able to reach her in over a week, but I wouldn't stop trying. I refused to believe that she was dead.

A warm hand rested over mine, stilling my agitated movements. "It's going to work," Bren said softly.

I swallowed around the painful lump in my throat. "Innocent people were electrocuted to death yesterday. They sacrificed themselves so we could get away. I still can't reach Iris, and we don't know whose side Ryker is on. I thought we stood a chance, but our numbers are dwindling already. Without enough inside help, how are we supposed to complete phase one of the plan, let alone—" I paused as the lump grew, cutting off my air.

Crap. The restraining chip.

Sensing my distress, Bren swept a thumb across my knuckles until the pain eased. "The villagers took a stand yesterday because *you* did. Their sacrifice means they believe in you. Have faith. We've come too far to give up now."

"I won't give up. It's just . . . harder than I thought."

"Anything worth fighting for always is," he murmured, picking up my hand to kiss my fingers.

For once, I didn't blush, despite Asher openly gawking at us. I was too busy memorizing the way Bren's lips felt against my skin, the way his face softened when he showered me with affection. These moments were precious, and I had a gut feeling that we didn't have many left. Every look, every touch, every whispered word could be the last I ever received.

"I'm going to, uh, head out now before anyone misses me," Asher said, walking backward toward the ladder with a dimpled grin. "I'll bring you more news tonight when I can sneak away."

Bren stopped kissing my hand long enough to say, "And maybe find me a shirt?"

Asher gave him a wink and salute. "I'll see if I can find somebody your size willing to part with one."

"What's it like out there?" I asked before he could open the cellar door.

He paused, glancing at me with a thoughtful frown. "Restless."

I nodded, mentally dissecting the layers of that one word. A few minutes later, he was back, clambering down the ladder so quickly that Bren went into protective mode. One second, I was leaning against the table, and the next, sandwiched between him and the wall.

I squirmed away, careful not to disturb his fresh bandages. When I caught sight of Asher's pale face and round eyes, my stomach dropped. "What is it? What happened?"

"It's the Supreme Elite. He . . . he . . ." Asher grimaced, scrubbing both hands down his face. "I'm so sorry, Lune. He just announced on the viewing screen that if you don't turn yourself in by sunrise tomorrow, the next person to be publicly disciplined will be Iris. I-I could attempt to infiltrate the bunker tonight when the handlers go home for the day. I could—"

"No way, Ash," I hissed, striding toward him. "No. Way. Everyone will be on high alert after that announcement."

He gave me a helpless look that crushed my lungs. "Then what are we going to do? It's your sister. We can't just let her—"

"We won't," I said firmly. *Too* firmly.

He didn't make a sound in his approach. It was the stirring of my hair that alerted me to Bren's close proximity. "Don't. You. Dare."

I locked my knees, refusing to bend under the commanding tone.

Asher's eyes widened in understanding. "You can't, Lune. Who knows what your father—I mean, the Supreme Elite—will do once he has you. Now that he knows what you can do, that kind of power in his hands could be . . ."

He groaned, yanking at the ends of his hair.

"I know," I said when the silence became suffocating. I couldn't even look at Bren. "But she's my sister, and I'll do whatever it takes to protect her."

I knew my choice of words would sting. Knew they sunk deep into Bren's heart, striking the most vulnerable part of him.

At least, I hoped so.

I knew that his need to protect me might exceed his empathy. And if that was the case, then there was only one thing left to do.

Take the choice away from him.

It was late. Maybe midnight.

The unspoken words between us had grown, but neither of us dared to break the silence. We both knew words were pointless right now. They would only add to the boiling tension between us.

All day, Bren had been a thick shadow at my back. He touched me often, reassuring himself that I hadn't slipped away. Even now, as we lay on the thin pallet provided for us, he used his body to keep me close. He'd imprisoned me from behind, one arm around my chest and the other my waist. For added security, he'd snuck a leg in between mine.

I shifted into a more comfortable position. He immediately jerked, then burrowed his face into my hair with a sigh. His panic and relief broke my heart.

"You all right?" he murmured against my skin. A lump formed in my throat. I couldn't speak even if I wanted to. He relinquished his hold, rolling me onto my back. The candle still burned, casting half his face into flickering light and the other mysterious shadow. It was still how I saw him, even if I knew many of his secrets now.

Propping himself on an elbow, he touched my cheek, offering me comfort. The gentle strokes of his thumb sealed my windpipe. I closed my eyes against the burn, turning my face into his palm. I placed a kiss there, like he so often did with me. His scent was almost too overwhelming, a reminder of all I had to lose.

When he reached for me again, I stilled him by pressing an open-mouthed kiss to his inner wrist. I took my time, kissing and tasting a path up his arm until I was blocked. Stupid new shirt. I opened my eyes to find his gaze aglow with desire and need. I purposefully licked my lips, drawing his attention to them as I tugged on the shirt's hem.

He reached for me once more, as if he couldn't help himself. I stopped him yet again by sneaking a hand beneath his shirt and running my palm over his abs. He quietly hissed in a breath when my nails scraped down his stomach. The sound sent warm tingles up my spine.

He leaned back, giving me room to carefully maneuver the shirt over his bandages. I tossed the material aside, hoping it got lost somehow. Through hooded eyes, Bren watched as I not so subtly checked him out. It was impossible not to, the golden swells and dips of his upper body a beautiful display of male perfection. Okay, I was slightly obsessed and didn't care if he knew.

Up until now, he'd been the one to explore, to send my pulse through the roof with sure sweeps of his hands. But I wanted this moment to be about him. He must have known what I was doing, but he didn't stop me. Didn't resist my efforts to comfort and show him how much he meant to me through touch instead of words. I knew it was something he understood.

I started at his full bottom lip, teasing until he sucked my index finger into his mouth. The warmth of his tongue momentarily distracted me. I quickly retreated, gliding the wet finger down to the pulse point of his neck where I planted an equally wet kiss. He loosed a throaty rumble, causing me to lose focus again. I knew he was on the verge of taking control, and that knowledge spurred me onward.

"Submit to me," I breathed, persuading him to comply by smoothing both hands down his chest and stomach. He growled, knowing that I meant more than just my touch. But when I skimmed the flesh below his navel, the sound cut off. Victory.

Shyness stole over me as I ventured further south, tracing the V that disappeared into his waistband. My fingers brushed the metal button of his pants, and his breathing grew uneven. I nibbled my lip, fighting off a blush.

In a swift move of rebellion, he undid the button for me, boldly guiding my hand even lower. If my entire body wasn't bursting into flames at the feel of him, I would have snorted at his unwavering stubbornness.

The display of dominance triggered mine, and I took control again. When his eyes fluttered shut and he finally let go, I was wholly entranced by the open emotion. The raw vulnerability. He hid nothing from me during moments like these, letting me see every facet of himself.

This level of intimacy was new and frightening, but I couldn't get enough. I wanted *every* moment to be like this—consuming from the inside out. A love that both destroyed and rebuilt, causing deepest pain and pleasure. A feeling like this shouldn't exist, a feeling so powerful, it weakened me.

Stars, when had Brendan Bearon become my addiction?

"I love you," I whispered, pressing a kiss over his heart. His answering groan sent a smile to my lips and more heat shooting through my core.

I'd rendered him incapable of speech, a willing slave to my touch. Words weren't necessary anyway. I knew how much he loved me, but I also knew how devastated he would be come morning to find me gone. He'd never willingly submit to me leaving, so this was my way of apologizing. Of pouring every last drop of my devotion into saying goodbye.

This was my moment to protect, honor, and love him.

Because my very last breath might come sooner than either of us was ready for.

WAKING NIGHTMARE

Dawn was a couple hours off when I emerged from the wine cellar undetected. As expected, the villagers were tucked inside their homes, still under curfew.

A part of me had hoped that it wouldn't work. That I had experienced a one-time fluke in controlling someone's mind.

But when I'd commanded Bren to sleep, he obeyed without argument. Seeing him so helpless against my ability's power had nearly destroyed my resolve. I knew what had to be done, knew that this mission was solely meant for me. But putting myself in danger and leaving him behind *again* would hurt him deeply.

I would carry that hurt every second we were apart, knowing I had no one to blame but myself.

Stealing his free will was monstrous and unforgivable, but I had to follow my gut. Ever since discovering where Iris was, I had a feeling that I'd end up there too. At least this way, I'd be infiltrating the bunker and not Asher.

What happened after that, I didn't know.

I easily snuck past the village guards, wondering if Renold ordered them to stand down in light of his announcement. Watching me crawl back to him of my own volition was something he'd take pleasure in.

What I didn't expect was Ryker. Halfway between the village

and my destination, I spotted him on Napoleon. Despite my tense body, I walked up and waited for him to escort me the rest of the way.

He didn't dismount and cuff me like a loyal Keeper should. Instead, he stared off into the predawn horizon for several silent moments. Then, "Go back, Lune. I'll turn a blind eye just this once."

"No." I firmly shook my head. When he opened his mouth to argue, I said, "Either you take me to Renold or I create a big scene. One way or another, I'm going to be arrested."

He scowled. "I could knock you out."

"You could try," I taunted, widening my stance.

After a moment of mutual glaring, he simply said, "Why?"

"Why did you challenge Rollie on that rooftop?" I threw back.

His expression immediately cleared. A muscle jumped in his jaw, but he reached a hand down without a word. I accepted the help, swinging onto the back of his charger. We rode to Tatum House in silence, but I drew comfort from his presence. Whether he was on my side or not, we had an understanding.

Running from our demons wasn't the solution. Only by facing what tormented us could we truly find peace. But we both knew there was always a price to pay.

For once, I welcomed his firm grip on my arm as he led me past a wide-eyed Dobson and into the house's foyer. His hand kept me from running back to Bren, my safety. His steady footfalls encouraged me to move forward. And his even breaths reminded me to *breathe.*

When we were face-to-face with Renold, Ryker tightened his hold as if deciding against this plan after all. Too late. I stepped forward, giving him no choice but to let me go. I stood before my adoptive father, oddly calm. The fear I always felt in his presence was missing, and by the pinched look on his face, he could sense the change.

"Search her," he said.

I didn't flinch as Ryker's hands traveled up and down my body. He wouldn't find anything. There were no weapons.

Only me.

Did Renold know I could destroy his mind in a matter of seconds?

He must have come to the same conclusion because he murmured, "Try anything and Iris will pay the price."

I ground my teeth together, smothering the urge to melt his brain.

With a snap of his fingers, he called a guard forward. "Cuff her, if you please, Mr. Cooper."

When a puckered scar on the man's cheek caught my attention, I gaped stupidly. There was something familiar about the scar's X shape.

"Hello, Mute."

A streak of cold slithered down my spine as I met Lars's dark gaze. His eyes unapologetically raked over my body while he restrained my wrists. When the metal dug into my skin, I bit back a cry, refusing to give him the reaction he sought. I hadn't forgotten what Bren said about him. How he might be a Berserker and wanted to claim me.

More than ever, I had to stay strong.

"Thank you for returning my daughter to me, Mr. Jones," Renold said to Ryker. "As always, your loyalty will be rewarded. Mr. Cooper will take things from here."

"I most certainly will, Your Grace," Lars replied with a slight bow.

Eww. Suck up.

I didn't fight his hold when he tugged at me to follow. But before we could leave, Ryker slid into our path. I blinked, surprised to find him glaring at Lars.

The grip on my arm grew painful. I refused to show how much it hurt, but Ryker glanced at me anyway. Lars tsked, chortling lightly. "Careful, Keeper. She's under *my* protection now." With a yank, he dragged me after him, boots slapping the marble at a sharp clip.

As soon as we rounded a bend, he jerked me close. "I've missed you, Mute."

Bile pushed at my throat. "I missed you about as much as I missed charger dung."

I didn't see the slap coming. Blood welled from where I'd bitten my tongue.

When the spots cleared, he was inches away. "I missed that *mouth* most of all."

Oh? I spat blood into his sadistic face. He reared back, shock, then fury contorting his features. Without warning, he clapped his mouth to mine in a bruising kiss. Rage flooded my senses, and I shoved him. Inflicting pain was one thing, but *kissing* me?

No. Freaking. Way.

I scrubbed a sleeve across my mouth, snarling, "I should turn your stupid brain into scrambled eggs for that, but I'd rather do *this*."

My knee was slamming into his groin before I could think better of it.

Satisfaction at hearing his lungs empty quickly turned into more pain as he backhanded me. I straightened only to receive a sharp prick to the neck. Flinching away, I stumbled on unsteady legs. A lethargic feeling slid through my body, slowing my movements and numbing my limbs.

Lars grabbed my arm again, forcing me upright. "Apparently you're *dangerous* now and must be sedated during the transfer process. I personally don't see what all the fuss is about."

"Wh-why are you here, Lars?" I slurred as he wrenched open the staff's stairwell door. While we descended, I goaded him into spilling information. Pride was his greatest weakness, so I aimed for a sore spot. "You didn't w-win a Trial. Shouldn't you be s-slinging dung in the stables or s-something?"

He cackled, not at all bothered by my jab. "You've been blind, Mute, too focused on avoiding the elites and winning the Trials. I was only trying to elevate my eliteborn status by showing my willingness to earn it. You never noticed me in the halls because I was a lesser elite, you stuck-up snob."

His fingers dug into my bicep as I missed a step, keeping me from plunging down the stairs. "Since you've been away, I'll tell you what loyalty gets you around here. Not only do I now have a room on the second floor, but a job very few even know about. Too bad you decided to betray your family by siding with that outsider. What do you see in the giant meathead anyway?"

I bit my tongue, refusing to comment. I'd forgotten that he was born into an elite family, but keeping tabs on Tatum House's residents was never a priority of mine. His presence here made sense now, but if he was tasked with bringing me to the bunker, then why were we in the sub-basement? Maybe my gut had misled me. Maybe Renold never planned on sending me to the bunker, but meant to keep me down here for the rest of my days.

The thought of rotting away in this place triggered my panic button.

I couldn't see straight as we veered down an unfamiliar

hallway. Bare bulbs lit our path, patches of light and shadow blurring and spinning the farther we went. The floor swooped underneath me, and I pitched forward.

Before I could hit the ground, Lars wrestled me over his shoulder. Blood immediately rushed to my head, further spotting my vision. "You're heavier than you look, Mute," he grunted, sliding his hand too far up my thigh.

A wave of exhaustion stopped me from putting up a fight, so I settled on mumbling, "Well you look like a charger's—"

My head suddenly smacked against the cement wall. I groaned as pain splintered my vision.

"Oops," he said flatly. "What's the point of a sedative if it doesn't shut you up?"

Keys jangled. A lock scraped open. Despite the fierce pounding in my skull, I noted the room we entered. The heavy steel door at the far end.

I swallowed another wave of panic as metal groaned and moldy air wafted up my nose. I glimpsed a tunnel lined with fluorescent lighting before Lars sealed the door shut and spun around. A tunnel?

"Wh-what is this place?"

"That's for me to know and you to find out," he said brattily.

"You remind me of this outsider I m-met. Same obnoxious laugh and soulless eyes. He was always scheming, uncaring who was hurt as he sought to gain his leader's attention."

Lars squeezed my thigh. "Sounds like my kind of guy. What happened to him?"

"He stuck his neck out too f-far, and his leader snapped it. I only w-wish I could have snapped his neck myself."

One moment, I was staring at boots and concrete. And the

next, everything went dark.

A terrifying scream jolted me awake. When another pierced the air nearby, a cold sweat doused my body. Those screams. They weren't human.

"Wakey, wakey, Mute," a voice singsonged. For a horrible moment, I thought I was back in the correctional center with Skervvy.

But the voice wasn't quite right. And the smells were all wrong. The air was a new kind of foul—old blood and rotten meat. The more I blinked, the clearer my vision became. But I had to be dreaming. This was too horrific to be real. Yet I couldn't blink it away. It *was* real. I'd much rather endure a cell with flesh-eating vorax than *this*.

Lars dropped me, not bothering to catch me as my legs gave out. The screams rose to a feverish pitch. Lars swore and stepped back, then must have thought better of it. He grabbed my arm and dragged me sideways. I tried to dig in my heels, but the floor was slippery. Wet.

Blood. Some dry, some not.

And . . .

Bones.

Something heavy rattled a cage nearby. Lars swore again and dropped my arm. Before I could stop him, he swung a gate shut in my face. A lock clicked, sealing my doom. He leered at me through the thick metal bars, jangling a set of keys.

"A couple nights in here should give you some perspective." A pause. "Just don't move, speak, or breathe. Maybe they'll forget you're here."

He cackled, loud and long, setting off a chorus of roars as he strolled out of sight. A door slammed, and I knew—just *knew*—that I was alone. Alone with a roomful of hungry, carnivorous beasts that wanted nothing more than to rip apart my flesh.

I curled into a ball in the middle of my cage. Because on either side of me . . .

Don't look, don't look, don't look.

Stars help me, I looked.

I saw the massive tan paws designed to shred first. Then the muscled chest built for climbing and pouncing. The dagger-like fangs were as long and sharp as ever. And the bright yellow eyes . . . were staring directly at me.

I jerked as one hissed and batted at the bars separating us. This close with nowhere to run, I was forced to face my childhood fear at long last.

Memories—memories I'd buried deep—clawed their way to the surface.

Pale green eyes and rich brown hair. An open smile and booming laugh.

Those were my memories of him.

Mum always said he and I were exactly alike. Adventuresome and reckless. Attracted to danger.

But I was rash and dumb that day, sneaking past the community's outer fence to follow his hunting party. I was only five, weaponless and completely untrained. The two saber cats cornered me, knowing I was an easy kill.

My screams alerted the hunters.

And my father . . .

My father darted in front of the beasts without hesitation, bravely taking them on to save his foolish daughter. And all I could do was watch. Watch as they tore him down and ripped out his jugular. Blood splattered the snow. Close enough to touch—like the cats on either side of me right now.

An object in the corner of my cage dragged me from the painful memory. Something round with two gaping holes. A human skull.

The pressure in my chest became unbearable.

I screamed.

But no one was going to save me.

Not this time.

THE BUNKER

This was meant to break me.

At a different time in my life, it would have. I would have done anything, *anything* to be free of this nightmare. But things were different now. I was stronger than I ever thought possible, even with my body locked in a cage.

So I waited for two days.

Listened to my companions hiss and pace.

Lars came by a couple times only to jab a pole through the bars and inject me with more sedative. I was treated like a wild animal, kept calm so I wouldn't harm the handlers. The sedative fogged my mind, leaving me too weak to access my abilities.

At the end of the second day, Lars came back, this time without a pole. Hunger clawed at my stomach from lack of food and water. A headache threatened to crack open my skull. He had to drag me from the cage and let me lean against him, I was so weak.

Drugged and starving, I was a poor excuse for an infiltrator. But my opportunity was coming. It had to. I was adaptive and resilient. Quitting wasn't an option.

We left the room of caged beasts behind, descending a floor in silence. Still cuffed, I didn't attempt to escape. That wasn't my mission right now anyway. Instead, I worked on settling my too rapid pulse before I passed out. I needed to memorize the layout of this place so that when the time came, we could easily find the prisoners and lead them to safety.

But all plans were tossed aside when we exited the stairwell and I saw *him*.

He simply stood there, secured between two guards. They all stood as if waiting. Waiting for *me* to arrive. To taunt his capture in my face.

We lunged for each other at the same time.

"Bren!"

"Lune!"

Our captors tore us apart. Lars caught me around the waist and started dragging me down a hallway. The harder I struggled, the more punishing his grip became. As my ribs bent under the pressure, I cried out.

A roar echoed off the walls. I twisted around in time to see Bren ram a shoulder into the guard next to him. The man flew sideways, rebounding off a wall before crumpling to the ground. He lashed out at the second guard, but the man was ready with a volt stick.

I screamed as blue electricity lit up Bren's chest.

He was struck again and again until his body twitched and fell. I felt every hit, felt the searing heat charge through my limbs and freeze my breath. Lars continued down the hall, forcing me to lose sight of Bren. I growled and cursed, fighting to break free despite the waves of dizziness threatening to pull me under.

"I thought this moment would never arrive," Lars purred in my ear. "You. Me. Him. He's not so high and mighty now, is he?"

I wet my cracked lips and spat, "You're not fit to lick his boots."

He slammed me to the ground. Before I could catch my breath, he planted a boot on my chest, forcing the air from my lungs. As I fought to dislodge the boot, he bent down and grinned wickedly. "Well, you're not fit to lick mine. But if you do, I'll let you up. Better hurry, your face is turning purple."

Righteous anger filled me, and with it, a snarling whoosh of adrenaline. I grasped at the feeling, pulling the energy to me until a trickle of my newfound ability arose. The water-like force built in volume, shoving aside my body's weakness and reinforcing my mind. I wrestled for control of the energy, like reining in a charger.

This time *I* would be in control.

I zeroed in on his boot. "Step back."

His leg slowly lifted. When both his feet were on the floor again, I let go of my tight grip on the energy. Restlessness still buzzed through my veins after it was gone, strengthening my lethargic muscles. When I glanced up to find Lars's expression completely blank, I used the opportunity to scramble down the hall toward Bren.

I was inches away, *inches*, when a volt stick froze me in place. Control was ripped from me as my entire body seized. I fell into a convulsing heap, close enough to Bren's prostrate form that my twitching fingers brushed against his shirt.

"Stop," a voice commanded. The pain switched off, but my muscles continued to spasm. Before I could touch Bren, something sharp pinched my neck. I jerked away to see a needle retreating. The sedative whooshed through me, stilling my movements. Groaning weakly, I blinked up at a frowning Renold.

"She was to remain sedated at all times, Mr. Cooper," he said, fixing his glacial stare on Lars.

"She was, Your Grace," I heard him say. "I followed your orders explicitly—"

"Apparently you skipped a dose," Renold cut him off, his usual calm replaced with a hard edge. "If you're incapable of following orders, perhaps I can find you a different position."

"No, sir, I won't fail again."

"See that you don't. It would be unfortunate if I had to replace you." Weighty silence fell as the thinly veiled threat settled between them. Then, "Make sure they're *both* safely delivered to the interrogation room."

He strode off without another glance at his *daughter,* half-starved and delirious. Lars hoisted me up, bearing most of my weight as he led me down the hall. Everything spun, but I caught glimpses of wide-eyed faces trapped behind glass. I struggled to focus, searching for familiar dark red hair and hazel green eyes. Frustration and panic built when the hall ended and I couldn't find her.

We turned left down a shorter hallway, the lights dim and ominous-feeling. Nausea rolled in my empty stomach. When Lars pulled open a metal door, I expected to see blood. Perhaps a discarded finger or toe from an especially gruesome interrogation.

But it wasn't an interrogation room we entered.

Lars closed the door behind us and grabbed my wrist to remove the cuffs. I stiffened, alarm flitting through me.

When my restraints were gone, he said, "Strip."

What the—?

"No," I snapped, flaring my nostrils to show my disgust.

He jabbed a finger straight ahead. "All prisoners must be clean, and to be honest, you smell pretty rancid. Strip and get in the shower or I'll do it for you."

He'd probably like nothing more than to *help* me undress. Yeah, that wasn't going to happen. Ever. He huffed when I willingly slid open the opaque-glassed stall door and stepped inside.

With the sedative still heavy in my veins, removing my boots was a challenge. I placed my belongings on a white-tiled shelf away from the showerhead.

The water, of course, was freezing. Only Tatum House had warm water in this city. Still, I took my time, hoping the cold would chase away some of the fog clouding my brain.

Before I was ready, Lars barked, "Time's up, Mute." He rapped a knuckle on the shower door, and I'd never been more thankful for opaque glass. "Put these on. Leave your belongings."

I mashed my lips together to keep sarcasm from leaking out. But when I reached for my new clothing through a crack in the door and saw what he intended me to wear, it physically hurt to keep my mouth closed. This had to be a joke. I held nothing more than a white, midriff-baring tank top and tight matching shorts.

My body began to shake. With rage.

Lars smacked the glass, making me flinch. "*Now*, Mute."

Clenching my jaw, I slipped on the material that could pass for underwear. When I exited the stall, Lars raked his eyes up and down my body. I might as well have been naked. Despite my anger, humiliation burned my cheeks.

"I never would have guessed *that* was under there," he goaded, fishing for a reaction. My expression remained blank. When I refused to take the bait, he grabbed my arm and led me from the room. I thought he'd made a mistake in not cuffing me again, but we entered another door across the hall, which he swiftly closed.

He marched me straight to a metal table, the room's sole piece of furniture, ordering me to sit. When I didn't comply fast enough, he used the opportunity to manhandle me onto a chair. I landed hard on the metal surface, but still refused to engage him.

This seemed to irritate him to no end. He grabbed my wrists

and yanked them across the table. Before I knew what was happening, he had them locked in metal cuffs attached to the table's surface.

I finally reacted.

My chair tipped back as I sprang up, struggling to free myself. But the heavy table was bolted to the floor. Thoughts of what Lars could do to me in this position slithered through my mind. The restraints bit into my flesh as I strained back. His gaze dropped to my chest and I froze. Panic sealed my windpipe shut as he reached for my breasts.

Before I could attempt to bite him, he made a fist and yanked.

I gasped as the leather around my neck snapped.

He dangled the bear tooth necklace inches from my nose. "What's this? I told you to leave your belongings, so this must be special. Is it, Mute? Is it *important?*"

My rapid breathing filled the silence, and a slow grin bled across his face.

"I think I know just what to do with it," he said before tossing the necklace to the floor. He raised a boot.

"No, wait!" Adrenaline surged through me. I scrambled to grasp the feeling and wrestle the energy to my will. But it was too late. His boot came down. The heel struck the bear tooth with a resounding *crack*.

As he revealed the damage, I could only stare.

The tooth was broken. Destroyed. Jagged pieces clung to his boot as he scattered the remains.

The sight was a terrible omen. A warning that I'd lose more than a necklace from a golden-eyed boy before the end came.

As if to confirm my gut feeling, Bren staggered in, wearing nothing but white shorts. A guard thrust him into the chair next to me and secured his wrists to the table. Lars righted my chair but I refused to sit. My focus was on a barely conscious Bren whose forehead now rested on the table. He probably didn't even know I was here.

I started to tremble again. And this time, anger wasn't the only emotion boiling to the surface. I channeled hatred toward the people who hurt others for their own selfish gain. The feeling was hot in my chest. The fog blanketing my mind began to lift.

"What's she doing?" a muted voice said.

Lars swore. "Get the Supreme Elite! Hurry, you idiot. The sedative isn't working!"

He slapped my cheek. The sting only fueled my hatred. My eyes snapped to his.

"Stop breathing."

The command rang hollowly in the void between us. Almost immediately, he grabbed his throat and began to choke. He stumbled back against the wall, mouth and eyes wide as he stared at me incredulously. In the back of my mind, something whimpered at me to stop. I flicked the weak voice aside.

This man—this foul creature—had to pay. They *all* had to pay for hurting my loved ones.

Lars was on the floor now, bucking and writhing. Like the snake that he was.

Cool fingers slid over my neck. I winced, almost losing my concentration. Despite a flare of alarm, I didn't look away from my prey. I had to finish this. One less monster to taint the world.

I heard a *click*.

And then there was pain.

Slicing hot. Razor sharp.

I screamed in agony and rage as I lost my connection with

Lars.

More pain seared my wrists, but nothing compared to the feeling of knives shredding apart my brain.

Someone next to me started shouting. So loud that I squinted my eyes open. It was Bren. Our gazes collided. He was afraid. I was too. Something was wrong, so terribly wrong.

My head. It hurt. Worse than anything I'd ever felt.

Like a switch being flipped, my body shut down.

INTERROGATION

"State your full name and date of birth."

"Brendan James Bearon. August fifteenth."

"And why did you come back after your mission failed, Mr. Bearon?"

A throat cleared.

"The longer you delay in answering, the more painful it will become."

Finally, "To—to complete my mission."

"And what mission is that, exactly?"

Silence. A hacking cough.

"Be vague, Mr. Bearon. I know about the restraining chip."

The coughing hurt to hear. I almost lifted my head.

But Bren forced words out in a rush. "To destroy you."

"Ah, the truth at last. It's good to finally have that out in the open. One final question since you've been so cooperative. Would you do anything to protect my daughter?"

"No."

A light chuckle. "Let me rephrase. Would you do anything to protect my *adopted* daughter?"

Pause.

"No."

A grunt of pain and more coughing.

"Lie. Try again, Mr. Bearon."

Long pause. A sigh.

"Yes."

"Thank you. That's all I need to know. Lune, I know you're awake. No point in pretending."

My eyes cracked open. I waited for the pain to register, the pounding headache and empty pangs in my stomach. Nothing. I blinked, slowly lifting my head to take in my surroundings. The metal gray room was square and unremarkable, except for a long mirror on one wall. We must be in the interrogation room. I caught my reflection and about leapt out of my skin. There was something silver around my neck. And *tubes* were attached to my body. Bags of liquid hung from a pole behind me.

Saliva rushed into my mouth. I tried to breathe past the rising nausea and panic.

Something brushed against my little finger. I looked down to see Bren's finger stretching toward mine. My eyes traveled over his body, searching for injury. Both of our wrists were still cuffed and scraped raw, but the rest of his injuries must be internal. A round device was stuck to his neck. Did it force him to tell the truth?

I almost caved to the pull and met his eyes, but I stopped myself just in time. If I did, I wouldn't have the strength to face the room's other occupant.

"Welcome back, Lune. Feeling better?"

I schooled my expression as best I could before fixing my gaze across the table. For once, it wasn't his icy stare that grabbed my attention but the white knee-length coat he wore. I'd never seen Renold in anything but a perfectly tailored suit before.

He laughed lightly. "You don't have to hide your surprise. I can feel it."

My eyes flew to his. The wide smile on his face sped up my heart rate.

"The time for secrets and tests are over. Now that I have your abilities under control, we can speak openly. Yes, I know all about what you can do, but do you know what I can? I share my family's Sensor gene, but I've managed to simulate Empath and Intellect DNA as well. The only DNA my body doesn't carry is the Visionary gene."

Holy mother of mutant babies.

He had *three* abilities?

Well that wasn't freaky or anything. It was only a small comfort that he didn't have my ability to control minds. What troubled me the most was that he knew so much. Dr. Stacey had been working for him, but was Dr. Moore working with him too?

"And before you get any ideas of controlling my mind," he continued, "know that the collar prevents you from doing so. After learning that adrenaline fuels the energy needed to project an ability, I installed an electromagnetic pulse into the collar that suppresses the hormone. It's what you felt before passing out."

A growl rumbled in Bren's throat, which Renold promptly ignored.

"And I should warn you. Tampering with the collar will emit a strong electrical current that could potentially kill you. Now, let's get down to business."

He rose from his seat to stand beside me. Bren's knuckles whitened. Despite what I'd just been told, I wanted nothing more than to access my mind-controlling ability. Before I could do anything stupid, Renold placed a round device on my neck just above the collar and retreated.

He sat, picking up a clipboard with pencil and paper attached.

As a whole, the city was illiterate, but I wasn't surprised to discover that he could read and write. "I'm going to ask you questions, and I need you to be quick and honest with your answers. If you don't, you'll receive a very unpleasant zap that seals your windpipe. It's similar to Dr. Moore's restraining chip, but I've perfected the model. Are you ready?"

Holy crap, of course I wasn't ready. This was insane. A sudden sharp pinch at my neck startled me. I inhaled, but the air snagged halfway down my throat.

"You might want to answer," Renold prompted.

"Y-yes," I stuttered. The pressure eased.

He didn't waste any time. "First question: State your full name and date of birth."

"Lune Avery. October second."

His grip on the pencil tightened. But he jotted down my answer anyway.

"Why did you return to Tatum City?"

"To protect Iris." The answer rang true, even though it was only a fraction of the truth.

"Who is she to you?"

Dr. Stacey had no doubt told him already, so I didn't hesitate to answer. "She's my sister." Before he could ask another question, I blurted, "What do you hope to gain by kidnapping children with abilities and forcing women into a breeding program?"

In all my eleven years of knowing him, I'd never dared ask him such a bold question. But he was already torturing me. Enduring more pain to gain a little control over this interrogation would be worth it.

Apparently Bren didn't agree. His leg gave mine a warning nudge.

Renold simply blinked, no sign of anger in his expression. "I'll make a deal with you, Lune. Promise to cooperate with me and I'll explain everything."

My mouth instantly dried.

His gaze hardened when I didn't speak. "We can be allies in this or enemies. The choice is yours."

I wanted to laugh in his face. "When have we ever not been enemies? This isn't a choice. It's another way to control me. To *weaken* me."

At that, he almost looked apologetic. More fake benevolence. Sickening. "I may have done some unorthodox things over the years, but I only ever sought to make you stronger. Every decision, every obstacle, was a test. To see if you were everything I believed you to be."

I frowned. He truly believed in what he was saying which was the most twisted part of all. But it was his belief in *me* that gave me pause. "I just need to know one thing before I make a decision. Why me?"

"You're what I've been searching for. Someone whose DNA mutated in a way I didn't think was possible. You're *more*. With you, I can finally pass on my family's legacy."

More questions than ever battered my brain, but an impatient gleam had formed in Renold's eyes. I'd pushed him as far as he would let me. For now. If I was going to free Bren and Iris from this creepy place, then there was only one thing for me to do. I wet my lips before saying, "I need a few reassurances first."

"Name them."

"As long as I cooperate, you won't kill anyone I care about."

"Done. Anything else?"

"Bren stays with me."

Anger finally reached his eyes, but he simply said, "I'll see what I can do. Is that all?"

"I want out of these cuffs."

His probing stare sent chills crawling up my spine. If he had the Empath gene, could he hear my thoughts? *Crap, crap, crap.* I forced my mind blank. After a solid minute under his scrutiny, he set down the clipboard and stood. His gaze never left mine as he produced a key and unlocked the cuffs. He stepped back and waited.

I raised an arm laden with tubes and offered him my hand.

"We have a deal," I said. When his fingers clasped mine, revulsion shuddered through me.

Because I'd just made a deal with the devil.

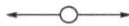

"Are you angry?"

The private holding cell we were in for the night offered little room to pace, but Bren managed anyway. I sat on the narrow bed, reaching for the familiar comfort of my bear tooth necklace. My fingers found cold metal instead. Sadness twisted my gut when I remembered that it was gone. Forever.

The pacing stopped.

Bren crouched in front of me, carefully laying a hand over mine where it gripped the collar. "You'll hurt yourself. Let go," he whispered.

My hold tightened. "Maybe I deserve to feel pain."

"Lune," he growled quietly, squeezing my knee. "Don't go down that road. It promises relief but it's empty. You'll only lose yourself in the end."

I shook my head. "But don't you see? You once said you feared destroying me, but I'm the one destroying *you*."

He frowned. "How so?"

"I controlled your mind and took away your free will."

"Yes."

"I left you. Again."

"You did."

"And now we're in trouble."

"We are."

"You should be furious."

"I am. I could punch a hole in the wall, I'm so mad."

I glared at him, hissing, "Then *show* me. Yell. Punish me. Tell me how awful I am!"

His lips thinned. "Would it make you feel better?"

"Yes! I want to feel your pain so I can comfort you. So I can fix the terrible things I've done. I'm sorry. I'm so sorry that you're here because of me. I want it all to go away. I want—"

The hand on my knee suddenly slid up my inner thigh, pulling a gasp from me. He slowly parted my legs and settled between them. "You want to forget?" he breathed against my neck, successfully disentangling my fingers from the collar.

A nod made its way past the haze already crowding my senses.

"I'll make you forget." His thumb swept inside the bottom of my shorts, awakening my desire. "I'll show you how angry I am." He bit my shoulder, hard enough to make me tremble. "If you say that you're mine."

I whimpered pathetically, willing to say or do whatever he wanted.

"Say it," he said, the rolling timbre of voice doing all sorts of crazy things to my insides.

"Yes," I sighed, placing my hands on his chest. "I'm yours."

He grabbed my wrists and pushed me back. I bounced onto the bed, blinking up at him in surprise. His leg came down between mine, pressing until I arched against him with a low groan.

"You can destroy me all you want, little bird. As long as you're mine, I can endure anything," he said before pinning the rest of me to the bed and stealing my mind with a scorching kiss. My wrists were shackled above my head. My body unable to move. But in this moment that slowed time and warped reality, I was the furthest thing from a prisoner.

THE FAMILY SECRET

My leg bounced nervously.

Not because I was face-to-face with the devil, but because I'd been separated from Bren. Now that Renold knew without a doubt that Bren was a spy, the only thing stopping him from killing the man I loved was our flimsy deal.

After learning about my restraining chip this morning, he'd ordered a doctor to surgically remove it. Bren was probably having his removed right this very minute. But instead of using our alone time to grill me for information, Renold chose to uphold his end of the deal.

I sat at the interrogation room table, uncuffed except for the thin silver collar around my neck. Either he was stupid or incredibly confident that I couldn't take him down with my bare hands. I wasn't willing to find out which. Not yet anyway.

"Shortly after I adopted you," he began, slowly pacing the length of the room, "I knew it was time for the next phase in my plan. I needed more resources, and when I heard rumors of a technology-advanced city, I sent Dr. Stacey, one of my best elites, to infiltrate their stronghold. She quickly learned that they couldn't be trusted. Dr. Moore has repeatedly tried to gain access to this city's secrets with the intent to exploit them. None of the attempts were successful until I allowed Mr. Bearon entrance."

Did he know that Dr. Stacey was dead? I was tempted to ask, curious how he'd react, but I wouldn't jeopardize the advantage he was giving me. The more he shared, the more fuel I had to find a way out of this mess.

"So you knew all along that Bren was a spy?"

"Dr. Stacey warned me, yes. But with his past ties to the Recruiter Clan, I had to see if you remembered him." He stopped to pierce me with a look. "Using him to test you failed, though. He's become your weakness."

He clasped his hands behind his back and resumed pacing. "Still, knowledge is power. If I'm to remain in control, I must know my enemy's agenda. The weak are afraid of change, and Dr. Moore is against the next step in our evolution. Before the Silent War, money and social status ruled the world. But hierarchy balanced on material wealth is easily destroyed. It is the very essence of a person's DNA that defines one's worth and ability to rule over another. Which was why we sought to unearth mankind's true potential."

A cold chill snuck up my spine. "We?"

"My great grandfather was a part of an elite group of scientists dedicated to advancing the human race. Back then, a military branch of the United States funded their efforts, but when the government deemed the project too dangerous, it was shut down. Undeterred by simple-minded thinking, the scientists continued in secret. When the formula was ready, they released it on the world.

"The timing was convenient. War was already brewing, so when the virus spread, it was easily blamed on the government who betrayed us. Ninety percent of the population died as a result, but with change comes great sacrifice. The virus chose to spare the best of us. Sadly, no one was exempt from the selection, and my great grandfather was the only original scientist to survive. He groomed his son to carry on the family work, and now the cause rests on my shoulders. It's been our family's secret for a hundred years, but not even my wife and daughter know. Only the strongest heir earns the right to such knowledge, which is why I adopted you."

No. Freaking. Way.

Renold's great grandfather brought on the *apocalypse*?

That explained a lot, actually. Renold was a diabolical monster. Maybe the trait ran in the family.

I must have been in shock because I managed to say in a completely calm voice, "Why not Rose? She's your flesh and blood."

He brought his hands forward to study his gold and sapphire rings. "Lineage isn't everything. Superior DNA doesn't always get passed down, and Rose was born unchanged. Defective. When my wife couldn't have more children, I began searching for the perfect heir. Many children have been brought into this city, but none as strong as you."

His pale eyes gleamed as they met mine. He was like a teacher basking in his student's success. A proud father. Never in my life had I experienced mental whiplash this severe.

"If you want me so badly, then why did you let me leave the city? Weren't you afraid I wouldn't come back?"

He flashed a disapproving frown, one I was much more accustomed to. "Fear is weakness, Lune. No, I knew Mr. Bearon would return to Blue Ridge Sector, and that Mr. Jones would bring you back. With Dr. Stacey's help, the risk of you staying at The Ridge was low. Your connection with Bren assured you'd be allowed access to their training facility, which needed to happen so I could confirm the extent of your abilities. But more importantly, I had to make sure that the girl destined to be my downfall was *you*."

Holy freaking crap, he knew. He knew *everything*.

He held up his hands in a placating manner, no doubt sensing a spike in my emotions. "Yes, I know it's you, but who's to say we can't change this premonition? Everything can be bent and shaped to our will. And now that you know the full story, I'm hoping you'll choose the path of enlightenment. Dr. Moore thinks I'm building an army to unleash war on the world. But as a division of Homeland Security, The Ridge is more likely to wage war than I am.

"Anything they consider a threat is infiltrated and shut down. They're ignorantly repeating history all over again, willing to destroy decades of painstaking research simply because they fear change."

"How could they not when you impregnate women against their will and kidnap children to contend in a trio of deadly Trials?" I couldn't help but point out. If he was going to punish me for asking a disrespectful question, now would be the time.

But his expression remained amiable, putting me on edge. The full might of his persuasive powers were being used to win me over. "I want to show you something. Come." He rapped a knuckle on the door, and none other than Lars poked his head inside. "Escort us to the research wing, Mr. Cooper."

"Yes, Supreme Elite," he said respectfully, but I didn't miss the way his eyes narrowed on my bare wrists.

Oh. Was he nervous? He should be. I made a show of leaving my seat and striding toward the door with confidence despite the tremor in my legs. We walked the halls in silence, running across a doctor and a few guards, but otherwise, we were alone. Then why did I feel like we were being watched? The hairs on my arms stood on end every time we passed a door. Each one had a narrow window, but the insides were dark.

"You look cold. Here."

The feel of Renold's white coat sliding over my bare shoulders sent a shiver through me, and not the good kind. I accepted the offer with a forced smile, stuffing my hands through the arm holes when I'd much rather stomp on the thing. His scent—biting, like a cold winter's wind—wrapped around me. I stopped breathing.

"Do you sense them?"

I grimaced. Talking meant I had to breathe. "Sense what?"

"Their insane minds screaming to be liberated. Don't worry, they can't get out of those rooms. They're escape-proof."

Dread trickled down my spine. "*Who* can't escape?"

"Berserkers, of course. The ones who lost all control of their abilities. Sadly, once madness grabs hold of the mind, instinct takes over the body, making them dangerous to others. It's the mutation's sole flaw, one that I've worked tirelessly to eradicate. The mind and body must be strong at all times, which is why weakness is not tolerated."

So the citizens who went missing were *Berserkers*? But at least a dozen people disappeared every year. Surely not all of them were insane. "What are you doing with them?"

"I keep them from hurting anyone and they provide me with blood and DNA samples. Occasionally, I have to run a test, but an able mind and body are better for such things."

They're not science experiments! I desperately wanted to shout, but the twisted man beside me was beyond reasoning with. Instead, I said, "So you breed women who have a greater chance of producing babies with strong, mutated genes?"

He nodded as if proud of my deduction skills. "Precisely. And the children who hold promise are brought to Tatum City."

"And the Elite Trials?"

"They're necessary to test an individual's worth, making the selection process easier. But the Trials you speak of are just a small part of the whole."

He chose that moment to turn and dismiss Lars, who looked ready to protest but simply bowed, marching off at an agitated clip. I wanted to join him. I wanted to grab his set of keys and lock myself in one of these rooms. Because Renold was pressing his hand to a print scanner, ushering me inside a door. Beyond was another set of glass doors. A woman wearing a doctor's coat was exiting those doors and approaching us.

And I knew, just *knew* that something awful was about to happen. My gut was a swooping mess of nerves warning me to run, demanding I save myself from the untold horrors within.

But I didn't move a muscle when the woman stopped in front of us, throwing me a curious look before acknowledging Renold. "Supreme Elite."

"Are the subjects under, Dr. Yale?" he said by way of greeting.

Her brown eyes flicked to me again, but quickly looked away. "Yes, sir. Subjects three-two-one and three-two-nine are ready for you. Do you require assistance?"

"No, I'll handle this myself."

She nodded and stepped aside. Everything after that was surreal. The glass doors swept open, revealing a brightly lit room sectioned off into square, glass cubicles. They were empty. Except for two. And inside those cubicles were two unconscious people.

The girl who looked like me and the man who carried my heart.

Iris was strapped to a bed, her dark red hair a smear of color against the white sheets.

And Bren was held upright by a harness across his bare chest. Chains from the ceiling were attached to the wrists above his head.

Even his ankles were cuffed.

Iris. She had a collar around her neck. Like mine.

But it was the varying shades of bagged liquid flowing down tubes and *into* Bren's body that drove blades of fear through my chest. I swallowed again and again until I was finally able to speak. "What is this?"

"The next to final phase in the Elite Trials."

My hands began to shake. "And what's the final phase?"

"Sharing my legacy with the rest of the world. There will be a careful selection process, of course. Only those who prove themselves worthy are fit to rule this world. Once order is restored as it *should* be, we can expand. Take back the lost cities. War won't be necessary because everyone will clearly know their place."

"And where's my place?" My voice trembled, but Renold didn't seem to notice. He was beaming. *Beaming.*

"I made you an Elite Guardian for a reason, Lune. Your job is to protect my legacy. You will stand by my side when we petition other cities to enter the selection. One thing people understand is power, and when they see what you can do, they'll want to follow you. *Be* like you. But only the chosen can obtain great power."

"Chosen?"

He turned to me, laying a gentle hand on my shoulder. I felt the weight like a thousand bricks. "Those with the ability to carry superior DNA within themselves. You and I," he said almost reverently, "are chosen ones. The world was meant to bow at our feet."

Metal chains rattled as Bren suddenly tensed up. A tremor went through his body. Tendons stood out on his neck. With his eyes still closed, he arched his back and screamed.

The harrowing sound shook me to the core. "What's happening?" I demanded, curling my fingers into fists. So help me, I was going to slug Renold in the face if he didn't answer me in two seconds. "What's happening!"

"Calm yourself," he said, a slight edge to his tone. "It's all part of the selection process. If he is worthy to receive the superior DNA, his body will adjust to the enhancement."

Wait. He injected Bren with *enhancement serum*? The same stuff that Ryker said would help him defeat his father?

I jammed my fists into the pockets of the coat I wore so they wouldn't do anything stupid, like break Renold's nose. "And what if he isn't worthy?"

Please don't say it, please don't say it, please don't—

"Then he'll become a Berserker or die."

All the air in my lungs rushed out of me. I would have lunged for the glass cubicle and tore out as many of the tubes as I could before Renold could stop me, but something unexpected happened. My knuckles brushed against an object in my left coat pocket. It was thin and metal, about the size of a key.

A key, or perhaps a tool. A tool that could unlock a collar?

Still unconscious, Bren continued to convulse as serum that could kill him pumped through his veins. The sight was too much, and I had to look away.

And that's when Renold moved, opening the glass door to Bren's cubicle.

This was my chance. I didn't give myself time to second-guess my decision. Deal or no deal, I couldn't stand by and watch the love of my life being tortured. While Renold was preoccupied with checking Bren's vitals, I palmed the tool. My other hand went to my neck, feeling along the collar's smooth surface for any holes. When I found one, I quickly raised the tool.

My fingers trembled. My heart thundered.

The tool slid inside the hole.

Perfect fit.

I twisted the thin metal and waited to hear a *click* that would free me, allowing me to take control of Renold's mind and—

Wild pain shot down my spine, freezing me in place. My knees gave out and I crumpled to the floor, writhing as agony tore at my brain. A face flashed before me. Eyes made of chipped ice. He wriggled the tool from my stiff fingers, shaking his head in disappointment. Then showed me a small, square device. His thumb was pressed over a button.

Hot tears welled up and I squeezed my eyes shut.

I failed.

The pain switched off before I could lose consciousness.

Aftershocks twitched through my muscles as Renold crouched, a heavy frown on his face. "Did you really think I'd be so careless? Maybe your only thought was to react, and that's why you continue to fail."

He sighed, shaking his head again. "If you won't cooperate of your own free will, then I have no choice but to enact my backup plan." He dragged me to my feet and over to the empty cubicle beside Bren's. I weakly struggled against his grip, hooking my ankle around his. He lurched forward, letting me go as he stumbled into a metal cart. Shiny objects flew everywhere with a resounding *clang*.

I was scrambling for a scalpel when pain streaked down my spine again. I crashed to the floor once more, screaming in agony and frustration. Renold picked himself up and loomed over me. His raw expression bled with an emotion I'd never seen him expose before.

Rage.

Fear flooded my veins when he continued to ooze fury

without releasing the button. I didn't know how much longer my body could withstand the pain. Renold stared and stared and stared, his face a mask of loathing and hatred.

For years, I used to think that I'd die by his hand. That one day, I would push him too far and he'd tip over the edge. Maybe that day had arrived.

Darkness crowded my vision. My eyes drifted shut.

"You *know* how much I value loyalty," he snapped, "and you betrayed me anyway."

I cracked my eyes open, if only to see his frustration at not bending me to his will. Even in my final moments, I refused to beg.

You cannot break me.

With a hiss, he released the button and pocketed the device.

I was too numb, too weak, too exhausted to fight when he picked me up and entered the cubicle. His coat was stripped from me. A harness was fitted over my head and snuggly strapped beneath my breasts. Chains rattled. My arms were raised. He stepped back and I sagged, but didn't fall. The restraints chafed my ribs and wrists, but held me aloft.

Eyes like twin pools of cold fire appeared before me. He was in control again, all emotion carefully tucked inside his intense gaze. "You haven't come this far simply to be destroyed. You're a chosen one, but you'll always be under *my* rule."

He smoothed a hand down his shirt, straightening his rumpled collar before adding, "All you had to do was cooperate. I would have given you everything, Lune. But, once again, you sacrificed it all for *him*. Now I have to punish you."

"Game on," I breathed.

His brow wrinkled in confusion. "Excuse me?"

My mouth slowly tipped up. Even that small effort was

tiring, but it was worth seeing Renold's growing bewilderment. "You heard me. Bring it on. Nothing you do will stop me from destroying you."

There it was again. That spark of rage.

But I didn't so much as flinch when he went nose-to-nose with me, saying coolly, "We'll see about that."

He stormed from the cubicle and sealed the door shut, pausing only to slam the tool that unlocked my collar onto a metal cart. "A simple wall separates you from your freedom. But can you get past it?"

A taunt. The start of my punishment. It was effective, reminding me of the very thing I'd fought, bled, and been willing to die for all these years.

But my smile remained.

Dr. Yale arrived shortly after. Her eyes widened when she spotted the mess on the floor. But when she saw my smile, her face drained of color, and she quickly ducked out of sight.

I continued to smile as my hands grew numb and sleep pulled at my eyelids.

Because Renold had revealed his cards.

Dominic had been right. I was the linchpin, the chink in his armor. His pride wouldn't allow him to kill me.

I would be the Supreme Elite's downfall because I was his ultimate weakness.

CHOSEN

Every time Bren screamed, a tiny piece of me shriveled up and died.

I was running out of pieces.

Endless hours passed. Maybe days.

Neither Bren nor Iris had regained consciousness, not when Dr. Yale continued to sedate them. She sedated me too, but only to keep me calm as she attached wires and multiple tubes to my body. Forcing me to hear Bren's screams was probably a part of Renold's punishment.

At one point, I dozed off, awaking to a stiff neck and nausea. The sick feeling wasn't from whatever they were putting in my body though. It was a warning. Ignoring my sore neck, I whipped my head to the right, seeing Bren's dangling form first, then Iris's bed.

She was no longer in it.

Just as panic squeezed my throat, the door to my cubicle opened and Renold stepped in.

"Good, you're awake." He fiddled with the bags feeding my tubes, replacing a few.

I licked my dry lips. "Where's Iris?"

"Safe."

"Where. Is. She."

At my clipped tone, he calmly met my stare. There was no need for rage—he was in control. "She's in the ability testing wing. I don't usually run tests on children, but if you prove to be an unsuitable heir, then I must get her ready to fill your shoes. She may not be my first choice, but her abilities are just as strong as yours. They're quite remarkable, actually."

Fear for my sister shot through me. As I twisted my wrists in their padded cuffs, the chains from above jangled, drawing Renold's gaze. With a faint smirk, he returned to his task.

Evil piece of charger dung.

"Test me instead," I said, hating that the words were almost a plea. "I'll cooperate. I'll be your heir if you leave her alone."

He chuckled lightly, wrapping a length of rubber around my bicep and cinching it tight. "The time for deals has passed, Lune. I will make use of you in other ways until you can be properly controlled." He positioned a needle at my inner elbow. When it punctured my skin, I grimaced, inhaling deeply to dispel a wave of nausea.

"In what ways?" I asked when I could speak again.

"I need your blood for a new serum," he murmured. Red liquid bubbled up a tube attached to the fresh needle. I tracked the blood, *my* blood being forced from my body and into a plastic bag.

Time slowly ticked by as I watched my blood drip, drip, drip into the bag. When the bag was plump and glossy, filled to bursting, chills trembled through me.

Renold returned to replace the full bag with another. Then he started to chat as if stealing people's blood was an everyday occurrence. Crap, maybe it was. "This will leave you weak but not completely drained. All the vitamins and minerals pumping into your system will speed along the reproduction of more blood. I'll need a lot if I'm to replicate your DNA exactly."

I swallowed past a dry throat. "And what is the serum for?"

He studied me a moment before saying, "It will be the ultimate test of one's inner strength. A careful selection of DNA strands from each of the known ability types will make up this new serum. It'll grant immeasurable power or certain death to those who take it. Only fate can decide which."

"I'm assuming you'll be taking this serum?"

"Of course. I'm one of the chosen."

I barked a short laugh. He frowned. "What if it kills you?"

"It won't," he said with a touch of annoyance. "Once I've taken the new serum, I'll be indestructible."

"You're bluffing," I goaded. "You'll still be human. Humans aren't indestructible."

"Oh?" His lips twisted into a devilish grin. "Shall we test that theory on Mr. Bearon? I enhanced his Sensor genes. His strength, predator instincts, and the swiftness with which he heals—all given a powerful boost. He'll make a formidable bodyguard once his memories are erased."

My heart forgot how to beat.

"You . . . you mean *blocked*, right? His memories will be blocked, like mine were?" Panic pitched my voice higher. I couldn't hide it. I couldn't mask the emotions welling up within me. "Memories can't be erased."

Renold gave me a knowing look. "Oh, but they can. Dr. Stacey convinced The Ridge's top scientist to perfect the memory serum I provided. He made an antidote, it's true, but only for the original memory-blocker serum. The new and improved serum that you and Mr. Jones so kindly delivered to me has no cure."

Stars above, *no!*

Before I could succumb to a full-blown panic attack, he strode from my cubicle, pausing to pick up a scalpel from the metal cart outside. His white coat swirled behind him as he entered Bren's cubicle.

It felt like someone was sitting on my chest. I struggled for air but found none. "Don't hurt him."

Ignoring me, he placed the sharp blade against Bren's stomach. "What will you do to stop this?" he said, his voice still loud enough to hear through the glass.

My chin quivered. "Anything. Absolutely anything."

Renold's eyes narrowed to slits. "Then *beg* me to spare him."

And with those words, he finally found a way to break me.

Because when he tightened his grip and dragged the scalpel across Bren's stomach, I knew that at last—at long last—I would do it.

I would beg my adoptive father for mercy to save my soulmate's life.

"Please stop! *Please!* I beg you not to hurt him!" I shouted, jerking against my harness. Tubes and bags filled with liquid swayed as I thrashed.

Renold stopped. He turned my way. But there was no victory in his eyes. Only cold fury. "What did you say?"

I searched for the wound he'd inflicted—Bren hadn't even cried out. When I found nothing but smooth skin, my mouth formed a puzzled frown.

"*What* did you say?" Renold repeated with heat this time.

I forced myself to look at him. "I said *please.*"

His lips peeled back in a silent snarl. "After all this time, you submit because of *him*? I warned you. Caring has distracted you from what is most important, and it's time I cut out that weakness."

Without even a flicker of hesitation, he raised the scalpel and stabbed Bren in the chest.

"No!" I screamed. Bren jerked awake with a grunt. "Bren!"

Renold pulled the scalpel free. The blade glistened red. I cried out again, yelling Bren's name, staring in horror at the puncture wound over his heart. Then it happened. I wouldn't have believed it if the miracle wasn't happening right in front of me.

The blood on Bren's chest stopped trickling as the wound sealed shut.

Renold released a surprised laugh. "He survived." He stabbed Bren again. I was too overcome with shock to even whimper.

Bren was staring at his chest. Silently observing the scalpel's retreat and the fresh wound's disappearance. I must have made a noise. Must have broken through the haze he seemed to be stuck in, because his eyes lifted. And found mine.

I gasped. His eyes. They pulsed with an otherworldly light. His pupils were pinpricks, barely there. He swept his gaze over my body, taking in the harness and tubes. He froze on the bags of my blood.

Suddenly, his eyes were fire. He swung them toward Renold.

Something else happened then. Something I never thought I'd ever see. Renold stumbled back, and there was fear, *fear* stamped on his face.

Tendons and veins protruded from Bren's neck and arms as he jerked against his restraints. The chains rattled menacingly.

Renold wheeled, grabbing a syringe from the metal cart. He quickly jabbed the needle into Bren's bulging bicep. And that wasn't the only part of him swelling with new muscle. His whole body was. His thighs had thickened, his chest and abs more de-fined.

And was I staring at an *eight pack?* Yes. Yes, I was.

Once Bren was under again, the visible tension in Renold's shoulders eased. He even chuckled a bit before saying, "Well, Mr. Bearon may be a spy, but he's proven himself worthy today. He's been chosen to be a part of the new human race."

My brain short-circuited. "New human *what*?"

He turned to me with a victorious smile. "The new Elite race. It's why the old world had to die. Nothing this monumental could have happened in a world focused on monetary gain. But after tireless decades dedicated to improving humanity and erasing defects, we are ready for a new era led by a master race."

I couldn't hide my disgust. "We're not *gods*, Renold." I remembered Bren telling me that his first day in Tatum City.

His gaze held fake sympathy, like he pitied my stupidity. "I can't expect you to understand. You haven't received a higher education and don't know the power of science. That will all change soon. The Elite race will be gifted with knowledge. They will receive everything the world has to offer."

"Sounds like you're creating *monsters*."

Anger sparked in his eyes. "Is it monstrous to want perfection? I told you from the beginning that it's about control. Control your impulses. Your wayward reactions. Why do you think I never punished you with my bare hands all these years?"

I jerked my head back as if struck.

He prowled toward me, looking every inch a predator in that moment. "I know my triggers and limits. My Sensor instincts demand submission, and when you wouldn't, it drove me mad. But I *controlled* those urges, same as any true Elite will."

He stopped just inside my cubicle. "Losing control is weakness and the path to becoming a Berserker. It's why you consider *yourself* a monster. But I didn't create that weakness, Lune. You did."

Hours later when all was silent with Bren still unconscious and Iris returned to her bed, I continued to replay Renold's words.

He was right. Fear of losing control had become my weakness, and ultimately, that fear had controlled me.

But not anymore.

I was going to embrace the chaos within me. Only then could I break free of the fear.

Weeping filled my ears. Ragged sobs of anguish. The cries grew louder, drowning out the animal roars and screams of dying people.

I jerked awake, eyes fluttering open to the sound of my own whimpers. The dream's vivid imagery still clouded my mind. I released a shuddering breath, blinking to clear away the tears. I checked on Iris first, relieved to see her still asleep on the bed. But when I checked on Bren, it was to find his golden eyes already on me.

My heart tripped and somersaulted.

We continued to stare in silence. There was something different about his gaze. Something preternaturally still. It was more than a predator's keen focus.

It was wild. Wholly wild.

I swallowed. When his eyes tracked the bob of my throat, I sucked in a breath. "Bren?"

He didn't respond. Didn't react. Simply stared. It was too heavy. Too intense. *Too much, too much*. I looked away. Nervous confusion fluttered in my belly. Did the serum alter his brain?

Maybe he was a Berserker. No, he couldn't be. Renold wouldn't have called him one of the chosen if he was.

Right?

Panicked breaths reached my ears. Mine. The more I tried to slow them, the faster they became.

He can't be. He can't be. He can't—

"It's . . . okay. I'm . . . okay."

My eyes widened at the sound of those familiar words uttered from a stranger's voice. It wasn't the deep, rolling timbre I knew so well. The voice was gruff. Like grinding stone.

"Bren," I gasped, frantically searching his face for answers.

His jaw hardened and he grimaced, turning away.

What the—?

"Bren, please. Tell me what's happening. I don't know how you're feeling and—"

"I'm fine." The words thundered from him and I flinched, startled by the unexpected volume. At my reaction, his head whipped my way. I swallowed a gasp at his crestfallen look. "Please don't be afraid of me, little bird."

My lips started to tremble. "Oh, Bren, I'm so sorry. I'm so sorry for what he did to you."

I saw the shame and vulnerability in his eyes before he hid his gaze from me again. It broke my heart. He was still him, I could see that now. But the voice that had comforted me for so long, that couldn't even be wiped from my memories, was gone.

"Everything is so . . . loud," he said, sounding more bear than man. I forced myself not to cry. Not to mourn the loss of something precious. The time for that would come—and it would hit me hard—but in his moment of weakness, he needed me to be strong.

"My skin . . . feels stretched too thin. And there's this buzz, right beneath the surface. It's wild and powerful."

He finally looked at me, his expression raw horror. "I'm afraid of what I'll do if I'm set free."

My chin was wobbling now, no matter how tightly I pressed my lips together. He was scared of who he was. I understood that fear all too well. "You're still you, Brendan Bearon," I said past the tears clogging my throat. "The man whose gentle strength thawed my cold heart. The man who reminded me that I'm not alone. The man who would sacrifice everything for the people he loves. That is who you were, who you *still* are—strong, brave, selfless. And I'll never give up on that man."

He studied me with those wild eyes, skittish and uncertain. But my gaze didn't waver. Not this time. Not when I needed to prove how much I meant every single one of those words.

I hadn't realized how tense he was until his shoulders drooped, the hard lines of his body relaxing. He sighed, clearly exhausted.

"What do you see in your future?" I asked him quietly, hoping to put his mind at ease as well. "When all of this is over, what's the one thing that you want to happen?"

His brow furrowed, then he shook his head. "I've never . . . I've never thought that far. I never let myself."

"Try," I whispered, encouraging him.

He frowned some more, deep in thought. Eventually, he cleared his throat, the sound like a tumbling boulder. His mouth tipped into the barest of smiles as he said, "I see a wedding. Our friends and family are there. It's outside, the trees a vibrant mix of golds, oranges, and reds. You're wearing a pretty white dress, and your hair is up so I can see the graceful curve of your neck that I love so much."

My laugh ended in a hiccuping sob.

He smiled softly and I forgot all about the gruffness of his voice. "When you walk down the aisle, you're holding flowers. I'm not sure what color they are, but they're not blue. When your eyes lift to mine, I . . . I stop breathing. Inwardly, I'm saying, 'How? How can this perfectly exquisite creature want me? She's so pure and good, and I don't deserve her.' But I marry her anyway, thanking the heavens for this precious gift. I sweep her into my arms and carry her all the way to our new home. There's pine trees and a little house that I helped build, nestled beside a sparkling lake."

I was openly crying now, silent tears dripping off my chin. Bren's voice was hushed, choked with emotion as he finished sharing with me the vision of his future—the vision I desperately wanted to become real.

"The lake is almost too cold, but that doesn't stop me. I carry you in, pretty white dress and all. And there, I make love to you. I don't even notice the water surrounding us. All of my past fears and failures have been washed away. In that moment, I only know peace and joy and happiness. Because my salvation, my everything, is in my arms."

Silence settled between us. A comfortable one filled with yearning hope. After a while, Bren sighed, a faint smile still playing about his lips. "What about you, little bird? What's the one thing that you want in your future?"

I didn't even have to think about it. "To be the lucky girl in your arms."

BERSERKER

The faint *click* of a door unlocking woke me from a rare dream of hopes and wishes. When my eyes opened, the darkness was absolute. My heart skipped several beats, panic setting in. I startled at the rustling of chains.

"It's just me." It took me way too long to identify the voice as Bren's. I ignored the swift pang of sadness, focusing on his words. "There's been a power outage. It could mean nothing, or everything."

"Can you see anything?" A faint scraping noise sent my heart to skipping again.

"Yeah. No one's in here but you, me, and Iris. But there's movement coming from beyond the main doors. With the power down, doors like those would have to be forced open. Wait. Someone's doing just that. Forcing their way in. It's . . ."

A fierce growl suddenly ripped through the darkness. Every hair on my body stood on end. The growl became words as Bren snarled, "What are *you* doing here?"

Cackling laughter echoed around us, bouncing off the walls and burrowing beneath my skin. I didn't need sight to know who had just entered. Bren growled again, the sound more animal than man. Nervous energy zipped through me when his restraints furiously clanged together.

"Don't touch her, you piece of filth. Don't you dare—"

Fingers touched my cheek. As I yanked away from the hand, Bren let out an unearthly roar that practically shook the floor.

"Shut your trap, outsider," drawled the voice in front of me. "I'll deal with you soon enough."

With a sharp *click*, light blasted my eyes, blinding me all over again. It took precious seconds to blink the spots away. When they cleared, Lars's gloating face came into view.

"Hello, Mute," he purred, placing a lantern on the floor beside him. "Miss me?"

I ignored the asinine question. "Why are you here, Lars?"

"Just doing a little research. Everyone's all frantic with the electricity out, giving me an opportunity to finally get some answers. I know the Supreme Elite has let you in on his secret plans. Tell me what they are and I'll leave the meathead alone. Well, after I rough him up a bit. Payback for giving me this *scar*." He jabbed a finger at the ugly X on his cheek.

I barked a laugh despite the frantic pounding of my heart. "Release me and I'll tell you. Don't worry, my *collar* is still working," I crooned, prodding his ego.

He hesitated, but I knew he'd give in. Knew he couldn't pass up the chance to prove himself. Sure enough, he reached for my harness. "Try anything and you'll pay," he hissed, purposefully dragging his knuckles over my breasts.

I bit back a snarl, but Bren didn't. He loosed a flurry of curses and threats. Lars ignored him, but I didn't miss the tremble in his fingers as they unbuckled my wrist cuffs. When the last restraint fell away, I swayed on legs that felt like rubber. Tubes still protruded from my body and I pulled the needles out, wincing at the sting. Lars had backed up a step, and I used the opportunity to stumble toward the door.

He gripped my arm, stopping me from leaving the cubicle, but I was close. So close. I slumped against the glass beside the door, catching my breath. My show of weakness was only partly an act.

"Now tell me," he ordered. "Tell me what your father is planning. He hinted at more Trials. I want to know how I can further my status."

"You can't."

He scowled, crowding my personal space as he snapped, "Why not?"

I leaned to the side, far enough to grasp the glass door frame for leverage. "Simple. You can't contend in any more Trials because you're not *worthy*."

He froze, his dark gaze boiling with shocked rage.

This was the time to strike. To try a maneuver I'd never attempted before. It was dirty and brutal. But it was the only way.

I reached between his legs and gave his jewels a sharp twist. He fell to his knees with a grunt, and I shoved him backward into the lantern. Light flashed and spun crazily as I lunged for the metal cart. But I was weaker than I thought. My shoulder glanced off the door when I exited the cubicle, causing me to lose my balance.

I fell sideways into the cart. Metal objects crashed to the floor and so did I. Something sharp sliced through my palm and I hissed. The floor grew slick with my blood, but I didn't slow.

"You're going to pay for that!" Lars shouted. He stormed after me.

My searching grew frantic. *Where is it, where is it!*

And then I saw it—my *freedom*—scant inches away, winking at me knowingly.

Before I could reach out, a boot stomped on my spine,

pinning me to the floor. Air gushed from my lungs, but I managed to palm the tool and slip it between my teeth.

Lars grabbed my other arm and wrenched it behind me. I groaned, my shoulder shrieking in agony, but I kept my lips firmly sealed. Hot breath hit my ear as he hissed, "You're not going to be so high and mighty after this." His laugh was demented. "You'll do whatever I say when I've humbled you a bit."

He bent my arm even higher before allowing his other hand to rove my body. Revulsion shivered through me. He yanked my tank top up, and that's when my thoughts switched off. I was running on instinct and barely restrained adrenaline. If I concentrated on what he was doing, panic would consume me. My reactions were under control. All I had to do now was free myself.

The process was slow and painful. Twisting my collar around to find the keyhole without him noticing took patience, and time was running out. Despite my best efforts to ignore him, Lars wasn't playing. He may not know what claiming meant, but Sensor instinct was controlling his movements.

And then there was Bren. He hadn't stopped roaring and yanking on his chains. I feared what the sight of Lars touching me was doing to him. Feared that he'd go Berserker in his need to protect me.

So I renewed my efforts, blindly feeling for the small notch. When I found it, I carefully slid the tool from my mouth and fit it to the hole. My fingers trembled uncontrollably. With Lars so close, any metallic noise could alert him to what I was—

Click.

Everything went silent.

Lars suddenly flipped me onto my back. I cried out as he dug a knee into my sternum. He reached for the collar, swearing colorfully when it fell open in his grasp.

"Gotcha." My lips formed a wicked smirk.

Before I could say anything else, his hands were around my neck. "Treacherous snake," he spat. "You think you can best me? Let me show you how powerless you really are."

And then he squeezed.

Adrenaline, sweet adrenaline kicked in.

Instead of fighting him, I dove into my mind. Energy whipped around and inside me, growing in volume despite my restricted air flow. The stronger the current became, though, the more my brain screamed for oxygen.

Hold on, hold on.

Just a few more seconds . . .

And I could make this all . . .

"Stop."

Lars released me immediately, but darkness crowded my vision, nearly breaking my concentration. "Get off me," I demanded, quickly dragging in air when his weight lifted.

I tried to sit up, but the world tilted dangerously. I lay back down as my control over him began to slip. If he broke free of my mind control, I wouldn't be strong enough to fight him off a second time.

There was only one thing I could do, regardless of the consequences.

"Release Bren."

His movements were robotic as he stood to do my bidding. Bren grew still, deathly so, watching Lars like a hawk. I should feel guilty—and I almost did—for making Lars unchain the thing, the *man* that could kill him. He looked so small and helpless next to Bren's hulking form. But I didn't pull back from his mind, didn't order him to stop as he deftly unbuckled the harness, then the ankle cuffs bolted to the floor.

Dizziness suddenly crashed into me like a tidal wave.

I lost track of time and space, floundering to reach the surface.

When I came to again, it was to find Lars's soulless eyes inches from mine. I'd lost control.

Without a word, he reared back and punched my face. I quickly curled onto my side, protecting my head. "You're done, Mute. Done!" he shrieked. Pain pulsed through me as he kicked my back.

Now I was the helpless one, too drained of blood and strength to defend myself. I tried burrowing into my mind again, but dizziness prevented me from absorbing more energy. I almost blacked out as Lars's boot connected with the back of my head. It was the musical notes of jangling metal that chased the darkness away. I peeked through my arms in time to see Bren grab the chains above his head and pull. With the rest of his body now unrestrained, he might have the leverage to—

One of the heavy metal chains snapped like a twig. He didn't bother unbuckling the cuffs. Simply snapped the other chain too.

Lars chose that moment to grip my hair. He yanked my head back and encircled my throat again. I clawed at his hold, but my hands were slick with blood from the cut on my palm.

I frantically looked to Bren.

I needed him. I needed him to save me.

But he had stopped. A glass wall separated us. Lars had shut his cubicle door, locking him inside. The fingers at my throat squeezed and squeezed. I kicked and bucked, but for once, Lars was protecting his weak spots.

Bren backed up. He charged. Glass shattered as he broke

through the wall. A few pieces pelted my skin, but I was too desperate for air to even feel them.

And then he was there, looming over Lars like a vengeful god. With one swift move, he pried the hands from my neck. And broke them. Lars let out a blood-curdling scream. The sound ended in a wet gurgle as Bren gripped his throat and lifted him off his feet.

I sagged, struggling to inhale through a bruised throat. By sheer force of will, I stayed conscious.

"You hurt my mate," Bren seethed, his voice like gravel.

Lars managed to wheeze out laughter, saying, "Well . . . she's soiled now. I had my hands *all* over her. And . . . I think she liked it when I—"

Bren exploded into motion with a roar. And that was when I saw them. The *fangs*. Before he sank them into Lars's neck.

It was so violent. So bloody. That I was transfixed.

With a swift jerk of his head, Bren tore out Lars's throat.

Blood sprayed. It glistened darkly on both men's skin. It dripped. From Bren's chin.

When Lars's body crumpled to the floor, I knew he was dead. His jugular had been ripped open. And not by a saber cat, but by the man I loved.

He stood over Lars like a mutant beast over its kill. Stars, he *was* a mutant beast. His very genetic code had forced him to become my childhood nightmare. He was trembling, a man-beast on the verge of losing control, but I was suddenly standing.

I was approaching him, not running away like any sane person would. I was reaching out, touching his blood-soaked hand. He recoiled like I'd hurt him, backing up a step, then another.

"Don't," he panted, his broad chest heaving. "Don't touch me. I might hurt you."

There was so much pain behind those words that I could scarcely breathe. Still, I pursued him. "You promised to never push me away again, Brendan Bearon."

He grimaced, dragging an arm across his mouth. When he saw the blood, fear flickered in his eyes. He stared at Lars's destroyed body as if seeing it for the very first time. "What have I done?" he croaked. "I didn't mean to. There was so much rage and I couldn't control it."

"Bren." I stepped forward each time he stepped back. No way was he running. No way was I losing him. No. Way.

He yanked a hand through his hair, flinching when strands stuck to his bloody palm. "Take Iris and go. I'll stay here, maybe try to lock myself in one of the holding cells."

"I'm not leaving you here, Bren," I said firmly, getting close enough to touch him again. "You're not a Berserker. I trust you with my life."

"Don't you dare trust me, Lune Avery!" he thundered. "I'm not safe." And instead of retreating, he grabbed my arms and shook me. My eyes were wide, jaw unhinged as he thrust his face near mine and bared his fangs.

I should have been scared out of my mind. I should have been disgusted by the coppery smell of blood on his skin. I should have been a million things—*anything*—other than relieved.

But his grip on my arms was gentle. And I knew, just *knew* that he was still him. Still my Bren. So I stepped into him. Raised my hands to his face and said, "You *are* my safety." When he didn't resist my touch, I carefully wiped the blood from his mouth. "Don't take that away from me just because you're scared." I rubbed at the blood on his chin in vain, only smearing it further. "You need something, and I'm going to give it to you now."

Those final words broke him.

He folded inward, dropping his hands as I drew him to me. His body, built for strength, speed, and predator-like precision, collapsed against mine. My arms were around him, my cheek pressed to his blood-spattered heart when a violent shudder shook him. He pulled me even closer and buried his face in my hair, choking back sobs.

My very soul ached at the wretched sounds. Weeped at its other half's misery. But it was here. *I* was here. And all we could do was comfort our soulmate, be there as he mourned the loss of his former self. We both mourned with him.

He suddenly stiffened, lifting his head. A growl rumbled in his chest, vibrating through mine.

"Brother."

Startled at the new voice, I tried to pull away.

Bren's arms tightened, trapping me against him as he said, "We aren't brothers. Not anymore."

SECOND CHANCES

Ryker stood inside the double doors, armed to the teeth.

None of his weapons were pointed at us, but I knew better than to trust his relaxed pose. "Are you friend or foe?" I asked, prying myself from Bren's grip to face him.

Ignoring the question, he said, "The villagers did their thing with the power outage, and everything else has been set into motion. But you know I can't speak of it." He tapped at where the restraining chip lay hidden. "So let's not waste this opportunity by bickering over loyalties. Is she able to be moved?"

I looked to where he was gesturing.

Iris!

I hurried to her, picking up the tool I'd dropped and the discarded lantern along the way. I touched her hair and cheek. Still unconscious. Covered in a white hospital gown, her thin frame was free of tubes except the one keeping her sedated and another for bodily fluids. My fingers shook as I twisted the tool to unlock her collar.

Or, at least, I tried to.

"It's not . . . it's not turning. Why is it not—?"

A hand stayed my movements, loosening my hold on the tool. Startled, I jerked away, clenching the tool in a death grip.

"Calm down," Ryker said, reaching for the tool again. "I'll do this while you—"

Bren was suddenly in between us, shoving Ryker back. Whether he meant to push him that hard or not, Ryker hit the cubicle wall.

In a flash, they were nose-to-nose, bristling with aggression.

"What's your problem?" Ryker growled.

"Don't touch my mate," Bren snarled, baring his elongated canines. Ryker tensed but held his ground.

Crap, we did *not* have time for this.

"*Boys,*" I snapped, getting their attention by wedging myself between them. "You can go at it when we're out of this mess. We have a lot of people to set free."

Ryker glared at Bren a moment more before holding out his hand. "Let me work on the collar. Your friend Asher made contact with you-know-who the way he usually does an hour ago. But they need an update on progress inside the bunker. Tell them we're on our way out."

I nodded, relinquishing the tool with a warning look. If anything happened to Iris because of him, I'd have his head.

Before I could form a mind connection that would suck more of my dwindling energy, Ryker murmured, "What happened to him?"

Bren heard but only snorted, crossing his arms. The action puffed up his chest even more, an intentional move if I ever saw one.

I rolled my eyes. "He was injected with an enhancement serum."

Ryker studied Bren with a shrewd eye, taking in the bulging muscle and blood stains. When his gaze flicked to Lars's body, I could have sworn Bren deflated a bit. "So it's actually real? It works?"

"Oh, it worked," Bren interjected, his voice hard as granite. "But the side effects almost killed me. Then again, that's probably a risk you're willing to take. You'd do anything to remain in control of the Recruiter Clan, after all."

A muscle thrummed along Ryker's jaw, but he didn't comment. Good. At least one of them was attempting to focus on the task at hand. Not that I could blame Bren. He had suffered greatly from Ryker's past actions. We all had. It was hard to see clearly on the other side of betrayal.

While Ryker tinkered with the collar, I formed a quick mind tether with Jaxon. "*The time to stop Renold is now*," I said in parting. Once they arrived, The Ridge's stealth team led by Yukiko would rappel over the wall. The mission was to open the gates and let in the rescue team before the guards could sound an alarm. Hopefully all those war games they played in the Abilities Competition paid off tonight.

So many things could go wrong, though. The electricity could turn back on and kill anyone in contact with the wall. The guards could spot them and open fire. I gave my head a shake, reaching for the extra clothes Ryker had brought. I couldn't afford to think of worst case scenarios. There were too many.

The people involved in this mission had made a decision to sacrifice everything for a better tomorrow. One where madmen like Renold couldn't dictate their choices. Some things were worth risking everything for. My eyes rested on Iris's limp form. And if it came to it, some things were worth dying for.

I finished lacing my knee-high boots—boots that Ryker must have taken from my room in Tatum House, along with the leather pants and steel gray shirt I now wore.

I was buckling on my dagger harness when Ryker said, "The tool wasn't made for this collar. I can't get it off." My heart sank. I quickly shook off the helpless feeling and grabbed a handful of throwing knives, their solid weight a small reassurance.

"We'll figure it out later. Bren, can you carry her?" I glanced over to see him fully dressed in all black. Probably Ryker's clothes. Still, the shirt could barely contain his new muscles. As much as I appreciated the sight, though, I had to focus.

He adjusted the leather straps across his chest, a quiver of arrows and the tip of a su-yari poking over his shoulder, before answering, "I don't think I should."

I frowned when he wouldn't meet my eyes. "Why not?"

His attention went to the hands splayed in front of him—hands free of shackles and caked in dried blood. "Look at me. I can't fix this. If I lose control for even a second, I could crush her."

I stepped forward, all too aware of the way he tracked the movement, of the way heat and raw power emanated from him as I slid my hands into his. My fingers were delicate and pale as milk compared to his, but he grasped them gently. As always. I peered up into his face, capturing his gaze. "I *am* looking. And I know with absolute certainty that there's no safer place to be than in your arms. You won't hurt her. I know you won't."

When his expression clouded with doubt, my fingers squeezed his in challenge. I tugged him over to Iris, feeling fear tremor through him. But when I guided his arms around her, he didn't flinch back. Once she was secure against him—a slip of a girl cradled in the paws of a beast—it took me a moment to collect myself.

"What's wrong?" The panic in Bren's voice dragged a strangled laugh from me.

I brushed a pesky tear away. "Nothing's wrong. You're

amazing, that's all."

He looked startled by the words, but before he could reply, Ryker emerged before me, slinging a bow and arrow quiver over my head. "Focus," he said. "I didn't sneak in here just to watch you two make eyes at each other. Once we leave this room, be prepared to fight. Anyone standing in the way of our mission is the enemy. This won't be like the Elite Trials. There's no rules, no controlled environment. If you want to survive, allowing the enemy to live might not be an option."

"But they're not our enemies. Not really," I countered. "Renold is the villain here. He should be our sole target."

"He is. But what do you think he's doing right now knowing that people are trying to sabotage his work here? He can't face the insurgents alone. With the electricity down, I bet he has every single elite and then some on high alert. And what lies do you think he's told them? What deals and promises did he make to secure their loyalty so they'd faithfully follow him into battle to protect this city? Yeah. Things are going to get ugly."

There was no arguing with that. He was right. "We're going to need more numbers then." Goosepumps peppered my skin as an idea formed. I turned and approached Lars. His body had fallen face upward and I tried not to look, tried not to notice the pool of dark blood beneath him. I crouched, holding my breath as I rummaged through his pockets. When I found the keys, I quickly stood.

My eyes betrayed me then and glanced at his. They were black, empty pits. I forced myself to look away and leave without a word. I had nothing to say to him.

Renold had said that war wasn't his intention, but he'd created power-hungry elitists like Lars who would fight for him if it meant securing their futures.

War was inevitable when minds were bent on destroying others to feed their own desires. War could destroy us, but at least we were doing something. At least we were fighting back, at long last.

And we were doing it *together*.

"Once The Ridge arrives with more weapons, we'll have the advantage," Bren said when I rejoined them, his earlier vulnerability replaced with a calm sureness. "And don't forget about the villagers. They'll follow you, Lune."

I nodded, despite the doubt and worry tightening my muscles.

"So let's get out there and show them you're still alive," Ryker said, holding the lantern out to me. "A revolution needs its leader."

I gaped at him. Crap on a cookie, nope. I was *so* not the leader. But I accepted the light anyway. At least I was fully clothed now. Leading an army in underwear wouldn't have been ideal.

I had standards.

"I'm a beast-taming, kick-butt warrior princess," I whispered as we exited the room I hoped to never see again.

"Heard that," Bren and Ryker said at the same time.

Gah!

The long stretch of hallway ahead was equally dark, but we weren't alone. I could still feel them behind their locked doors. Lars's keys bit into the cut on my palm as I squeezed them, indecision a dreadful weight on my chest. I cautiously peered into one of the windows. Pitch black. Silent. Something slammed into the narrow pane of glass and I bit back a yelp.

Ryker grabbed my arm, hissing, "What are you doing?"

At Bren's warning growl, I pulled away. "They're prisoners. We have to release them." The keys clinked together as I readied to insert one in the lock.

Ryker blocked my attempt. "I was told not to let these ones

out. They're mentally unstable. If—"

"Halt!" a voice shouted.

A sizzling blue ball of electricity shot toward us. Ryker slammed my back against the wall, shielding me from the blast. As I turned to make sure Bren and Iris were safe, Ryker yanked an arrow from his quiver and aimed down the hall.

I heard a *whoosh* and *thunk*, then a loud *thud* as the guard fell. Ryker melted into the shadows, returning with a new weapon and set of keys. I didn't dare ask if the guard was dead. Instead, I narrowed my eyes at him and said, "I don't care who you've been talking to or what other tricks you have up your sleeve. We're releasing these prisoners, dangerous or not. Besides, if you haven't noticed, we're *all* a little insane."

"She has a point," Bren said in a faintly amused tone. "We should give them a chance."

Ryker's face settled into irritable lines, but he grumbled, "Fine. If they cause a problem, though, I'm zapping them."

I snorted. "Fair enough. Now help me get these doors open before more guards come."

We worked in silence, the only sound an occasional thump and rattle of metal as we struggled to fit the keys in the locks. Every time a prisoner was freed, they were greeted by an enormous man with wild, flashing gold eyes. It didn't matter that he cradled a small girl in his arms. No one moved beyond the glowing lantern set on the floor.

When the last door was unlocked, at least three dozen people were huddled in the hallway. I avoided their haunted eyes still silently begging for help. I recognized a few of them, villagers who had disappeared some time ago. They were of varying ages, the youngest barely older than me. Wearing white shorts and a tank top, she looked defeated. Broken.

I pressed my lips together and picked up the lantern, wordlessly waving them forward. Nothing I said would ease their suffering. But maybe after tonight, just maybe, they'd get a second chance at life.

Problems arose as soon as we left the research wing behind. Two more guards spotted us, alerted to the hiss of three dozen shuffling bare feet. Three freed prisoners were hit by volt darts before Ryker and I could incapacitate the threat. We dragged the guard's unconscious bodies out of the way, picked up our wounded, and hurried on. Doctors and handlers shouldn't be roaming the halls this time of night, especially with the power down, but we were still vulnerable in these narrow passages.

I readied my keys again as we neared the location of the other prisoners I'd seen a few days before. We rounded the corner only to be stopped by a guard.

"Freeze!" he barked, pointing his volt gun at my head.

Before Ryker could shoot him, I immersed into my mind, pulling energy to me with a swift tug. "*You* freeze," I ordered. When the guard obeyed, I added, "Now zap yourself."

As he crumpled to the floor in a twitching heap, I let go of the energy with a weary sigh. Several gasps and whispers leaked past the fading rush of adrenaline leaving my body.

"Conserve your strength," Bren murmured, brushing his arm against mine. "You lost a lot of blood earlier."

"They needed to see," I replied quietly, moving forward again. "They have to know that we stand a chance against Renold when we ask them to fight beside us." By revealing my power, I hoped to restore some of their own. They had abilities and we needed them.

In less than half an hour, we had gathered over fifty people.

The sharp bite of chemicals and fear permeated the air.

As Ryker reached for the stairwell door, I said, "There's a tunnel. It might be safer if—"

"We stick to the plan," he interjected, opening the door. "Tatum House is crawling with elites and we don't have enough weapons. It would be a massacre."

I shook my head but followed after him as he ascended the stairs. "How do you know so much?" *Can we trust you?* I wanted to say but didn't.

He shrugged. "I've kept myself busy."

Well, I wanted to busy myself with planting a *boot* in his back for that cryptic response. But as we neared the first floor, a tense silence settled over our group. Not even the children whimpered. We all knew what resided on this floor. I wondered how many of them had been locked inside a cage like I had. I wondered how many hadn't made it back out again.

We were whispers of air breezing through the passageways. Still, the beasts caught our scent. A chorus of roars nipped at our heels as we scurried toward the bunker's main entrance. Ryker continued to lead the way, all sure steps and confidence. I couldn't help the unease tumbling round and round in my stomach. This could be a trap. This could be Ryker's final mission before earning the enhancement serum.

I was a coiled ball of anxiety as a pair of giant steel doors materialized before us. There hadn't been a single guard on this floor, which only fueled my misgivings. Maybe the whole point was to lead us here so the mutated beasts could eat all evidence of Renold's botched science experiments.

Stop thinking, stop thinking!

I was driving myself mad.

Ryker walked right up to a hidden panel near the doors and ripped the cover off. As he pulled a red handle, a loud *click* came from the doors. When he began forcing them open, I rushed to help. Soon, several hands were aiding in the effort and the doors were sliding back, back, back, allowing moonlight to spill inside.

Never in my life had I cherished the smell of dirt and pine as I did now. I wanted to close my eyes against the sting of tears and breathe it all in, but a hand from the outside jerked me forward and into a tight hug. Behind me, Bren growled, the sound more surprise than anger. When the scent of hay tickled my nose, I returned the embrace with a shaky laugh.

"You okay?" my best friend asked.

"Yeah. I am now."

THE REVOLUTION

"So where are we at with the plan?"

Ryker gestured at Asher who seemed eager to fill me in. "We're all set to create a diversion that will keep the Supreme Elite's focus inward and not on the wall. The amount of damage done to the solar panel field should allow your friends to breach the wall and open the gates before they can restore the electricity."

Bren stepped forward. "Where is the diversion taking place?"

"We're bringing the fight to them. Tatum House."

I gaped at my best-friend-turned-strategist. "We're going *inside*? How will we manage that? Sneak through the tunnel?"

"Only some of us. But there are too many ways for the Supreme Elite to escape. The majority of us will storm the house from the outside and block off all possible exits."

"And we already have a man inside," Ryker supplied. "He'll open the front doors for us."

My eyes were bugging out now. "Who?"

"The butler." He shrugged at my dumbfounded look, adding, "Told you I've been busy. He knows a *lot* of stuff and really isn't a fan of what happens inside the bunker. I might have promised him a more exciting job if he helped us out."

A snort-laugh left me. I never saw *that* one coming. "Okay, then we'd better get going before Renold has a chance to organize the guards and elites. We have miles of ground to cover and—"

"Actually," Asher said, drawing out the word, "we're not going on foot." He grabbed my hand and tugged me toward the trees.

"Ash, what are you—?"

"Wait for it," he said with obvious excitement. We were barely past the treeline when he paused and flourished a hand. "Ta-dah!"

"Uh . . ."

"Look!" He practically danced in place, pointing at the dense forest I'd feared for so long. His dimples sunk inward like someone had poked holes in his cheeks.

I squinted into the predawn gloom, but it was the sound of wet snorts and jangling metal that clued me in. My face split into a huge grin and I practically ran into the woods. At the sight of my beloved charger, my cheeks throbbed from smiling so hard. But she wasn't the only animal tied to a tree. Stalin, Napoleon, and at least a dozen others were there too, all scrutinizing me with their eerie yellow irises.

"How?"

Asher slung an arm across my shoulders, clearly pleased with himself. "All of the stable hands are in on the plan. Feels good to work together for a change, you know?"

"Yeah." My chin quivered. "It really does."

He pulled me into another hug, planting a kiss on top of my head. A year ago, I never would have allowed us to be this close. City rules aside, I'd been afraid that caring for him too deeply would make it impossible to leave this place. But now, all I wanted to do was make up for lost time.

And so I said, "Freedom."

"Hmm?" he mumbled against my hair.

"I named my charger Freedom when I first signed a Rasa

Rowe contract."

He chuckled lightly. "I know."

"What?" I twisted in his arms to see his face.

"When you were younger, I used to catch you whispering to her all the time. You weren't very sneaky." He reached up and flicked the end of my nose.

I batted his hand away and mock-scowled. "Good thing you never let on that you knew or I would've demanded your silence in a not-so-nice way."

He guffawed, not looking the least bit scared.

Stars, it hit me then. All those years of hiding who I was and this boy always saw right through my mask. If he hadn't shared the gift of his friendship, we probably wouldn't be standing here today.

Out of everyone, I owed him the most.

"Thank you for always being there for me, Ash." I had to clear my throat as it tightened. "I couldn't have asked for a better best friend."

Tears sprung to my eyes when he gave me the sweetest smile.

Ryker chose that moment to brush past, muttering, "Save the speeches for later. No time to waste."

"There might not be a later," I replied to his back, watching it stiffen. "There's no time but the present."

He swung into Napoleon's saddle without comment, but I didn't miss his curt nod.

A few moments later, I was astride Freedom and about to address the freed prisoners when two short whistles pierced the air. Freedom danced beneath me as a couple dozen villagers joined us, all carrying what looked like sledgehammers.

"You were right," one said to Asher who was riding a gray mare. "The guards watching over the solar field were lazy. We should have done this years ago."

"That was the easy part," Ryker interjected, glowering down at the man. "Are you ready to face a highly trained elite? Not just knock them out, but put that sledgehammer through their skull? Because that's what it's going to take to stop them."

Several gasps and wails rose up from the freed prisoners. I didn't need a Sensor ability to detect their abject fear. The gap between lesser and elite had never been bridged before. They believed change to be impossible, the price of failure their very lives.

I remembered Bren saying, *I want to change things for good. But sometimes, for things to get better, they first have to get worse.*

It was true. The process of change was painful, but what if all that pain was worth it in the end? My eyes drifted to Bren astride Stalin with Iris still cradled in his arms. If I hadn't accepted change, I never would have cared for them. My heart wouldn't be so full that I sometimes had to press a hand to my chest just to contain the feeling.

Yes. The pain was worth it. So very worth it.

I whirled Freedom in a tight circle, looking into the faces of the people around me. "You don't have to fight. The choice is yours," I said, surprised at how steady my voice was. "But if you do, know that it's for a better tomorrow, for a future where your children and grandchildren can feel safe. The Supreme Elite sees you as little more than slaves, and I'm but a tool in his grand scheme to create a new master race.

"But there's one thing he overlooked," I continued, facing Bren, Ryker, and Asher. "Teamwork. And if we all unite against him, we can reshape this city into a place where everyone is equal. DNA doesn't define your worth. Character does. And whether or not you fight today, be proud of who you are."

Silence fell. Crap, I was getting misty-eyed. Someone needed to say something and fast.

Bren rescued me, drawing everyone's attention as he said, "Those who want to join us, choose a weapon from the pile over there. Whoever can ride, double-up if you can. We're going in hot. We also need people to hold the underground tunnel between here and Tatum House. Renold and his elites must not get access to this bunker. Everyone else, find someplace to hide until this all blows over. Protect each other. Stay safe."

That got them moving. As people scrambled about, Bren nudged Stalin alongside Freedom and reached for my hand, pressing a lingering kiss to my knuckles.

Tears pricked my eyes. Again.

Because that small gesture said a great many things.

"You sure we should take Iris with us?" he whispered for my ears alone.

"No, but I don't trust anyone else to watch over her like you can."

He swallowed, then nodded. Straightening in the saddle, he looked for all the world like a man who finally believed in himself again as he raised our joined hands and roared into the fading night, "Who's ready to storm the castle?"

A chorus of cries shook the trees.

CHOICES

The earth trembled with the rumble of hoofbeats.

We burst through the trees, clambering across the bridge spanning the French Broad River.

We swept over hills, our mounts foaming at the mouth as we pushed them to greater speeds. Wind sucked the air from my lungs, tossing my hair back and plastering the shirt to my body. Laughter bubbled up and out of me. I couldn't help it. Even with insurmountable danger before us, I was in my element.

Danger, adrenaline, speed.

Where thoughts drifted away and instinct took over.

And I wasn't alone.

A black charger nose with flaring red nostrils came abreast of me on my right. A dark bay one to my left. From behind, I knew that a gray one kept pace with several others. And on the opposite side of the city, Yukiko and her team should be in the process of scaling the wall.

My hope soared.

We could do this. We could take on the elites and win.

As I caught sight of Antler Hill Village in the distance, though, my hope dropped.

"Bren . . ."

"I see it."

The village was awash in a pale orange glow. With the power down and curfew still in effect, all should be dark.

"Let's check it out," Ryker said over the pounding hooves. Without hesitation, we veered left. If something was wrong in the village, then that's where we belonged. Thousands of people were there who needed our protection.

As we neared, the glow only brightened.

Bren suddenly cursed and reined in Stalin. We followed his lead. Our mounts snorted, sides heaving as they flung their massive heads in the air, fighting their bits.

We all looked to Bren, relying on his superior eyesight.

"What is it?" My stomach twisted into knots as he struggled to speak.

"The buildings," he said at last, tucking Iris closer to his chest. "They're on fire."

My heart stuttered to a halt.

Several startled cries arose from our companions. Asher nudged his mare next to mine. "My family's in there," he whispered in a voice so heartbroken that I couldn't breathe.

I swung desperate eyes to Bren. "We—we have to put it out. People will lose their shelter and livelihoods. Some of them could still be trapped inside their homes. Come on." I prepared to kick Freedom, but Bren grabbed the reins. I frowned. "What are you doing? We need to go!"

"If we do this, the mission might fail. At least half the village is up in flames, even the hotel. There's no putting it out. The best we can do is round up the survivors."

It was a choice. A choice he was asking me to make.

Would we save the city or help the people?

"We go to the village," I said firmly, because it *wasn't* a choice.

The city wasn't worth saving if its people were dead.

Bren released the reins with a nod and we stirred into motion once again. But the mood was less certain now. Heavier. The fire couldn't have been an accident. If this was Renold's doing, then he was done playing. He was showing his hand, letting his mask slip, breaking his people's will by striking fear into their hearts.

And if he succeeded, this revolution was doomed.

Smoke hung in the air now, stinging my nostrils. Shrill cries and wailing came from inside the village. But surrounding the outskirts, trapping the citizens inside, was a wall of guards and elites. And in front of them . . .

The Supreme Elite.

A dark blue cape billowed behind him, his shock of white-blond hair a deceiving halo.

Even from several yards away, his electric blue eyes seemed to flash with triumph.

A short time ago, I would have cowered in fear under that knowing look. But today, I made a point of running a hand down my throat. No collar meant no control. His mouth twisted into a wicked grin. When he raised a hand, the people around me readied their weapons. But Renold wasn't holding a weapon. The object he held was flat and rectangular, similar to the one he'd used to—

"Lune," Ryker hissed urgently. "Her collar."

My mind blanked.

Then . . .

Oh stars. Oh—

Renold pressed the button.

A blood-curdling scream exploded in my ears.

Iris.

She arched in Bren's arms, shaking as electricity streaked

through her small frame. For an unbearable moment, fear froze me solid, then I was scrambling to reach her. My sister—my little *sister*—was in agonizing pain. And I couldn't think straight. I couldn't do anything but get to her. I needed the pain to stop, stop, stop.

Stop.

I could make Renold stop.

But I was suddenly there, pulling her from Bren's arms, falling to my knees under her weight. And all I could do was rock. Back and forth. Back and forth. Cradling her to me. "I've got you, sweetie, I've got you," I heard myself say, oblivious to everything but her.

Then there was a voice. A voice that chilled me to the core. "Come to me, Iris."

She stopped trembling.

I peered into her face to see her eyes open. She was looking at me. But something was wrong. Terribly wrong.

Her expression was . . . empty.

And then those hazel green eyes identical to mine rounded in fear. She let out an ear-splitting shriek and flailed against me. Not in pain, but to get away. She was trying to get *away*.

"Let me go, let me go!" she screamed. And I did. Stars, I did. Because I didn't want to hurt her and I didn't understand. She crawled several feet away before collapsing, whimpering when she saw the row of puffing, pawing chargers.

"Iris," I called, lurching after her. "It's me, Lune."

She waved me back, inching closer to Renold. "No! Please don't take me. Stay away!"

"Iris." My throat closed. "I—"

But she didn't let me finish. She turned and ran toward Renold, crying, "Father!"

I blinked in disbelief. I must have heard wrong. There was no way . . .

"Father!" she said again, flinging herself into his arms.

The sight tore a hole through my heart. I pressed a hand to my chest to keep blood from spilling out. Renold glanced at me over her head and smiled. Nothing, *nothing* was crueler than this. Getting shot would hurt less.

"What . . ." The word was pitiful. Broken. "What did you do to her?"

"Did you say something?" Renold called. "I couldn't hear you."

I gathered the fragments of pain, confusion, and fury burrowing into my heart and threw them at him with a roar. "What did you *do* to her?"

He shrugged. "Only what I should have done to you from the beginning."

I ground my teeth together as hatred for this twisted man came to a boiling point. "You can't have her. I'll unblock her memories."

"Actually, you can't."

Ice shot down my spine. "And why is that?"

His eyes bored into mine, forcing me to face the truth. "I think you know why."

"No." I shook all over as denial and adrenaline coursed through me. "It's not possible. I don't believe you!"

I lunged for her, not with my body but with my mind. The tether snapped into place. Lightning quick, I dove into her subconscious. Instead of speaking to her, I latched onto her emotions. Pain, relief, confusion, fear. I dug deeper, searching for images. *Memories.* Her mind, so cold and vast, was a wasteland of empty space.

I almost gave up, almost pulled back when a dark mass sucked me in. A memory.

"*Why can't I remember anything?*" Iris was saying.

"*The past doesn't matter. Only your power and loyalty matters. People will come to steal you away and plant false memories in your head. They will seek to destroy me, the only one who cares about you. Will you let them?*"

"*No.*"

"*No, what, dear?*"

"*No, Father.*"

The memory flickered out and I was sucked into another— of Renold. I shoved it away only to be plunged into memory after memory of Renold. No Mum. No Asher or Freedom. No Bren.

No me.

I fought to disengage from the painful inner shell she'd become and snapped back to myself with a strangled cry. Pressure squeezed my chest. It built and built until I was forced to heave a sob. I clutched at my throat to quiet the sounds but my grief refused to be silenced. I was helpless to stop the anguished tears from spilling free.

Arms came around me, grounding me to earth. "What's happening, little bird?"

"He . . . he erased us," I choked out. "He can't have her. Please. Get her back."

As Bren stood, Renold's voice cut through the air. "They're going to harm me, Iris. Stop them. Stop them now."

No. I jumped up. It was impossible, yet she turned to face us, her pale throat free of the collar. *No!* In a flash, I had an arrow drawn and pointed at Renold. "Iris, don't do it."

Instead of heeding my warning, she sucked in a deep breath,

more and more. Stars above, she was pulling energy to her. Then she released it all in a scream. "Stop!"

The arrow froze to my fingers. I was ice. A prisoner in my body. And I wasn't the only one. No one moved around me. Not even the chargers. It was like she had stopped time itself. Except the guards and elites stirred. Renold raised a hand and so did their weapons. Volt guns, arrows, throwing knives. All poised to take us out.

I thrashed against the invisible bonds. My body didn't budge, but my mind . . . it whirred awake. She was strong. I could feel her power now, a rush of water that swirled in and around me, holding me in place. But I could sense the weak spots, the water stretched to a mere trickle. She was controlling dozens of minds, and her hold was slipping.

If I was going to save us all from certain death, I had to do it now. *Now!* Aiming for a thin spot in Iris's mind control, I sent my power hurtling toward her like an arrow.

It buried deep, deep, deeper. I clung to her subconscious and shouted into that terrible void, "Sleep."

She crumpled like a ragdoll at Renold's feet.

Time restarted with a jolt. My bubble of power burst and I immediately blacked out. The darkness grabbed me but I kicked away, swimming toward the surface. I broke through only to emerge into chaos.

"Attack!"

Chargers screamed. Hooves pounded.

My body was lifted, borne into the air and held in a viselike grip. I struggled to see, to make sense of the world.

Zip, zip. Shots were fired.

"Get to Iris!" a familiar voice bellowed in my ear.

I jerked upright and the world refocused. Grays and browns painted my peripheral. Chargers. I was weightless, flying among them. No, I was astride Stalin. Bren must be at my back. A volt gun slid into place beside me as he fired at the guards and elites. One went down.

"Iris."

"Lune," Bren said with obvious relief. "You all right?"

"Yeah, I—"

Stalin suddenly reared, bugling a shrill neigh. As he started to tip over, Bren wrapped me up in a bear hug and jumped free. Gravity sent us tumbling over the ground, knocking the wind from our lungs. Bren was up in a flash, dragging me with him. Everything tilted but I shook off the dizziness, relieved when Stalin stumbled to his legs again.

"Where's Renold?" I shouted, reaching for my daggers.

"There."

I followed the point of his finger to where the Supreme Elite stood protected by a ring of his elites. Ryker, Asher, and several others fought to break the circle and reach Iris still asleep at his feet. I advanced on him only for a blond-haired behemoth to block the way.

"It's been awhile, trainee," said Drake, my old Trials instructor. He raised a massive broadsword with a challenging sneer.

Bren stepped beside me, twirling his su-yari in a lazy figure eight before widening his stance, prepared to fight.

The older man's eyes visibly widened at the sight of Bren's enhanced form. His gaze shot to me. "What, you can't take me on by yourself?"

"Oh, didn't you know?" I flipped my daggers. "I learned a new fighting technique. It's called *teamwork.*"

As surprise settled over his face, I rushed him. Steel striking steel shivered up my arms. I blocked out everything but me, Drake, and Bren locked in a fight that would surely end in death. I ducked as the broadsword swooped toward my head, popping up to see Bren engage him. He thrust the spear tip forward only to have it batted aside. But he wouldn't let up, swinging the staff around again and again with pounding force.

I snuck underneath Drake's guard and drew first blood. He hissed, freeing up a hand to throw a fist. Even as my head whipped to the side from the blow, he cried out. I pushed past the throbbing in my skull to see Bren yank the su-yari from his side. Bren's fury was palpable. His fangs were bared, eyes flashing with heat. To spare him more guilt, I lowered my daggers and dove into Drake's mind.

"Knock yourself out."

His broadsword thunked to the ground. Then so did he as my command was obeyed.

Bren was still fighting for control of his inner rage when I toed Drake's prone form, muttering, "Now *that* technique was all you. Fight dirty, remember?"

I threw Bren a wink despite my pulsing headache, then took off toward Renold. Halfway there, I saw an elite aim a throwing knife at Ryker. Barely breaking stride, I halted the throw with a, "Stop." Then, "Punch yourself."

I could get used to this.

Ryker glanced over his shoulder and our eyes locked. He nodded his thanks, wiping blood from his face before jumping into the fray once again. Some of the people from inside the village had broken through and joined the fight. They brandished tools as weapons, many getting shot down by arrows and volt darts. We were still outnumbered, the fire keeping our inside help at bay.

But The Ridge would come. If we could hold on for a little while longer, victory would be ours. I wouldn't accept anything less.

A villager next to me wailed as a guard jabbed her with a volt stick. I swept a dagger at the guard, catching his arm. He dropped the stick and my boot lashed out, striking his gut. Bren grabbed him then, knocking him out cold. An elite rushed me from the side, but before I could engage, Bren was there, whipping his su-yari through the air to block the man's weapon. As he continued to protect my back, I turned toward Renold.

He was already staring at me. The screams, spraying blood, and smoke-filled air drifted away as I held his stare. "Surrender," I said, knowing he could hear, "and I won't tear apart your mind."

His nostrils quivered with barely restrained fury, but he managed to smile serenely as he replied, "*You* surrender and I won't press this button." He waved the flat device to taunt me.

"Iris isn't wearing her collar anymore. Your days of playing fake daddy are over."

His expression flattened. "This device isn't for her collar. It's one I never planned on using, but you're giving me no choice. I'd rather see my city destroyed than let you take control of it. Their deaths will be on your hands."

"What are you talking about?" I snapped. "What does it do?"

"It unlocks every single cage in the bunker. Not even a power outage can stop these locks from opening if I were to—" He paused, glancing at the device before slowly raising his eyes to mine. "Oops."

Horror crashed into me and I stumbled back.

"Better hurry if you want to save them," Renold called. "The beasts go wild at the scent of fresh blood."

A hand gripped my shoulder from behind. "It's just me," Bren's voice rumbled in my ear. I didn't even flinch, my thoughts a wild disarray of disbelief and consuming fear. He came around, scanning my face and body, worry lining his forehead. "What's wrong? What was Renold saying?"

As I struggled to speak, a twisted mass of friends and enemies, spraying blood and undulating flames danced before me. In the center, swirling so fast that no one detected him, was my best friend. He dipped and pivoted, pulling my sister to safety. He carried her away, away, away. I felt nothing but dread. Because no distance was great enough. No one could escape what was to come.

"The beasts are loose," I whispered to the wind, the very thing that would draw our scent to the ravenous animals and doom us all.

I looked for Renold, the harbinger of death, but he was gone.

FLY, LITTLE BIRD

Ignoring Bren's shout, I whistled for Freedom and ran.

I caused this horror.

By pushing Renold over the edge, an entire city would pay the price.

"Lune, wait!"

"Protect Iris," I yelled, jumping over a fallen villager. "Protect them all!"

Because this wasn't about him protecting *me* right now. I quickly resheathed my daggers and swung into the saddle. Bren grabbed both the reins and my thigh, holding us captive.

I clenched my jaw, then steeled my gaze. "I need to warn the others. Nothing you say will make me stay. I *have* to go."

"I know."

My mouth fell open. I expected him to fight me tooth and nail, not—

The hand on my thigh shot up and gripped the nape of my neck. I sucked in a gasp as he brought my head down, kissing me soundly. His lips were hot and urgent against mine. He poured an ocean of words and feelings into that one soulful kiss. A plea and a prayer and a thousand whispered confessions of love.

When he pulled back, I clung to him, desperate for one more moment. But he gently removed my hands and wrapped them around the reins. He stepped away, giving me the most devastating half smile.

"Fly, little bird," he said. Then slapped Freedom's backside.

We shot down the road like a bullet. Away from the fight. Away from him.

He was finally letting me go. Not because he wasn't scared or didn't love me. But because he *believed*. Utterly and completely believed in me, harnessing his worries so I could fly freely.

And I ached all over from the joy of it.

I carried the feeling with me, holding it tight when panic threatened to unhinge me. The entire city was in grave danger. Most were unaware of the upcoming threat, and I needed help warning them.

Trusting Freedom to fly true, I gave her control, retreating into my mind to form a tether with Jaxon.

Please tell me you're in the city, I quickly spoke into his mind.

His reply was instant. *Affirmative. There were a few casualties, but we're heading your way.*

Meet me at Tatum House. I'll tell you more when you arrive.

I disconnected and leaned over Freedom's neck, urging her to sprout wings. When we arrived at the main entrance, I reined her in sharply. She skidded on the gravel road, rearing as bright headlights sliced our way. I slipped from her back while she pawed at the air.

Four black vehicles ground to a halt before us, and I grabbed Freedom's reins before she bolted. Jaxon jumped down from the driver's seat of his Rover, striding toward us with a slack-jawed expression.

Slinging the longest gun I'd ever seen across his shoulders, he pointed at Freedom. "That's a . . . that's a—"

"Charger?" I supplied helpfully. "Ogle her later. Right now, we have a bigger problem than Renold, the elites, and a village up in flames."

"Flames?" Yukiko came up alongside Jaxon, straightening her black bulletproof vest.

"I'll tell you everything on the way, but I need you to send half your team across the river to defend the bunker's main entrance. There are people over there unaware of what's just been unleashed."

"Help me out here, Lune," Yukiko prodded, even as she waved one of The Ridge's guards over and handed him a map. "What are we walking into?"

I realized then how frantic my voice sounded compared to hers. I worked on slowing my galloping heartbeats before saying, "Every single mutant beast inside the bunker has been released. There's a tunnel on the sub-basement level of this house that leads directly to the bunker. We need to get down there *now* before the beasts find the men we sent to block off Renold's escape."

"Where *is* the sneaky villain anyway?" Jaxon asked while Yukiko stepped aside to issue orders.

I opened my mouth to fill him in, but lost all track of thought as someone new joined us. "*Bells?*" I said incredulously before scowling at Jaxon. "What is she doing here?"

Jaxon groaned. "For the love of salami sandwiches, I told you to stay in the Rover, Bells. Under no circumstances are you to leave its bulletproof sanctuary."

"But I have a vest on," she argued, inching forward. "And I can shoot. Bren made me learn, remember?"

Jaxon dragged a hand down his face. "I blame this on Prince of the Bad Boys. Ever since he came back into the picture, *this* keeps happening."

She perked up. "Is he here? In the house?"

The growl of an engine drowned out my reply. I tightened my grip on Freedom's reins as two of the Rovers kicked up gravel and sped away. Yukiko rejoined us, rolling her eyes at Bells before handing her a gun. "Stay in the *center* of our group. And don't even think about sneaking off to find Ryker. He's a big boy and can take care of himself."

"I wouldn't—"

"I mean it, Bells. No heroics. Even if there's a lost fluffy kitten."

"Is there—? Okay, I promise."

I was only slightly reassured when she checked the gun with practiced movements. At least she had a bulletproof vest on. Someone held one out to me but I declined. I had too many weapons strapped to my back and no time to readjust them. I barely had time to loop Freedom's reins around Lennie's statuesque lion head before we were mounting the stairs.

"Once inside, be prepared for anything," I warned, sparing a second to accept the gun Yukiko handed me. "I don't know how many elites or guards were left to defend the house."

"Roger that," Yukiko muttered. "Just like our war games but with real ammo."

When we reached the front doors, I paused, hoping Ryker was telling the truth about his inside man. If not, this could get awkward really fast. I bypassed the annoying bell and knocked.

Almost immediately, the doors swung inward. Guns cocked, ready to fire. Hooded gray eyes peered down at us all with a bored air. "Your name and business, miss?" Dobson droned.

"Beast-Taming, Kick-Butt Warrior Princess, here to save the

day."

"So epic," Jaxon whispered in approval.

The doors widened further. "Of course. This way, Warrior Princess. I've been expecting you."

Was this a dream? I must be dreaming.

Dobson swiftly led us to the staff stairwell without instructions. He was observant, I'd give him that. Maybe he was a closet Intellect. It explained why Ryker confided in him though. Besides their quiet and broody nature, they both knew more than they let on.

Other than the faint squeak of boots against marble, the house was silent. We could be walking into a trap, but I doubted it. Dobson was stuffy, but he'd never been malicious. Maybe he felt like a prisoner too and was jumping at the chance to set himself free. At the stairwell door, he bowed, holding it open for us.

I saw him in a different light then. Instead of bored, his well-worn face simply looked tired. For the first time in several years, I gave him a genuine smile, speaking without sarcasm. "Thank you, Dobson."

He wordlessly inclined his head, but I could have sworn his mouth twitched into the barest of smiles.

A light clicked on, illuminating the stairs. Jaxon tapped my shoulder and handed me a flashlight. More switched on behind me, casting bright beams as I swallowed my trepidation and descended.

When we hit the basement level where most of the in-house staff slaved over the elite's needs, the usual clank of pots and pans as the cooks prepared breakfast was missing. Was *everyone* at the village? Ironically, it was probably the safest place to be now. Every single one of those elites knew how to wield a weapon.

The sublevel was pitch black. Not even faded moonbeams

from a window broke through the inky depths. Only the flashlight, slightly trembling now, chased away the shadows. I veered in the direction Lars had taken me, hardly daring to breathe.

I almost leapt out of my skin when Jaxon whispered, "So tell me about this bunker."

"Now isn't a good time," I hissed, expecting to see flashing yellow eyes at any moment.

"Now's the perfect time," Jaxon insisted. "You're super jumpy and animals can—"

"Smell fear. I know, I know." I huffed, training my light on the door leading to the tunnel. Crap. It was open.

Yukiko slid around me, signaling us to halt as she crept through the doorway. No one moved a muscle. I held my breath. As silently as she went in, she returned. "All clear."

She took the lead then, entering the tunnel. Stars, it was creepy in the dark. A tube. We were in a cement tube with a possible horde of ravenous beasts on the other end.

"Tell me, Lu Bear," Jaxon said, walking beside me now. His voice echoed faintly, and I cringed. "Yukiko will warn us if anything with pointy teeth is coming. I need intel on that bunker."

"Why?"

"'Cause it's my job," he replied, all seriousness. "I watch, listen, and piece together information to better understand what's going on in the world. I wasn't kidding about that. But it's all to discover threats that could wipe out humanity again. The bunker seems suspicious, so I'm hoping you can tell me a few things."

I snorted softly. "I could tell you a *lot*. It's where I spent the last week—or longer. Which reminds me. Don't stare at Bren's teeth when you see him next."

Before he could pepper me with questions, I told him the

short version of Renold's diabolical family history, from the Silent War virus to plans for creating an Elite human race. When I finished, he was eerily quiet.

Finally, he made a sucking noise with his teeth. "Wow. I was totally wrong in my theory."

"Not really. He *is* trying to build a cult, in a way. And . . ." I drew in a tight breath, focusing on Yukiko's back. "He turned Iris into a mindless robot. Bren was going to be next, then probably me."

Jaxon suddenly stopped. "Sugar Plum," he called softly, but Yukiko heard, reversing course.

"What is it?" she said, still on high alert as she scanned our surroundings.

"I have an idea." He turned to me. "Do you have the ability to check if there are any humans left inside the bunker?"

"Uh . . . since I've been inside, I could probably feel my way through the darkness and search for anything living. Why?"

Before I'd even finished speaking, he was removing a backpack, unzipping it to rummage inside. "I'll tell you later. Hurry, we don't have much time left."

"I need someone to watch over my—"

"I've got you," Bells said reassuringly, slipping an arm around my waist.

And surrounded as I was by friends that I knew without question could be trusted, I didn't hesitate to leave my body behind for them to protect.

It was surprisingly easy to cast my mind out, like stretching a well-used muscle. The desire to check on everyone at Antler Hill Village was strong, but I wouldn't be able to tear myself away if I did. So I forced my consciousness to stay on target. Upon arrival,

I felt the beasts. Their minds were all the same: instinct and blood-lust. They were on the hunt, and the only thing available was human flesh.

Several had made it to the lower level where the prisoners had been kept. One was focused on something with an intense territorial possessiveness. Which could only mean that it had found its prey. When I couldn't detect another life force, I assumed its kill was dead. I swept through the research wing, mentally cringing as I reached the room we'd left Lars's body. A beast had found him.

On my way back to myself, I detected a cluster of humans in the tunnel. Their minds were relatively calm. Safe. For now.

"It's clear," I panted, swiping at the blood trickling over my lips. "And the men we're looking for are just up ahead." Bells let me lean on her as exhaustion pulled at my limbs.

Jaxon and Yukiko engaged in a whispered conversation, but I was too tired to eavesdrop. The whispers soon became heated and frantic. Yukiko shook her head, baring her teeth in a silent snarl. Jaxon suddenly grabbed her face and kissed her. A beam of light remained steady on the two lovers, their kiss needy and desperate. Several throats cleared when tongues appeared.

Then Jaxon was pulling back, oblivious to everything but his girlfriend. "I love you a lot, you know," he said, loud enough for us to hear.

"I know, you dumb idiot." Despite the harsh reply, her voice trembled. "You'd better come back alive."

He kissed the tip of her nose and flashed a brilliant smile. "I'm a sleek, stealthy panther. Nothing can touch this." Then he was moving. *Away.* Heading down the tunnel without us. Before the darkness could swallow him up, he glanced over his shoulder and met my widened eyes. With a wink, he was gone.

348

Then everyone was speaking at once.

Yukiko raised a hand for silence. "New plan. Jaxon's going to slip inside the bunker and set a charge, which will destroy the beasts *and* Renold's work. Kill two birds with one stone."

"What's a charge?" I didn't care if the question was stupid. If I didn't get answers soon, I was bolting after him.

"A bomb," she explained. "Explosive devices are just one of the many things he likes to tinker around with." She sighed, shoving spiky bangs off her forehead. "It'll work. If he doesn't get eaten first."

"So he's going to *blow* up the bunker?"

"Yup. He never does anything halfway." Her nose ring winked as she inhaled deeply, struggling for composure. "We'll wait a few minutes for your people to arrive, then head for the village."

At the one minute mark, gunshots dispelled the silence. *Bang bang bang.* We froze as shouts and screams from up ahead echoed throughout the tunnel. Yukiko slowly turned, her dark eyes round and glittering. I thought she would go after Jaxon, overcome with fear for his safety. But then I heard it—the scrabbling of claws on concrete in the midst of pounding boots.

"Run!" Yukiko roared.

When my body seized with indecision, she yanked me toward the way we'd come. Crazy beams of light ripped through the darkness as we ran.

Yukiko glanced behind us. Swore. "Go, go, go!"

A man's piercing cry chilled my blood.

Too close, too close.

I whipped my light around, illuminating a dozen pair of frightened eyes. If I stopped to aim, they'd trample me in their fear. I couldn't do a single thing as a saber cat leapt and dragged down one of the men. A shot of adrenaline zipped through me and I whirled, putting on an extra burst of speed.

We were sitting ducks in this blasted tunnel. Without an unobstructed view of the beasts, I'd accidentally shoot a human. But I could see the exit and the team spilling through. In a matter of seconds, we were scrambling to close the tunnel door.

It slammed shut behind us.

"The lock is automatic," Yukiko shouted. "There's no way to seal it—"

Bam!

Bells shrieked as a heavy body collided with the metal door, pushing us back.

After an eternity of throwing our weight against the beasts, Yukiko barked, "Go. They're too strong!"

We were halfway down the hall when the scratch of claws reached my ears. *Don't look, don't look.* I looked. Four saber cats were in pursuit, fixated on our retreating forms. We were giving them the ultimate chase of their lives.

Oh *crap!*

No one dared slow to face them in these cramped quarters and neither did I. We took the stairs three at a time. From behind came a cat scream. Someone had stopped to swing an ax at the beast. They stumbled as the animal swept out a paw, catching their leg. I readied my gun, waiting until the only person in my way was the man caught in the cat's clutches.

Bang.

I missed completely.

My heart rammed against my rib cage as I steadied my trembling fingers and aimed again.

Bang, bang.

The animal dropped.

"Move it, Lune!" Yukiko shrieked as the remaining beasts clambered up the stairs. I grabbed the man's arm and yanked him to his feet. Only twelve steps to go. Seven. Three. The second we burst through the door on the main floor, Yukiko slammed it shut. She cursed when there was no lock to be found. It wouldn't hold for long.

And then it hit me—what we'd done. We led the beasts inside the house. "Dobson!" I ran for the entrance, praying I'd find him there. "Get out of the house *now!*"

Nearing the entryway, I yelled his name again. "Dobson!"

My shout was obliterated by the sound of a door splintering. I whirled as three saber cats crashed inside, sliding on the marble floor.

And there, standing feet away, was Dobson. The saber cats took one look at him and pounced.

"No!" I screamed as he fell. I fired at the beasts, hitting their backsides, afraid to aim higher in case I shot Dobson. But in their blind need to feed, they continued to tear him apart.

There came a blood-curdling scream from the base of the main stairs. One of the cats, blood dripping from its finger-length canines, spotted Blanca, Renold's wife. Rose was a few steps above her mother, pale as a sheet. My stomach dropped as the animal prowled toward them. I opened fire, striking the beast's shoulder. It hissed, but didn't slow. With one swift blow, Blanca was flat on her back, sliding down the remaining stairs. The animal shredded through her pretty dress, coating it red.

Rose stood stock-still as the cat mauled her mother, not even flinching when blood sprayed her bare legs. I lurched forward, emptying the last of my bullets into the cat's side. More shots joined mine, striking the other two beasts. They collapsed in pools of their own blood, but we were too late to save Dobson and Blanca.

Pressure built in my chest at the brutal loss of life. At the way they'd suffered. So many pointless deaths tonight.

And then there was Rose.

Rose.

My childhood tormenter. I almost left her to stare at her mother's mutilated body as penance for all she'd done to me. But I refused to be that monstrous.

"Rose," I called, eyeing the gaping stairwell. More beasts could arrive at any moment. "Rose! You need to get out of here. Let's go."

She showed no sign of hearing me as I approached cautiously, gun at the ready.

I touched her shoulder. "Rose." She lifted her big brown eyes, not a shred of disdain in them—only fear. Crap on a cookie, my heart turned over for her. She'd seen her mother die, after all. I grasped her hand. "Let's go."

She threaded her fingers through mine and pressed into my side like a frightened child. I supposed she *was* a child, in a way. A spoiled little girl who never had to grow up, who always got what she wanted but not what she needed. Change would be harder for her than most.

I led her across the room, pausing at the open front doors where Yukiko stood. She finished speaking with a member of her team before turning to me.

"I want you to lead everyone to the village, Lune," she said, not quite meeting my gaze.

"Okay." I frowned. "What will you be doing?"

She looked lost as she said, "Jaxon rescued me from the darkness, and now it's my turn to rescue him." She shrugged, her expression clearing. "Besides, I need to finish what he started if something happened to him. Setting a charge can't be harder than learning to drive a stick shift."

"Yukiko . . ."

She threw an arm around my shoulders, locking me into a fierce hug. "I'm really glad I didn't shoot you up on the mountain." With a sniff, she pulled away and inched backward. "Please go, Lune. They need you."

Then she was gone.

MY DESTINY

Dawn slashed across the sky, a brilliant, bloodthirsty red.

Charcoal smoke belched from the hellish pit before us while white ash rained down from the heavens.

Villagers streamed past, most of them in their soot-covered nightclothes. They cried and screamed. They clutched at each other or simply walked about in a daze. One man had an arrow sticking out of his leg and didn't seem to notice. I veered Freedom around a wide-eyed child no older than five. Shocked. They were all in shock.

I probably was, too. I couldn't feel my injuries.

A dark shape streaked toward a small herd of livestock. Magnawolf. More screams.

I had dreamt of this very thing happening, and now it was.

The segregating war for power had become a mutual fight for survival.

Shots fired, announcing our arrival. Heads turned. When they spotted me astride Freedom, their eyes filled with devastating hope once more. The sight crushed my lungs.

Appearing out of nowhere, a tawny magnawolf charged us. I whirled Freedom around, using her serrated tail as a whip. The beast recoiled with a sharp yip. It lunged again, but I was already in its mind, destroying, destroying, destroying. The animal soundlessly dropped dead.

Humans should not possess such deadly power. It could corrupt even the purest of souls. Taking a life should never be this easy, but it was. With a simple thought, I could control them all. With a simple thought, I could end the chaos and suffering.

But I didn't.

For better or worse, God gave the world free will, and I had no business taking it away.

I mentally checked on Iris again. Awake and disoriented, but safe. She was inside the village, the very place I was headed. I wasn't coming for her, though. Not yet. Along the village border, I found Bren and Ryker facing off against a pair of those freaky giant bears. Bren had said they were no longer brothers, but as they fought side by side, protecting each other's backs, that's exactly what he and Ryker looked like. Brothers, not through blood, but through trials by fire.

I skirted around them, utterly focused on one person. One target. I couldn't save the entire city, but I could answer destiny's call.

He was in the middle of Village Square, one of the last spots still untouched by the raging fire. Behind him, the Arcus Point viewing screen flapped in the breeze, a gaping hole in its middle. The crackling flames at my back stole his words, but as I neared the tight circle of elites—listening to him with such rapt attention that they didn't even notice me—I saw what he held.

Vials of serum.

I slid to the ground. Tugging on Freedom's bridle, I brought her head down. As she butted her nose against my chest, I smoothed my hands over her prickly cheeks. "Thank you, old friend. For everything," I whispered. Her ears twitched.

I shoved her head away. "*Fly*, Freedom." My loyal friend

obeyed without question. My throat ached as she tossed her mane and whirled, cantering past the Square and out of sight. I was on my own now, but this way, those I loved couldn't be used against me.

Hiding my gun, I drew near enough for him to hear me, making sure no one was at my back.

"Are you done yet?" I yelled. "I grow bored of your idiot-ology."

The effect was instantaneous. Dozens of heads swiveled my way, including Renold's. To say their stares were unfriendly was an understatement.

I shrugged despite every bone in my body on high alert. "What? It's true. I've never heard of a more hairbrained plan."

Renold's mouth tightened, his lips almost blue. Now that I was looking, his skin was pasty and glistened with a fine sweat. His voice lacked its usual grace as he said, "Ah, Lune, I thought you'd be cowering in a corner from the mutant beasts. Well, I'm glad you're here. I have a gift for you."

Goosebumps shivered up my arms. The last *gift* he'd given me had been the thumbs of my former hairdresser and seamstress.

He snapped his fingers and two elites appeared, dragging a tall, lanky boy. He was bound and gagged, his face brutally beaten. With both his eyes swollen shut and one cheek a bloody mess, I didn't recognize him. But it was his hair—ash-blond and sticking straight up—that I recognized.

Asher.

Despite my locked knees, I jerked forward a step. It took every last ounce of strength not to react further than that. Renold was still playing a game, but this would be our final match. I would make sure of it.

"I did this myself, actually," Renold said, gesturing proudly at my best friend's face. "He wouldn't tell me where he hid Iris, so I was forced to dirty my hands. I don't know why I resisted for so long. Losing control feels good."

Crap. *Crap.* The madman was becoming a Berserker.

"Your wife's dead," I said, hoping to divert his attention from Asher. "The beasts mauled her to death in your house. And you should probably know that your breeding program is no longer operational. Rollie and Dr. Stacey are dead, too."

The blue of his eyes flared so brightly, they were nearly white. "And Rose?"

I snorted. "Do you even care? She's not one of the *chosen.*"

His jaw clenched. I got him there.

Then I drove the nail home. "Your precious bunker is next."

The mask slid off, and his gaze sharpened. "What do you mean?"

"Oh, I forgot about our deal. You tell me how your family decimated the world a century ago and I stop anyone from destroying your plans to destroy the world again. That's the gist of it, right?"

The elites stirred, murmuring amongst each other.

In a blur of motion, Renold grabbed Asher and placed a gun to his head. The whispers grew louder, interspersed with shocked gasps. That wasn't a volt gun. It was a *real* one inside a gunless city. The Ridge had only just arrived, which meant he'd had it this entire time. His voice was a low hiss as he said, "Tell me what's happening to my bunker and maybe I won't blow his brains out."

Every part of me was visibly shaking. *Asher, Asher, Asher,* my mind whimpered. *Save him!* But I needed to expose Renold for the monster he was first. I needed to strip him of everything he held dear. His city, his elites, his legacy. Only when he had nothing could I put an end to this.

This was my mission.

My destiny.

Freeing the world of Supreme Elite Renold Tatum was *my* legacy.

As if in agreement, the ground rumbled. I glanced at my feet, expecting a ground-dweller beast to pop up and swallow me whole. How anticlimactic would that be?

But then . . .

An explosion rocked the air.

My heart kicked against my chest. That explosion could only mean one thing: Jaxon or Yukiko were still alive. I dared to hope that they *both* were.

Over the startled shouts and shrieks, I heard Renold scream, "What did you do, you ungrateful, disloyal child? *What did you do?*" His face turned an ugly red. Veins protruded from his neck and forehead.

As he jammed the gun against Asher's temple, I knew my moment had arrived.

My moment to play God one last time and end this.

I raised a hand. "Stop!" The energy already swirling around my body filled me with a heady sense of control. I threw the command out and Renold froze. "Put the weapon down."

The gun lowered. Then paused. Renold released a dark chuckle. "I took the enhancement serum containing your special DNA, Lune. It burns through my veins like molten lava, and not even *you* can stop me now. No one can. But you've betrayed me for the last time. After I'm finished killing your friends, you'll *beg* me to inject you with memory-erasing serum. And I will. Oh, I will. And you will never, *ever* disobey me again."

Blood trickled from his nose. Slowly, then faster and faster.

My eyes widened. "You're not worthy."

His face reddened even further as he swiped at the blood now gushing from his nose.

"Did you hear me?" I shouted. "You're not a *chosen* one!"

He glared at me and snarled like a rabid animal. "I *am* a chosen one. I'm stronger than you, which proves my worthiness!"

Emotions flooded me, the greatest of them fear as he lifted the gun to Asher's head again. And this time . . .

He pulled the trigger.

Blood exploded. Asher's blood. His head snapped to the side and he fell, fell, fell. My best friend. He'd just killed my beautiful, sweet, honest best friend.

My knees struck the ground and I screamed and screamed and screamed.

With a sickening jolt, I was on my feet again, sucking in a ragged breath. I blinked in disbelief at a standing Asher. *Standing.* My heart thundered.

A vision.

I'd had a *future* vision.

Which meant I could change it.

When Renold's gun began to lift, so did mine.

I leveled it right at his heart. "Stop or I'll shoot!"

Everything slowed. His face blanched with fear. His gun swung my way. He fired. But so did I.

We gazed at each other for an endless moment, two forces unwilling to bend.

If our bullets found their marks, I couldn't tell. He wore a midnight blue suit and I felt nothing.

Out of nowhere, a double-bladed su-yari was thrown, sinking

deep into Renold's gut.

From my other side, a gun appeared. Not a whisper of sound could be heard as it fired, but I saw the damage. A clean hole through Renold's forehead.

As he fell, I followed his eyes. That icy blue I'd dreaded and feared for eleven years dulled to a murky gray. They stopped seeing me. They would never see me again.

And then warm, honey-gold eyes filled my vision. Bren. The man who held my heart. My soulmate. I smiled at him but couldn't feel it. He didn't smile back. Lines furrowed his brow. Worried lines. Scared lines. I wanted to erase them but couldn't.

Why couldn't I?

Because I had no hands. Nothing was left of me but my eyes. I could still see, and I wanted to see everything.

My gaze flew over his head to the russett sky streaked with gold. A flock of birds soared past. Beautiful. Free. They were so breathtakingly free. I felt free. Free of pain, free of cages and walls, free of torment. I could join the birds now.

Because that's what I was. A little bird.

They beckoned to me.

"Don't leave me," I whispered, hoping they heard. But I couldn't see them anymore. Even my sight was gone.

As my eyes fluttered closed, I felt something on my face. It was familiar. Comforting. It gave me peace.

I knew everything would be all right then.

It had started to rain.

BREATHE

I was swimming.

It was warm and safe here. A quiet place where thoughts weren't needed. But it was different this time. I couldn't feel. Or remember. And that bothered me. Although the water was peaceful, it was empty. Before, I wouldn't have minded, but things had changed. There were people, places, *dreams* that weren't here.

Something was wrong.

I jerked against the water's hold. Normally so languid, it clutched me tightly, refusing to let go. Panicking, I thrashed and depleted the last of my oxygen. My lungs burned, desperate for air. I denied them. Holding my breath underwater was a game of mine. I could go a while longer.

"Come back to me."

But I didn't want to. I wanted to be free of this water. It was holding me back from something, something that I wanted very much.

"Please don't leave me. Please."

If it would just give me the *choice* to decide for myself.

"Breathe, Lune, *breathe.*"

Breathe? Well, now the water was trying to kill me. And here I thought we were old friends.

"I don't want to live a future without you in it. I need you, little bird."

That was different. And yet familiar. Real? Yes. That was it. *Real.* And wherever it was, that's where I wanted to be.

A voice, a crazy voice in my head said, *Just breathe.*

Yeah, right.

"It's going to be okay, little bird. Just wait and see."

Oh. I remembered that.

And the voice—I remembered that, too. I wanted to hear it again.

Just breathe.

Ugh, this water was murderous.

Just. Breathe.

Doing so could mean death, but what if it brought me to that voice? I wouldn't mind dying if I could reunite with that voice. Something told me I'd experience all the things that were missing here if I took a chance and dared to take a breath.

And so—against every instinct I possessed—I took that first step, that leap of faith.

And breathed.

———○———

Home.

I was home.

EPILOGUE

"Lune, you're going to be late!"

I gripped the railing and drank in the breathtaking sight a moment more, then hurried inside. "I can't help it, it's *perfect*," I said, closing the French doors of the observatory. "Besides, my hair was still wet."

"Yeah, because you couldn't stop training for *one* second to take a decent bath." Bells glanced over her shoulder to roll her eyes at me. "Seriously, though, you couldn't take today off?"

I shrugged as we scurried down the stairs. "I'm an adrenaline junkie."

She groaned but didn't comment, too busy herding me to our destination like a mother duck. An hour later, she was still fretting.

"Stop fiddling with it."

"But it doesn't look right," I muttered, fiddling some more.

"It looks exactly like it's supposed to." At my exasperated sigh, Bells' hands went to her hips. "Hey, who's the fashion expert here?"

"Me," a male voice said, startling us both. Jaxon waltzed into the room, a pronounced limp to his step. His prosthetic leg must be bothering him today. With a grunt, he lowered himself onto the flowery yellow couch. "I say stick with the metal armor and cape look. It's who you are."

"It's not what you wear that matters," Bells said in a deep, scratchy voice, "but what you do. Isn't that how the saying goes, Jax? And you shouldn't be in here. It's bad luck or something like that."

"If that's the case," I interjected, "then I don't need to wear this thing. I'll just take it off, and—"

"No!" both Bells and Jaxon shouted.

Through the floor-length mirror, I saw Yukiko pop her head into the room. "What's going on in here? Do I need to kick some butts? If these goons are bothering you, Lune, just let me know."

I smirked at her reflection. "Maybe kick their butts afterward. A boot print might show on that flimsy pale fabric they're wearing."

"Pshh, I ain't wearing flimsy fabric. It's airy," Jaxon said with a lofty tone, making room on the couch for Yukiko. She bypassed the seat for his lap instead, careful to avoid what he called his "battle wound." He pulled her close and waggled his eyebrows. "It lets certain body parts *breathe* better."

A chorus of female groans filled the semi-crowded room. Iris giggled from her perch on the canopy bed, and I turned my head to grin at her encouragingly.

"Did I miss something?" Another head poked through the doorway, then spikey, ash-blond hair was streaking across the room. Iris squealed when Asher landed beside her. The bed creaked loudly under his weight and they both laughed. "Where's your brother and sister?" he asked before flicking her nose.

She shrugged, a blush staining her cheeks. "They're playing with your sister and brothers. I just needed a break from the noise." She would never admit it out loud, but I knew that socializing was still overwhelming for her. Everything about her past self was brand new, and the one person she'd latched onto during this confusing time in her life was Asher.

I pressed my lips together, sharing a look with him. We were both aware of her budding crush. While he winked at me, Iris studied the marred side of his face. The raised scar—which stretched from eye to chin and cut right through a dimple—definitely made him stand out in a crowd now, a fact he was extremely proud of.

I fiddled with the comb thing in my hair again, certain it wasn't in the right spot.

"Stooop," Bells moaned. "It's perfect. He won't be able to take his eyes off you."

My heart suddenly tripped all over itself.

"I know what he'll be looking at and it's not your—" Jaxon's drawl ended in an *oof*.

"Knock it off," Yukiko warned.

"What? Baby cakes, I was going to say hair!"

A laugh bubbled out of me, drawing everyone's attention. My dress rustled as I turned around despite Bells' protests. "Thank you all for being here today. And you should know that I love you, in case I don't get to—"

"In case Bren never lets you see the light of day again?" Jaxon offered.

This time, his girlfriend chuckled in agreement.

A knock came. "You all ready? It's getting late."

At the sound of the deep, grumbly voice, a myriad of emotions lit up Bells' face. To top it off, her cheeks flushed a pretty pink. She expertly teetered across the room in her high heels and threw the door wide.

Ryker stood just outside. He inclined his head to me, taking in my attire with a swift glance that missed nothing. His wide shoulders were tense, but when his blue and black eyes landed on Bells, they noticeably softened.

She buried her hands in the folds of her skirt. "Hi," she whispered.

His lips twitched into a faint smile. "Hi."

"I missed you," she blurted, then ducked her head.

Ah, if only she could have seen his face after those words. There was such raw devotion and adoration. He was without a doubt falling in love with her. But they were still learning how to communicate—mostly him. That didn't stop him from expressing his affection in other ways. Never once taking his eyes off her, he placed a hand on the small of her back and pulled her out the door. After a few shuffles and giggles, all went silent.

I blinked. Well, then.

They hadn't seen each other in a month, though, so I understood their enthusiasm. After The Great Daring Rescue, as Jaxon called the liberation of Tatum City, everything had changed. The city was a mess, the citizens even more so. Some up and left without a word—like Elite Instructor Drake and others who'd fought against us—but most stayed. Despite the horrors of that day, many were still scared to step foot outside the walls. Slowly but surely, though, they were learning. Books had been brought in. Jaxon had even lent out a few of his movies.

Tatum City had been renamed New Hope—another of Jaxon's suggestions—and the house was now a sanctuary for the homeless. My old room technically wasn't mine anymore, but Bells had commandeered it for the day. Because there was one minuscule difference about today, a milestone that everyone here knew about—thanks to Jaxon.

It was my birthday.

I'd been alive now for nineteen years, and I *chose* to spend today in this city that was no longer a prison. And even with its many scars, New Hope had the ability to recreate Bren's future vision exactly how he'd pictured it.

Everything had to be perfect. Because there was one other thing different about today.

It was our wedding day.

After almost dying in Bren's arms from a gunshot wound to the gut, we were both living in the moment. Every day was a miracle, our time spent together precious. He was often busy doing what he did best: fixing things. The village needed rebuilding and he'd thrown himself into the project with zeal. But each night, no matter how tired he was, he never failed to show his gratitude that I was still alive.

The treaty between the Recruiter Clan and The Ridge still held, but Ryker spent the majority of his time keeping the men in line so his mother Evie could birth a thriving kingdom. Bells was struggling. She so desperately wanted to stay with him there, but he wouldn't risk her safety like he had last time.

Rumors of a rogue clan that continued to traffick humans kept both groups busy, especially Jaxon and Dr. Moore who were cooking up another mission to infiltrate a suspicious walled city. Thankfully, Bren hadn't volunteered to spy for them and didn't seem at all inclined to for the future, either.

The biggest change was having my mum nearby. Now a citizen of New Hope, she and Asher's mother—who was on the mend after receiving better health care—had grown close. I saw them often and helped babysit their five rambunctious children, but my new job required the majority of my time.

As the founder of Holland Academy—named in honor of Dominic, my late instructor—my days were filled with endless lessons, questions, and confusion on how to organize everything. With her teaching background, Bells helped, but I handled most of the hands-on training. Anyone was welcome to learn, no matter their age or status. The classes ranged from ability control, learning how to read, to surviving the outside world.

A few months ago, the unlikeliest of people had signed up for a survival course. She was uncoordinated and whined every time I knocked her down, but Rose was almost tolerable when she concentrated on something other than herself.

The prison I'd hated for so long was now a place for people to thrive. The city was still without a leader, and I still had nightmares, but I was healing. *We* were healing.

"You ready, Lune?" Asher said, jogging me from my thoughts. He studied me curiously, probably sensing the dozens of things I had felt in the last few contemplative minutes.

I tucked it all away, every single important memory, for another time. And accepted his offered arm. "Yeah, stable boy. I am."

The wedding ceremony was a blur of sensation and overwhelming emotion.

It was a crisp autumn day, the trees brilliant shades of gold, orange, and red. The sky was a fathomless blue and the breeze sent my gauzy veil fluttering—oh, that's why Bells positioned the comb there. I experienced an abundance of feeling that I was still getting used to: Contentment. Certainty. Joy and happiness. And, above all, love.

And then there was Bren.

My Bren.

My soulmate.

The colors and faces surrounding us fell away when I saw him at long last. His white suit beautifully contrasted his deeply tanned skin. His face was clean-shaven, his wavy hair tamed except for a stubborn lock slowly inching down his forehead. I saved his eyes for last. Stars, I would never grow tired of those intense golden eyes. Every time he looked at me, I caught on fire. The entire ceremony, my face flamed red as he stared and stared and stared like a man parched, waiting for the moment when he could slake his thirst.

After the ceremony, we danced until winking stars and a delicate half moon graced the night sky. The skirt of my lace dress swished in time to the violin's haunted strains and I was carried away, away, away on the soaring notes.

Butterflies fluttered in my stomach when Bren dipped me low, whispering in my ear, "I have a confession to make."

I shivered, distracted when his lips found my earlobe. "What's that?"

His teeth gently bit the soft flesh before I was righted and whisked away again. "I didn't think my future vision thing all the way through. You see, I can't carry you all the way to the house."

I frowned. "Are you saying I've put on a few pounds since becoming an instructor?"

He saw my put out expression and quickly shook his head. "No, not at all. It's just—"

I couldn't hold in my snort a second longer.

He stopped. Then scowled. "You were joking." The scowl tipped into a smirk. "Two can play that game."

"I'm counting on it," I purred, throwing him a wink as I whirled away.

A low growl was my only warning before he lifted me into his arms. As he spun me, I threw back my head and laughed, uncaring who heard. He carried me to the stables, setting me down to throw a blanket over Stalin's back.

I bit my lip. "Well, this feels familiar."

"I brought Freedom to the house earlier today so you had no choice but to ride with me." He twirled a finger with a smirk. "Turn around." When I gave him a skeptical look, he laughed softly and grasped my shoulders. I rolled my eyes but didn't resist as he positioned himself behind me.

What was he going to do? Launch me onto Stalin's back?

Before my mind could get too carried away, his fingers feathered over my neck. A slight weight settled between my breasts and I glanced down. And gasped.

"Bren." I carefully lifted the familiar object that dangled from an equally familiar leather cord.

He kissed my bare shoulder. "Happy Birthday, little bird."

My chin quivered and I whirled to face him. "How?"

"Well, I had a run-in with a bear recently, if you remember. And I've been waiting for a special occasion to give this to you ever since."

Speechless, I cradled the bear tooth in my palm and dropped my gaze, his tender expression too much. He knew me so well now, knew how much I'd cherished that necklace and would cherish this one. Knew that I was seconds away from crying and needed a moment to collect myself. He tucked a strand of hair behind my ear and kissed my crescent moon tattoo before hoisting me onto Stalin's back.

The trip wasn't long. We had found a spot not too far from here, perfect for starting our future together as husband and wife. Although private, Bren and Jaxon had secured the property with an alarm system.

I snuggled close to him as a cool breeze tickled my bare skin. He rested his palm on my stomach like he did every day since I'd been shot. His fingers idly traced the spot just below my navel. The days following the event that almost killed me were forever etched in my memory. Bren didn't leave my bedside once, standing vigil day and night until his body would force him to sleep.

When I'd regain consciousness for a few moments, he was always there, holding my hand, resting on the bed beside me, or gently tending to my body's needs. The utmost care he'd given me—the commitment and sacrifice, the outpouring of love—had restored my strength. From that moment forward, I let him see everything. Good or bad, there wasn't a single wall between us. I wanted him to know, without a doubt, that I would do anything, *anything* for him in return.

When we arrived at our three-stall stable, Freedom greeted us with a nicker. She and Stalin had become extra friendly lately. I'd have to keep an eye on them.

Bren jumped down and swooped me into his arms, all business. I bit my lip to keep from laughing again. I knew where he was headed. Every bone in my body knew.

As we exited the stable, I caught a glimpse of our newly built cabin through a stand of pine trees. Wisps of smoke curled from the stone chimney, mingling with the stars.

"Did Jaxon light the fireplace?" I squinted at the softly glowing windows.

"I did it earlier. Why, are you not keen on an audience?" he said with amusement, flashing a bit of fang.

My cheeks turned a rosy hue again. Ugh. Now I was picturing us completing the final part of his vision with the wedding party shouting encouragement. The rest of my body burst into flames. A rumble began in Bren's chest, further stoking the heat that blazed through me.

A dunk in a cold lake sounded heavenly right about now. To distract myself, I began counting.

"Twenty . . . sixteen . . . nine . . ."

"Why are you counting?" Bren asked with a chuckle.

I shifted my eyes from the calm lake that glistened under a waning moon to his curious gaze. "I simply want to know how many steps stand between us and our happily ever after."

He slowed, feet away from the gently lapping shore. "So you're happy?"

I nodded, fighting a grin when his irises brightened with emotion. "Are you?"

His eyes slid shut and he pressed his forehead to mine with a sigh. "Yes." He erased the space between our mouths and captured my lips in a heated kiss. "Happier than I ever thought possible, little bird."

Our lips refused to separate as Bren moved toward the lake again, my body tingling with anticipation for what was to come. Still, I couldn't help counting. Only a handful of feet stood between us and the beckoning water.

"You're my everything," I whispered against his mouth, even as I finished the countdown.

Three, two . . .

One.

The End

ACKNOWLEDGMENTS

First, I just want to take a second to *breathe*. Wow, this trilogy has been a whirlwind of sweat and tears, joy and laughter. When I first started it, I had no idea what I was doing. I just knew there was a story inside my head that wanted out. I had no intention of pouring so many of my fears and desires into the characters, letting them struggle the human condition and become stronger for it. To be honest, I'm jealous of them. They are so much better at taking action than I am, at facing their fears and making their dreams become reality. In many ways, they're the ones teaching *me*.

I thank God every day for free will. It is a gift to make our own choices, to fail and try again. Our decisions define who we are, and I'm thankful for the endless opportunities God has given me, especially the ability to write. It has been such a lifeline to me the last couple of years, an escape from my overactive mind and an experience akin to freedom.

I want to thank my loyal friends, family, street team, writing buddies, and readers who made this journey far from lonely. Your excitement and support means more to me than words can express. You are the reason why I fought so hard to make this story as epic as possible. Hopefully I succeeded. A special shoutout to my best friend, Melissa McMurry, for being there since day one. And last but not least, I want to thank #teamelitebanana. I am extremely lucky to have you all in my life. Love you, guys!

ABOUT THE AUTHOR

Becky Moynihan is the award-winning author of *The Elite Trials* trilogy (a YA dystopian romance), and co-author of the *Genesis Crystal Saga* (an NA urban fantasy series). She lives in central North Carolina with her family. Find more info on Becky's website: www.beckymoynihan.com. And sign up for Becky's newsletter to learn about upcoming releases!